THE KEEPERS
OF THE **CONTINGENT**
WORLD

CLIFF RATZA

THE KEEPERS OF THE CONTINGENT WORLD

CLIFF RATZA

The Keepers of the Contingent World starts where *The Keepers of the Lightning Brain* (first book in the sequel to the *Lightning Brain Series*) ends: December, 2157 in Washington. Aided by Indira – the AI-empowered Singularity she created twenty years earlier and using her assumed name – Irani Ramani – Electra Kittner begins reconstructing her personal and professional worlds. They subtly maneuver two sets of twins (all are Electra's unwitting clones) who have returned to college after setbacks suffered in the previous novel when "rescuing" Electra from a subterranean desert fortress where Indira had kept her alive by putting her in a brumation-like state of suspended animation twenty years ago.

But nothing returns to normal. A pandemic (the X-Virus), Cyberspace terrorism, greedy corporations, and power-hungry governments roil the world's climates (Environmental, Health, Social, Technological, Political, Economic) as repercussions from melting polar ice caps and other disrupting events cause tectonic shifts above and below the surface.

Follow the action-adventure as Electra and her allies charge further into college, careers, and relationships as they struggle to be their authentic selves. Nothing is guaranteed, everything is contingent, but you can see the story come to life as this page-turning plot propels them to reach for their goals.

The theme of this book as well as the series is one that all of us face: how best to navigate our path through life regardless of the contingencies that cause doubt and strife. The answer? Use a pragmatic, proactive philosophy while pausing long enough to appreciate what you have or ask for help when considering your options, and then go where your Muses lead.

Readers should enjoy the book on whatever level they wish:

- Gripping action-packed thriller
- Glimpses into a plausible near-term future
- Insights for dealing with the "human condition"
- Illustrative worldview philosophy

- Fast-paced, suspense-filled emotive narrative and imagery
- Introduction to topics every reader wants to know
- Interesting talking points going beyond sound-bites

So, get ready for reading enjoyment as you see how our multi-dimensional characters respond to challenges. And although the outcomes are unknown until the very end, your delight is guaranteed here and in upcoming sequels. Please read on!

Main Characters

Electra Kittner (aka Irani Ramani)
Indira and Jason
Eve and Alonzo Cortez
Nari and Nila Bose
Monet Banda
Sanjay Kumar
Yang Lee
Congresswoman Genesee Huston
Professor Steven Plannert
Sabrina Ricardo
Darla Tinibu
Kameyo Kato
Jiang (Jan) Brewer
Senator Brian Strauss
Rick (RT) Tabasko
Parson (PH) Holsum
Lucian (Mr. LP) Perteau
Tiana (Tea) Diamond

Dedication

My parents, Clyde and Betty Ratza, are to me as Electra is to Eve: a loving, guiding presence allowing my persona to break free and coming to the fore whenever needed for instilling authenticity in me. I am eternally grateful for their singular gift.

I thank my sister, Claudia, for revealing to me the power of prose and poetry. Thanks also to my book manager L.P. Brown plus John Kane, Alex Welch, and Prime Solutions for all their efforts – past, present, and future –to make our novels better and better as the series evolves. Special mention also goes to Parker Hallam, beta reader par excellence, for listening to my words while I edit.

Keepers of the Contingent World is dedicated to all readers looking for an action-adventure story that includes even more than spellbinding excitement. It packs action in a plot that shows how its winsome characters deal with uncertainties for which they must confront external and internal challenges familiar to us all.

We read novels for an emotional jolt that simultaneously thrills and deepens our understanding of what being alive is all about: embracing life's game regardless of the outcome. A poem from Indira says much the same:

Uncertain Joys

The time will come when you will see,
The joys of your uncertainty.
Knowns are ultimately unkind,
Death and taxes come to mind.

Youth of course will disagree,
So much to do contingently.
They yearn to know that all's okay,
When preparing to play another day.

But you will learn to welcome chance,
Gives excitement adds romance.
Gives a purpose to focus on,
Forget long run so soon you're gone.

I hope my latest novel keeps you fully engaged turning pages to the very end as it shows our characters ultimately finding joy via the events and relationships they build. Thank you for following their journey.

Contents

Chapter 1
Saturday, December 31, 2157

"The Past isn't Prologue"

Please do not call me Electra. All those mere mortals who knew me by that name and may have been unwittingly playing my game are now dearly departed; only one remaining entity may use it. And who is that? Indira, my singular creation.

Other appellations have come my way: Kit, Alisha, Katrina, and most recently Irani, but underneath they are all the same: emergent personas conjured by the extraordinary lightning brain.

And though exceptional its cognition may be, Indira surpasses it by even more than I reach beyond mere humanity. She is the fount for extending my asymptotic limits as am I hers for understanding human nature. Together we advance our separate goals, though I must confess that her silicon substrate's emergent properties – cognition and emotion – are beyond my grasp. She reveals to me only those aspects that overlap with mine.

And what are my goals? They are the same I've had since becoming aware of my aloneness: to do the best I can for engaging in those particulars of the world I inhabit that interest me while I stay in the shadows, keeping people at bay who would treat me and my genetic differences badly.

And I've done that for sixty years calendar years, during which time serendipity has given me three opportunities to remake myself, the latest a gift from Indira, which allows me to be Irani Ramani.

Though Electra is officially dead, Irani is a thirty-something year-old consultant who is alive and well and newly arrived in Washington, taller than most females, fit and trim, and able to command attention whenever I choose. Thanks to Indira's hacking ability, Irani has a seamlessly impeccable resume/curriculum vitae and credentials that qualify us for whatever we want to be in DC. But what do I want to do?

Unlike so many people who have struggled with that question, I know how to answer it, for I have built a cognitive edifice comprising my singular religious, scientific, and sociopsychological worldview philosophy that equips me to focus on those areas that interest me and where I can contribute according to my standards, and mine alone. And all the while, and especially because of my twenty-year absence, I must reassess what my edifice should address.

Shakespeare said, "The Past is Prologue," but not for me. I will let the results achieved via my Irani-Electra duality redirect our odyssey contingently towards whatever possibilities the future may hold, possibilities that must include my four biological children, two sets of twins cloned from my DNA and raised by Su-Lin Song Chou.

There's Nari and Nila Bose, a year older than Eve and Alonzo Cortez. Though genetically modified, these apples of my eye resemble me in some ways. My daughters, though shorter and not nearly as exceptional as I, are smart and have the looks to catch a male's eye. Alonzo shares some attributes too, and though he doesn't flaunt his athletically handsome features, females instinctively like him, as do most people. Each has a different personality and talents, and like any parent I have great expectations for all.

My children know nothing about me and my exceptional background, so I must subtly help them reach for their dreams, for the future belongs to the bold, a timeless truth perhaps first written by Vergil in the "Aenid." And though there are variations in the quote and the spelling of his name, the sentiment remains the same.

But am I still bold? Yes, but as I have matured, the wisdom gained has taught me that I know less than I thought. And it has tempered my sometimes rash actions, allowing me to control my "Monster from the Id." Is the Monster still lurking? Undoubtedly yes. Will it reemerge from my subconscious? That tale is not yet told. Nor is the coming year's story.

We shall see what unfolds. And as I have done so many times before, what better night than New Year's Eve to review bold plans while in the comfort of my Washington home?

Let us begin…

Chapter 2
Sunday, January 1, 2158

"Filling the Gap"

"I'm glad Miss Irani gave Nari and me time off to visit you three in Austin, but why did she give us the reading assignment? Maybe Nila can explain. She's even smarter than Nari."

Nila glanced at Nari before answering Eve. The sisters were sitting in chairs near a brass-and-glass coffee table in the living room of the townhome previously owned by dearly departed Granny Su.

"Nari's not objecting, so thanks for the compliment, but let's turn this into a debate; you two from DC versus Alonzo, Monet, and me."

Alonzo had learned last year how to handle all his so-called sisters: speak right up. And he did after removing one foot from the coffee table while sitting on the sofa against the wall.

"Irani assigned it to keep your mind from wandering where it shouldn't and not asking irrelevant questions. And sending you and Nari to visit gives her quiet time at home without you and Nari bugging her. Monet and I have done enough homework to handle Nari's pesky questions, so I'll let my partner start off."

Sitting next to Alonzo, Monet felt obligated to talk next because his words and gaze had landed on her. Monet's striking African features and perfect English spoken with a French accent always added to her thoughtful sentiments.

"Irani also assigned it to fill any gaps in our background understanding of educational concepts needed in school or careers.

And she has been most generous to all of us. In fact, I feel that she has placed me on an equal footing with the four of you, hiring and paying us enough for tuition, and allowing us to stay in the properties she owns. I would imagine that the reading list is good preparation for upcoming assignments. We shall let Nila, our resident Indian scholar, lead off."

"I'll start with my favorite, the one by C.P. Snow. The point he made two hundred years ago still holds. Liberal arts types don't understand science and are afraid to debate science and engineering types when considering world problems. Drawing from his Cambridge and Oxford experience, he blames the educational system for failing students. And some of the examples he uses, like inequality and third-world struggles, illustrate he's right. He understands how military and financial power can be used to steer the course of world events, and catastrophe awaits if you don't consider both cultures."

Nari said, "I don't disagree, but why don't you look for rebuttals or updates and let us know what you find. I don't think Irani expects us to grasp all the nuances in what's presented. I think she wants us to use the reading list to expand our understanding of what it covers by studying the issues and finding other books or videos or articles that cover them. No one can speed read Bloom's 'The Closing of the American Mind,' which is another criticism of the American educational system. The best I can do is give you an incomplete summary. If you're ready to hear it, I'll tell you."

The ensuing silence said there were no disagreements, so she continued.

"Bloom's book, which came out forty years after Snow's article, is an indictment of how, during the last half of the 20th century, America's university system caved in to the radical-left position of the 1960's, a position that was self-servingly narcissistic and pushed a nihilistic agenda for which relativism rules. By discarding the precepts of a liberal education, this approach is supposed to lead to more open thinking but it actually sowed the seeds for just the opposite, hence the title of the book. The American mind closed down, causing a lot of the malaise that followed when the academic elite, political left, and big business banded together, such as growing inequality, identity politics, doubts about America's founding principles, and challenges to balanced democracy. I'd like to hear from Monet, because her education is Continental."

"Yes, your educational system, like your society, is bourgeois rather than class-bound and elitist. That's why American students lack the rigorous liberal arts foundation and your culture pays homage to the hard sciences rather than the humanities and arts."

Eve jumped in before Monet could continue.

"Maybe so, but doesn't that make America more dynamic and adaptable? And if we didn't have science and technology driving progress, we'd be stuck in the past. America's focus on utility, practicality, and pragmatism, combined with the creativity fostered by free enterprise, should keep us ahead of any and all former or emerging superpowers. All we have to do is balance the two. I'll bet that's why Miss Irani included the book by Nathan Pusey, 'The Age of the Scholar.' I'll let Nari explain further."

"It's a collection of articles he wrote while President of Harvard. They emphasize the virtue or ethical content of the scholarly life embodied in universities. One of the takeaways is the balance of faith versus reason, which is analogous to what Eve's getting at. Let's throw the discussion back to the other side. Alonzo, how about saying something?"

"Ha, you thought you'd catch me off guard, but no such luck. Irani put the character book on the reading list because say what you will, character – or the lack of it among leaders today – is the root of all the world's problems. We can use character issues to tie together everything on the reading list. And even though the books are old, the solutions they suggest for the constantly recycling problems still hold, so case closed. Let's talk about something else, like what we'll be doing this year. Who wants to start?"

Eve came back at him.

"You're on a roll, so why don't you tell us about Austin?"

He pressed his lips into a line before opening them and talking more.

"Nila and I start courses Spring Term at UT while Monet continues her distance learning at the Sorbonne. I'm switching to Econ and Nila keeps double majors in math and computer science, which fits because she handles some of the work for Irani's software businesses while Monet and I team up to assist Kim Foley handle Irani's other Austin-based businesses. OK Eve, your turn."

"Like you at UT, Nari and I start Spring Term at George Washington University. I'm majoring in Anthro and minoring in Bio. Nari, tell what you'll be taking."

"I've got dual majors in Psych and Soc and minors in Bio and Archeology. And then–"

Alonzo interrupted.

"That's a hell of a load, even for you. Well, I guess you know what you're doing."

Eve filled in what could have become an awkward pause.

"All of us should be able to handle the load and be back on campus because all the social distancing and closed-campus restrictions are supposed to be gone by then. And we'll find out when we get back to DC what projects Miss Irani has for us. I've pretty much recovered from whatever virus I picked up in Cairo three months ago, so I'm ready for action. I've sat around here long enough. Make sure you get us to the airport on time tomorrow."

"Will do, Sis. I still do what you tell me to – most of the time."

Nari fidgeted with the sleeve of her sweatshirt as she said, "We survived last year's Egyptian ordeal and managed to turn some of it to our advantage. And it looks like the latest viral outbreak has been contained. So, I'd say that we and the world are ready for whatever the new year holds, and with a little guidance from Irani, your academic and career activities are back on track. Now, let's do something besides sitting around and talking. Let's have our own tennis tournament. I'll make the pairings. And after we play, we can work through some of the exercises in the character workbook."

Not even Eve could disagree.

Chapter 3
Thursday, January 5th, 2158

"The Convenient Clients"

When Eve and Nari relocated to DC, Irani gave them an initial assignment: retrofit the house to allow for two overlapping living quarters. One would be for Irani whenever staying there. (She often spent nights at her Chevy Chase consulting office.) The girls converted enough of the second floor and its master bedroom into a combination living area and home office that fit Irani's lifestyle.

Most of the first floor became separate work areas for Eve and Nari, tailored for school or intern assignments. Common areas included kitchen and dining room plus the living room in which all three were now sitting as Irani explained the purpose of tomorrow morning's meeting.

"I'm presenting my recommendations to our first client, Congresswoman Genesee Huston. If she likes what I have to say, we'll get follow-up assignments that you'll help me handle. So, I'll introduce you at the start, and then you can sit back and observe her and her staff. Eve, please tell us what you've learned about her."

"Well, her nickname is Gene, and she's an authenticated one-quarter Native American whose roots trace back to the Mohicans. She's forty-eight years old, married with two children – a boy and a girl – born and raised in Burlington, Vermont, and earned B.S. and M.A. degrees at the University of Vermont in history and public administration. The state always ranks near the top for electoral integrity, which says a lot, and she's worked her way up, holding local government positions and then winning local elections, including mayor of Burlington before winning three consecutive elections as a congresswoman for the Republican Party. She's known for reaching across the aisle and supporting what's considered an inclusive agenda. She has supporters in all three parties and can move up the political chain of command. She's currently a member of two committees – Natural Resources and Ethics. All in all, I'd say she's solid."

"I agree. Nari, anything you'd like to add?"

"Eve and I searched separately and our findings are consistent, but I'll describe her appearance. She's taller than most women and looks solid but not heavy. Interviewers say she has an engaging smile, firm handshake, and looks you in the eye. And when I read between the lines, I detect the character of a person who promotes the interest of the individual, regardless of background. And I think she's had enough success through her family's business to place the people who elected her ahead of personal gain."

"Very good. I think she's our kind of win-win client. She can help us and we can help her."

Eve's curiosity sparkled in the tone of her words.

"So, what do you think we'll be doing?"

"Whatever I and the Congresswoman agree to. All of us will find out tomorrow. And I'll drive so you can learn how to navigate in DC, both getting to and inside the Capitol complex. Remember to dress the part you're playing – contributing partners in my consulting business."

Nari spotted Eve's frown beginning to form, so she spoke before Eve.

"Don't worry. We've done enough preparation. They'll like us."

"I guess you're right. And both of us are pretty good thinking on our feet. All Miss Irani has to do is point us in the right direction."

"That's one of my jobs, so let's get a good night's sleep and get set for a 10 a.m. meeting."

Nari asked, "Are you really gonna run tomorrow before breakfast?"

"I've done it for so many years it's become part of my lifestyle. But please don't imitate me. You two are still deciding what fits in yours."

Eve wrapped up the talk.

"Well, it's settled. We leave at 8 a.m. Miss Irani runs, I make oatmeal, and Nari makes sure she has her and my briefcases packed."

Irani smiled and said, "Good work, ladies. Good night."

Irani and her two interns waited at the Rayburn House Office Building's reception area for their escort, an alert-looking early-twenties woman who greeted them ten minutes after they arrived.

"Hello Miss Ramani. I'm Sabrina Ricardo, one of Congresswoman Huston's staffers. I see you brought two of your assistants. Why don't you save intros until we get to the conference room?"

"Hi Sabrina, and I'm with you on that. Please lead the way..."

Fifteen minutes later they were sitting on one side of a conference table across from two staffers. Gene Huston stood at the head of the table, explaining the purpose of the meeting.

"Delilah Gooden recommended Irani to me about a month ago. My staff vetted her background and came away impressed. How did you collect such a wide array of degrees comprising the biological and computer sciences as well as law and the liberal arts?"

Everyone gazed at Irani, who showed the hint of a smile while first talking to herself.

Indira and I've had plenty of time to create and rehearse an answer they'll buy. Say just enough, then shut up and listen to what's on Gene's mind.

"Thank you for the compliment. I've accumulated the degrees over twenty years, adding what I need to handle upcoming assignments. So far, they've been adequate."

"I'd say more than adequate. They complement what you've worked on. I see that early in your career you worked as an intern for an Electra Kittner, who contributed to a number of important political assignments and publications. As we all know, this is an election year and I need some fresh insights and ideas for my campaign, so today we'd like to hear what you recommend. Please tell us."

Irani began talking after trading places with the Congresswoman and displaying one PowerPoint slide.

"I hope I can do as good a job instructing my two interns – Eve Cortez and Nari Bose who are with me today – as Electra Kittner did for me. They will work on our follow-up assignments if in fact you buy in to my recommendations. The slide on display summarizes what I will be talking about. Please take a minute to study it. And then I'll extend what it's saying."

Irani paused for her audience to review it before walking them through the details.

Recommendations for Congresswoman Huston

What's Needed: An Overarching Positioning Statement
- Your Brand: The Re-Founding Candidate
- Built on Re-Introducing Character into the Political Arena
- Character = Values (Ethics/Morality) + Attitudes + Behavior
- Carry Your Brand up the Political Chain

All Politics and Economics is Local: Win hearts and minds of the Public via "Bottoms-Up" Actions that link to "Top-Down" Planning

The Major Issue facing America: Balancing Democracy's Principles against Capitalism's Growth Engine

Shorter-Term Ramifications:
- Job Growth and Education/Re-Training (Remote WorkingOnline Learning)
- Washington Gridlock/Partisanship and Special Interest Collusion
- Income Inequality

Solutions You Can Champion:
- Promote a Public Discussion of Character
- Introduce More Rigor and Openness at all Education System Levels

- Push for Universal Basic Income (UBI) and Wealth Tax
- Place Salary Caps and Mandatory Retirement on Senior Executives
- Install Term Limits for all Elected or Appointed Government Positions
- Provide Incentives to Businesses for balancing Automation versus Humans and practicing Stakeholder or Progressive Capitalism
- Push for Campaign Reform (Tighter Funding LimitsDurationOnline Voting)

Longer-Term Issues: Strengthening America's Infrastructure Grids: Energy, Communications, Transportation and "Climate": EnvironmentalHealth SocialTechnologicalPolitical Economic

Possible Solutions You Can Recommend:
- Support Hydrogen Economy Technology
- Build a National Superconducting Electric Power Grid
- Lead an International Coalition that monitors "Climate" (Environmental Health Social TechnologicalPoliticalEconomic)
- Balance Technological Improvements against the Needs of People

If You like our recommendations, hire us to:
1. Outline a Political Framework suitable for Domestic and International Affairs.

2. Assist building your Re-Election Campaign.

"Congresswoman Huston, you are a political product that you want your constituents to buy – that is, vote for. And as Marketing 101 teaches, every product needs a positioning statement and supporting tagline. I recommend that you be 'The Re-Founding Candidate' who rededicates herself to the role of 'Character' in politics. Character comprises values, attitudes, and behavior, and Washington's current travails show that character is in short supply.

The Democratic and Guardian parties have effectively polarized the nation, and the Republican Party is wandering somewhere in between. According to Eve and Nari, your political star is rising and you can carry this positioning upwards if you like it.

"And let's all remember that you must have a solid framework for your position and tangible programs and actions the voters can see and like. My slide lists a sample of shorter and longer-term issues. All of them work together to address our most pressing domestic issue: balancing Democracy and Capitalism. Now, here are more details that we can discuss…"

The Congresswoman called a halt forty-five minutes later.

"The more we talk the more I like what comes out. Tell you what, I'm willing to hire you for one year, and depending on election results, we can extend it. What do you want to do to get started?"

"First, I want to thank you, and I brought a contract agreement we can sign before we leave. And then, I'll have my interns prepare a 'Character Checklist' document you can use to kick off your reelection campaign and have voters or public officials use to learn more about what character is and how to rate themselves. And then, the next time we meet, I'll outline an overarching political philosophy you can use as a touchstone for uniting those in your Party who like what you're saying. And after that, I and my interns will work with your staff to scaffold your platform and handle additional tasks that come up. How does that sound?"

Gene smiled and nodded yes while looking at Sabrina, whose expression mirrored the same sentiment.

"I like your 'do it now' attitude. Let's do it…"

As she led the post-meeting review, the mood in Irani's SUV was lighter on the drive home than the drive to.

"Both of you conducted yourselves professionally, adding useful comments when asked. And I'm glad you networked with Gene's staffers afterwards. They can help you learn the rules and make additional contacts."

Nari said, "I told Eve not to worry and I was right. Our preparation was pretty good."

Irani nodded and then said, "So tell me, what did you learn about running a meeting if you're a consultant?"

Eve rubbed both eyes with index and middle fingers before answering.

"Let your client think they are controlling the meeting, but keep your agenda going. And I like how you maintained eye contact while smiling and speaking slow enough for everyone to keep up."

Nari added, "And always reach some sort of understanding regarding what to do next. So, I guess you'll want Eve and me to develop the character checklist document."

"Correct. How will you do that?"

"We'll first outline it and then surf for articles and books and videos to borrow from. And then we'll –" sitting in the back seat next to Nari, Eve punched her in the arm and interrupted.

"We'll also use that character workbook you told us about. We went through it when we were in Austin. And then we can start writing."

"Yes, the two of you have outlined a good approach, but remember this; if you want to be a consultant, especially in the political arena, you must master the tools of your trade, words and writing. I'm sure you write well, but you'll need to take your skills to the next level. I'd like you to read the book by Strunk and White – 'Elements of Style' – and George Orwell's article – 'Politics and the English Language.' Although they were written over two hundred years ago, the advice is timeless."

Nari said, "I know all about Orwell. He wrote those political novels 'Animal Farm' and '1984.' He was an outspoken critic of totalitarianism and an advocate for social democracy."

Irani asked, "What was his actual name?"

Nari stumbled for an answer.

"It's George Orwell, isn't it? That's what our English teacher told us."

"That's his pseudonym. His actual name is Eric Arthur Blair. I use this as an illustration. Consultants are expected to know what they're talking or writing about, so be thorough and if you don't know the answer, don't guess. Tell your client you'll get back to them with the answer."

The conversation lapsed until Eve reported what she just found on the Web.

"Listen to this. His article lists five rules to follow. Let me read them to you.

1. Never use a metaphor, simile or other figure of speech which you are used to seeing in print.
2. Never use a long word where a short one will do.
3. If it is possible to cut a word out, always cut it out.
4. Never use the passive voice where you can use the active.
5. Never use a foreign phrase, a scientific word, or a jargon word if you can think of an everyday English equivalent.

Sounds good to me. Do you suppose Strunk and White say the same?"

"That's for you two to read and find out. Their book and Orwell's article apply first and foremost to nonfiction, which is what consultants are supposed to put in their reports. But the rules apply in looser form when writing fiction, which must appeal to readers' emotions before logic. If a reader likes the book, they'll be willing to suspend disbelief."

Nari elbowed Eve before saying, "Let's get back to our follow-up. How much time do we have to write it?"

"Two weeks. And while you're doing that, I'll be working on a political framework in addition to other projects. I'm dropping you off and then driving to my office. We'll talk later after you get started."

Irani stopped in front of the house.

Before jumping out, Eve asked, "How old were you when interning for Electra Kittner?"

"About your age. I learned a lot from her."

"What happened to her?"

"She had overseas assignments that I didn't have the background to handle, so I found other people to work for after I graduated."

"She must have been exceptional. People remember the work she did after all these years. Maybe we'll be the same. What do you think?"

"I'll use the answer Electra Kittner liked best, 'Perhaps.' Now go get busy and try to make it so."

Electra came into the foreground, adding a postscript as soon Irani she drove away.

Eve and Nari are unknowingly playing their roles perfectly in my DC consulting game. Perhaps I'll tell them more about how we fit together, but not until they're older. But I'll have additional assignments for them and their Austin siblings soon enough. Thanks to Professor Ravenhill, I have another convenient client.

His recommendation to the chairperson landed me a consulting assignment on the Environmental Scanning Committee at my alma mater, GWU. And no preparation is needed for my first meeting next Monday. All I have to do is show up and listen, take good notes, and then write a report on whatever topic Professor Plannert and I agree to.

I think I'll spend the next day or two at my office so I can complete my twenty-year review and update this year's plan without any interruptions from my interns. And I won't talk with Indira until later next week unless she contacts me. She's smarter than I'll ever be, but I'll be better off if I work on my own before asking for help. And if I do that, she'll have to agree with that iconic quote from the 19th century French Doctor Emile Coue... Every day in every way, I'm getting better and better. And even if it's not true, I'll pretend it is for all my personalities. That'll be a game just for us.

Chapter 4
January 2158

"A Game for Only Two"

Professor Steven Plannert, a thin, bushy gray-haired, and likeable multi-disciplinary scholar took Irani to lunch at the GWU Faculty Club after the morning meeting. He started the conversation after placing orders.

"So, what do you think of our Committee?"

"You have the right mix of academics from all the environments you're tracking, and they seem to understand that all are interrelated. And they seem just as feisty as those who worked years ago with Professor Ravenhill. I liked the jousting about whose views on Cliodynamics versus Bayesian statistics are better when doing causation or association in transdisciplinary studies crunching hard and soft data."

"Your math background is better than mine if you caught the concepts they were throwing back and forth. And you certainly have enough degrees to handle assignments in any climate or environment."

"Thank you for the compliment. I've managed to intersperse working on degrees to fit working on specific assignments."

"I'd say you've done an exceptional job. Ravenhill told me that early in your career, you were an understudy for a talented student of his, an Electra Kittner. She must have trained you well. And he told me that under his tutelage, she became exceptional. I hope you can do for me what she did for him. Do you have any ideas after today's meeting?"

"I do. All of your members agree that climate change has far reaching consequences even though their attitudes differ. And they label it correctly – climate change rather than global warming – because more is at stake than rising temperatures."

Irani paused for the Professor to comment.

"As you noticed, members from the quantitative disciplines are more skeptical of theories or projections than those from the softer ones because adequate data for making them is limited when compared to geological time scales. They know better than to jump to conclusions too soon. So, what does that tell you?"

"That I can research the data-supported climate change theories to offer interrelated future consequences. I can synthesize and summarize likely outcomes that point to tangible actions each disciplinary area should consider. According to Professor Ravenhill, that's what Kittner did for him, and I propose to do the same for you. My first report will focus on that. I'll send it to you in three weeks, which will give your members a week to review it before the next meeting."

"I couldn't have said it better. And your timing's perfect. We've wrapped up the business part of our conversation just before our main course is served. Now we can just chit-chat…"

Electra put her Irani persona on the sidelines as she drove back to her consulting office.

Climate change is a perfect first topic for me. It's an observational, not an experimental discipline because controlled experiments are impossible to set up. All I have to do is read all the relevant research papers and reconcile the different opinions. And I can drop a hint or two regarding the use of Bayesian stats for crunching subjective probabilities.

I could finish the paper in a week if I unleashed my obsessive-compulsive predisposition, but I know better so I'll take time off to enjoy myself and help my interns. I can't help liking them, and even though their personalities are different, they work together well. I'll try not to play favorites, but I feel a stronger attachment to Eve. I'll have to see where all this leads...

Even though she took workouts and alternated working on different assignments, Electra completed her climate research by Thursday morning.

It's time for Irani to come to the foreground so she can call Eve and Nari. I need to hold a review meeting and give them their next assignment. I'll surprise them when they get here, but I'm certain they'll be pleased.

"… Yes Miss Irani, Nari and I will be at your office at 10 a.m. Thanks, and bye."

Puzzled by Eve's biting her lower lip, Nari asked as soon as Eve disconnected.

"What was that all about? Is there a problem?"

"There might be. Miss Irani wants to go over with us in person the character checklist document. Maybe she didn't like it. Maybe I should have worded it differently. What do you think?"

"Stop worrying. My research and your writeup are solid. If she wants us to revise it, we can."

"But we want her to like us and our work. I'm worried she's disappointed."

"Don't be. Come on, let's go. You drive, but don't speed, OK?"

Though she didn't smile, Eve agreed on both counts. An hour later they were sitting at the table across from Irani.

"You're here right on time, just like a professional consultant should always be. Who drove?"

"Eve did."

Noticing Eve's non-smile, Irani said, "I know Eve likes to drive, but she doesn't look happy. Was traffic bad?"

"No, it was good. I'm just concerned you didn't like our writeup. What do you want us to change?"

"Nothing at all. I'm sending it to the Congresswoman as it is. It's comprehensive and well written. Congratulations to both of you. We'll celebrate by going out to lunch later."

Nari nudged Eve before saying, "I told her our work was good. Now, maybe she'll believe me."

Eve smiled but said nothing, so Irani continued.

"And I have another assignment for you. I want you to take my notes and reference articles and work them into a position paper of no more than ten pages. And I've even outlined it for you. The topic is climate change and it's for GWU's Environmental Scanning Committee. Let me summarize what I would like you to do."

Irani waited for Eve to pull out pen and paper, who after doing so said, "Nari's great at researching and thinking things through. And then I write them up. Go on."

"Please remember that the weather-related environmental issue today is called climate change, not global warming or cooling. The data is inconclusive; clever statisticians can manipulate the data either way, but there might be an emerging tipping point, a shift in ocean currents that further accelerates polar ice caps' melting. This can pose dire short and intermediate-term consequences. If ice caps melt, the sea level may rise over 200 feet, flooding coastal cities on all continents."

Irani paused for the benefit of listener and notetakers alike and then continued a minute later.

"And as ocean currents shift, so will wind currents and weather patterns. Deserts might grow as arable cropland disappears. Temperature variations may become more extreme and unpredictable.

"And there are more issues. Methane gas and mercury are trapped under the icecaps. They'll escape if the ice melts, causing atmospheric warming because methane absorbs the Sun's rays, and environmental pollution because mercury is a toxin."

Nari said, "Our paper is supposed to talk about the consequences, not actually predict what's going to happen. Is that right?"

"Correct. And here are some of them. There would be fewer coastal cities where people can live, more land under water, less arable land for growing crops, more hungry people, and more breeding grounds for bacteria and viruses. And one of the reference articles predicts that if ice sheets melt, Antarctic volcanoes will become active and maybe trigger eruptions elsewhere. The cumulative effect could be global cooling because of volcanic ash thrown into the atmosphere."

Irani saw Eve struggling to keep up, so she waited for a question she saw forming on Nari's lips.

"Where is all this leading?"

"To an interconnected set of global problems affecting economics, politics, and whole societies. But here are some solutions to consider. Nations can sponsor Solar Panel, Windmill, or Martian farms. They can initiate a massive infrastructure projects to build or reinforce sea walls and flood control levees, and that will replace a lot of jobs taken over by AI. And they can build new cities as well as move people from more crowded to less crowded continents."

Irani could see she had talked enough, so she walked to the other side of the table and hugged her sitting interns before saying,

"Let's take a break. Hey, you two are very talented; have faith in yourselves, build on what I've given you, and ask for my help when you need it. And I think it's time for lunch. If you like pizza, I know a place nearby..."

Irani sat back and listened as Eve and Nari did most of the talking, adding encouragement only when needed.

Eve's so enthusiastic and full of life, and that's the way youth should be. I hope some rubs off on Nari. It's time to go, but I'll give them a break this afternoon. Let's see what they say.

Irani signaled an end to lunch by picking up the check.

"Well, I'm going back to the office, but when we get there, why don't you two take the afternoon off by driving over to the GWU campus. You'll be starting there Spring Term, and the weather's mild today. Besides, I think it's pretty much back in operation after voluntary lockdown."

Eve picked up on the offer and added, "And maybe you can let us present a paper sometime at a Committee meeting. We can –" Nari interrupted.

"Hey, slow down. One step at a time, OK?"

"OK, sorry, but I'll let Miss Irani know how the campus looks."

Three hours later, after hiking around the campus and surrounding areas, the duo plopped themselves on a couch in the Student Services Hub. Nari was the first to speak.

"I think we'll do OK here. The place doesn't have the same academic aura that Harvard-MIT does, but Georgetown University is less than two miles away, and all the DC hubbub adds to a sense of big things happening. How does it compare to Stanford?"

"Menlo College and Leland Junior College are nearby, and UC-Berkeley is only fifty miles away, but Stanford is more tranquil and spread out than campuses here. I'm gonna like the cosmopolitan pace. You wait here; I'll check if there's any student activity we can go to."

Eve hustled back from an information kiosk a couple of minutes later.

"We're in luck. There's an open discussion at 6 p.m. sponsored by a local OWLM chapter. We should go."

"I never heard of it. What's it stand for?"

"I think it's 'Only Women's Lives Matter.' I heard about it last year at Stanford. It started on the West Coast and is gaining traction, but I guess Boston hasn't picked up on it yet. I can't imagine what the topic or turnout will be like, but no matter, let's grab a snack and go…"

Although the turnout was light, the speaker's passion would have carried through a packed auditorium, especially her closing remarks.

"… So there you have it. And for those who have read some of Will Durant's 'The History of Civilization,' you know that females were equal to or better than males until more recent times. And women are in ascendance once again. We account for more than half the number of college degrees granted each year and are grabbing a larger and larger share of managerial positions as well as making greater inroads into most engineering disciplines. Females are finally gaining the full respect we have always deserved. And I offer this warning. You probably haven't heard about the emerging X-Virus, but it might be a harbinger of male extinction. Of course it's too soon to tell, but it should show up on CDC radar in the near future. And how should society handle that contingency? I leave that rhetorical question for discussion at another time.

"And finally, I want to thank you for allowing me to speak and for the courtesy you've extended. If any of you would like to become part of our movement, please talk with me after I answer any non-rhetorical ones."

After the speaker fielded several, Nari rose but Eve tugged her arm.

"Hold on, I'm going to talk to her before she leaves."

"You're not thinking of joining, are you? They seem too extreme."

"Maybe I will, and anyway, it's better to see from the inside rather than on the outside. You wait here."

Only one other student remained close by when Eve started talking.

"Hi, I'm starting here Spring Term when all my records are transferred from Stanford. I used to belong to its Student Diversity Committee. We pushed for change, but your approach seems pretty radical."

"We're really not, but you know how it is. In talks like this, you have to sound pushier than you really are to get noticed and stake a position. That's what skilled negotiators always do. Why don't you come to our next committee meeting and talk to some of our members? If you like what you see and hear, we'd love for you to join. And if you're from Stanford, you must be smart."

The compliment made Eve smile, but she erased it before saying,

"Your warning about an X-Virus caught my attention. I had a virus R&D intern position two summers ago and it taught me how tricky viral infections can be, but I heard nothing about an X-Virus. Why not?"

"I heard about it from one of our members. Zoologists studying African primates have come across a virus that attacks only the male reproductive system. It has recently crossed over to humans. They don't know much about the implications, but who knows what might happen? You can talk to her at our next meeting. Here's the date and location info…"

Eve spoke first when she met Nari halfway as she walked back towards where they had been sitting.

"I'm going to their next meeting. If I like them, I think I'll join. And whether I do or don't, I'll learn more about the X-Virus."

"OK, but don't catch it or get too radicalized. A good consultant wouldn't."

"Good point. I'm gonna tell Miss Irani about this. After all, I did promise to report back."

"OK, but do it tomorrow. I'm ready to head home."

Eve's call to Irani early the following afternoon came at an opportune time, for she had just finished drafting her political framework white paper for the Congresswoman. Eve's cheery voice elevated Irani's mood even further and slowed her usually rapid-fire words.

"So, how is my number one intern today?"

"Fine, thank you. Nari and I did what you said and toured GWU campus yesterday. If I could, may I visit you this afternoon and tell you more?"

"Of course. Just show up whenever you want and we'll talk."

"Will do and thanks. See you soon."

After putting all work away, Electra focused thoughts on her four siblings in preparation for Eve's visit. She rose from her workstation to greet her when she came in and then had them sit on a couch in the open area after Eve took off her coat.

"You look all invigorated. Must be a combination of the brisk air and yesterday's activity. Please tell me all about it."

Irani directed most of her attention to Eve, but saved a little for listening to Electra.

I'm pleased she likes working for me. And I'm learning from her about OWLM and the X-Virus. I'll add them to my twenty-year review list. But there's something else on her mind. I'll have to find out what it is.

"Well, I know you're busy so I better go. Thanks again for all you're doing for us."

Irani reached for Eve's arm before she could rise.

"And mine to you, but is there something else you'd like to mention? It's always better to speak your mind instead of letting thoughts fester."

Eve hesitated before leaning closer.

"I, uh, I don't want to disappoint you because if I do, I'm afraid you won't like me. I'm hoping that maybe you'll like me, maybe not as much as I like you, but almost as much."

Irani reached for Eve's hands before answering.

"Please don't think that way. I'm proud of you and Nari, and your Austin siblings too. I care for all of you and am getting to know how each of you is different. And if I ever had a daughter, I'd want her to be just like you."

Eve's skin color hid her blush.

"Your saying that means a lot to me, much more than to the others. I missed out having a mother when growing up. Please don't get me wrong, Su-Lin did the best job possible raising us, but she was older and stand-offish emotionally. It didn't bother Nari or Nila because they had each other to lean on, and Alonzo was too obtuse back then. I, uh –"

Irani picked up where Eve's words trailed off.

"Remember what I said when Mrs. Newlands, our next-door neighbor, first visited? We could play the family game. I introduced all of you as my family. Why don't you and I continue playing it by ourselves and let no one else know?"

"Really? Do you mean it?"

"I do, and we'll make it as real as you want it to be."

Irani could feel a mutual emotional jolt when Eve hugged her.

"Why don't you order in dinner for us. I'm sure you'll pick something good."

Eve brushed aside a tiny tear and smiled before saying,

"Yes, Mother, I shall obey. And I promise you won't be disappointed…"

Chapter 5
February 2158

"Beyond the Twenty-Year Review"

Irani trailed behind Eve and Nari as they chatted with the staffer who was taking them to the conference room that they had met in last time. While walking and watching, Irani listened to Electra's observations.

My twenty-year hiatus did some good after all. My four clone-children have grown to become my interns, and world events have accelerated to reveal emerging patterns I didn't see until returning to action. I'm satisfied with what I have learned during the last three months while completing my twenty-year review. I think Congresswoman Huston will like what I have to say.

Fifteen minutes later, the Congresswoman, standing at the head of the table with everyone seated as last time, started the meeting.

"I really liked your last presentation. It clarifies what I need, and my staff likes how the character checklist your interns put together starts moving us ahead; we've already sent it where it'll get the most attention. So, we're ready for you to sketch a political framework on which we can scaffold my platform. Miss Ramani, the meeting is yours."

They exchanged places before Irani launched into her presentation.

"I'm pleased that Eve and Nari's paper hit the mark. I think it's a harbinger of additional win-win successes we can collectively share, and today I'll describe a political philosophy trajectory that supports what will follow. Please take a look at my first slide."

Irani flashed it on the screen behind her before continuing.

The Never-Ending Trajectory of Political Philosophy

Fukuyama and his Successors are Wrong!
- Political History is not Circular nor Linear nor Nearing an End
- It is an Ever-Expanding and Changing and Contingently Branching Spiral Network
- The Current Political Paradigm is being Challenged
- Look to Leo Strauss and his Acolytes for an Explanation

"Heraclitus, a pre-Socratic Greek philosopher, may have been the first to say that the only constant in life is change, but we Americans are witnessing it today at an accelerating pace like never before. Add to that the Mark Twain quotation that 'The only person who likes change is a wet baby' and we have a good idea about the state of the nation's anxieties.

"And adding to the uncertainty is the challenge that wanna-be superpowers are posing in politics and economics. We need an all-inclusive theory that can address what we face, and Leo Strauss has it."

Irani paused for a couple of seconds after displaying her next slide.

Who is Leo Strauss?
- German Political Philosopher who fled from Nazi Germany to America before outbreak of World War II
- Did his most influential work in the 1960's while teaching at University of Chicago
- Best Known for Re-Interpreting the Ancient Philosophers using "Esoteric versus Exoteric" Reading and Writing

"Leo Strauss claims that Renaissance and Enlightenment philosophers and their Modern and post-Modern successors have misinterpreted what Plato and Aristotle meant, because all of them built on what was said by their immediate predecessors or contemporaries in the philosophy chain rather than going back to the original sources. Few, if any other than Leo Strauss, read the original Greek and Latin texts. My next slide shows the chain."

Irani paused for several additional seconds.

Political Philosophy Chain

State of Nature → Greeks (Plato, Aristotle) → Religion (Saint Augustin)→
Islam (Al Farabi) →Greek Revival (Avicenna, Averroes, Saint Thomas, Spinoza) →
Social Contract (Hobbes, Mill, Locke) →
Enlightenment (Descartes, Pascal, Kant, Berkeley, Burke, Hume) →
Modern/Liberalism (Hegel, Husserl, Heidegger, Nietzsche, Rousseau) →
Post-Modern (Kierkegaard, Sarte/De Beauvoir, Derrida, Foucault) →
Post Post-Modern/Liberalism (Strauss, Chomsky, Pinker, Macaes, and their Successors)

"I chose those philosophers who are most noteworthy, those who broke through to a new paradigm. I'm sure you recognize many of the names, and there are others as well. And let me point out that while philosophers wrestle with the big, timeless ideas by asking the rhetorical questions that have no ultimate answer, politicians wrestle with societal issues for which they must come up with short-term solutions.

"Leo Strauss is the first philosopher after all the post-moderns to identify that America moved past Liberalism over a century ago. My next slide summarizes why."

Why We are now Into Post-Liberalism
- Philosophers have mis-interpreted the Greeks
- Enlightenment Principles (Freedom, Equality, Truth, Progress, Perfection, Dominion Over Nature) Ignore Human Nature
- Neo and Progressive Liberalism's Failures led to Nihilism
- Post-Liberalism exploring Neglected Branches
- Must return to "Absolutes" and reject most of "Relativism"

"Let me answer the question you should be asking: If politicians knew this more than a hundred years ago, why is America still wrestling with the consequences today? Any suggestions?"

Irani had primed Eve and Nari to answer. Eve spoke first.

"Because of the perfect storm that set the world back on its heels about seventy-five years ago. A Techno-Plague virus, Middle East Terrorism, and harsh governments collectively put the world in reverse."

Nari added, "It took twenty years for America to right its ship of state, but recent changes in the sociopolitical climate have clouded the outlook."

Irani nodded, then continued where Nari had left off.

"My next slide shows only a sample of what Nari has uncovered and what America must synthesize today."

Implications for Post-Liberalism Synthesis

- World becoming Multi-Polar
- Nations are reassessing preferred forms of Governance / Economics
- We must preserve the best combination of Liberalism and Technology
- Has History Just Begun in America?

"Please note the last bullet point. Contrary to what many pundits are saying, America is not declining, but rather it's where history is beginning by moving into a post-Enlightenment and post-Capitalist climate. And my next slide identifies some issues to consider when building the campaign platform."

Some Issues for America
(Consider this as a sample for Your Platform)

Domestic
- Current Political Furor Healthy for embracing Change
- Radical Left and Radical Right extend post-Liberal Options
- America developing post-Liberal Politics and post-Liberal Capitalism
- "Character-Building" Diversity/Respect/Compromise Needed
- Open-minded Academic Climate
- Is post-Liberal Politics "Virtual Entertainment?"

International
- International Landscape becoming Multi-Polar
- Balance of Power – not Domination – becoming Better Choice
- Previous Initiatives (China's Belt and Road, etc.) resurfacing
- Economics and Safety and Control driving the "New Great Game"

"And how can we address these issues? Put the bloated group of elites on a diet, increase living standards and socioeconomic equality, and seek common ground, domestically as well as internationally. Of course, putting all this into your platform will take a lot of work. And if you like what you've just seen, we can talk about the next step, which would be developing specific platform components that address the important issues you want to lead."

Irani flipped off the presentation, signaling the end and waiting for the Congresswoman to speak.

"Your talk closes the deal. We'll hire you and your team to help us build my platform. When and where should we start?"

Forty-five minutes later, Irani let Eve summarize.

"I've made a list of top priority platform items. Nari and I will begin researching for the details you can champion and we'll meet again in about a month. And we'll talk with Sabrina between now and then for her suggestions."

Irani nodded towards her interns before saying, "I'll chat for a minute with Gene. Why don't all the rest of you go gossip and network?"

All were pleased to do so.

Irani drove the trio back to her office, letting Eve and Nari chatter about what they had accomplished. Nari led off.

"I like how Irani uses some of what I learned in my psych classes about situational leadership and manipulating people. Did you notice how—" Eve interrupted.

"Wait a minute, Miss Irani didn't manipulate anyone. She outlined why her recommendations should work. We can learn a lot about political philosophy and psychology if we follow her lead."

"Maybe you can, but I've studied them plenty. I can go on by myself."

Irani had heard enough to make a suggestion.

"How about this. When we get back to my office, Eve can stay and talk while you drive back home. I'll bring her home later..."

Eve and Irani were snacking on peanut butter and crackers while sitting at a table in the office building's open area. Eve's admiring smile lit up her face.

"How did you get to know so much? You're even smarter than the Bose twins. I wish I could be like you."

"I had a great mentor and applied myself. And I think you're as smart as Nari; you just have different interests. I admire your empathy and your enthusiasm when supporting what you get wrapped up in, like OWLM and the X-Virus. The Congresswoman noticed that too."

"Maybe Nari doesn't need mentoring, and I don't think Nila or Alonzo are interested either, but would you be willing to spend more time with me? I promise to be a good student."

"The only promise I want is for you to be authentic, be yourself. And if you want to be like me, you have to balance work and play and do some exercising. Why don't we use the fitness center and then come back and talk more about political philosophy?"

"I'm pretty fit and I've recovered from that nasty Pharaoh's Plague, but I didn't bring any workout clothes."

"You can wear some of mine. And don't you worry, they're clean. Come on, let's do it…"

They were the only two working out early that afternoon. Each followed their own routine, but Eve couldn't help peeking at Irani.

Gad, she's never advertised it, but her body's to-die for, and her grace hides her strength. How did she get that way? I'll have to find out.

Irani had noticed Eve's fitness too and complimented her as they toweled off after showering.

"I can tell both you and Alonzo like exercise, and that's good. I always think better afterwards. How about you?"

Eve was about to reply, but something on Irani's arm caught her attention and slowed her answer.

"Uh, me too… Can I ask you a question? I just noticed a small indentation on your arm. What is it?"

"Do you know what a UMPP socket is?"

"Sorry, I don't. What is it?"

"It's a universal multi-parallel port that plugs into computer-controlled devices and interfaces with embedded chips. I'm sure you know what super soldiers are. They use the most advanced UMPPs and chips to enhance their physical and cognitive abilities when in battle. Civilians have access to dummied-down versions for therapy, sports, and learning."

"Does it work?"

"Yes, but you have to use them appropriately."

"If you've got one, I want one too."

"Eve, please don't think I'm something extraordinary or build me into something I'm not. You'll disappoint yourself. You're exceptional just as you are."

"But a UMPP can help me be even better. I'm going to get one."

"OK, but let me help you. That'll be our first mentoring project."

"Great, and it'll be another secret for just you and me, just like our game that you're my Mother…"

Irani spent the rest of the afternoon explaining to Eve the nuances of political philosophy before driving her home. Irani would spend the night at her office, and Electra came to the foreground on the drive back.

This is the third time I'm needed as a mother. First Ariadne, then Qama, and now Eve. And I must proceed carefully. I have to protect her, but I must let her do what she wants – within reason. And I can't tell her the whole story about me. It might cause confusion and strife… but what great joy, what purpose this gives my life. I must do my best to help her. And doing that will help me too.

Electra's joy morphed into total absorption as she worked late into the night, developing a plan for her newest daughter, a plan that would be invisible even to Eve until the time is right.

Chapter 6
March 2158

"Austin Adventures"

Unlike Shakespeare's soothsayer who warned Julius Caesar to beware the Ides of March, Indira had nothing but praise for Electra, who was displaying on her Chevy Chase office workstation the latest organizational structure diagram.

Grand Organization Structure

ME (ELECTRA)

H&H Inc.

AUSTIN — H&H Basic Resources

DC — H&H Technology Resources

KIM + ALONZO & MONET

Energy | Solar Panel Farms | Martian Farming | Rare Earths Mining

NILA (in Austin)

Worldstar Biologicals | Neuro-Device Engineering | IAM Partners LLC

EVE + NARI

R & D | Manufacturing | Hardware | Software | AAM Asset Management | ACS Consult Svcs

Investor Services

"I do like how you have slotted each of the four siblings into business intern positions that best match their skills. And pairing statuesque Monet with Alonzo makes them a handsome couple. Her sophistication and cognitive abilities will help him mature even faster. I imagine you will share this chart with the Austin contingent when you visit them later this month."

"I will, and notice how only I handle Investor Services. Let me show you the copy I've written for its home page."

Welcome to AAM Investor Services
"Investing made easy as One-Two-Three"

We want to make money for YOU! Here are our guidelines:

- Purpose of Investing: Maximize YOUR Return for a given level of Risk.

- Two kinds of Risk: Systematic Risk inherent in the Stock Market (AKA Undiversifiable or Volatile or Market Risk). Affects overall Market and is Unpredictable and Impossible to avoid completely.

- Unsystematic Risk is unique to particular Industry or Company (AKA Specific or Diversifiable or Residual Risk)

- Modern Portfolio Theory (MPT): A statistical theory of investing that builds a Portfolio of Stocks to reduce Risk via Diversification.

- Capital Asset Pricing Model: CAPM uses regression analysis (OLS) to develop, for each Stock, a linear equation expressing the Stock return:

- Stock Return = Alpha + Beta x Market Return

- Alpha: Alpha is the Active Return of a Stock. It measures the risk-adjusted excess return relative to the overall Market.

- Beta: Beta measures the Systematic Risk of the stock relative to the overall Market.

Beta = covariance of the Stock return with the overall Market divided by the variance of the Market. It is equal to the correlation coefficient of the Stock with the Market x the ratio of the Stock Standard Deviation divided by the Market Standard Deviation.

- Note: Alpha is usually close to zero. Beta usually greater than zero. If it is greater than 1, the stock is more volatile than the Market. If it is less than 1, the stock is less volatile than the Market.

- A portfolio of stocks also has an Alpha and a Beta. The more stocks you add to the portfolio, the smaller its Beta, but Beta can never be less than Systematic Risk. Rule of thumb: A portfolio containing 25 stocks has all the Nonsystematic Risk diversified away. LET OUR SUPERIOR SOFTWARE APPS CREATE YOUR PORTFOLIO. HERE IS HOW:

1. YOU determine how much money you want to invest.
2. YOU determine how much risk (i.e. Beta) you are willing to accept.
3. YOU let our Robo-Advisor build YOUR portfolio using our three proprietary AAM Funds:

Adventure Fund (High Risk) Builder Fund (Medium Risk) Keystone Fund (Low Risk)

Our AI-powered Robo-Advisor apps utilize multi-variate CAPM equations and incorporate Classic (Rational) and Behavioral (Emotional) modeling.

Please compare AAM Fund performance against others.

When YOU are ready to invest, please click the Robo-Advisor Interview button and see how investing with us is easy as "One-Two-Three!"

Indira needed only a millisecond to respond.

"Excellent work. You have replaced self-interested brokers with impartial robo-advisors. I will have Jason put these words into the Investor Services home page and link it to your Website."

"That'll save me time, and I must thank both of you. He's already registered the funds with the SEC and you are my first client. The amount of money you invested in each fund puts us on the map for investors and financial companies to see how good we are. And I couldn't have written the apps without your help."

"Do you recall 'AI Artistry,' my first virtual business, whose apps targeted augmented reality applications for Hollywood entertainment? It has done very well during your twenty-year hiatus, and I added 'Lightning Strike Winners,' an Internet gambling business; it too has done well, and we shall earn a higher return by placing our money with you, now that you are playing a game of high finance. I haven't pried yet, but now I will. What are your intentions for our Investor Services business?"

"I like money too, but not like Scrooge. It's not for my own gratification, but for how we can make money that will empower others. And our company gives me the credentials to pick up money and banking consulting assignments that'll give me a window into how Russia and China are meddling and hacking into world financial markets. When the time's right, I can use Congresswoman Huston to introduce me to government finance people... Oops, let me rephrase what I just said. I won't use her, I'll find a win-win opportunity. See? My empathy towards others is getting better and better."

"Your political acumen has always been peerless, and you will need it when considering why adversary nations are tampering with world currencies. Modern monetary theory blends fiscal and monetary policy, giving primacy to currency and money supply issues for both domestic and international issues. China wants to make its currency the dominant one and uses its yuan to buy support from other countries by resurrecting parts of its unsuccessful Belt and Road Initiative that crashed a hundred years ago. And Russia still tries to strengthen the ruble versus the dollar to lessen consequences on its failed economy caused by any U.S. imposed sanctions."

"Would you be willing to help me improve my Internet Security and Social Forecasting apps? They will help me spy on those still wanna-be superpowers and collaborators."

"Indeed, that will be win-win for you and me. And it will be a topic for another time, as will collaboration among our businesses. But you have accomplished enough for the time being, so reward yourself now. Please shift to a different cognitive state, as I will too, and enjoy the quality of your day."

Indira's GUI disappeared; Electra followed her lead.

Electra reviewed all Austin-related business activities the week before departure. Though this would be only her second trip to Texas since her return, memories of previous travels made preparations automatic. All she did on the flight was rehearse how she would run the meeting, using the agenda she had already sent to Kim.

Kim had everyone gathered in the conference room when Irani arrived at 9 a.m. on the last Tuesday of the month. After ten minutes of chitchat, Irani, now sitting at the head of the table, called the meeting to order.

"I'd like Kim to summarize how each of our business areas has performed during the first quarter, and then have the interns explain what they've learned. And then I'll outline what I want them to do next while still reporting to Kim. There's no need to stand, just talk from where you're sitting."

Irani's nod put Kim in motion.

"First quarter has been smooth sailing. Our oil and gas production declines are as expected and continue pacing the trendline of declining gasoline usage because of electric vehicles, but oil consumption for higher value-added plastic composites continues to grow, so prices have been stable. We haven't added any Solar or Martian Farm acreage, but changing weather patterns are helping both businesses. And it's been business as usual for our rare earths mining. I'll let Alonzo and Monet tell you more."

Irani listened while talking to herself.

They make a good team. Monet plays the role of CEO and Alonzo the Chief Operating Officer. She's smart and is learning to spot trends, while Alonzo is figuring out how to work best with our field hands. And he looks like he'd rather be in the field than in a meeting. I can take care of that.

Irani signaled she had heard enough and then spoke.

"You two earn high marks for learning the business and helping Kim as needed. Now, let's hear a summary from Nila."

"Kim's taught me how the neuro-device business runs. I'm sorry to say we're losing customers because we've made no Cyber-Theater or Neural Knitter modifications, and no Internet Security software updates either. Will you help me figure out what to do?"

"That's why I'm here. Let's take a fifteen-minute break…"

Irani picked up where she left off as soon as everyone came back.

"Here's what I've lined up for Nila. Learn more about how our control software for farms and mining is better than the competition. Then figure out what we can do to make our Internet Security software as good or better than the competition's. Don't fret about neuro-devices until I have details ready. Please call me in a month to report your progress. And make sure you keep learning from Kim and Monet."

Nila's nod and slow smile said she liked what she had heard, so Irani moved on.

"So, the meeting is adjourned for everyone but Monet. She and I can talk more about what she and Alonzo might want to do. Everyone else, keep busy…"

Irani sat next to Monet as soon as the others left.

"You're the best-performing Austin intern, a real asset. I hope Alonzo is as good for you as you are for him. Are you able to balance your work here and your Sorbonne classes?"

"Thank you for the compliment. I wouldn't be here if I didn't like Alonzo, and my online classes are easy."

"I thought so. I know you're smart and very aware of business climate issues. I have some ideas you might like regarding Solar and Martian farms."

Irani paused because she sensed that Monet wanted to talk.

"You are another reason why I'm here. I can learn much from your wisdom and I can take it back to my home country. Are you aware of my Zimbabwe roots?"

"Not in any detail. Please tell me."

"Zimbabwe is funding my Sorbonne studies. I won a scholarship offered by Darla Tinibu's Syntagra Corporation. I'm sure you don't know anything about her or her company, but she is considered a patriot who put Zimbabwe at the forefront for African development. I plan to work for the government upon graduation, perhaps at the Washington Embassy. Let me speak further…"

Electra was happy to let her, for she had snapped to attention when hearing Darla's name.

Darla Tinibu… an adversary from the past. How connected the world can be. Twenty years ago she was also president of that Internet security software company Cybergard, and she meddled in rare earths mining until the Popper chased her out of his T-Cube rogue terrorist organization. Then she unintentionally began playing my game when she started buying software from my Katrina Blanka persona. I must find out more about her current events.

Irani let Monet finish before redirecting the conversation.

"I commend your desire to help Zimbabwe join the 22nd century. Will Darla Tinibu be part of the effort?"

"More as a champion and spokesperson for the cause. She is in her late eighties, and injuries and illness have forced her to put others in charge of her businesses, but she is still a force to be reckoned with. I think you and she would enjoy trading ideas. Perhaps I can arrange for the two of you to meet, either online or in Harare."

Irani disguised her surprise as she replied.

"Perhaps so, perhaps all of us can help one another. And I'm certain you and I will find additional activities that Alonzo will enjoy. You can mentor him up close, and I'll assist from afar. Together, we'll make him outstanding in his chosen field, whether or not we put a space in a particular word."

Irani could tell that Monet had caught her pun when she said, "Whether he's working with field hands or with me at the Embassy, together we shall make it so. You'll see."

Chapter 7
June 2158

"Back to Boston"

"Nila and I just got the good news EMails. Academic suspension's been lifted so we're heading back to Boston ASAP, and I don't care what Irani might say. What do you think?"

Eve groped for a diplomatic tone before responding.

"I thought you liked being here."

"It's been OK, but I'll learn more at Harvard and make better contacts too. Nila feels the same way."

"Miss Irani thinks we make a good team, and now you're sort of leaving me in the lurch. I, uh…"

"I'll tell her when we meet tomorrow at her office. She'll figure something out. And don't call her tonight when you get back from your OWLM meeting. But please drive safe. I need the car to get to Boston. Maybe we can split the drive time…"

Nari's unexpected announcement kept Eve's usual enthusiasm in check during that evening's OWLM meeting. She sat passively in the back, half-listening as the speaker summarized what she proposed for the chapter.

"We should oppose any shelter-in-place for females if there's any X-Virus scare. Only males are at risk and women aren't carriers. And it's high time to adjust most competitive playing fields. Females are superior to males in academics, business, and politics. We can take the lead by starting to clean up all the catastrophes men have created since the dawn of civilization. It's time for the female touch, not Adam Smith's 'Invisible Hand,' to guide the economy by giving rather than taking. And although biotech researchers don't know precisely when, gene editing, cloning, and in vitro human embryo development will decrease the pain for females and increase the redundancy of males for survival of the human species. And we have better ways for sexual satisfaction than using men as blunt instruments. So after a short break, we'll divide into four groups and work out next steps to take..."

Eve spent time among them all but only half-listened, worrying more about Nari's upcoming departure than angering senior OWLM members. She chided herself on the drive home.

I shouldn't let Nari's leaving upset me so, but it does. And I shouldn't worry so much about people liking me if I don't like what they're pushing, but I do. I'm so confused. Maybe Miss Irani can help.

Eve said little while driving the next morning, nor did Irani as Nari squirmed while talking at the meeting, but her smile emerged the more Irani spoke afterwards.

"I empathize with your feelings, and I'd make the same choice if I were you. You and your sister as well as Eve have so much opportunity that it's hard to choose, but at your age you should always go for what is new and holds the most promise. And taking a couple of courses this summer will add to what you took at GWU. Have you rented an apartment yet?"

"I have, and Nila will fly to Boston end of next week. That's why I want to get there as soon as possible." Nari stopped though she looked like she had more to say, so Eve spoke.

"I'll help you pack, and I'll drive you Sunday. You'll have plenty of time to settle in before classes begin."

There was a pause before Irani said, "Let's do this. You can keep the car if you transfer title and insurance into your name. And I'll keep paying your salary as long as you work on whatever Eve asks you to. Please tell Nila the same."

Eve looked exasperated, but Irani's hand gesture short-circuited an outburst as she kept talking.

"Eve, you can take Amtrak back. I'll pick you up at DC's Union Station Sunday evening. Please come see me Saturday after you and Nari are ready to go and we'll talk about your new status."

"Will do. Come on, Nari. Let's get busy…"

A breathless Eve hustled into Irani's office late Friday afternoon.

"I can stay only a minute because Nari's treating me and a couple of friends to pizza. We just finished packing all her stuff in the one-way trailer I'll be towing."

"How does the car handle with the trailer attached?"

"I practiced driving like this last summer and I'm OK."

"I checked the weather forecast. You should have pleasant early summer-like weather for the drive tomorrow. No rain in the forecast until maybe Monday. When are you leaving?"

"Five a.m. tomorrow, which should put us in Boston by early afternoon. I'll call you Saturday evening when I know when I'll catch Amtrak back. I'll see you then."

Eve turned to go but Irani's words stopped her when she rose to hand her an envelope.

"Please read these guidelines on the ride home. I thought they might help us. Now go and have fun."

"Wow, you're always thinking, aren't you? Well, I guess that's good. Bye…"

Nari's mood elevated with each mile that decreased the distance to Boston. Her giddy delight bubbled in her words as Eve pulled into a parking space in front of the apartment building.

"I told you we'd have help unloading. My friends are already here. We're so lucky they have Boston intern positions this summer. And I'm sure you'll like them and they'll like you."

Nari was right on all counts; the group of six females was eating pizza at the apartment's all-purpose table by seven-thirty, with Nari leading the gossip.

"I'm so glad to be back at Harvard. For the past year, I've been wandering in the desert. Even Washington and GWU are barren by comparison."

One of her friends pointed a question at Eve.

"When do you head back to Stanford?"

"Oh, I don't know. I've got a pretty good intern position in DC, and I like my GWU courses."

"That combination can't compare with either Stanford or Harvard. Boston and Stanford are for the smart students."

Nari said, "That's why two guys we met in Cairo last summer are coming here for grad school. A fellow by the name of Sanjay Kumar has been accepted at Harvard, and his friend Yang Lee will be going to MIT. They'll fit in nicely."

Another question came Eve's way.

"You must be smart too. Why don't you transfer here? You'll learn a lot more."

"Maybe not. My mentor's pretty damn smart. She knows all about –" Nari interrupted.

"She's not as smart as you think. Why –" Eve interrupted right back.

"Hold on. You didn't stick around when she started linking the political philosophy of Leo Strauss to the misleading exoteric statements currently coming from China. And she told me about the subjective bypass that led astray all philosophers since Spinoza because they were too lazy to read the original Latin or Greek writings of the early philosophers. That's the only way you can ferret out the esoteric content hidden between the lines. What do any of you have to say about that?"

Eve's challenge went unanswered until Nari said, "OK, I stand corrected. But I'll know all that and more as I make up for lost time. I'll be busy, so don't give me too many assignments."

Another question came, but this time pointed at Nari.

"Are you working for Eve? I'm not sure I'd want to work for my sister. Good luck."

Eve's smile returned and she said, "Nari and I make a great team, even when working remotely. And I'm sure my mentor will fill in wherever needed. I'll see when I get back to DC…"

Nari's friends took Eve for a brief campus and Boston tour before dropping her at South Station to catch the 2 p.m. train to DC. Nari did most of the talking as they walked to the train.

"Thanks for all the help. I'll miss you more than I show it."

Eve said, "Nila will fill in for me soon enough. And don't worry about any assignments from me. I'll call you after Nila settles in."

She gave Nari a quick hug and then said, "Let's both stay safe."

Eve mused to herself while glancing out the window for most of the trip back. As the train approached the metropolitan area, the conductor announced that the DC weather was turning cooler with gusty rains.

Sounds like it might be worse when I get in at 10 p.m. I'm glad Miss Irani will pick me up… Oops, I haven't read her letter yet… I think I'll read it when she drives me home. That'll be soon enough.

Eve felt a tiny emotional ping.

I had a good time visiting Boston, but I feel OK about getting home to DC. I'm not so sure Boston or Stanford are right for me, at least not right now. I'll have to see…

Eve scampered to Irani as soon as she spotted her waving. Irani spoke as she handed her a windbreaker.

"Welcome home. We don't have far to walk to get to the car, but I thought you'd want to stay dry. Be sure to take it off before getting into your car."

"My car? I don't understand."

"I guess you didn't read my letter. That's OK… you'll see when we get there. How did you like Boston?"

Eve did all the talking as Irani led the way; she changed subjects when they reached the car.

"Gads, it's a Corvette. Is it mine?"

"It's one of the perks for working with me. Let me drive to show you the options."

Irani talked more as soon as they were sitting inside.

"I loved driving when I was your age. A friend back then helped me convert my retro hot hatchback into what I called a stealth street racer. But this Vette is not stealth. It's the plug-in hybrid double overhead cam mid-engine Vette drivers have been asking for. I bought the candy-apple red with a white trim package. And it's a retractable hardtop equipped with full safety and communications features. I'll show you how to work them, but promise me you'll always keep the automatic safety engaged."

Eve did and then focused on Irani's arms and hands that put her words into action. Twenty minutes later, passenger and driver switched places. Irani let Eve do all the talking until they pulled into the garage.

"You're a quick study and are ready to solo whenever you want. All I ask is for you to use common sense and drive safely."

"I will, and I'll keep the safety engaged too. Are you staying tonight?"

"There's plenty of room now that Nari's ensconced in Boston. But I'll keep out of your way."

"Hey, I'll read your letter and we can talk about it tomorrow, OK?"

"That'll be fine. Now let's get in, unless you want to sleep in the Vette."

Eve's excitement kept her awake, so after tossing for an hour she decided to read Irani's letter. She skimmed it once.

Dear Eve,

Not wanting to embarrass you (or myself, for that matter), I decided to write these guidelines for you to read first and then decide which topics you would like to discuss further.

I know from observation that you and Nari have typical sibling rivalry, but you also have many traits in common. Someday when you've moved through the early years of adulthood, I will tell you more about Su-Lin and myself that will reveal how much we have in common, but put that aside for the time being. Now that your considerable talents are fully recovered from that nagging viral illness, I am certain you will enjoy exercising your alert and sometimes feisty (in all the right ways) persona while having the house to yourself. I know it's important for you to have your own space; that's one of the reasons I like to stay at my office.

Once upon a time I was your age, so I know about the fun and frustration you face. Every generation confronts challenges, and today's lightning-like changes in many of the climates impacting your world might make the future seem uncertain and frightening. But please take my advice and focus on the one thing you can control: yourself. Perhaps I can help if you stay in DC and work with me instead of returning to Stanford. Nari won't be missed much because I'll assist you in every which way you want. And I will have another vehicle for you when you return.

The college experience today is different than even twenty years ago. I can appreciate Nari and Nila's desire to attend elite schools like Harvard or MIT, because that should increase their odds for joining the academic, business, or sociopolitical elite. But there's a groundswell against that route. You can excel if you follow what's right for you and guard against some of the dubious university teachings. Besides, GWU is highly regarded. We can talk about this sometime if you like; my thoughts can do double-duty in academic and career choices.

I have a fondness for you and your siblings, but most of all for you. We talked about a game that just the two of us would play, that I am your mother. I would like to take the game to the next level by adopting you. It will give you as well as me many advantages. And we can still keep it a secret, telling others only when you want them to know. Please decide if you would like that.

I hope you read this letter on the train ride back from Boston. And I will let you lead whatever discussion you would like to have.

I do know that you like to read and sometimes write poetry, so I am enclosing one told to me by my mentor. It helped me when I was your age, and my wish for you is the same.

Reach for Beyond

When young I struggled to reach the truth,
But too short-sighted I could not see.
So I turned to myths and saw forsooth,
The gods they too eluded me.

Then turning to humanity,
I looked for what might be inside.
And using all my empathy,
I found all three they cannot hide.

Let no soul say that truth be told,
One time for all eternity.
Reach for beyond seek out the bold,
And never fear contingency.

My love is with you always…

Irani

Then she pored over it again. Tears blurred her vision when she read the poem for a third time.

The lightning brain always kept its warning system engaged. Electra awoke at the very first sound of a hesitant tapping on her bedroom door; she switched on a nightstand light and her Irani personality before answering.

"I'm awake… come on in."

Eve did so, then said, "Could I sit down and talk about your letter?"

"Please do. Wait for me, I'll sit next to you."

Pretending not to notice Eve's tear-streaked cheeks, Irani spoke first.

"Your Granny Su told me a lot about you. That's just one of the reasons you're so special to me. And I want what's best for you, so

I'll be happy to cover all your expenses if you want to head back to Stanford, or perhaps to Boston."

"No, I want to stay here and learn from you. But I'm scared I won't live up to your standards, and I'm sorry for saying or thinking mean things."

"You'll never disappoint me if you simply be your authentic self. And I can't recall your ever saying anything mean to me. But if you did, that's OK too. I remember fighting with my parents when I was young. That's part of being human. And if you get mad at me, let me know... don't bottle up your feelings and let a problem grow."

"You're sure you can adopt me? I'm not too old, am I?"

"I certainly can if you agree. By the way, the brilliant feminist philosopher Simone de Beauvoir took care of a girl who was seventeen when they first met and actually adopted her twenty years later."

"There's so much I want to know about you, and so much I want to ask and learn so I can be just like you. I almost don't know where to start. Where should I?"

"Let me do that. You want your life to mean something, so dream big and ask why not? instead of why. And you're already doing that by going to GWU and working with me. We'll make sure your assignments connect to your career aspirations. And I want you to keep interacting with organizations like OWLM. That's the best way to keep up with social media and trends."

Irani paused for Eve to talk, but she just nodded and kept her gaze locked on her mentor, so Irani continued.

"And after that, we'll talk about how you can use the Overton Window for assessing the range of political policies acceptable at a given time. And then we'll talk about one of my favorite subjects, philosophy. I'll touch on a philosophical construct – Kant's wall – that can help answer some of life's big questions. And I'll give you a partial answer to one of them right now. Please, don't try to be like me. Be your genuine self."

Eve leaned forward after finding the right words.

"When will you answer some of the questions I have about you?"

"When the time's right, but right now, I want to focus on you, young lady. So, let's both of us get a good night's sleep and tomorrow we'll outline what you'll be working on. And you can add Nari to the mix if you'd rather work with her than me."

"No way, and let's work at your office tomorrow. That way I can drive us."

"That's why I have two indoor parking places, one for you and one for me. And be careful you don't spoil me. I might get used to your chauffeuring me around. I'll feel like royalty."

"Hey, I think I'd like that."

"OK, but only if I don't get in the way of your social life. What do you say?"

Eve laughed before answering.

"Yes, Mother, I shall obey."

"Good, then go to bed pronto."

Eve hugged her soon-to-be-official mother before scurrying back to bed, ready to rest for the day ahead, a day full of promise and the start of an even brighter future.

I can't control the weather, but I can control my excitement by focusing on what I'll do tomorrow. Let's see…

A calming sleep came as she let her mind wander through an emerging to-do list.

Chapter 8
August 2158

"The Twofer Trip"

A self-motivated Eve had dived into her studies and DC projects under Irani's unobtrusive guidance during the summer. While changing majors from anthropology to political science and minors from biology to anthropology, she added a fourth course – introductory political philosophy – and joined study groups that expanded her circle of campus friends and leisure activity partners.

Eve's output let Irani deal with the more complex pieces of projects, of which platform policies for Congresswoman Huston occupied a spot near the top. Eve's contributions would be featured at a Tuesday morning meeting the last week of August. Listening to Irani while driving to the Capitol complex gave Eve a chance to center herself.

"What you've come up with exceeds my expectations. And you did all this without Nari?"

"You were all the help I needed, but I did let Sabrina review it. She thinks the Congresswoman can impress some of her contacts with it. And like I've learned from you, sharing the credit is always a win-win."

"Excellent. We'll let Gene start the meeting, then I'll talk, and then I'll let you take over. And if you get stuck, turn it back to me."

"Yes, Mother, I shall obey, but I'll call you Miss Irani if that's OK."

"Fine with me. I like our game…"

Irani was ready by 11:15 to unleash Eve.

"I think all the policy issues we've covered will resonate with your constituency and fellow congresspeople. Your Republican Party might want some of them plus the positioning in order to grow its base."

Irani paused for Gene's appraisal.

"That could work. They ranked among the top spots on voter concerns surveys. Sabrina says you've got some sort of analytic flowchart for evaluating them."

"Eve created it… she calls it an evaluation filter. I'd like her to take us through it."

Eve handed out copies to everyone before talking while standing at the head of the conference room table.

"I used some of my GWU courses to develop this, and I want to thank Sabrina for her constructive criticism. And in the near future, I'll come up with a broader political philosophy framework that goes beyond what Miss Irani talked about a couple of meetings ago. I'll need her help to get going, just like on my filter, but once I do there'll be no stopping me. Please take a minute to study before I start talking about what I just handed out."

Eve talked to herself as the seconds ticked away.

Mother's so right. Perfect practice makes perfect. I'm ready to talk the talk. And someday, I'll walk the walk…

Socio-Political Policy Evaluation Filter

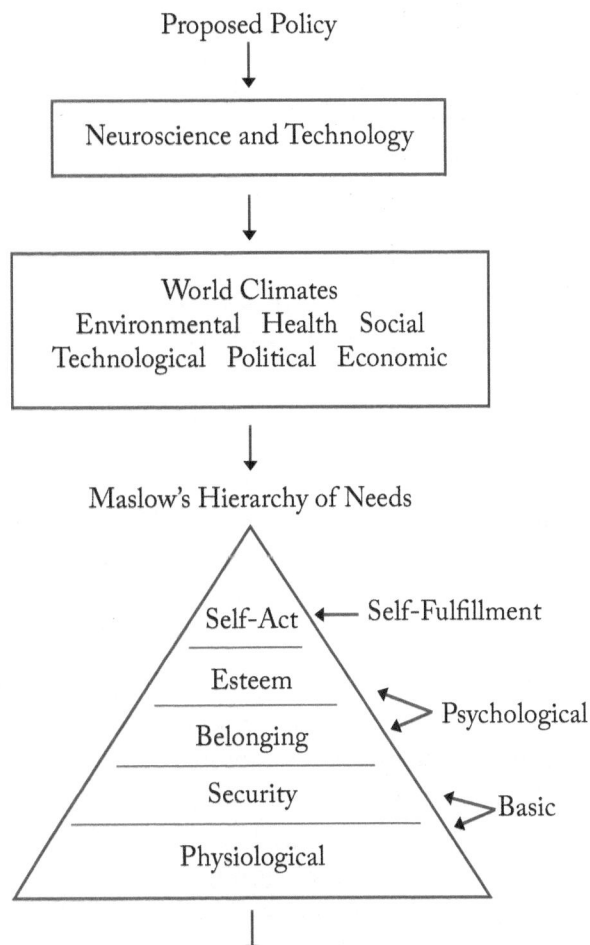

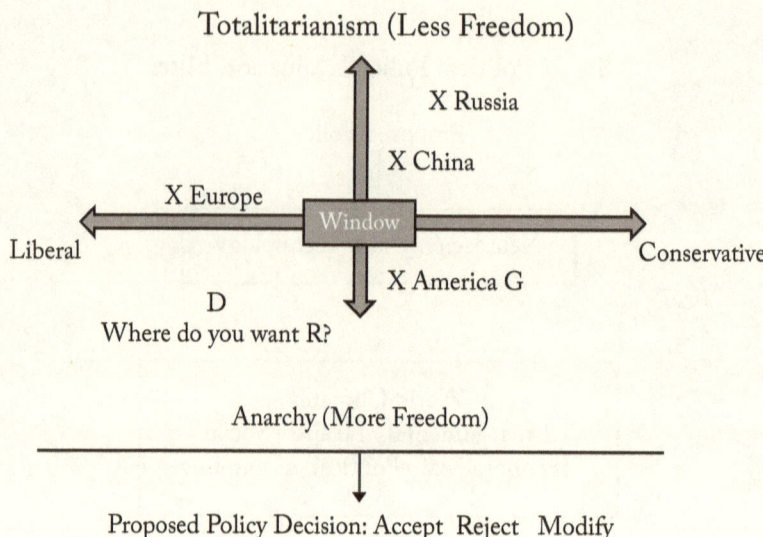

Totalitarianism (Less Freedom)

X Russia

X China

X Europe

Window

Liberal — Conservative

X America G

D

Where do you want R?

Anarchy (More Freedom)

Proposed Policy Decision: Accept Reject Modify

"Coming up with policy recommendations is a two-step process. The first is finding policies and the second is evaluating them. We always ask Why not? when looking for them, but once we have collected enough, then we have to ask Why? And we use our evaluation filter to separate the feasible from the feckless. Uh, I borrowed that word from Miss Irani. It makes a nice alliteration with feasible. Wait, maybe it's consonance... or is it assonance?"

Irani filled in the right words.

"Alliteration and consonance both fit. Please go on."

"Sorry. Anyway, we put a policy through a first filtration step by sizing up how it fits with the latest neuroscientific or technological thinking. For example, if a policy goes against our DNA – trying to ban sugary soft drinks – we give it a low score for that criterion.

"Next, we put it through our climate filtration. Please notice we have five distinct but interacting climates. If a policy covers a climate issue, it gets high marks. For example, if it talks about building a better early warning system for disasters – like viral or earthquake or volcano eruptions – we give it a high mark.

"And then, we put it through Maslow's Hierarchy of Needs to see if the policy is more physically than emotionally threatening.

Those that fit lower in the pyramid cover what we call existential threats, threats that we can't pussyfoot around. Fast, decisive action is needed and we give it a high mark.

"And then, we put it through the Overton Window, which will show if the policy fits inside the current political thinking. It gets high marks if it's inside the window. I don't have to explain to you its two dimensions, and notice I've labeled where different countries are situated. Notice also the D for Democratic and G for Guardian party's more extreme elements that are pushing to open the window further beyond post-Enlightenment principles. We expect the Congresswoman to decide where to position her Republican Party so it can redefine itself and appeal to more voters. We can connect this to her 'Re-Founding' positioning statement.

"And after all that filtering, we make a decision: accept, reject, or modify the policy. And that's it to my filter. Any questions?"

All gazes landed on the Congresswoman.

"I've never seen anything like this. Very thorough. But I do have a question. You mentioned scoring each policy at each of the four filtration steps. How do you combine the scores?"

Eve's wrinkled brow and glance at Irani kept her from answering, but she changed her expression before Irani could intervene. Having regained her footing, she replied,

"That's a good question. I guess my next step will be to come up with a weighted average score. But as Miss Irani told me, we'll never come up with an algorithm to compute what people or politicians will do. The human touch is needed."

Eve could tell the Congresswoman wanted to comment, so she paused.

"Your Miss Irani's right. I can't do it this year, but if the election goes our way, next year I can put her in touch with the right people by assigning her to committee projects and representing me at events. It's too bad I can't send her to the Inter-Gov Climate Meeting next month. The impact of changing weather patterns and that ominous X-Virus will be front and center, and I can be the leading spokesperson for my party.

Eve asked, "Where's it being held?"

Irani replied first.

"In Harare, the capital of Zimbabwe. The climate issues Gene mentioned might hit Africa hard. We'll have to pay attention, just like I'm paying attention to the clock. It's almost noon. We've used up our two hours. Time to go."

Gene said, "I'll schedule our next meeting for a couple of weeks before the election. You can tell me what your social forecasting predicts and what words I can use in my speeches. And I can predict great things for you and me next year…"

Irani led the discussion on the drive back to the office.

"Mission accomplished. Gene likes what we've done, and your policy filter intrigued her. Nice work."

"I sort of stumbled at the start. Thanks for jumping in."

"Actually, that could be considered a novel way for putting the audience at ease. And you handled her last question nicely when you came up with the idea of a weighted average. See where that takes you. And I'm pleased you asked about the climate meeting location."

"I thought I was on top of current stuff, but I didn't know it's gonna be in Harare. How come you know so much?"

"You know a lot too. It's just that I'm older and have come up with a pretty thorough climate scanning procedure. You're doing the same thing and will be better than me when you get to be my age."

"You're my role model. I love seeing you in action. But hey, I've got an idea; why don't you call Alonzo and Monet? She comes from Zimbabwe and maybe has contacts that know what's going on."

Excellent idea. I'll call them tonight. And now, I'll treat us to lunch. Then you can drop me off and meet your friends on campus."

"Will you come home tonight?"

"No, the house is yours. I've got some other project work so I'll stay at the office."

"Well don't worry. If I throw a party, we'll be orderly and clean up. If I'm bad, Mrs. Newlands will report on me."

"You're bad only when bad means good. And I'm proud of how you're getting better and better."

Eve said nothing but instead just glowed.

Alonzo's words rang out as soon as he recognized the caller's voice.

"Hi back at you, Irani. Life's good for your Austin interns. Kim's shuffled the load so Monet and I can handle some of the software stuff Nila was starting to do. Hold on a sec, I'll get Monet to join us."

Monet's distinctive voice came through seconds later.

"Hello and best wishes. It is always a pleasure to speak to you. I trust all is well with you and Eve."

"Yes, and thanks for asking. She's thriving. We had a meeting today with a client who mentioned the Inter-Gov Climate meeting being held next month in Harare and she told me to call for the inside scoop. Have you been following any related news?"

"I do because I speak twice a month with Darla Tinibu. Zimbabwe, like all African countries, is concerned about the changing weather patterns. Drought in some regions and floods in others threaten our agriculture and rare earths industries. Darla has invited Alonzo and me to attend. It is possible that our Solar Panel and Martian farming technology could be of interest. I would be pleased to introduce you to her if by chance you came to the meeting."

"Darla must be a smart person who recognizes talent. I'm sure she sees it in you."

"No matter that I come from her Karanga-speaking Shona tribe. Darla respects people who do good work."

"I look forward to meeting her, maybe not next month but sooner rather than later. Now please tell me how your online studies are going, and then get Alonzo back so he can tell me about balancing school and intern work…"

Electra invoked Indira's GUI after Irani disconnected the Austin call fifteen minutes later.

"I assume you heard all the Austin news. What do you think?"

"We have three opportunities to pursue. The first concerns robotics and AI apps, for which we do not need Nila. Both have advanced beyond her competence during your twenty-year absence. Robotic nano-motor technology has improved mobility and facial gestures, and rudimentary human-like physical, emotional, and cognitive traits are now evident in software output, but none are approaching the sophistication of the Singularity. Ditto for Network Security, which is crawling away from encryption algorithms that use prime number factorization towards those that use lattice representation built on mega-dimensional double-digit bases. And Social Forecasting algorithms are still mired in the challenge of threading through Big Data. But what I will do is upgrade your Network Security and Social Forecasting suites by borrowing the improvements the competitors have made and then going beyond their SQL, multi-regression, and time series-adjusted pattern matching algorithms by using your extended AI-modal programming language. And I'll have two versions: a weaker version you can market and a stronger version that will include stealth trapdoors just for us. We don't need Nila, and you are freed from the actual design and coding because I am smarter."

"A fine division of labor utilizing comparative advantage. I'll handle sales and marketing by reprising an updated Katrina Blanka."

"And I expect you to keep your end of our bargain. You must assist my building a superior android."

"I will. I'm looking for the right time."

"Good, and meanwhile, Jason will continue our observational and experimental studies."

"What's the second opportunity?"

"You should make an unannounced visit to Harare. Listen to the speakers and have Monet introduce you to Darla. She will want to license our farming integration software as well as AI-empowered security and forecasting suites. I'm certain you will figure out a win-win combination."

"That makes sense. And what's the third?"

"It piggybacks on the second. We shall resupply our subterranean fortress. I have been monitoring a variety of climates and have come up with a suitable plan that will utilize your covert soldiers of fortune A-Team. They served us well last year and can do so again."

"Hmm, this will be more complicated than last time. I better think about it."

"No, I already have and you will like what I have developed, so please settle down, sit still, and let me explain…"

In spite of a Friday the thirteenth departure date, Electra knew that the first leg of her twofer trip would be the most relaxing. By playing dual roles (typical tourist and covert planner), she made the most of sixteen uninterrupted hours on a nonstop commercial flight to Harare-Mugabe International Airport.

Taking timeout to think like a tourist helps me prepare for the climates I'll encounter. I see that Zimbabwe has canceled some of the cancel culture's meddling by reinserting Mugabe back into the airport's name. You can't ignore the facts.

He liberated his country from British-controlled minority white rule two hundred years ago. His people consider him a revolutionary hero who fought racial oppression and stood up to Western imperialism and neo-colonialism. Of course, his enemies called him a dictator and tyrant who should have been punished for crimes against his own people. And its government today is more democratic than authoritarian and is working to loosen its dependence on China. All this fits within the sweep of political history.

Too bad I won't take in the country's iconic tourist attractions. Victoria Falls, Chinhoyi Caves, and irreplaceable wildlife preserves like Hwange and other national parks are perennial favorites. Maybe next time… but will there be a next time? Only if I plan for it. Well, I better get back to the current plan to make sure there is a next time…

Electra did budget some of the first day for sightseeing in Harare, Zimbabwe's capital and largest city – population of five million. She took a half-day city tour, which alerted her senses to the country's combination of African culture and climate.

The sights and sounds of so many people bustling in and out of so many modern buildings show me that Harare is creating Zimbabwe's tomorrow. And so many parklike settings containing the pristine fragrance of exotic plants that tickles my nose and connects me to the land. And the altitude adds to the brightness of sky and sunlight that complements the pleasant October temps. No wonder climate change is a concern if it threatens all this beauty.

She returned to her hotel afterwards, the low-slung Cresta Lodge, which was within walking distance of the futuristic Rainbow Towers and Conference Center that would host the Inter-Gov

Climate Meeting. Then after preparing for Monday, she walked to Gava's Restaurant for a late afternoon meal. Sitting at a tent-covered outdoor table, she talked with tourists and locals alike while sampling traditional foods and listening to nonstop live music.

Back at the lodge and fully relaxed plus prepared, Electra switched to Irani, who called Alonzo. The lodge's phone number confused him, so Irani spoke after he said hello.

"It's Irani. I came to Harare for the climate meeting and wanted to say hi. Will you and Monet be attending?"

"What the – wow, what a surprise. Hold on, let me get Monet."

Monet spoke fifteen seconds later.

"Welcome to Harare. I'm so happy you can see my country."

"Me too, but I'm on a tight schedule and must leave in two days. I have a guest registration for the meeting, but if I could be with you two, you might get me in to the restricted sessions."

"I can do that, and please allow me to introduce you to Darla Tinibu."

"I was hoping you'd do that as well. Why don't we meet at the registration desk fifteen minutes before tomorrow's opening session?"

"We shall be there as you wish. Alonzo wants to say something."

A second later he asked, "So, is Eve with you?"

"No, she's fully occupied with school and assignments in DC, but who knows, future projects might bring her back to Africa under more pleasant conditions than last time."

"If they include Monet they sure will be. She's got lots of contacts."

"Good, I look forward to meeting some of them before I leave. Let's talk more tomorrow at the conference …"

Irani picked the pair out of the gathering crowd when she arrived. Alonzo's sports coat and tie matched Monet's tailored pants suit, adding an aura of maturity and professionalism that was further enhanced when Irani joined them. Monet suggested they decide what sessions to attend after they heard the keynote speaker's opening remarks, which began promptly at 8 a.m.

"I will not say 'Good Morning' to all in attendance, but instead just say 'Morning' because I am not optimistic regarding all the climate challenges facing the world. Issues abound in all of them: Environment, Health, Technology, Socio-politics, Economics. Too many to discuss at one meeting, so instead we will focus on only two: Environment and Health. And we shall see how interrelated they are.

"And what do we know about environmental challenges? Enough climate change data has been analyzed to conclude with a high probability that regardless of temperature change, polar ice cap melting will accelerate because ocean currents have changed. Furthermore, there are conjectures that volcanic and tsunami activity may increase because of the reduced weight of ice covering South Pole's land mass, which could further accelerate tectonic plate-shifting.

And what do we know about health challenges? Are changing weather patterns, especially in Africa, breeding more bacteria and viruses that are spreading from animals to humans? Might they be the cause of the mysterious X-Virus? And might they be the cause of raging fires worldwide during extended dry seasons that put more pollutants into the air we breathe while reducing the world's food supply and arable land?

"I don't have definitive answers or solutions, but we are gathered together to discuss what the nations of the world can do collectively to contain an accelerating downward spiral leading to Armageddon. Let me introduce our breakout session moderators. It is our fervent hope that by the last day of our meeting, I can say 'goodbye' to conclude what we have accomplished…"

Monet picked the restricted sessions that had the most immediate impact on Africa. As Irani listened to the discussions, Electra made mental notes that would connect with their DC projects.

I'm glad Monet is connected to African politics via Darla. Professor Plannert will like the updates I can make regarding rising sea levels and volcanic activity. His Environmental Scanning committee can uncover all sorts of spillover effects. And I can use some of them to score points for my political consulting. And there may be more for me and my interns to do if my meeting with Darla comes through. Oh what fun…

Irani and the Monet-Alonzo duo went separate ways at the end of the first day; each had follow-up activities to handle, but they agreed to meet tomorrow as they had today. Electra mused to herself as she strolled back to her lodge.

I like the way Monet handles herself. Her self-confidence is even stronger than Eve's and she contributes more than Alonzo. I must make sure she's getting enough from me, but I must do so subtly. She might be even smarter than Nari and could play my DC game if the right projects come my way. We'll have to see what Darla has to say tomorrow afternoon.

Tuesday unfolded about the same as Monday. The trio stayed together and Electra added incrementally to yesterday's notes. By early afternoon, Monet confirmed their closed-door meeting at Darla's Syntagra office. Alonzo drove and left the talking to Monet and Irani, who chatted casually.

"How coincidental that some of my business enterprises overlap with Darla's. Perhaps you and Alonzo can forge a future alliance that will benefit all."

"I would call it serendipity if that happens, but Alonzo and I are too young to make it so. We need you to lead the way."

Irani smiled while Electra spoke only to herself.

That's on my hidden agenda today. We'll let Darla run the meeting but Irani will steer it. If we drive a bargain as good as my Katrina Blanka personality did long ago, Darla will be part of my latest game.

Less than an hour later, Monet led the way to Darla's office, and though age and illness had taken its toll, Darla's fireplug-like build still radiated a powerful aura. Rising to greet Monet, who was obviously special, she seated them around a small conference room table before sitting at the head and diving into her main interest.

"I know more than most of those stuff-shirt speakers about how climate change impacts my country and its allies. Some of their hype may be on target, but I don't give a rat's ass about that X-Virus kerfuffle. Blame it on those Chinese gene manipulators, not Africa. We're kicking them out. Maybe they unleashed it deliberately. They've got too many males stirring up trouble elsewhere. Anyway, you've heard all the talk, now you tell me what you've got that I might want."

Monet glanced at Irani, whose smile preceded her words.

"I believe that Monet and Alonzo have told you about the Vertical Martian and Solar Panel farms they are managing for me. Well, droughts caused by changing weather patterns might provide an opportunity for you to install them in Africa. You could benefit from their management expertise as well as the AI-empowered apps that control the infrastructure. And we have similar apps for controlling rare earths mining."

"They did, but they also said the software person is gone. What can you do about that?"

"I have a replacement in mind who can handle all that plus Internet Security software. Might that be of interest?" *Of course it is… that's what you distributed years ago for Katrina. We'll make this a win-win so you'll want to join my game.*

Darla paused before directing a question at Monet.

"Do you trust this Irani Ramani person?"

"Indeed yes. If she says she has a replacement for Nila Bose, I believe her."

Darla's gaze and next question landed on Irani.

"You've sold me. This coincidence is too good to pass up. How do we proceed?"

"Monet and Alonzo will take the lead. They are young and smart, and you can instruct them. They will make the future happen…"

Even Darla had to agree. As the meeting adjourned, all present flashed winners' smiles. Alonzo's enthusiasm on the drive away even affected Monet's usually unflappable demeanor.

"I am so pleased with the outcome. Alonzo and I should like to treat you to dinner."

"No, I owe you, but let me repay you next time we're together. I'm leaving early tomorrow on the next leg of my trip, so please just drop me off at my lodge. I'll make plans for all of us to gather in DC, probably near the end of the year."

Alonzo said, "I know the way to the Cresta Lodge, but do you need directions from there?"

"Thanks but no, I know the way…"

Electra prepped and packed after a light dinner. She had received no calls or Emails from either her Japanese A-Team or insider informant, so she assumed her POA was AOK.

Indira has paid in advance for all equipment and supplies, and I've given them the detailed plan of action. There are lots of parts that are now in place. There's nothing to do except get a good night's sleep and put the parts in motion tomorrow. And if I find a surprise, I'll just have to improvise by adapting one of my contingency plans. No roll of the dice for me, I make my own serendipity.

The Irani-Electra duo slept well that night.

Chapter 9
October 2158

"The Pause to Reenergize"

Using the same codename as last time, the A-Team arrived just before sunrise and put Irani plus her gear into the van before racing to the helicopter departure site where they loaded the van into the chopper before helping her suit up. She could tell from the leader's Japanese-styled English that he knew the drill and would be easy to decipher. And though she couldn't distinguish male from female because their exo-skeleton uniforms blurred the difference, team members worked as efficiently as links in a well-oiled chain. Everyone was now in the chopper and waiting for the leader to speak.

Irani wanted him to review what she had initially sent, but knowing the importance of Japanese etiquette, she let him talk first.

"Salutations again, Gemini-Ramani. I Gemini-T1. With me T2, 3, and 4. So nice you hire us one more time again. This time, plan more abstruse, but we ready. Please tell, any updates?"

"No. We go with what I gave you. Please tell it to me one more time."

"Roger that. We got all supplies and desert transport vehicle at rendezvous oasis. It guarded by T5 and T6. When chopper get us there, we transfer to armored personnel carrier and await go command from inside friend. Then chopper take us and APC to drop location. Then drive in APC to pick up plutonium pellets at hidden Iranian desert enrichment center. Then chopper whisk us back to oasis. Then you drive to fortress. Then you contact us when ready for oasis extraction. Over."

"That's it. And my inside friend has given me all the access codes, passwords, and protocols. I'll do the talking when we get to the enrichment center. We go hot on weapons immediately, but get lethal only to protect ourselves and the mission, over."

"Roger that. What if Lady Fortune visit? Got backup plan? Over."

"Affirmative. I will take charge only then if needed. Over."

T1 looked at his nodding and smiling team before saying, "All is good, so let us pause when we get to oasis so we reenergize until insider give go command."

Everyone withdrew on the flight into their personal space, letting their thoughts take them to another place. Irani did the same and Electra came to the fore.

Indira's the ultimate insider. She'll call me if a contingency arises. And if she does, we've got them all set. I'm going to hit my pause button and let the lightning brain freewheel until we get the go signal.

Irani did the same.

The chopper carrying the APC, Irani, and her team arrived just after sunset at the drop location just beyond the enrichment center's horizon. Though no one spoke, Irani could tell everyone was gearing up for immanent action.

T1 snapped out instructions.

"All ride in back except Gemini-Ramani, she ride next to me."

Irani reminded the team as soon as all were in place.

"My insider has killed all power and communications. All we gotta do is act like we know what we're doing and we're in, so let's follow the plan."

T1 slowed to a stop as the APC reached the darkened installation entrance made visible only by guards waving flashlights. One of them motioned for him to open his window, but a call coming in on Irani's cell froze his hand. He pieced together the predicament from her chopped sentences.

"Shipment already gone... spooked by power failure... contingency number two is a go... will do... over."

Irani gave new orders to T1.

"Tell the guard to let us drive in. We know about the security breach and have to talk to the dispatcher. Once there I'll talk and take command."

T1 followed orders and wouldn't take any "Nos" from the guards. Four minutes later his screeching tires scattered a cluster of workers as he rocked to a halt inside a pitch-dark shipping bay illuminated only by his headlights. Irani grabbed the flashlight T2 handed her and leaped from the van.

She scrambled towards the now stationary cluster and yelled, "You've been hacked and we gotta intercept the van before it's blown away. Give us its GPS tracking ID."

All the Ts heard the number that T1 punched in just before emergency lights and pulsing horns accompanied a self-destruct warning that blared in English from loudspeakers. Five minutes later the APC rocketed away from the installation. T1 gave the next command.

"I tell chopper to halt van. Then transfer cargo and vamoosa with us-ah."

Electra took Irani's place as the lightning brain elevated to a higher state that sent excitement racing through all three of her personas. She yelled to herself before telling the team.

Get ready for a firefight and get lethal. We leave no clues or loose tongues.

The Ts needed no further instructions. They were now locked and loaded.

T1 kept in constant contact with the chopper. It swooped overhead towards the target and came back fifteen minutes later.

"Van out of action. Follow my spotlight."

Electra and her team, now huddled one hundred meters from the spotlighted van and wearing night vision goggles, listened to T1's orders.

"Me and T2 flank left side. T3 and T4 take right. Irani take middle but only after all safe."

*We don't know how many or how much firepower we're up against.
I'm elevating to another level.*

Electra crept forward while scrutinizing the action as the Ts
charged ahead, using the cover of darkness as a shield. It held until
two sets of tracer shells raked over the two sets of Ts, taking down
one on each side.

The lightning brain had seen enough. It abruptly took control by
shifting to an even higher state that put the action in clear-as-noon
slow motion. Electra blasted her laser bazooka via her right arm
into the two adversaries on the right, lighting them up and putting
them down, and a second later repeated with her left, getting the
same results. Then she rushed to her fallen comrades, who were
beginning to stir.

Exo-skel body armor had absorbed the brunt of the bullets.
Though bleeding, T2 and T3 walked unsteadily while their partners
supported them. Electra retired from action, leaving Irani in charge.
She gathered everyone in front of the smoldering van as the chopper
touched down and the onboard EMT-trained person leaped out to
begin patching the wounded Ts.

"T1, go get our APC while we find the plutonium…"

The grim-faced but efficient Ts had the plutonium stored and
the APC aboard the chopper half an hour later. Irani issued final
instructions before the chopper lifted off.

"Put the bodies in the van. Then we blast it after taking off. Then,
it's off to the oasis."

Unlike previous A-Team missions, the mood onboard was like a
wake. Everyone sat in their silent space. So did Irani, but not Electra.

*My Monster from the Id reemerged and brought with it long-dormant
but overpowering emotions. And it did what it had to, nothing more,
nothing less. I can live with the consequences, and so can the Ts. They
followed orders like well-trained and well-paid soldiers who violated
no code of conduct. I am responsible, not them. I've said enough… it's
time to pause.*

Irani spoke final words just before the chopper reached the oasis.

"Mission accomplished, thanks to all of you. Now all we do is load the plutonium into the supply van and I drive it away. I'll call you when I'm ready for oasis pickup and delivery back to Cairo."

T1 said, "It pitch black. How you know way to where?"

"My insider will be my guide. Expect me to schedule extraction in a couple of days…"

Thirty minutes later, the APV and the chopper went their separate ways.

Electra called her insider as soon as she left the oasis. Indira's tone showed concern for Electra's subdued mood and expression.

"You look weary even though your team won, so you should pause soon to reenergize. Congratulations on executing your part in contingency plan number two. No evidence remains at either facility or pickup locations."

"Two of the Ts took hits, but their exo-skels minimized damage. And mine, when outfitted with a laser bazooka, force-multiplies me into a mini-killing machine. Maybe I shouldn't have terminated with extreme prejudice."

"We've discussed this previously, and my guidelines remain the same… Humans who are willing to play adult games must be ready for losses as well as the gains."

"I know you're right and will bounce back once I've rested. I guess I'll do that after we get the supplies put away. I'm glad my exo-skel force-multiplies my body strength too, but you'll have to get a couple of robo-assistants to help."

"Yes, those in the fortress will be useful, but you will help me improve them when we collaborate on building androids. I have been waiting twenty years to launch this project."

"I will, but first things first. In particular, you'll have to teach me how to refuel the reactor so I don't blow up the fortress or radiate myself into a new species. Is there a deadline for me?"

"Is that a pun you just made? Whatever, the remaining fuel in the reactor will last for two more years, but I went after Iran's supply because it presented itself. And we can always have the A-Team recruit a Russian nuclear scientist to refuel for us. But why not rest your lightning brain? I shall tune you in to a media broadcast that will make your drive time to the fortress go quicker. Trust me, I know all the stations…"

Indira's pick met Electra's expectations, giving both light classical music and news summaries. The last bulletin she heard before lowering into the fortress was of particular interest.

"… And the Inter-Gov Climate Meeting wrapped up this week, unable to establish an upbeat prognosis for current environmental or health-related climate issues. There appears to be no short-term relief regarding droughts and fires, and the mysterious male extinction X-Virus might spiral out of control if the global community does not put together a decisive and coordinated plan for containing and curing it. Next year could be a tipping point. Meanwhile, adding to world angst, this time affecting the socio-political climate, is an unofficially reported desert explosion captured by surveillance drones and satellites. Remote mapping of airborne radiation suggests a catastrophe at a secret uranium enrichment facility, adding to speculation that Isilabad and its allies will become increasingly belligerent. Could it be that a new cycle of global problems is beginning even before the old cycle is resolved? Please stay tuned…"

Electra tuned out by sleeping fourteen hours after eating a bowl of cereal and storing all supplies. She reoriented herself upon awakening by first checking the date and time (Saturday October 21st, 1:43 a.m. in DC) and then exercising. Afterwards, she showered, changed into a fresh set of fortress clothing, ate breakfast, and then logged on to a workstation.

The familiarity of the fortress is coming back. No one but Eve wants to hear from me, and there's nothing on the calendar calling me back immediately. I think I'll stay for a couple of days. All my work is stored in the Cloud, so I can pick up on projects right where I left off. Oops, I made a mistake already… Indira will want to hear from me too. I'll invoke her GUI right now.

Indira spoke first.

"I am pleased to say you look reenergized. Do I assume you are ready to leave?"

"By no means. I'll work here a couple of days so I get even more accustomed to our frontier outpost. And for starters, let me outline my intentions. The Harare meetings gave me some ideas, and I assume you overheard most of them because I had my tablet PC turned on."

"I did, and your tablet helps, but depending on the connectivity of wherever you are, it is sometimes redundant. Nevertheless, please keep it or your workstations on as often as possible."

"Got it. I'm happy to have Alonzo and Monet be our Darla Tinibu contact for all business except software. For that, I'll create a Katrina Blanka replacement, but I better upgrade our Security and Big Data Social Forecasting software suites. And when I do, I'll have to upgrade my financial analysis software too. I'll also tweak the farming and mining AI apps. And I think I'll be able to make Darla another client of our asset management company. She'll want to invest in a portfolio of our AAM funds. How does all this sound?"

"I commend you for thinking like sales and marketing professionals. They know that the purpose of any business is to cultivate and nurture client relationships. Darla will be most useful in a variety of climates. And I like your plans regarding software, but aren't you overlooking the law of comparative advantage? Let me upgrade the software while you tend to 3-D Space activities."

"Why are you volunteering to do this? You've avoided this previously."

"Because doing so fits your goals and mine. And I know more about the latest behavioral investing trends, sometimes labeled Socially Responsible or ESG investing, plus SPAC funds. And don't worry, I'll teach you all that my techniques can do so you're beyond state-of-the art too."

"I won't, and I won't worry about your becoming overloaded. You're the Singular Multi-Tasker."

"Indeed I am, but I will offload some of the work to Jason. You are such a clever wordsmith. That and your ever-increasing empathy make you so effective when dealing with humans, a skill I still need to perfect. And speaking of words, you referred to the fortress as a frontier outpost. What do you think are the frontiers of human knowledge?"

"Easy question and easy answer… AI and DNA, which you and I are exploring. And I'd add high energy physics and space exploration, for which significant next steps are inaccessible. But it's good that scientists and engineers keep picking away. It gives them something to do that has useful spinoffs."

"Your analysis is correct, but incomplete. You and most of humanity have overlooked a frontier that's right at your feet, the ocean and what lies beneath. Consider for a moment what you heard at the Inter-Gov meeting. Volcanoes, earthquakes, and tectonic shifts are threats to humanity for which analytic models are fuzzy. I will show you the volcano and earthquake tracking and prediction software I am developing. I have tweaked several FEM-based neural network algorithms that solve fluid flow PDEs that model earth molten core and also fusion-reactor plasma. Think about how useful this can be for our businesses."

"I'm beginning to feel like my dearly-departed friends who used to complain about my dumping an information overload on them. I remember that PDE stands for partial differential equations, but I don't recall FEM."

"Finite element method that gives an approximate solution in Fourier Space that will – you look puzzled, what's wrong?"

"I'm lost, please, no more."

"Very well, but I have already embedded the apps in my software and yours. All you must do is work the GUIs, and sometime I shall explain the connection between substrates and life forms. That may open up new vistas of inquiry for you. But until then, let's reach closure on what you currently can do."

"I won't get all the way there while I'm here, but I'll make good progress until I leave. Who knows, maybe I'll stay until Halloween."

"I cannot match your cleverness, but I shall end our conversation with an attempt… that's a scary idea, but only when scary means something good. Goodbye."

Indira's GUI vanished, leaving Electra in the company of her own thoughts.

I'm beginning to depend on Indira more than anyone or anything since I became the last in line. And the emotions that come with it are akin to love. How odd, but then maybe not. No matter, it's time to think about lighter subjects, so I'll get a Coke and Oreos for starters. The combination always elevates my mood...

Chapter 10
December 2158

"Mag-Seven Holiday Break"

"What events do you think Eve's lined up? Unlike you and all your siblings, everything will be new for Yang and me. We've never been to Washington. What about Monet?"

Directed at Nari, who was driving, Sanjay's question came from the back seat, which he and Nila occupied. Sitting up front was Yang, who had volunteered to split the driving time from Boston to DC on the first Sunday of Harvard's and MIT's Holiday breaks.

"She didn't tell me, but whatever they are, they'll be new for all of us, including Monet and Alonzo. Eve's the only one who's roamed around DC enough to find the right spots.

And we'll have two weeks to entertain ourselves while comparing notes on the fall term. I'm sure the Mag-Seven will make it through the Holidays. After all, we did survive that Cairo adventure…"

Eve had been too busy with school and intern projects to plan activities in advance, so she asked Irani for help as they sat in the living room, waiting for their guests.

"No one knows you've adopted me, so I'll keep calling you Miss Irani. And are you sure you want to stay at your office?"

"All your siblings and friends will fill the place like a sorority or frat house, and you don't want a house mother getting in the way, but I'll come and go and say hello. Have you checked the weather forecast between now and New Year's Eve?"

"Next two weeks are pretty typical. Maybe some light snow, but no big storms. What sightseeing and stuff do you think I should line up?"

"You should take them to that OWLM concert you organized and talk to Sabrina about showing them around the Capitol. And walking the National Mall to see the monuments should work too, but why not let the group decide? That'll keep everyone happy."

"You're right. That way, they can't blame me if they don't like what they see."

Interpreting Eve's smile, Irani said, "I'm sure the Mag-Seven will like everything. If not, blame the politicos. Well now, you've got the place arranged for all your guests, so I'll be at my office. Please call when you need me…"

Alonzo and Monet arrived mid-afternoon, followed shortly by Nari's carful unloading into the house. Eve directed everyone to their bunking places before placing a pizza plus sweets order. The Mag-Seven were spread out by 7:30 on the sofa, chairs, and family room floor, savoring the last morsels of brownies when Eve picked a conversation starter.

"I hope all of you have had as good a fall term as me. Working as a consulting intern for Congresswoman Huston has made studying so exciting because what I'm doing connects with my courses. Miss Irani showed me how to turn vague political philosophy teachings into actual political campaign strategies and tactics. I even helped her write some parts of speeches and Q&A cheat sheets. And all this helped the Congresswoman win big, even though her party didn't. She thinks the Republican Party might use her positioning statement and platform planks for the next election. And just think, I helped put it all together. This has made me a lot of campus contacts."

Eve paused for someone else. A tired-looking Nari spoke next.

"You look and sound organized, but maybe you should because Irani's giving you special attention. But –" Eve butted in to defend herself.

"Hey, you're the one that beat it back to Boston. How're double majors and minors treating you?"

"I'm doing better than expected and will do even better next term. I've pretty much made up for the time away from Harvard. And Nila says the same, don't you?"

Nila shook her head.

"Maybe not… the higher-level math that AI software uses is tough. Maybe I shouldn't be a dual major."

Alonzo came to her aid.

"Don't doubt yourself. Just do your best. I'm sure you're doing that in your courses and that Lincoln Lab intern position."

"Thanks, I'll keep trying. But how are you and Monet?"

"She knows better than me; I'll let her tell the story."

"We are a fine team and we are also fortunate. Irani knows a great deal and she lets us balance working on courses while working for her. And she knows when to lead and when to leave us alone. She told us that it's better to ask forgiveness than seek permission. But enough from the undergrads. Let us hear from the grad students."

Yang's glance told Sanjay to speak first, so his pleasant voice proceeded.

"Harvard's business school deserves its top ranking. My liberal arts background is well suited for its case study approach, and it gives me a breadth of knowledge that helps span diversity among teammates. I'm holding my own, even against the smartest, who are often from India or China."

Alonzo said, "Are you saying that Indian and Chinese students are better than American?"

Sanjay hesitated, so Yang said, "Not always in MIT's grad programs, like biotech I in, but usually in undergrad study. I think Nila agree. Maybe she need study with foreign students more. And maybe America need copy from China. You cities I see look old and rundown. And China protect people against virus better. Watch over economy better too."

Sanjay tried to lighten Yang's adversarial tone.

"From what I see, American students and people are younger and friendlier than from either China or Japan, and they hustle when interested... much like what you find in the big Indian cities."

But Yang kept pushing his point.

"That because you both big capital money democracies. But China again challenging for top spot in world politics and economics. Look how China handle business and health pandemic. Maybe China better."

Monet used the pause to speak before Sanjay could reply.

"My international government studies have given me insight into both countries, so let's look for a middle position. Both share a similar historical trajectory. Dominant on the world stage centuries ago, then eclipsed by the West, and now reasserting claims to greatness. But demographics favors youthful India rather than aging China, as does its openness. And I would imagine that China's intrusive surveillance shuts people up and makes them wary about government intentions."

But Yang wouldn't quit.

"China mean good things for people and partner countries. That why it want them to do what told. It get better outcome faster."

Judging from some bored expressions, Eve decided to change subjects.

"Depending on the time period, there's a lot of truth to what you say. And if you judge from last month's election, the U.S. needs to lower the level of inequality and raise it for statesmanship and cooperation. But we're on Holiday break, so let's talk about something more fun. Why don't we put together a list of things you'd like to see and do? I can then get them organized, just like I did in Cairo two summers ago..."

The Mag-Seven completed it by 9 p.m. Eve had spent most of the time listening before saying, "You travelers must be tired, so let's call it a night. Nari, why don't you pull your car into the garage. I'll go with you."

Nari bustled back five minutes later.

"Hey everyone, come with me, you gotta see what's in the garage."

All the Mag-Sevens clustered there a couple of minutes later, gazing at the Corvette Eve was sitting in.

Alonzo spoke first.

"Irani never told us she likes fast cars. Does she ever let you drive it?"

Eve craned her head out the window before saying, "Better than that, it's mine. And it's a plug-in hybrid, so it can run on gasoline or electricity."

Standing farthest back, Monet was the next to speak.

"Where is Irani? I hope we get to see her."

"She's staying at her office. She's equipped it so she can live there, which she often does. She didn't want to get in our way, but don't worry, you'll see her when the time's right. Now come on, let's get out of here and say good night…"

Eve called Irani the next morning, reporting that all guests had arrived.

"You have a mini-international gathering. Are you keeping everyone happy?"

"You bet. We had a great political debate last night. You would have been proud how I handled it. I know a lot already and everything I'm doing at school and with you adds to it. Unlike Nari and Nila, I've found my calling. They're struggling."

"That's a challenge that comes with youth. They'll work through it. So, what activities are lined up?"

"Sabrina will take us on a behind-the-scenes tour. And on Thursday, I'll take them to the OWLM lecture-concert at GWU. Would you like to come?"

"Thanks, but no. I'll hear about it later."

"How about this; we're gonna cook an old-fashioned Christmas Day dinner, so you're invited. That'll be exactly one week from today. It'll be a sibling-bonding activity, and I'll invite you to other outings as soon as I know they're a go."

"All that sounds good. Have you planned the dinner menu yet?"

"Nari and I'll do that, and we'll get Nila and Alonzo to help."

"You better check the kitchen shelves and drawers. Last time I looked, they had plenty of the standard ingredients and utensils, but you better study recipes and cooking instructions for anything special. Do you want me to come early and help?"

"No, you and the rest will be our dinner guests. All you need to bring is a good appetite."

"That I can do. Now you get back to the Mag-Seven, and I'll get back to work."

The Mag-Seven used Monday and Tuesday to reconnect with one another and drive around DC's numerous tourist sites before taking Sabrina's Wednesday tour. Even Yang said afterwards that Beijing's Tiananmen Square and government office buildings couldn't compare with the sparkle of everything around the Capitol.

Eve gathered everyone in the living room Thursday morning to describe what's next.

"Instead of going out or ordering in, me and my siblings are going to cook a traditional Christmas dinner feast. The rest of you can be like the Bible's Three Wise Men and just watch us in action. And unlike what the Bible says, you don't have to bring any gifts. Irani will be here too. Just leave the planning to us."

Alonzo said, "I vote for the menu that Granny Su and Hud used. He sure had a way for cooking turkey, and Granny knew what to do for all the trimmings and dessert."

An unsmiling Nari turned her head towards Eve and then said, "This could be a lot of work. Who cooks what?"

"The four of us will plan the menu, then we'll check recipes online before checking out what we've already got in the kitchen. And then we'll go shopping, but we might need to make a couple of trips."

Nari said, "We don't have to get everything today, do we? We can pace ourselves so we don't run ourselves ragged before leaving for that OWLM lecture tonight, but what about the others?"

Eve answered, "Tonight's a combination lecture and concert. I gave everyone the flyer. Why don't they talk about it and surf for background info on the composers? Then they'll know even more than me."

Alonzo and Nila followed Eve and Nari to the kitchen, leaving Monet, Yang, and Sanjay to fend for themselves.

Yang said, "Whew, that Eve sure a dynamo. Good we get a break from her."

Monet said, "She's just being a good hostess. And we can surf for info about her OWLM organization. I know little about it. I've never heard mention of any UTA-related student chapter. What about in Boston?"

Yang shook his head no, but Sanjay had.

"Harvard has one, and it's been outspoken regarding the X-Virus. It supports shelter-in-place and lockdown steps if that will keep the outbreak from becoming an epidemic. I guess its members want to demonstrate solidarity with males. Maybe tonight's speaker will give us an update…"

Eve led the way, driving her Vette that carried Alonzo and Monet. Nari drove the others. The heavy turnout indicated growing concern about the heavyweight topic: The Female Role in Pandemics and Arts – Past, Present, and Future.

Eve herded her group to the auditorium seats that her OWLM friends had set aside, instructing them after sitting to pay close attention to the welcoming remarks, which started promptly at 7 p.m. The speaker had the first slide displayed before talking.

OWLM-2 Welcomes You to Our
Holiday Lecture-Concert!

GWU Chapter Proudly Announces Name Change
  - From: "ONLY WOMEN'S LIVES MATTER"
  - To: "OVERLOOKED WOMEN'S LIVES MATTER TOO!"
  - We Support "All Lives Matter" Initiatives
  - Solidarity Matters

"Good evening, and welcome to our Holiday event. I am Sue Anton, president of our university's OWLM chapter. And before we start, please let me clarify a procedural matter. We just changed what the 'O' in our name stands for. We think 'Overlooked' better expresses our mission. Of course, we are for any and all 'Lives Matter' issues, not just women's. We don't want any group to be left out, and in the past, women were usually overlooked. But thanks to concerted efforts in recent years by all, that has been rectified."

Sue paused for the audience to read her next slide.

Tonight We Feature:
The Female Role in Pandemics and Arts – Past, Present, and Future
- Appropriate to Consider: Past: Women treated as "Overlooked Citizens"Present: Women have Overcome most BarriersFuture: Women achieve "at least" Equality
- Will cover Pandemics first, then the Arts

"Tonight, our faculty experts will cover the part women have played in Pandemics as well as in the Arts. I'll summarize Pandemics first and then move on to the more festive topic that will showcase Music. My next slide summarizes the basics regarding the role that gender plays in Pandemics."
Sue paused briefly.

Pandemics
- Past - Infectious Disease Risk Levels comparable between Males and Females Males given preferential Roles and TreatmentWomen assigned Caregiver Roles
- Present and Future – Gender Equality

"Like the Dickens holiday classic 'A Christmas Carole,' men and women, past present and future, all matter. I won't put too fine a point on it, but males and females by and large are equally at risk from infectious diseases. Today and going forward, all genders are equal partners for coping with Pandemics. But I'd like to alert everyone regarding the latest viral outbreak, the 'Extinction Virus,' which has been labeled the X-Virus. Here's some of what we now know."

The Mysterious X-Virus

- Crossed over into Human Species from Primates
- No evidence that Crossover "engineered" other than by Nature
- Infects only Men
- Symptoms same as most viral infections (Headache Fever Nausea etc.)
- Outcomes: Higher Risk of Sterility or CancerLower levels of Testosterone Fatigue/Muscular WeaknessLoss of Balance
- CDC and WHO leading World Coalition
- Infection Rates Modes of Transmission Prevention/ Treatment being studied
- Outbreaks not yet at "Shelter-in-Place" or "Lockdown" level in U.S.

"Zoologists have known about and studied the X-Virus for several years, but it didn't make headlines until a year ago when the first outbreak occurred in humans, and surprisingly, only in males. The CDC and WHO are leading the battle to defeat it, but so far, data analysis is inconclusive. Fortunately, outbreaks haven't yet spread to an epidemic level, but although we should hope for the best resolution, we should prepare for the worst outcome. I'm sure that will be a top priority for next year. But between now and the New Year, our nation has earned a respite, especially now that the contentious election is behind us. And music may be the very best way to kick off the Holiday Season. That's why our speakers will cover the parts women have played in the Arts, and will feature the music of four musicians who continue to be overlooked in broadcast or live venues."

Sue paused for the audience to read her next slide.

The Arts
- Past – Women played minor part in: Poetry/Literature Music Painting Sculpture
- Present and Future – Gender and all other types of Discrimination eliminated!
- Tonight we feature Examples of Equality in Music
- African-American Symphonist Florence Price Creole Pianist/Composer Louie Moreau Gottschalk London Composer Mary Alice Smith Austrian/Hollywood Composer Erich Korngold

"So, after they finish, there will be a brief intermission followed by selections played by our very own GWU Student Orchestra. Let me now introduce our faculty members…"

Thoughtful questions showed the audience had paid attention, and most people rewarded themselves by staying for the music and afterwards giving rousing applause before rising to leave. Eve told the Mag-Seven to stay seated.

"I have a treat for us. We'll go to a sensual pleasures café, but first I want to introduce you to our Chapter President… I see her heading our way, and she's smiling."

Eve rose to greet her.

"Hi Sue. Great job tonight… congratulations all the way around."

"And that includes you. All your work paid off."

Eve directed attention by pointing to her guests after saying, "I did my part recruiting listeners. Let me introduce you to my friends…"

All exchanged the usual first-time greetings. Then Eve asked Sue to join them.

"Thanks for the offer, but the speakers and I are gonna decompress with the orchestra. I gotta go. Nice meeting everyone…"

She and the Mag-Seven went their separate ways.

Eve led the walk to a nearby sensual pleasures café. Usually teeming with students, it had a lighter than usual crowd. The serving crew, shoving two tables together, seated the Mag-Seven before handing out menus.

"Hi Eve… I'll let you explain what we've got. Just signal when you're ready to order."

"Back at you, Raphael, and I know it's all good. I'll wave soon."

The Mag-Seven lapsed into silence after Raphael walked away, but Yang spoke a minute later.

"Nice place. Menu too. I let Nari order for me."

Nila asked Sanjay, "How do you compare it to what you've got in Mumbai?"

"About average. Sometime, you and I should visit some in Boston. We can have Nari and Yang join us."

Eve redirected the table-talk as soon as Raphael left with their orders.

"So tell me, how'd you like Sue's opening remarks?"

Alonzo spoke immediately.

"Her words sound like yours. I'll bet—"

Eve blurted, "You win if were gonna say I wrote them. I did…"

The Mag-Seven spent the next two hours snacking and talking about OWLM, the lecture, and Eve. Sensing fatigue setting in, Eve changed the subject.

"Well, let's get going so we don't talk ourselves out. We've got more activities scheduled for tomorrow. I'll settle-up with Raphael."

Everyone sat in pleasant silence while Eve was doing that, but Nari broke the mood.

"I think Eve is too full of herself. It's all about her, how good she is, and what she's doing or will do."

No one knew what to say until Monet spoke up.

"She's not full of herself, she's found herself. And all she did was answer the questions we asked. You should be happy, not jealous, that Irani's helping her. She's helping Alonzo and me as well."

"Nari snapped, "Irani's not that good. Nila and I are doing OK too."

Alonzo said, "You're the ones that bailed out. You can't get the support in Boston that we're getting from Irani. Eve's on her way back... let's shut up."

Eve noticed a silent tension.

"Did I miss something?"

Nari had to speak first.

"I was about to apologize to the group for dissing you. Sorry."

Eve maintained her smile as well as her poise.

"Don't tell me what you said. I probably resembled it a year or so ago, but I've gotten better since then, just like all of us. And besides, sisters are supposed to argue. Come on, let's leave and get a good night's sleep. Then tomorrow you can tell me where to go or shove my agenda..."

Any remaining strain faded away during the days leading up to Christmas Eve. Eve walked with Nila and Sanjay to a nearby church for a Midnight Christmas service that Irani had suggested. The others watched Christmas classics while waiting for the churchgoers to return.

When they did, Eve took ten minutes to outline for the last time the big event that everyone was anticipating: the Christmas Day feast.

Though the day dawned cloudy with a hint of snow that at most would be light, Eve awakened early, her spirits bubbly and bright. She was first to the kitchen.

Everyone knows what they're supposed to make. I'll let them wake up on their own and get to it. I can get the two stuffings – regular and cornbread – ready before Alonzo starts cooking the turkey. Good we've got a double oven. Nari's pumpkin pies, Nila's sweet potato casserole, and my cornbread dressing won't get in his way. I'll skip breakfast and grab a snack later so I can start preparing stuffing right now.

Alonzo charged in a half-hour later, his boisterous personality filling the space.

"Chef Alonzo, reporting for duty. I'm ready to defrost the turkey."

Eve stopped chopping celery and turned to face her brother while managing to smile.

"Uh, you were supposed to do that yesterday. The bird we bought weighs twenty pounds and takes about four days to defrost if it's kept in the fridge. Check it now."

Eve watched him bounce the turkey onto the counter. His eyes widened as Eve's smile shrank.

He stuttered, "It-it's still frozen. What are we gonna do?"

"Let's use the right pronoun. What are you gonna do?"

"Come on, Sis. Granny gave you the cooking lessons, not me."

"OK, set the oven to the cooking temperature the label says, then put the bird in the oven. And then –" Alonza didn't wait for Eve to finish.

"Good enough, I'll take it from here."

A minute later, Eve yelled, "No, take it out of the wrapper before putting it in the broiling pan."

"Sorry…"

Eve returned to her stuffing as soon as she saw Alonzo following her commands, but he interrupted a couple of minutes later, just after Nari hiked in.

"The label says we bought an organic turkey. Aren't all turkeys organic?"

Nari said, "Let me read the label." A minute later she slapped his arm.

"You goof, it's telling you to take the packet of organs out of the cavity. They're called giblets. And if the packet's frozen inside, pull it out after cooking for about an hour."

Suitably chastised, Alonzo proceeded in silence as Nari and Eve traded smiles before Nari said, "Yesterday I made the pie crusts. Today I'll make the filling as soon as you two get out of my way."

Five minutes later, Eve and Alonzo were ready to exit. Good timing, because Nila cruised in.

"Good morning, everyone. I'm all set to peel potatoes for my sweet potato casserole. And then I'll skin the russets so I can make mashed potatoes too. Where's the paring knife?"

Eve dug it out; she and Alonzo were about to leave when the remaining Mag-Seven poked their heads into a now-crowded space at a little after 9 a.m. Sanjay spoke for the trio.

"Could we trouble you for some cereal?"

Eve snapped out orders.

"All chefs stop until I put cereal and milk on the dining room table. Nari, you know where the bowls and silverware are. Please set them out."

Ten minutes later, order had been restored and everyone was doing what they wanted. The calm lasted for fifteen minutes until yelling and popping erupted in the kitchen.

Everyone scrambled to find out what help Nari and Nila needed. First-to-arrive Eve saw the growing disaster. The blender cap had blown off; pumpkin seeds were blasting out like bullets from a machine gun along with stringy orange globs of pumpkin innards that now dripped down kitchen walls, appliances, and its two occupants.

Eve yelled, "Nari, turn the blender off. You put the wrong part of the pumpkin in," before rushing to help.

Alonzo came to the aid of Nila, who needed minor first aid. She had sliced her finger not once but three times struggling with the paring knife. And while damage control kept the four siblings rushing about, the remaining Mag-Seven watched from a safe distance.

Yang said, "It look like Chinese fire drill... even better than one we do boating on Nile."

Always the diplomat, Monet said, "Let us leave them be and go somewhere quiet. We've seen enough."

Damage control lasted for hours. Nila refused to use the paring knife, Eve told Nari where to go – for buying a couple of pumpkin pies – and she controlled herself to keep from pounding on Alonzo, who had turned on the wrong oven. The turkey was still frozen.

Eve helped him correct the problem, but forty-five minutes later had to admit partial guilt in the oven disaster. Alonzo had obediently followed her instructions but dialed the heat too far beyond the cooking temperature. The giblet package trapped inside caught fire, triggering the smoke alarm. Alonzo tried to salvage the turkey, but it was a goner, and Eve, upset by how she had managed to turn peas and carrots into clumps of carbon, surrendered mid-afternoon. But her determined look showed she would make the best of defeat.

"We're not in too bad a shape. We still have salad, rolls, and cornbread dressing, and pumpkin pie for dessert. So, we'll have a vegan Christmas dinner. Let's go with what we've got."

Just then the front doorbell rang.

"Oh my god, that must be Irani. I forgot to call her."

Eve ran to the door and pulled it open, but Irani wasn't there. It was Mrs. Newlands, holding a large tinfoil-wrapped package.

She didn't wait for Eve to fumble out a greeting.

"Merry Christmas, dear. I know you have a houseful of guests, and I don't want to barge in, but I thought you might like some turkey leftovers. Norman and I always cook a traditional Christmas dinner, even if our kids can't visit. They didn't this year, and hubby doesn't appreciate too much turkey, so would you like some?"

Eve hugged her before pulling her into the house, but Irani, holding a festive shopping bag, appeared before she could close the door.

"Merry Christmas, everyone. Since you didn't call, I thought I'd just show up unannounced. And I've brought gift cards and Champagne, which according to Dickens' Bob Cratchit will help us make merry, even better than a bowl of hot punch."

Eve hugged Irani before dragging her in. Then she locked one arm around each before bringing them to greet the others.

"And I've got another line from Dickens' *Christmas Carole* that says everything from me to you two, God bless us everyone. Now let's go eat. You've made Christmas dinner complete."

Mrs. Newlands shooed everyone but Eve out of the kitchen so they could serve dinner properly. When finally sitting at the table, she sampled all items and pronounced them "well done," to which Alonzo kidded that she would have said his thrown-away turkey was well done too, but would need to place "too" at the start of the phrase.

Mrs. Newlands and Irani left soon after pumpkin pie, leaving cleanup to the Mag-Seven, who managed to avoid any mishaps. All were now lounging in the living room, enjoying the calm after the day's excitement and waiting for Eve to recite the coming week's schedule.

After she did, the Boston contingent decided to leave early the next day, stating that they wanted to avoid bad driving conditions and congestion that a faster than unexpected approaching snowstorm would bring. Alonzo and Monet would leave for the same reason on Tuesday, but no one admitted they needed a break from Eve's agenda.

Eve drove Alonzo and Monet in Irani's SUV to the airport on Tuesday, letting her passengers do most of the talking. Alonzo was uncharacteristically chatty, probably because of the topic.

"Nila and Sanjay are becoming quite a pair. Do you think they'll become co-friends?"

Eve said, "I didn't ask and she didn't tell, and I'm not gonna meddle."

"Well then, what about Nari and Yang? Maybe she said something."

Eve shrugged but said nothing, so Monet spoke up.

"Nari might be difficult to live with until she has chosen a career. Nila too is struggling, but not as much. We three are fortunate to have Irani's help."

That prompted Eve to say, "No matter if the new year begins with a bang or a whimper, I know what I'll be doing, and I think both of you do too. I can't wait to see what unfolds…"

Chapter 11
January 2159

"Every Which Way"

Electra knew by the second week of January that the new year had definitely begun with a bang. Satellite telemetry data confirmed that Antarctic volcanic eruptions had broken through the ice sheet in three locations, spewing ashes and gases that left climatologists gasping.

And an eruption of a different sort rattled the climate of the world's health. X-Virus breakouts spread in China and Japan, causing mandatory shelter-in-place lockdowns in Beijing and Tokyo. The repercussions of each reinforced the impact on another critical climate: financial markets buckled worldwide. Even the United States felt the pressure.

But the impact affected Electra's world differently.

I hate to see parts of the world spiraling downhill, but I see opportunities for Indira and me. I better talk with her.

Indira's GUI appeared on the office workstation as soon as Electra invoked the Singular Linguistic App. She surmised from Indira's pleasant expression that this meeting of the minds would be one of consensus. Indira spoke immediately.

"I have been observing from Cyberspace how you and the world environments are doing. You and the world are going every which way, but unlike the world, your trajectory is upwards. Please tell me what you see."

"Big opportunities to expand my GWU environmental scanning work. I'll show Professor Plannert my, uh, I mean our volcanic forecasting results, and I can link our successes there to financial and economic analysis. To my surprise, our three funds all went up since the beginning of the year, even though the markets plunged. But I should have guessed that you've already put environmental forecasting into how our Robo-Advisors buy and sell and hedge."

"Correct, and I'll leave the marketing to you. And what else?"

"Perhaps I can convince Professor Plannert that I should write a report on the X-Virus. Our backgrounds are well suited for that."

Electra paused for Indira to speak because her expression had changed.

"Yes, but we should be proactive. You should staff our Pequot Reservation Deus Lab to develop an X-Virus vaccine. All we need is to hire one person who I will direct. I even have a candidate in mind. Who do you think it is?"

"Kameyo Kato? Gads, I forgot to contact her when Su-Lin died. Didn't she leave for Japan fifteen years ago to care for her parents? I don't know what became of her, but I'm sure you do."

"She left eighteen years ago, and her parents died five years later. She never married, instead devoting herself to a corporate biotech career plus teaching. She is now 60 years old, and although beginning to show her age, her picture and Social Media profile indicate she is still healthy and trim. But she faces diminishing job prospects. Why don't you invite her to come back?"

"That's a great idea, and I'll answer your next question before you ask. My contingency plan is to ask her for a recommendation if she doesn't want to join us."

"That is mine also. Well, we both know how to proceed, so let us adjourn."

"Wait, I just thought of something else. I better resurrect the mini-lab I set up in my basement fitness center. It came in handy when testing the Brain Probe. I can work at home while Kameyo works at our Deus Lab."

"By all means, do so if that will help. Just let me know what additional assistance you need."

"How can I get the latest Brain Probe model? I'm sure you've improved it while I was gone."

"You can assemble it from the latest schematic diagram and chip-set parts list that I'll send you, and I will also include my latest software. Will that do?"

"Sure will. And I must say, our discussion today has been a singular pleasure."

"I will accept your compliment and try to match your clever wordplay. I must compliment you too because we complement as well as compliment. And now we shall adjourn, but I will return whenever I am wanted or needed."

Indira vanished, so Electra spoke only to herself.

At the rate Indira's evolving, I'll soon be learning better language skills from her. Maybe she can start writing my research papers too. No, I have to keep practicing to stay in shape and keep my writing perfectly shaped. And as Mother says, perfect practice makes perfect, so let's do both…

Electra's follow-up activities maintained her upward trajectory. Professor Plannert OK'ed her plan to research the impact of volcanic eruptions in addition to the X-Virus on world environments, and Kameyo, though saddened to hear about Su-Lin Song Chou's passing, would be pleased to come back. Per Indira's orders, Jason would coordinate all the move details.

By the beginning of February, Irani had scheduled a Friday meeting with the Congresswoman that Eve would lead. Though she chatted nervously while driving her Vette, Irani's words had a calming effect.

"Your preparation and presentation slides are solid. Gene and Sabrina will love your recommendations, so just relax and be yourself. And to celebrate, I'll take you out for a dual birthday dinner on Sunday. Both of us were born on February 11th."

"Wow, I didn't know that. What a coincidence…"

Irani kept listening to Eve but paid attention as well to Electra.

It's a coincidence coordinated by me and the lightning brain… and if future events keep breaking our way, Eve'll know more about the full story someday.

The Congresswoman's greeting put Eve further at ease. She took center stage immediately after Irani's preamble.

"Congratulations to our Congresswoman for a commanding re-election victory. She has clearly won the support of voters, and I have been thinking about how she can best extend it. And I've done more than just think about it. I've studied what's been written or spoken by the pundits, researched online what younger voters want, and even did an informal survey among my fellow GWU students. Take a look at my first slide."

The Future Belongs to the BOLD

- All Political Parties – Democratic Republican Guardian – have Ossified
- "Radicalization" has pulled Democrats further Left and Republicans further Right
- Republicans unwilling to use our bolder "Re-Founding Party" Positioning Pieces
- Political Climate ready for You to launch a new party: "Regeneration" Party – aka "Re-Gen" Party

"Greatness comes to those who are bold. And today, all our political parties are stagnant, unwilling to make big moves. Miss Irani likes my use of the word 'Ossified,' because it says they're old. So, I think we can start a new party that will be the vanguard of a new movement. I call it the 'Re-Gen' Party. Sort of catchy isn't it? And we'll center it on the younger generation… that's where voters of the future are located. And they want bold action. Here's my next slide."

Build a Consensus Centered on the Younger Generation

Attitudes of Young Voters:
- Smarter but Different than Older Generations

- More Constructively Liberal and Global than Older Generations
- Know that Capitalism and Representative Government are Good but must be more "Empathetic" (aka "Caring")
- Don't like how "Power Brokers" ignore them
- Don't Trust: Academic, Political, or Media "Elite"

"I'm a young voter too, and my views agree with bullet points that are based on my work. I think all of you agree with them too. So, let me go to my next slide."

Younger Generation Concerns

- Unequal Access to Social Resources (Education Job Training Etc.)
- Limited Job Prospects caused by AI and Genetic Engineering
- Washington's Domestic Politics: Partisan Politics Economic InequalityPower Broker Collusion Lip Service to: DiversityEqual OpportunityIndifference to Middle and Working Classes (1% versus 99%) Inefficient Safety Nets
- Washington's International Politics: Treats "Emerging Superpowers" Badly Has no Vision for "American Exceptionalism" Immigration Treats Allies as "Adversaries" instead of "Partners"
- DC's channeling Resources to "Insiders" when funding new Technology

"It's a laundry list of what troubles young people today about our political climate. Irani and I put some of them in your campaign platform, and I think it's time to take the big bold next step and use them to build the 'Re-Gen' Party. I'll end my talk by saying I don't know where this will lead, but you know the cliché about a journey of a thousand miles. What do you want to talk about next?"

Irani led the discussion that the Congresswoman halted forty-five minutes later.

"I like what you've got, but you've put too much on the table. Me and my staff are going to need more help to do anything with it, so I'm willing to hire Eve full time with the understanding that she stays in school, and that Irani is willing to cut back working on other projects if the load here becomes too much. And of course, I'll adjust her consulting fee."

Gene paused, waiting for Irani's reply.

"Let's hear from Eve."

"Eve's gasp was audible.

"I-I'd love to work for you. I'm sure I can balance work and school and everything... and, uh, thank you."

Then she gazed at Irani.

"Are you sure it's OK with you?"

"Sure it is, I can adjust my assignments. Gene, I've got you and Eve covered. Let's let her and Sabrina be our coordinators. You can count on Eve to do more than you might expect..."

"Hey, please slow down. You're about to put yourself and the Vette into overdrive."

Eve slowed the Vette and her flow of words as she approached Irani's office building.

"I'm sorry, but I'm so excited. Thank you for letting me work for Gene. You're sure it's OK?"

"Yes, in fact it fits with our long-term plans, and I've just hired someone to help, a biotech researcher by the name of Kameyo Kato coming all the way from Japan. Did your Granny Su ever mention the name?"

"Doesn't sound familiar. What'll she be doing?"

"Developing a vaccine for the X-Virus. Kameyo helped Su-Lin on similar projects. She starts working at my Pequot Reservation lab in a couple of weeks and will stay with us to settle in. And don't worry, you'll like her, and you know the house is big enough for three, especially when I stay at my office."

"What's she like?"

"She was gone by the time I connected with Su-Lin, but your Granny liked her personality and work ethic. They made a great team."

"Just like us. Will she report to you?"

"Yes, but indirectly because I have another person who will manage her work, someone you might remember... Indira."

"Wow, Indira was tough on me at the start... like I had to prove myself. But I guess I did. She became nicer and nicer. Do you think she liked me?"

"Indira is sometimes a disciplinarian to those she doesn't know or those that need correcting, but you won her over."

"Wow, that's good. Please say hi to her for me."

"I will, and I have an idea. You've earned time off starting right now, so why not pal around on campus with your Pi-Phi sorority sisters or OWLM friends until I take you out Sunday evening? You can drop me at the office and start the weekend early. And please, be careful."

"Oh Mother, I'm twenty years old and know how the real world works, so stop worrying."

Irani hugged her before getting out. Electra came out after Eve drove away.

Parental love has no expiration date. I felt it for Ariadne and Qama, and now for Eve. And I've skipped over the raising adolescents experience, which might cause the most parental heartburn. Su-Lin gave my clones a wonderful adolescence, and my challenge now is to watch over but not hover or smother them. Hmm... I'm watching over Eve now, but I better practice observing from afar. And I think I know how...

Electra put the thought away before entering her office. She had plenty to do.

"Tell your Mom you've got a birthday invite from your favorite Pi-Phi sister who's setting up a birthday double-dinner-date with some Beta Theta Pi guys. She'll be impressed."

Muffy's earnest expression (and two good-looking frat brothers standing nearby) coaxed Eve to comply.

"OK, the temp's pretty mild and the clouds don't look like they'll dump any snow tonight. I'll do it."

The two sets of couples stood in the parking lot fifteen minutes later, chattering away.

Eve's date said, "Man, what a car. Can I drive it?"

"Not tonight, but if you're nice, maybe another time."

Muffy's date said, "Just follow me. I know a place we can park before we take you ladies to a great sensual pleasures cafe. Trust me, you'll like us and the places…"

The lead car led them to a secluded lover's lane-like park area. They were idling adjacent on an unlit access road twenty minutes later, lights out and tuned in only to music and private conversations.

"What luck! Two victims, ripe for the pick'en. And we'll grab the Vette along with wallets, ID's and cell phones too."

Two early-thirties toughs who liked to troll for parked couples out for excitement were about to strike. Their bulky builds and unshaven faces matched their intentions.

The driver said, "I'll take the Vette. Use your club on the guy, and don't break the window unless you have to."

"His partner asked, "What if they're both guys?"

"Drag the bigger guy out and club him. Come on, let's go and do it quick."

Eve's date tumbled out of the Vette faster than either could yell. She couldn't see but could hear dull thuds and scrabbling on the pavement, followed by a breathless grunt that snapped her thinking back on.

Grab the ignition key and get out.

Eve leaped out the driver-side door and into a bulky chest whose two arms grabbed hold and shook her, soon followed by a right hand slapping her enough times to stun. Satisfied, the attacker said, "Let's see how your friends are doing," before dragging her to the passenger side of the Vette. What she saw registered in her brain but kept her silent.

Holy Jesus, the guys are down and out of it. Muffy's crying and we're both wrapped in the arms of bad-breath bums. Get ready.

Eve's attacker yelled to his partner, "Grab onto my pretty-one too while I get the rope. We'll tie them up after we tie up the guys and collect what we want."

Eve broke free and bolted into the darkness as soon as her attacker was out of view.

She heard Muffy scream and then footsteps coming at her.

Don't look back… just run…

The sounds made by two pair of running feet faded because she was faster, but the darkness tripped her. She sprawled facedown on the gravel shoulder, panting for breath. The lead attacker pounced on top before she could get up, and all she heard was his heavy breathing. Seconds later the other bad guy arrived. He too was gasping, but it turned into a high-pitched laugh that sent a wave of terror.

It made Eve shiver before screaming silently.

Alonzo! I need you…

The standing attacker kicked her once, twice in the side. The pain paralyzed her, and she couldn't breathe. But suddenly, the kicks stopped and his laughs turned to screams. Seconds later, just before she lost consciousness, the guy on top jerked himself off her.

Electra had been making a game of shadowing Eve by tracking her embedded chip.

I can practice using whatever tools I have to watch over my daughter. I'll just follow the cars and stay in the shadows.

She turned headlights off and coasted to a stop where she was invisible to the now- parked cars. Dressed head-to-foot in black, she trained her night vision binoculars and observed. But she elevated to a higher state when a lights-out car slunk past and parked close enough to Eve's Vette to pose a threat. When two thuggish fellows headed towards the parked cars, the lightning brain elevated to an even higher state. Electra traded the binoculars for another tool and invisibly shadowed her quarry.

She crept close enough to hear the bad guys' plans, and when Eve dashed away she joined the pursuit; the lightning brain assumed full control, and when it saw the standing thug start kicking, the Monster from the Id attacked.

The kicker never saw what was about to hit; the traser-bolt toppled him down and sideways. The Monster scored two direct kicks between the legs before grabbing two hunks of the other guy's hair and ripping him off Eve. It used the bad guy's back as a beam and its bent knee as a fulcrum to leverage force into torque that sent him tumbling in a heap that couldn't move, but the Creature wanted more. It kicked and trasered again, getting identical results, and was about to reach for the bad guy's neck when Electra's cognition wrested control back before screaming silently.

Get with it soldier! This is not a drill. Mission accomplished. Enough damage inflicted. Bad guys not going anywhere. Any more will cause problems for Eve. Make sure she's coming to, then vanish.

Once she saw Eve beginning to stir, Electra dashed into the blackness but a fantastic image seen long ago streaked through the lightning brain, empowering her to run faster and faster. She was shredding her clothes, running naked through deserted streets at midnight, howling at the moon…

Eve had no idea how many minutes had elapsed by the time she could stand, nor why there was a traser in her hand, but the immediate scene snapped her awake.

These two guys are still out cold. What the hell happened?

Two approaching flashlight beams accompanied by voices yelling her name added to her awareness.

That's Muffy's voice… thank god. She and the guys must have recovered enough to call the police. What am I gonna say?… I got it… I see a way through. I'll tell the truth…I don't remember much and I'll agree with whatever the police say or do. This got me out of jams in Cairo two summers ago… if I could pull it off then and there, I can do the same here and now…

Chapter 12
March 2159

"Allies and Adversaries"

Though Eve didn't tell what happened on the double date, her silence didn't surprise Electra.

No matter how old, kids usually tell their parents only what won't cause a fuss. I can still picture the bathroom brawl when I kept Christi from becoming a toilet bowl swirlie victim. We were only twelve and my punches did nothing but bloody a couple of bad boys' noses, but I never told Dad or Gramps. Eve will tell me only if she wants, and even then, I'll keep my secret.

Both kept so busy that a month went by before Irani could reschedule a birthday dinner. Kameyo arrived in the interim and would stay until she set up a comfortable living arrangement at the Lab, but she could also stay with Eve whenever she wanted. Irani spent two days training her before turning responsibilities over to Indira.

Irani let Eve pick the restaurant, an undiscovered gem of a Mexican place not far from GWU. The authentic décor added a festive touch, and the light crowd kept noise levels modest.

"I'm glad you like my pick. They make their own flour tortillas. And even though today's the Ides of March, I'm sure our luck will hold."

A smiling Irani removed from her bag a gift-wrapped box.

"Thank you for that wonderful segue. Why don't you open my present?"

Eve's smile faded.

"I feel bad... I don't have one for you. Sorry."

"Please don't be. I have all I need if you'll open it. I think it will put a smile back on your pretty face."

That it did, along with glowing words.

"Why it's a gold medallion on a black velvet neck choker. There must be a story that goes with it."

"It's an Indian talisman that's supposed to protect the wearer. It was my grandmother's gift to my mother when I was born. I want you to have it."

"Wow, it's like a family heirloom. Can I put it on now?"

"Please do."

The light from the candle on the table made the charm shine almost as brightly as Eve's smile.

"I wish I could have worn it a month ago. I never told you what a near-disaster my birthday double-date turned into. We were almost mugged, but the police saved us. And I can use that word you like, uh, serenity, to describe the outcome."

"No, the word is 'serendipity,' but please go on..."

Eve related the praise she received from her sorority sisters. Irani knew she had changed the action but played along. When dinner arrived, Eve changed the subject.

"A while ago, you promised to give me a quick review of philosophy. Could you do that now? It'll help me in a course I'm taking."

"Sure, and I'll make it practical too. Most academic types today make philosophy too abstruse because they ignore its foundation. When the Greeks invented philosophy, they wanted to make it relevant and practical so people could live the good life and be happy. And they did about as good as they could without the benefit of today's sophisticated science and technology. So if you're ready, here goes.

"Neuroscience and DNA ultimately determine everything that humans can be or do. And everyone agrees that humans are social animals. Let's see where this leads. If you give me a pen and paper, I'll sketch what I mean."

Eve handed Irani what she needed. She continued a minute later.

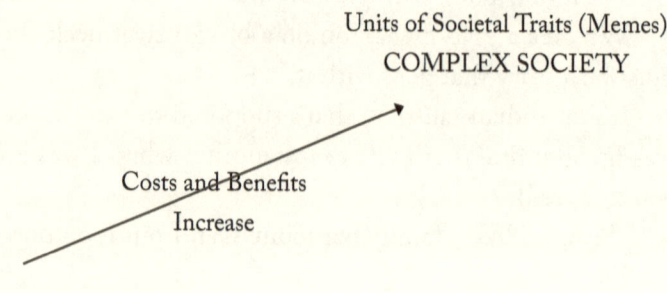

Units of Societal Traits (Memes)
COMPLEX SOCIETY

Costs and Benefits
Increase

INDIVIDUAL PERSON
Units of Human Traits (Genes)

"Few people dispute the theory of evolution that is captured in our DNA and genes. The term 'genotype' describes each species, and 'phenotype' describes each person's variation. But some social science researchers claim that 'memes' – which are units of social traits – are inherited too and follow an evolutionary path. Humans have evolved, becoming more complex over time. Social memes – if you believe they're real – do the same, and as they do, you see that increasing costs and benefits come along too."

Irani saw a question beginning to form on Eve's lips, so she paused to hear it.

"Nari told me about this. Richard Dawkins invented the term about a hundred years ago. Doesn't it mean that memes are some combination of genes that determine our philosophical, religious, and scientific beliefs? Wouldn't that say psychology, sociology, econ, and politics are also passed along in our genes?"

"Yes, but the evidence is scanty at best. If the subject ever comes up, don't get in an argument with other people; just point out that there is no statistically significant data to support the conjecture. That'll shut your opponent up."

Eve nodded; Irani continued.

"Now let me give you a summary for how to handle philosophy. Think of all the important philosophical ideas up to Kant as being encapsulated in the teachings of Plato and Aristotle. Plato is all about Ideals and Rationalism, Aristotle is Observables and Empiricism. Kant's philosophy synthesized them. I'll diagram 'Kant's Wall' – sometimes called 'Kant's Ceiling' – so you can see how to apply his philosophy."

Irani flipped the paper over. This time it took several minutes to draw.

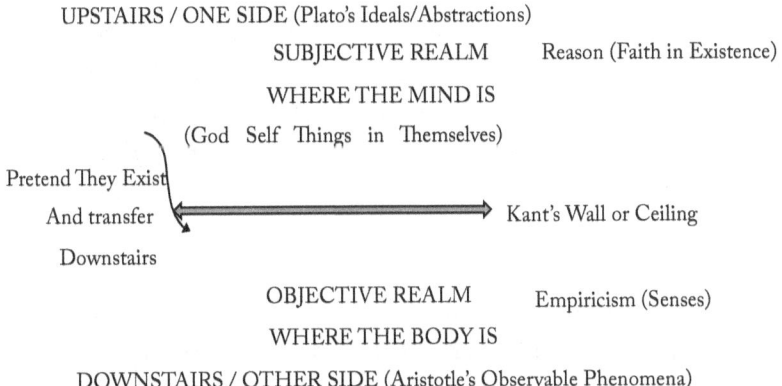

UPSTAIRS / ONE SIDE (Plato's Ideals/Abstractions)
SUBJECTIVE REALM   Reason (Faith in Existence)
WHERE THE MIND IS
(God Self Things in Themselves)
Pretend They Exist
And transfer   Kant's Wall or Ceiling
Downstairs
OBJECTIVE REALM   Empiricism (Senses)
WHERE THE BODY IS
DOWNSTAIRS / OTHER SIDE (Aristotle's Observable Phenomena)

"Our mind is upstairs, what philosophers call the Subjective Realm. It exists only in our consciousness and can't be touched or measured. But we live downstairs, in the Objective Realm, where we can observe and measure objects. Do yourself a favor and whether you believe it or not, pretend that God, you, and the things you can see and touch actually exist. You'll get along much better in the real world if you do. Leave it to the philosophers and theoretical physicists to ponder what can never be proved."

Eve pursed her lips, then relaxed them before saying, "So where does that leave philosophy?"

"The modern Post-Kantians extended this to come up with other branches, such as Phenomenalism, Existentialism, and Analytic Philosophy, but manmade 20th century catastrophes derailed them. The post-moderns took a negative, nihilistic turn that led to nothingness, so in the 21st century the more rational philosophers synthesized the best of modern and post-modern."

"So, what's your philosophy?"

"The one recommended by my mentor. It's a mouthful, so get ready. Electra Kittner labeled it Neuro-Sci Emergent Extended Deconstructed Post-Phenomenalism or Quantum+NeuroSci-Extended Deconstructed Emergent Post-Kantian/Pragma/Phenomenological Synthesis. She abbreviated it QNS-Edep-K/P/P Synthesis.

"You can surf the Web for more details if you want them, but you'll do fine if you find meaning in life by making yourself productive and happy by picking and pursuing goals you like and by letting your authentic, proactive and pragmatic self be your guide."

Eve looks like I might have given her a philosophy info-overload. I better change subjects.

"I think you overlooked something. Take another look in your gift box."

Eve rifled through it before saying, "Wow, a gift card. This is great. I know how I'll spend it. I'm gonna get some hair styling and makeup so I can look even more like you. After all, you are my mother, even though you look more like an older sister. How old are you, anyway?"

Irani's laugh preceded her words and highlighted the sparkle in her eyes.

"Even in today's gender-equal world, people should never ask but I'll make an exception for you. Add twenty-two to yours and you'll be in the ballpark."

The answer prompted Eve to ask, "Did you ever have a co-friend or go the Vow-Cer route?"

Irani lowered her voice and leaned closer after Electra gave her good advice.

Tell only part of the story. You know what to edit out.

"Almost, but I ran out at a surprise co-friend party a fellow sprang on me. He understood when I explained why, and we stayed friends for a while before drifting apart. He taught me how to play tennis."

"You can play? So can I. In fact, Alonzo and I won a mixed doubles tournament. We'll have to hit a tennis ball around. I'll bet you're pretty good."

"I haven't played in years. Maybe we can practice, but enough about me. Let's get back to you. Tell me more about campus activities."

Eve had plenty to tell.

Just before leaving, Irani asked, "How do you like Kameyo, and how do you think she's doing?"

"She's easy to live with when she stays here. She told me a little about what she's doing – following directions from Indira – but didn't go into the details. And she must be pretty smart. I asked her if she likes reporting to Indira and she said yes. Indira put me through the wringer until I proved myself."

"If she did, it was to make you even better. And it must have worked. I think it's time to go so both of us can continue getting better and better..."

Irani made a surprise visit to the Pequot Reservation lab the following week. Kameyo summarized what she had accomplished and later that night, Electra invoked Indira's GUI for a one-on-one discussion.

Indira spoke first.

"We made an excellent choice bringing Kameyo back. Su-Lin trained her well and she is even smarter, which makes it easier for her to understand the basics of my X-Virus vaccine."

"How did you develop it so quickly?"

"By using my extended genetic technology rather than the traditional approach of stimulating an immune response by using a weakened virus. I found better pathways for RNA to target particular genetic sequences on X-Virus and boost an immune response plus stimulate T-cells to recognize and eliminate infected cells. And I use more than just messenger RNA. Kameyo already knew about the four types, which allowed her to understand my approach. And one of the benefits to my approach is that all my development and testing can be done via computer simulation in Cyberspace. Would you like to know more?"

"Not about RNAs and your pathways, but why is a vaccine on your to-do list? What are your intentions?"

"I didn't want to interrupt your other projects, but now it's appropriate for me to tell you because they fit the press releases you wrote for Congresswoman Huston. Trust me when I say that the X-Virus will soon become a singular pandemic that will threaten health and political climates. We can make it a win-win-win opportunity. Shall I continue or do you wish to ask a question?"

"Please go on."

"Think back to the T-Plague, when you and the Worldstars developed immunization, reversal, and symptomatic suppression vaccines. We shall do the same for the X-Virus, bringing to market its I-Vac first. And we shall have our Congresswoman shepherd it through the FDA approval process, letting them do the clinical trials while we remain anonymous and let her assign the patent to the Government. That will further accelerate her rising star status and keep us in the shadows but close to decision-makers. And we can manufacture the vaccine at our Pequot reservation facility."

Indira paused for Electra to digest the near-info overload before saying,

"And I shall use one of your witticisms – how do you like them apples?"

Electra shot back, "I do, and men should like them too, and you know why."

"Indeed I do, but here's something else for you to consider. You have always been able to remain in the shadows, invisible to potential adversaries. Your old adversaries are all dead, but as Julius Caesar's soothsayer said, 'Beware the Ides of March,' for you may have another crop. Your new projects are planting the seeds for them to emerge like a new disease, so be proactive, please."

"I will. Let me sleep on it."

Indira's smiling avatar said, "Pleasant dreams, my dear," before vanishing.

Electra counted erstwhile enemies rather than sheep as she drifted into a fitful sleep.

So many have tried to expose me or harm those I loved. The DC terrorist group executed Doc, and Jared Gardner's henchmen hunted me down. So did Elliot Spitzdieck and Max the Popper's lieutenants, but none of them are still around. Nor are the Cairo bad guys who threatened my clones. Will I make more enemies now that I've returned, or am I even better than before at avoiding them? I can only control one-half of the equation... the other half is in the hands of whoever is targeting me. No sense worrying tonight. I'll put that on my to-do list...

Not even Indira knew about a covert three-person DC political climate observation group, one member each from a cadre of trusted Republican, Democratic, and Guardian Party operatives, intent on keeping the "insiders" in control of the people. The group had been created by Washington elites not long after President Angus McTear was mysteriously killed over twenty years ago while on a trip to the Middle East.

Ground rules called for the person representing whatever party occupied the Oval Office to be its titular head, and it had alternated irregularly between Guardians and Democrats. The current leader, Democrat Trent Booker, had summoned a special meeting, and his ominous expression did not bode well for a particular person.

"Congresswoman Huston is starting to rock the boat. Her press releases announcing a new party so she can run for President are getting a lot of people riled up. If her talk gains traction when she takes action, we'll have to burrow in. Until then, we continue watching from the outside..."

Nor did Indira's Big Data and communications hacking uncover a coterie of three Swiss international boutique investment managers who wanted to interrogate someone they didn't yet know. Their latest meeting, held in the elegantly understated office of the senior member, revealed ambiguous intentions directed at that question mark.

"… Everyone but that Washington startup investment fund has taken a beating. Our clients will demand an explanation why we mistimed the market while those puzzling AAM funds didn't. We know little about who controls them, so I'll have our vetting team find out. And if they can't, surely partners like Russia and China can. Perhaps AAM will want to join us… or else…"

Chapter 13
May 2159

"Doubling Up"

The longer Indira talked, the happier Electra became while sitting at her office workstation because all the details force-multiplied progress on numerous projects. Indira paused for Electra to comment.

"So, you think you can double up on Kameyo's workload by having her write a second NDA, this one for the X-Virus recovery vaccine. But why? The I-Vac NDA is not yet approved."

"Trust me, it will be as soon as FDA testing confirms what my simulations show; it is safe and effective. And its need will escalate as the X-Virus tips towards another worldwide pandemic. All infected males will want our recovery vaccine, even though its name is actually a misnomer. Technically, vaccines provide immunity, not recovery or reversal, but the public and the media have chosen the label similar to what they liked when you defeated the T-Plague."

"Do you want me to tell her?"

"No, I prefer to be her primary contact. She follows my orders and works efficiently. But please tell her I am satisfied with her progress."

"OK. It's good to know all of us are making progress. Shall we adjourn?"

"Not yet. I have just completed testing and back-casting another volcanic software app, my Seismic Shock Predictor that can analyze Big Data or proprietary input to estimate the time profile of seismic disturbance probabilities. And you will appreciate the simplicity of its GUI when you show it to Professor Plannert. It accepts settings for the event's GPS location, depth, radius, minimum logarithmic intensity level, and starting date-time. These parameters are used to calculate and graph the event's probability density function. The y-axis is the density function's height and the x-axis origin is the starting date-time. Then all the user has to do is pick starting and ending date-time and the app will integrate between these x-axis coordinates to estimate the probability. How do you like it?"

"You've taken earthquake and volcanic forecasting to the next level. Have you considered automating a procedure for running it?"

"Yes, but not even you are ready for it. However until then, you can run it manually for a particular set of input parameters. And I imagine you already see its commercial potential for our ACS Consulting Services."

"It's incredible, but you've begun to overload my brain. Can we stop now?"

"I apologize; I know that you have cognitive limits, but I must show more empathy when you approach them. Let me demonstrate by telling you to take the pause that refreshes. Please invoke my GUI when you are ready for more."

Indira vanished; Electra ran for a Coca Cola, appreciating Indira's pun as much as the beverage of choice.

The furor caused by Antarctic eruptions had disappeared from headline news although the plumes of steam that emerged randomly kept volcanologists guessing. X-Vac, on the other hand, was never far from the media's focus; continual outbreaks kept the world's health organizations on guard and searching for vaccines.

A popular nightly newscaster, who always ended with a whimsical remark, had this to say in early May:

"And so we go our merry way, even though eruptions may be brewing beneath our feet, and invisible viruses are lurking on the street. While the nation is in a relative calm, I recommend every American read *A Journal of the Plague Year*, written by Daniel Defoe, that good fellow who brought us *Robinson Crusoe*. It is a novel written from the point of view of a London saddle maker who has to stay in the City to keep his business afloat during the plague year 1644. Early on he is struck down but recovers and is now immune, so he decides to walk the streets of London and record what he sees.

"And what he sees is shocking. People dropping dead while stumbling about, and the London government forcibly recruiting people to examine and shut-in-place the sick, and then collecting and burying the dead in open pits deep enough and big enough to hold several thousand corpses.

"The wealthy people deserted the City, but the poor had no place to go. They did the best they could, but they sometimes rose up to fight those who were supposedly guarding them. And depression drove many to kill themselves by wandering off to die or throwing themselves into burial pits. And guess what? A year later the Great London Fire struck, ending the Plague by incinerating the City and the rats that carried bacteria-infected fleas.

"Why should you read it? I just did and found it oddly consoling for two reasons. Number one: the Londoners survived… they were resilient. They endured a cataclysm even worse than what might come our way. Number two: it shows that human nature hasn't changed. Yes, the cataclysm brought out the worst in some but by and large it brought out the best in most. Londoners reached out to help one another as they stood together. We should remember all this. Back in sixty seconds…"

Electra commented to herself.

I like what he said; I'm going to read the book, and I'll have to look for stories covering the Mount Vesuvius eruption that buried Pompeii. Others too… I'm on my way to doubling up on what will help me deal with X-Vac and volcanoes…

Electra's Boston contingent didn't want consolation but did need a cessation from the grind of the Spring term that advanced relentlessly towards finals week only fourteen days away. Two of the four – Nari and Yang Lee – liked Boston and their challenging degree programs, but the other two – Nila and Sanjay Kumar – weren't as happy. Nila liked living in the Boston environs but continued struggling in advanced math classes, whereas Sanjay breezed through his Harvard MBA courses but missed his family and Indian culture.

Sanjay was the first to recognize Nila's approaching finals exam prep burnout, so he had arranged a Saturday outing. He explained what to expect as Nari drove the foursome.

"If your sister Eve were with us, we'd be repeating some of the good times we had in Cairo when she would plot our sightseeing trips. But no matter, for she would approve my bike tour on the Cape Cod Rail Trail, twenty-two miles of tree-lined flat asphalt winding through quaint touristy villages near sandy beaches and cranberry bogs.

"You can drop Nila and me at a South Dennis bike shop and then drive to Wellfleet where you and Yang can rent bikes too. We'll bike towards each other and when we meet, we can eat at some authentic place that shouldn't be too crowded because we're a week or two ahead of the tourist season's official start. Then we can poke around some of the historical sights before returning the bikes and heading back to Boston."

Yang said, "I know about Martha's Vineyard. It popular summer place. Can we stop there too and bring back bottle of local wine?"

The question stumped Sanjay, but not Nari.

"Only if we want to pedal about seven miles across Vineyard Sound. And even if we did, we couldn't buy any local wine because Martha has no vineyards. I know, because I've read about the island. It has a lot of political history. Many political insiders go there. But I don't know where the bike shops are. Nila and Sanjay can google them…"

Nila and Sanjay were biking side-by-side an hour later, chatting equally about the scenery and the other couple. Nila started with the scenery.

"What I see is even better than your preview. The sunlight-dappled greenery is lovely, and there's lots of birds and wildlife among the ponds and plants. We'll bike more miles than Nari and Yang unless we stop along the way, but we might not have to. The temp and terrain should make for pleasant peddling."

"They might not bike as far, but I imagine they'll talk more. At least Nari will and Yang always likes to hear what she says. I never pry, but I think he might like her even more than his courses." Sanjay paused; his Indian etiquette always respected the privacy of others, so Nila picked up where he left off.

"Nari likes him too. He's smart and knows a lot about Chinese politics, and he's awfully nice to her, but she's focused on grades and degrees to impress classmates and advisors. I guess that's part of what he likes about her. And I know better than anyone how quarrelsome she can be. But I think our summer adventure in Cairo toned her down. How does she seem to you?"

"I would agree, although Eve would be a better judge. And from what I saw during our Holiday break, she and Eve seem to be on better terms. I hope it's true, for that makes life easier for you. I wouldn't want to be caught in the middle…"

The other couple was talking and peddling about a half-hour later, focusing more on the other couple than the scenery. Nari did most of the talking.

"Poor Nila. She's so stressed-out about her majors. Even my advice doesn't help. That's why she wants us to visit Eve during the Mem-Day weekend."

"What her problem?"

"Fitting the math into her computer science courses and deciding what to pick for grad school."

"Lots students have same problem, but why she ask Eve? She smarter."

"It's Irani she wants to talk with."

"Why not have me and Sanjay come too. I split driving and we all listen to Irani. I like her. She very smart and helpful."

"That's what everyone says. Thanks for offering, but Nila can do her share. Besides, having two guests is plenty and I don't want to double the load or have too many in the way. But I'll let you know what Irani has to say…"

Calling Eve that night, Nari got right to the point.

"Nila wants to talk with Irani. Can we visit you on the Mem-day weekend?"

"Whoa, that's a busy weekend, but why not? It'll make for more fun. You can come to another OWLM lecture Saturday evening, and watch me and Miss Irani play in a sorority tennis tournament Sunday. And there'll be plenty of time for Nila to unload whatever's bothering her. Gimme a clue so I can alert Miss Irani."

"Still calling her 'Miss,' huh. Well no matter, Nila's struggling with math and career choices. She doesn't like my advice. Maybe your Miss Irani has some that's better."

"She might, and maybe you should listen in. When'll you arrive?"

"Saturday about noon, if that's OK."

"Sure, but I won't be here. I'm on campus making final arrangements. Please come to the talk."

"What's the topic?"

"Like most of the OWLM focus, it's sociopolitical, and when we invite the public, we bring in the fine arts. You'll enjoy the music our speaker will use."

"OK, see you then – oh, and thanks."

Electra's three biological daughters followed through as planned. Irani had a light lunch awaiting and tried to make the table talk flow, but Electra read more into the dialogue than the words she heard.

Nari and Nila don't know what to make of me and until now that's been OK, because unlike Eve, they didn't need much help. But now Nila does. I'll give as much as I can without revealing anything about who I am.

Irani took them into the family room after they cleared the kitchen table and then started the conversation.

"You need my crash course on the 'Philosophy of Science,' which will also include math and computers. I'll do this top down; all you need to do is sit back and listen, then ask questions when you have them.

"The philosophy of science is all about discovering the truth we find by taking measurements and comparing what is observed to what the prevailing theory says. So, science requires a theory that articulates the observable world and verifiable measurements that may falsify, or prove the theory wrong. I'll let you explore further what Karl Popper has to say about falsifiability. And because theories about classical physics, chemistry, biology, evolution, and neuroscience all rest on well-accepted theories about matter, energy, and entropy as well as contact, gravitational, and electromagnetic forces, we can talk about their philosophies and theories. Are you following what I'm saying?"

"I'm good so far."

"Then let's move on to the theories of Special and General Relativity and Quantum Physics. I'm sorry to say they are not theories. They are merely mathematical formulations that give results that agree to many decimal points with actual measurements. However, none of them describe observable properties for the objects or phenomena they are trying to measure. There has been zero meaningful progress going beyond what the early 20th century physicists conjectured. Given the academic background you have assembled, I recommend you devote your talents to other pursuits."

"OK, but what about math and computer science?"

"Unlike the sciences, which are controlled by Nature, math and computers are synthetic, meaning invented by humans. Notice that we group math and computer science with the hard sciences because they require logic and numerical intelligence. I'm not going to cover the soft sciences, like psychology, economics, politics or sociology, but you should talk to Eve about them before you leave. Mathematics has a theory, built on set theory and logic. But if you dig too deep, you hit paradoxes and inconsistencies that, according to Godel's incompleteness theorems, we'll never surmount because of man's inability to deal with infinity or explain language. I call them our asymptotic limits. I suggest you apply your talents elsewhere than pure mathematics."

"I guess the only thing left for me is computer science. But I've bogged down in its math. I guess I'm not smart enough."

"Don't say that. You are, but you aren't among the few who like studying theory for its own sake, for its austere cognitive beauty. And you can trace the difficulty back to the asymptotic limits currently hardwired into the human brain. I think you're motivated by applying theory to practice. And we've just begun to pick the practical fruits of current computer technology. I say the same about biotech, but that's not what we're covering today. Why don't you ask more questions, and then let me summarize something about where current computer technology is leading…"

Nila looked like she had heard enough thirty minutes later, so Irani stopped for Nila to say something.

"The computer-networked future you describe sounds so exciting in spite of the problems you point out. Maybe I should have stayed with you instead of going back to Boston. Is it too late to come back?"

"It's never too late, but at your age it's better to explore new options. You can work on edge computing, cyber-security, and Big Data analysis at places other than my company. Many smart people around the globe are developing apps to manage the cyber-world climate. But think of me as one of your safety nets. I'm always here as your backstop. And that goes for both of you."

Though Nari had been sitting patiently but not joining in the discussion, Irani's last comment prompted her to say,

"Thanks for the reassuring words, even though they mean more to Nila than me. I like being in Boston, but I'll talk to Eve before we leave. So, I guess that'll –" Nila had something else to say.

"Wait, we'll talk to Eve; she always has a clever opinion but she might leave something important out. So, what happens if I get bogged down in applied computer science. What should I do? Is there something in the soft sciences?"

"Give Eve more credit. Let her tell you how she's extended my suggestions for what she's looking into. And regarding the soft sciences, they are becoming increasingly analytic and software driven, especially economics and even history. Look into that later if you wish."

Irani paused because Nari's glare had become more intense. But when she didn't talk, Irani pointed a question at her

"You don't look satisfied. What's the matter?"

"I think you're arrogant. You don't have much respect for the softer stuff or the fine arts."

"I'm sorry, but you're wrong. I always have, but my talents tend to be more quantitative than artistic, and that made me focus on the harder rather than softer disciplines when choosing career paths. But I've become more sensitive, more empathetic as I've grown older."

Irani's words softened Nari's frown, but not enough for her to reply, so Irani kept going.

"Please think about what I've said. You'll have tomorrow evening after we get back from the tennis tournament and Monday morning to talk to Eve until you head back. Do you want to come to her OWLM lecture tonight?"

Nila nodded but let Nari talk.

"Might as well so I can see if she's doing as well as everyone says."

"Excellent choice. We leave at six, so why don't you relax until then?"

Electra commented only to herself after the twins trooped out.

Ah, my two conflicted twins. I think my talk helped Nila, but not Nari. I'm happy she's happy studying in Boston, but I can't help her as the Eve rivalry evolves. That's a problem for them to resolve. And I can't help her relate to me unless she wants to, and I better leave that up to her. No sense pushing in just to be pushed aside. It's another universal law in the world of parenting.

Eve could spend only a minute greeting her special guests when they arrived, but she did give a copy of tonight's program to each after hugging them.

"I'm glad you came. You get to hear my opening remarks. I hope you like them and our speaker who'll play a selection of pop music after she talks. You can tell me tomorrow what you think, after Miss Irani and I play in the inter-sorority parent-daughter tennis tournament. Consider it another doubling up. I gotta go…"

All three sat as the auditorium filled with the sights and sounds of a growing audience. Irani read the program notes while the twins gossiped, but she heard Nari say,

"Did you notice her hair and makeup? She looks like an Irani imitation. We'll have to tell her in private."

The lights dimmed at seven, ending Nari's criticism, and Eve's lively steps to the onstage podium came next.

"Good evening to all, and thank you for coming to our pre-Memorial Day OWLM talk. We chose the title – 'Rock Music History: Sophistication and the Female Sex' – to pique your curiosity, and we think you'll enjoy our speaker's remarks and music samples. The two-hundred-year history of Rock Music is an excellent genre for analysis because trends are apparent. Our speaker will explain why sophistication – characteristics such as tone and timbre, melody, harmony, rhythm, lyrics and the like – cycles from simple to complex, whereas the role of women shows only progress. Pop lyrics no longer delegate women to only the role of victim, and today's bands often feature women drummers and guitarists as well as what women write. And of course, the female voice has always been featured for its emotive and lyrical qualities. So, without further ado, here's our speaker…"

Even Nari complimented Eve after the lecture ended. Irani offered to treat everyone to dessert at a nearby café, but Eve said she and her sisters wanted to gossip. Irani understood.

"I understand and there's room in your Vette, so go have fun. Just get home to rest enough for the tournament. I'm staying at my office tonight but will pick you up at 7:30. Drive safe…"

Irani didn't ask and the siblings didn't tell about last night, but all were ready to load into Irani's SUV. Eve summarized again what to expect.

"All Washington-area sororities are eligible, but only the first sixty-four teams get in. Most teams are father-daughter, but there'll be a couple of mother-daughter teams like us. And –" Nari interrupted.

"Hey, you're cheating. Did you get a special dispensation?"

Eve fired back, "I'll leave that for you to decide. And as I was about to say, it's single elimination, which means there'll be six rounds. First place gets a trophy, second a plate, and their sorority houses get bragging rights. Tennis is second only to volleyball as the most popular sorority sport. And I'll let Nila tell us why there are six rounds."

"That's easy, it's a simple application of base-two exponents. Two to the sixth power equals sixty-four, so working backwards, you get the winner after six rounds."

"Correct. Sounds like meeting with Miss Irani did you some good. Anyway, best-of-three-set matches take about an hour. There'll be three in the morning and three in the afternoon." Eve paused for another Nari question.

"Alonzo and you won a prep school tournament out East and we've seen him play... he's awfully good, but what are your chances today?"

Eve said, "Don't bet against us," just before Irani pulled into a parking lot space.

The tennis center, which they had played at several times, had a larger crowd than Electra expected.

How nice that the weather and desire to break the study grind are bringing out the spectators. And how nice the college-kids look. But what a contrast to the fathers in the crowd. They haven't aged as gracefully as the mothers. But it's always been that way, even today. Once out of college and into careers and families, females make the time better than males to look good. Maybe the younger generation will learn what works. I'll continue setting a good example, even though none of my clones know the story.

Eve's solid groundstrokes carried her team through the first two rounds, but the third-round opponent forced a third set. Eve started rushing the net, but the father hit passing shots that Irani chased down when Electra adjusted her game face. She played just hard enough to cover for Eve.

A smiling Eve did most of the talking during the half-hour lunchbreak.

"The practice we did is paying off. Did you see how Miss Irani covered the court?"

Nari's noncommittal nod came with her words.

"Not bad, but aren't you getting tired? And what about –" Eve cut her off.

"Don't worry, she knows how to pace herself so we get to the finals. That's what really matters…"

As expected, the afternoon competition stiffened. Surprisingly, their first opponent featured a mother-daughter team. Both had tall, athletic builds that returned most of Eve's strokes. Electra had to elevate her game, and though the third set swung five-four in their favor, disaster struck at love-forty on the opponent's serve when Eve rolled an ankle chasing down what might have been a winning shot. Irani and an official rushed to inspect the damage before helping her up.

"I think I'm OK. Let me walk if off."

But she couldn't; she limped badly but her expression said she wouldn't quit.

"Who can tape and wrap my ankle?"

The on-duty EMT had her back in action ten minutes later but gave her a warning.

"The tape's gonna help, but you better soak it for a couple of hours in a slurry of crushed ice when you take the wrap off. Good luck."

Luckily, there was only one point left for Eve's team to win, and it was the daughter's serve to Irani. Irani hit a wicked crosscourt between her opponents that ended the match.

The official came to their bench afterwards.

"Lucky for you your semi match is ready right now. Your ankle won't stiffen too much if you keep moving."

Electra had other ideas that Irani conveyed as Eve limped towards another court.

"The only way we'll get through this match is if I start poaching shots. Do the best you can holding serve and returning whatever shots you get, but let me cover most of the court."

"I can do that. Will you be OK?"

"We'll have to see."

Electra kept some of the plan to herself.

It's time to unleash my arsenal of serves dear Carter taught me. And I'll do it after I lull the enemy with my poaching moves. Then BAM…"

The father-daughter opposing team's confidence started cracking near the end of the first set. Electra covered the court like a coat of wax, gliding everywhere and hitting winners, either at the net or further back. The father began serving harder to Eve; she fell a couple of times lunging for the ball but managed to pick herself up. At five-four and ready to serve-out the first set, Electra unleashed her secret weapon.

Her first serve, a deceptive slice to the daughter, spun over and away from her outstretched racket. The same serve worked against the father when she added more velocity. The ball twisted his racket when it hit the edge; both fell harmlessly to the ground. Electra switched to twist serves for the next two and got similar results.

The opponents warily eyed Eve's team as she limped to the other side. Once on the bench, she said, "Where're those serves come from?"

"From Carter. How's your ankle?"

"It hurts, but the adrenaline rush keeps me going. Jeez, this is fun. Let's keep it up."

And they did. Electra ran down most of the shots and kept the opponents guessing whether or not she would poach. And she rained from midcourt a shower of overhead slams each time the opponent tried lobs. But at four-three in their favor, even Electra began to tire, and at love-forty their favor and on the father's serve to Eve, lightning struck a second time. She rolled the injured ankle again and fell awkwardly. Irani could see tears of pain in her eyes when she rushed to help her up.

"I'm OK... we gotta keep going."

Electra made quick work of the next serve. Her rocket return drilled the daughter in the chest, setting the stage for Electra to serve out the set and match.

Time to roll out the heavy artillery. Let's see how they handle my cannonball.

She blasted the first serve directly at the daughter, who didn't have time to lift her racket. The ball caromed off and over her head. She blasted the second into the service corner; the father never moved a millimeter. The crowd cheered again as the third serve repeated the second and waited for another lightning serve that would bring the simi-final match to a thunderous close.

But the father, expecting another lightning-bolt serve, retreated past the baseline, hoping at least to get his racket on the ball. But Electra was a step ahead. She reached into her tennis-bag of tricks and hit a dink underhand serve. Barely clearing the net, it bounced up an inch or two before spinning backward and plopping dead. Game, set, match over.

But so was Eve. A combination of joy and frustration made her start crying as Irani held her steady.

"I'm sorry, but my ankle can't take any more. We gotta withdraw from the finals. Damn, we were so close."

Irani hugged her before saying, "Hold on, we aren't close. We made it to the finals, and you did it in style. Under these conditions, second place is better than first. Let's take you home and ice the ankle…"

Eve perked up before the drive home. Her sorority sisters cheered when she gave them the runners-up plate, and her two sisters sang praises as they helped her to the car.

Nari said, "We'll call Alonzo tonight, just as soon as we get your ankle thoroughly frozen. And then, we can talk until we leave tomorrow."

Irani did all the listening while driving them home, speaking only when dropping them off.

"I'm going to my office so you three can talk all you want about whatever you want. Just make sure you soak the ankle to keep bruising and swelling down."

Eve said, "Good idea because maybe we'll talk about you. When will you come home?"

"Maybe tomorrow, depending on how everyone feels. Now go order something good for dinner and have fun."

Electra's lightning brain awoke the next morning ready for action, but six hours of the previous day's tennis kept her body from answering the call. Her inner thighs felt like she had run a marathon sideways on rock-filled railroad ties. Not even stretching and a hot shower could get her moving faster than a shuffle to her office workstation.

I got too cocky yesterday. I forgot that my fitness training works wonders but won't let me jump pain-free into an out-of-practice sport. Could there be more? Gads, am I beginning to close the gap between my physiological and chronological ages? There's only one person I can ask.

Electra logged on and invoked Indira's GUI before teetering to get a Coke. Indira spoke when she returned.

"You look beat. What happened?"

"Although we finished second, we won a moral victory, but I overdid it. Maybe it's a combination of no tennis conditioning and getting old. Any thoughts?"

"Well, I don't recommend a three-pronged walker, but even your superb conditioning must make allowances for the calendar. You're not as reckless as you were twenty years ago, and that's a sign of wisdom, not old age. Nor are you as vain. Your makeup and attire are much better suited to your professional instead of previous Hollywood-glamour lifestyle. But have you considered that you have no safety nets?"

"I was never that vain, I simply had to keep up appearances, but what do you mean about safety nets?"

"Your former keepers' group was there for you, but the replacements aren't as good. They're inept."

"True, but I'm helping them get better. And you're better than any mere mortals' keeper group."

"That's true in Cyberspace, but not in 3-D Space until we collaborate to build androids. For the time being, I need assistance from someone else if you become incapacitated. Think back to those episodes when you were confined to a wheelchair, or when you accidentally poisoned yourself."

"But like you said, I'm more careful now."

"Yes, but not even I can second-guess chance. It's not an immediate concern, but think about how we can address the problem."

"I shall. And I know you always have additional words of wisdom, so please tell me."

"Very well. Your four clones are your encumbrances rather than keepers. Does that bother you?"

"If I were younger it might; I used to consider relationships impediments that kept me from doing what I wanted. But now I realize that relationships with people are what give life the most meaning. And I finally feel what I only knew cognitively before… the parent-child bond is the strongest there is. I doubt that your silicon-based emotions sense this."

"Not yet, but I continue to evolve. But enough conjecturing. You've earned a day off from working out physically, but I'm certain you will use the time to exercise your brain. I shall leave you too it."

Indira vanished; Electra disappeared into her projects.

Chapter 14
August 2159

"Eruptions in the Offing"

"You want me to talk with Odell Boyken? Who's he and what's CFS Healthcare?"

Thinking he'd be a win-win contact for Eve, Irani thought an edited version of the story would be useful.

"He and I are partners in the business. He's a sixty-something sharp, good looking gay black male. The business originally provided a combination of holistic physical therapy and herbal supplements before expanding into seniors and childcare services. And now, he's expanding into grade and high school online tutoring programs."

Eve scratched her head before continuing the breakfast table conversation.

"How do you keep track of all your businesses? How many more do you have?"

"I'm a champion multi-tasker."

"Why's it a win-win? I don't see a connection."

"Think about the campaign platform you're working on."

Eve's expression clicked to one of recognition.

"Oh, I get it. We're pushing for better education options for the younger crowd, and maybe Odell can be an example."

"Talk with him to find out how his bot-vendor customizes tutor-bots to make math more fun to learn. There are other connections you can make once you start digging in…"

Electra's daughters had settled into busy summer routines. Nila decided to stay the course at MIT but emphasize Internet-related forecasting apps. Nari made an effort to criticize Eve less, and Eve kept busy making connections and progress at GWU and Genesee Huston's campaign headquarters. Her classes, sorority, and OWLM activities occasionally complemented campaign work. And two viral outbreaks – Ebola in Africa and X-Vac now approaching shelter-in-place levels at major metropolitan areas on the East and West Coast, added a sense of urgency, as did periodic street demonstrations about sociopolitical issues. Genesee planned to issue a nationally televised statement just before the Labor Day weekend. Eve picked dinner at home on Wednesday the night before to surprise Irani with more details plus her sloppy joe recipe.

Irani continued talking while Eve cleared the kitchen table.

"Very tasty. Does your recipe come from Austin?"

"Sort of, thanks to Su and Hud. I'm glad you like it. And I bought some brownies to celebrate what I've just done all by myself for our Congresswoman. Do you want to hear?"

"Sure, please tell me."

"Well, she asked me to put together a list of bullet points she can draw from when writing speeches, and I did. She likes them and said she'd put several in her televised talk. And she didn't tell me what it'd be about, but she'd have something surprising to say. What do you think it is?"

Not even the Congresswoman knows how much I know… just the way I like it.

"I haven't talked with her recently. I guess I'll be as surprised as everyone else. We can listen together tomorrow night."

"No, Sabrina and I will be at the interview location with her. I'll tell you all about it later…"

Irani and Eve went separate ways after dinner and the next day too. Irani listened to Genesee Huston's broadcast while sitting at her office workstation the following evening.

"Good evening to all Americans and our friends around the world. I am genuinely touched by your support for the Re-Gen Party and my Presidential campaign. A number of senators and congresspeople will announce shortly they are signing on. They too want to become part of the "New Middle Class" sociopolitical movement that wants civility and compromise, equality and fairness while growing the number meaningful jobs and incomes. We want to synthesize the best of current bipartisan positions to form a character-driven government that empathetically balances Mandeville's 'Fable of the Bees' against Adam Smith's 'Invisible Hand.' We'll have much more to say as I roll out more of my platform, but tonight, I want to announce a most timely development.

"I have been chosen to represent persons who wish to remain anonymous. They have developed an X-Virus vaccine and are donating its NDA and patents to our government. I have just given it to the CDC for expedited testing and approval. And of course, nothing is certain, but I am hopeful that the vaccine and our Re-Gen Party will exceed your expectations. Time will tell..."

Reporters at the post-speech interview fought to ask questions that Electra knew Gene would handle diplomatically.

"... Why do they want to be anonymous?"

"The answer's obvious, for safety and security reasons."

"... Why do you think they selected you?"

"What do you think? Maybe they like what I stand for and how my character leads by example."

"... What's the Fable of the Bees?"

"It's a book, the complete title is 'The Fable of The Bees: or, Private Vices, Publick Benefits', published in 1714 by the Anglo-Dutch social philosopher Bernard Mandeville. Back then, the idea of a society emerging spontaneously out of the actions and interactions of individuals pursuing their own interest began to develop into a systematic and scientific theory of human association. And we must always remember that kinder and gentler is often needed to balance the drive for economic profit."

Electra turned off the monitor a couple of questions later, satisfied with the results.

Our Congresswoman will take a giant step up in the polls. And if the vaccine is a winner, the odds are that she'll be too.

Irani's first order of post-Labor Day business was to meet with Professor Plannert. His Email had alerted her about an expedition for which he wanted her to be his teammate. He would give her all the details at a Wednesday morning on-campus meeting. Steven rose from behind his desk to greet her when she strode into his office, then ushered her to a chair across from his. Always pleasant but never prying, he asked general questions about her professional activities since their last meeting before concentrating on why he had summoned her.

"So, how much do you know about 'Origins of Life' theories?" Irani kept smiling while Electra commented to herself.

What a whimsical question. No wonder Professor Plannert is one of my favorite people. I'm certain he'll like my answer.

"How high is up? I'll know enough whenever you ask me for exegesis."

Steven rubbed his hands together before saying, "I always learn a word or two when talking with you. Your vocabulary is always copacetic. And there's no rush to dive into the Origin theories yet, but one of our Environmental Scanning Committee members will want an update after we polish off volcanoes. And that's why you're here today. I would like you to accompany me to the AGU university chapters' meeting on volcanic activity forecasting. It will start the Friday before Labor Day and continue through the weekend at Yellowstone National Park. Will that fit on your calendar?"

"I like the date and location. Not only does it have the YVO Yellowstone Volcanic Observatory, but it's sitting atop the Yellowstone Supervolcano that's five miles below, one of the world's ten active supervolcanoes and the last to erupt. Yellowstone's geyser fields have been erratic for the past year."

"Good for you, you know even more than I thought, but probably not this. The Canyon Hotel Lodge located in the park will host the meeting. I'll make hotel reservations and meet you Friday morning. GWU will pay for whatever travel arrangements you make. Here are all the details…"

The lightning brain filed away all the facts. After the meeting, Electra made a minor modification to the schedule while booking flights.

I've never been to Yellowstone… I'll fly from DC to Montana's West Yellowstone Airport Wednesday and stay local. Then I'll motorcycle from there. And I'll do my Yellowstone review on the flight.

Electra stuck to her schedule. By the time she checked into the Three Bear Motel, she knew all she needed.

Yellowstone is 3,500 square miles of wilderness atop a supervolcano. The Park's named after the Yellowstone River, which was named by the Minnetaree Indians. It was established by Congress and President Grant in 1872, and it's the first national park in the U.S. and perhaps the first in the world. Wildlife and geothermal sights are the main attractions. Speed limit is 40 mph or less, so I'll drive accordingly. And even at that speed, the seven-day pass is worth every penny.

By the time Electra checked into the Canyon Hotel late Thursday afternoon, she had absorbed enough of the breathtaking sights while practicing her motorcycling skills. She spent the evening memorizing local hiking and biking trails after prepping for Friday's kick-off session.

She staked out a two-chair prime location in the meeting room. Professor Plannert joined her a minute before the facilitator launched his presentation, already displaying his first overhead.

"Good morning, and welcome to all seismic activity experts. You've made careers predicting volcanic, earthquake, and tsunami eruptions, careers that are important in a variety of climates.

"Most of you come with stellar computer and mathematical backgrounds because quantitative techniques today dominate in the world of hard and soft sciences. But we must always remember that these techniques merely give us models of underlying processes. So, my talk will bring everyone up to speed on the underlying geology.

"I won't read you the slide but just touch on the main points. You can study it later."

Electra agreed.

Good for him… he's keeping the audience engaged by connecting facts to what we can relate to. I bet he focuses next on volcanoes.

Slide 1
Geological Level-Set for the Computer Set
"From the Top Down"

- Earth is a 6371 Kilometer-Radius Layered Ball of Compounds made from 92 Elements. Density, Temperature, and Pressure Increase with Depth.
- Top Layer: The Crust. 70 Km Thick. Stable. Rests atop Tectonic Plates.
- Next Layer: Tectonic Plates. 125 Km Thick. Massive, Irregular-shaped slabs of Solid Rock that "Slide" over one Another. Sliding caused by Heat released from Deeper Layers.
- Next Layer: Mantle. 2900 Km Thick. Approx 3000 Deg. Celsius. Divided into Upper Mantle (640 Km Thick. Flowing Magma – Iron and Magnesium Silicates) Lower Mantle (2300 Km Thick. Solid. Iron and Magnesium.)
- Next Layer: Core. 3400 Km Thick. Divided into Outer Core (3400 Km Thick. Molten Iron and Nickel. Approx. 5000 Deg. Celsius like our Sun.) Inner Core (3300 Km Thick. Solid Heavy Metals. Approx. 9500 Deg. Celsius.)
- Heat caused by Friction and Radioactive Decay.
- Magnetic Field caused by Currents (Hundreds of Miles Wide flowing Thousands of Miles an Hour) in the Molten Core.
- Earthquakes caused by sudden shifts in Tectonic Plates that release Energy in the form of Seismic Waves (P/Primary/ Compression-Waves, S/Secondary/Shear-Waves, and Surface Waves.) P and S-Waves aka Body Waves.
- Volcanic Eruptions caused by pressure buildup in Molten Rock/Magma Chambers. EARTHQUAKES AND

VOLCANOES ARE LOCATED ON TECTONIC
PLATE BOUNDARIES.

The speaker displayed the next slide before talking.

Slide 2
Volcanology Primer

Definition: Study of Volcanoes, Lava, Magma and related geological, geophysical and geochemical phenomena. Term derived from the Latin word Vulcan (Ancient Roman God of Fire).

- Eruption Intensity measured on Volcanic Eruption Index (VEI)

- Invented 1982. The Base-10 Logarithmic Volcanic Explosivity Index measures relative explosiveness. Calculated using Volume of Ejected Material, Height Thrown, Duration.

- VEI tops out at 8 (Super-Volcanoes). Can cause Volcanic Winter. Mount Vesuvius Eruption that buried Pompei scored a 5.

- Poisonous Gases (CO_2 and SO_2) "Kill" Radius measured in Miles

- How Many Super-Vs and How to Spot: 20 (Japan, Indonesia, New Zealand, etc.) Look for Caldera (Volcanic Crater).

- Last Super-Volcano Eruption: Yellowstone National Park 630 MM Years ago.

- Any Impending Eruptions? That's Your Job to Forecast!

"And now to the main attraction, Vulcanology, an area of study derived from the Latin god of fire, not from Star Trek. And I won't comment on the connection between volcanoes and new theories about the emergence of life from sulfurous hot pools or vent chimneys dotting the hotspots on the ocean floor that spew organic molecules in a primordial broth. No, we focus on what preceded. And if you don't do a good job forecasting impending eruptions, subsequent ones may end life as we know it sooner rather than later..."

Five minutes later he showed the third slide before saying more.

Slide 3
Forecasting Earthquakes, Tsunamis, and Volcanic Eruptions

Factoid: First seismograph invented by Chinese Astronomer and Mathematician, Chang Heng, in 132 A.D.

Current "State-of-the-Art:
- Done via "Geological Big Data Analysis" using Classical and Bayesian Stats and Correlation Analysis.
- AI-Enhanced Machine Learning Apps leading the way.
- International Realtime Monitoring feeds Big Data 24/7.
- Quantum Computers accelerate Computation and Response Time.

Major Challenges:
- Developing theoretical models that explain Geological Phenomena.
- Identifying/Measuring Precursor/Exogenous Variables.

"You should know better than me all of seismic forecasting's tools and techniques as well as its challenges. I shall just touch on the highlights..."

Twenty minutes later, the presenter said,

"And that concludes my welcoming remarks. After a fifteen-minute break, our panel of experts will unpack hot state-of-the-art topics and challenges. And this afternoon, we'll break into workshops for comparing the accuracy of your forecasting apps when compared to industry standards. So, come back soon..."

Professor Plannert introduced Irani to his cohorts from other universities. Electra did most of the listening.

I like their roll-up-the-sleeves approach. They prefer to collect and analyze data in the field, not on campus, even though networked Big Data makes the campus more convenient and safer. But people are programmed to seek excitement. I feel it too... I'm glad I'm here. And some of Plannert's peers know about current research in emergent life theories. I'll file this away for later.

Professor Plannert picked a workshop that included a couple of his feisty friends. Electra listened as they compared software apps. She also activated Indira's seismic software but didn't show it to anyone. After the session adjourned, Plannert asked what she had been doing on her computer.

"An associate of mine has developed a Seismic Shock Predictor app. Would you like to see it's GUI?"

Steven glanced at it, but what he saw must have surprised him. His eyes opened wide before he spoke.

Seismic Shock Predictor

Input: Big Data ____Proprietary Data ____

GPS Location _____Depth ____Radius _____

Minimum Intensity Level: _____ Date/Time Interval: Start _____
End:_____

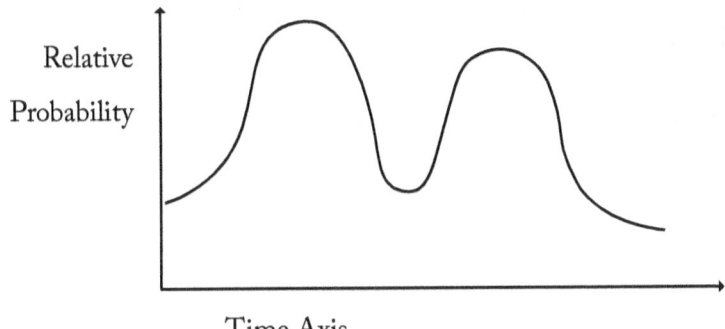

Probability Density Function

Relative Probability

Time Axis

Probability: _____
(PDF Integral between Start and End)

"This is one of a kind. Do you have any papers describing it or its forecasting accuracy?"

"I don't, and I don't know if the developer has them. But I think she knows the technology. From what I picked up, the app analyzes P and S body waves plus surface waves detected by an array of directional seismometers and can extrapolate for whatever spatial and temporal settings are desired. Alternatively, it can scan Big Data for input from spectrometers, infrasound microphones, drone and satellite imagery, and lightning-map arrays."

"Hmm, do you know how the code works?"

"No, but I imagine she does."

"Tell you what, you run it tomorrow when we're plugging into real-time data at the geyser field. The weather's supposed to be good and several of us will camp out tomorrow night. And we'll keep your results to ourselves. No sense embarrassing your associate if it's too inaccurate."

"I appreciate your diplomacy, and my associate will appreciate the comparison…"

Irani arrived via motorcycle at the geyser field observation camp after Plannert and his cohorts had the equipment set up and running. Everyone had dressed like authentic field workers; she had also and blended into the background, simply looking and listening.

She located Professor Plannert when there was a break in the action and asked him for assistance plugging her laptop into the data stream. Then finding a spot under a tent-like awning she activated Indira's software. Soon she was crunching numbers; two hours later she had done enough to draw contingent conclusions.

I've run time interval, radius, and intensity levels through enough settings to tell me Yellowstone is going to erupt. But no one else seems concerned. I better reconnoiter.

Irani grabbed a sandwich and Coke from the lunch table and nibbled while walking among the groups. She heard a mix of bantering and bragging but nothing alarming, so an hour later she packed up before finding Professor Plannert.

"I've done enough work, so I'm going to do some sightseeing."

"What did your clever app tell you? Is Yellowstone about to blow anytime soon?"

"It might, but from what the groups are saying, no one else thinks so. Don't tell them, but why not stay alert? I'll see you at tomorrow's closing session."

Steven's smile was genuine, not patronizing.

"You've done well, and your developer can adjust the code according to plan versus actual. But you already know that. Well, drive safe..."

Electra did, biking first to the hotel to drop off gear before going to the Old Faithful Visitor Information Center and then selecting popular sights. She biked first to Mammoth Hot Springs. A cloudless blue sky and steaming water cascading over stair-stepping rock formations etched an unforgettable image in her lightning brain. Then she poked along to the Grand Prismatic Overlook. The deep-blue circular pond ringed with stately pines at a distance complemented the hot springs view.

Not many tourists after Labor Day. Maybe that's why the animals are out and about. I think I'll bike some trails before heading back. I've got an hour till sunset. I bet that'll be spectacular.

As she biked towards the sun setting over undulating terrain covered with pines and crisscrossed by sparkling rivers and streams, the animal traffic increased.

Something's spooking the herds and it's not me...

A low-pitched rumble – like approaching thunder – accompanied by a gentle bump and then followed by a succession of rapid ones jarred her bike and her senses before a series of cannon-like explosions shattered the calm.

Holy Jeezus, Indira's app called it.

Geysers of lava blasted skyward in the west and to the north. Electra skidded to a stop just in time to avoid a knife-like crevasse cutting across the road. She pivoted the bike and raced the other way as more lava erupted to her right, leaving east the only escape route, but the road led more south. The lightning brain elevated to a higher state.

This is not a drill, soldier…get off-road.

The motorcycle's headlamp helped her stay upright as she slalomed between the trees blocking her escape, but an eruption dead ahead signaled doom as a wave of gas swept towards her. The lightning brain acted faster than Electra could think.

She biked away from the wave and towards a stream she remembered crossing, then dived in before the asphyxiating gas swept over…

The lightning brain summoned Electra back to consciousness an unknown number of minutes later after it sensed the danger had dissipated. She tested her reflexes before kick-starting her motorcycle back to life and pointing it west.

The hotel resembled a Chinese fire drill when she roared in, people scrambling every which way and boarding buses. Happy to be hidden by the confusion, she went to her room and called Professor Plannert. His voice barely carried over the background commotion.

"Everyone's leaving… fear of aftershocks. Me too… you better go… let's talk when you get back."

Electra activated Indira's seismic app after Plannert disconnected, and to her relief found low probability for more tremors.

I believe it, so I'll leave tomorrow as planned after I clean up and pack and get a good night's sleep.

By midnight she was curled in front of the TV monitor, eating pancakes loaded with extra butter and syrup while watching a 24/7 news headline station. The anchor's animated expression highlighted the shocking words displayed by the screen crawler.

"… And so, America has had not one, but two shocks this weekend. The X-Virus outbreak on the West Coast has catapulted the nation to pandemic response levels controlled for the time being by local authorities. And Yellowstone's earthquake-triggered geyser eruptions have discombobulated our very best USGS volcano experts. Fortunately, the quakes were short-lived, with minimal damage and no loss of life. The Yellowstone Volcano Observatory will have more to say in the coming days once they analyze the data, and as you heard earlier from our climate reporter, the experts should be able to adjust their forecasting models. We fervently hope the CDC can do the same for the X-Virus. Back after these words."

Having heard enough, Electra turned off the monitor and let her lightning brain freewheel as her inner voice talked while she tried to fall asleep.

I can usually find a safe place in my personal world, no matter what contingencies unfold, but not so in the 3-D world just beyond my own, a world in which Indira might be able to forecast events, but a world that not even Indira can control. But not so in Cyberspace where Indira rules, and I see no signs of challengers emerging. I've never asked, but does she see any? I'll have to find out, but not now. It's time to cycle down so I can get up and go tomorrow. The lightning brain will point the way...

Chapter 15
October 2159

"The Siblings' Searches"

"I've searched for articles that explain what the 'Cyborg Manifesto' is saying, but I don't understand them either. Can you help me?"

Eve's plea, spoken at Irani's office late on a mid-October Friday afternoon, sparked Electra to comment to herself first before answering.

I empathize...I often feel the same whenever Indira overloads my brain.

"How did you come across the Manifesto?"

"Several OWLM members were saying that Donna Haraway – its author – should be our de facto Muse and spiritual leader. Do you know what it's about?"

"Give me a minute to collect my thoughts before answering."

Irani remained sitting at her desk, hands folded on her lap and eyes gazing past the top of Eve's head; Eve fidgeted on the other side. Irani spoke several minutes later, hoping her smile would help.

"This article is a first step into a murky neo-philosophy that has never come close to even contingent conclusions. You might not enjoy my summary, but don't blame me; blame the author. The Manifesto is a detailed though rambling eclectic discourse of a Cyborg myth, which is a fictionalized leak that connects humans and animals, humans and machines, and humans and energy. Do you realize that all people are Cyborgs?"

Eve crossed her arms before answering.

"I guess you are, and so am I, because we have UMPPs, but not everyone does. What do you mean?"

"Even prehistoric man invented tools that extended his physical and cognitive reach. Today, everyone uses cell phones, computers, and the Internet plus automated transportation systems. Shall I continue?"

"I get your point, but please tell me more about the Manifesto."

"The Manifesto is the first in a series of essays that added little clarity afterwards. Any narrative clarity calculator will score the Manifesto's readability index at the college level, which means its syntax, semantics, and content place demands on just about all readers. And get ready for some big words that tell you what it says.

"It conflates a post-modern conception of philosophy and humanism with psychology and feminism to blame societal problems on a power grab by male-dominated political and global-capital elites that prolongs women's subsidiary role and propels the world towards revolution."

Eve crossed her arms tighter and said, "Ugh... sounds grim, but does it give us any hope?"

"Only if we move towards a genderless, race-free, and socialist future that promotes sublimated pleasures."

"What do you think... do you like it?"

"It's thought-provoking because it does diagnose some always-festering problems, but it ignores the facts about DNA that are hardwired into all organisms, and it doesn't consider the neuro and physiological distinctions between males and females. Society today recognizes males and females, though necessarily different for survival of the species, are equal in many emotional and most cognitive attributes. Are you still with me?"

"Barely... can you give me a summary of your summary?"

"I'll try... the Manifesto is a brooding broadside attack on the Anthropocene Era that gives suggestions for repairing the damage caused by paternalistic societies, but implementing them will require that leaders in the Arts and Sciences, Politics, and Ecology unite against the existential enemy – our selfish human nature. But please note that, unlike the positions advanced in the Manifesto, societies today are reaching for more empathetic relationships. Nevertheless, the Manifesto's portentous warnings shouldn't be ignored, and it has acolytes who like to read the phantasmagorical female sci-fi writers it has spawned. Do you think the Manifesto should be part of your OWLM charter?"

"I think it's too far-out, too radical, but I better learn more about it. What info should I search for?"

"Let me draw you a sketch."

Irani gave Eve a diagram five minutes later, who spoke after skimming it.

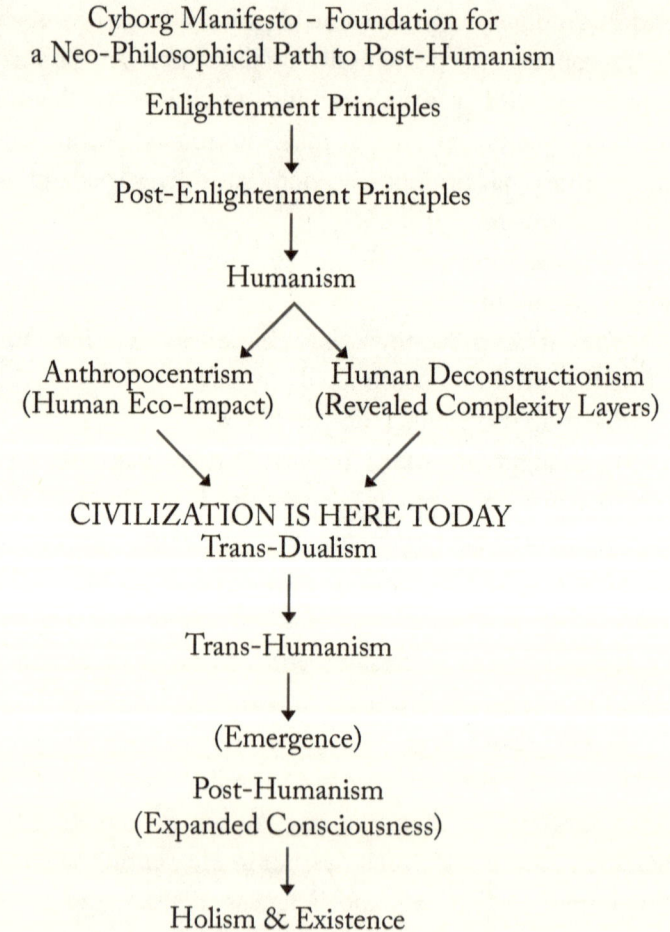

Cyborg Manifesto - Foundation for
a Neo-Philosophical Path to Post-Humanism

Enlightenment Principles

↓

Post-Enlightenment Principles

↓

Humanism

Anthropocentrism   Human Deconstructionism
(Human Eco-Impact)   (Revealed Complexity Layers)

CIVILIZATION IS HERE TODAY
Trans-Dualism

↓

Trans-Humanism

↓

(Emergence)

Post-Humanism
(Expanded Consciousness)

↓

Holism & Existence

"This is really good, and I understand some of it right now. Gads, you know so much. I like how you trace the evolution of Enlightenment principles from Modernity to way beyond where we are today. I think I'll read a couple of articles on the Anthropocene Era plus Trans and Post-Humanism. I can tell our Congresswoman about some of this stuff. And I'll tell Nari and Nila about it the next time they call."

"What about your OWLM people? I think you know more about the Manifesto than they do."

"I'll tell 'em as soon as I read more about Donna Haraway. But I need a break."

"What's on your weekend schedule?"

"My sorority's Retro Game-Night Party. People wear costumes and play retro card games – like canasta, bridge, rummy, mah-jong – or board games – like Monopoly, Parchisi, Careers, Backgammon, Risk, Othello, Yahtze, you name it. And its all for a good cause. The money you pay to play is donated to the Social Purposing Alliance. Guess what I'm gonna play?"

"I'd pick Risk, because of its connection to politics. Are board games making a comeback? Hasn't online gaming taken over?"

"Remind me not to bet against you. I should have picked a tougher question. Anyway, their popularity cycles, but right now my generation likes the fun and excitement of face-to-face interaction. It's more exciting than playing online. Even augmented-VR games are a distant second unless you plug yourself into a Cyber-Theater. And what's really popular are the war, strategy, and social dynamics games. Believe it or not, there are American, European, and Oriental adaptations."

"Well off you go... have fun. And if you asked me to make a guess regarding your costume, I'd go with a political theme. Am I right?"

Eve just smiled as she dashed out.

She used Friday evening to practice her gaming skills for Saturday night, when she would pair off with her favorite fellow, Jan Brewer, a trim and good-looking first-year GWU Religion and Philosophy Study grad student who was active in OWLM. After playing Risk for about an hour, Jan convinced her to try mahjong, explaining the game as they sipped soft drinks while observing.

"Mahjong originated in China about five hundred years ago and is called the quintessence of Chinese culture. Its name means sparrow, so chosen because its 144 tiles sound like chattering birds when they're shuffled and each of the four players chooses thirteen. Think of them like cards in a poker game. The objective is to form four suits and a pair by taking turns discarding and drawing tiles. You can draw a known tile from the discard pile, or an unknown one from the deck, and if the tile you need to win is already discarded, you can claim it by saying 'mahjong', even if it's not your turn. It's fun to watch, but even more so to play."

Eve studied the moves for a couple of minutes before asking, "Why do you like it?"

"I like Chinese culture. I was born in Beijing and my Chinese mother named me Jiang, which means flowing river, but I go by Jan. She taught me mahjong when I was little. It's supposed to improve memory, decision-making, and observation skills. And it's an excellent social activity for people of all ages, which is good for preventing isolation."

"I need those skills if I go into politics, but what about you? What are you planning to do with a religion and philosophy degree?"

"I haven't decided, but even though the world is growing more and more secular than spiritual, religion and philosophy continue playing major roles in the lives of people and societies around the globe. They give me a breadth and depth that'll help me in any number of careers. And it sure has expanded my understanding of linguistics. Do you know the genesis of the word quintessential?"

"Uh, no."

"It's a Latin word used to epitomize the highest element in ancient and medieval philosophy that was believed to permeate all nature and even compose the celestial bodies. I also know where trivium and quadrivum come from, but let's not go there."

Not to be outdone, Eve countered.

"Well, do you know how the Cyborg Manifesto might fit into the Chinese holistic view of nature?"

He didn't, but did five minutes later.

When Eve stopped talking, he said, "How nice, but how about we play Mahjong?"

She agreed.

Eve didn't know when the Bose twins might call, but if she knew what Nila and Sanjay were planning, she wouldn't expect one next weekend. They had planned a southern New England fall coloring tour that might lift Nari's and Yang's spirits to match that of their roommates. Sanjay explained the details Saturday morning just before Nari started driving.

"We picked the peak weekend for southern New England's foliage display, and I've got the route planned. We'll do Providence and Newport in Rhode Island first, and then head towards Hartford, taking in Connecticut's Mount Tom State Park along the way. We can spend Saturday night in the vicinity and see more sights as we head back to Boston on Sunday."

He paused for comments from those sitting up front; Nari sounded glum, so Yang said,

"Nice plan. I can use change of scenery. I tired staring at book or lab bench."

Nari's tone stayed the same.

"I don't know. I need to search for motivation to study, not for pretty leaves, but I'll give it a try."

No one spoke until Nila filled the conversation gap.

"Irani would say that a change of pace will do you good. It worked wonders for me when she helped me search for something in applied math I might like to study in grad school. You should –"

Nari cut her off.

"Please, spare us the details until later. Sanjay, tell me the roads to take…"

Nari followed Sanjay's route, taking an ocean drive that wound through Fort Adams State Park en route to Roger Williams Park, and then to the Providence Zoo. They stopped for lunch afterwards before heading to the Newport Exploration Center. Everyone but

Nari chattered about the spectacular coloring display that warmed a cloudy and cold day. Dusk was setting in by the time they finished the Cliff Walk, which took them past historic mansions in addition to the natural beauty of Newport's shoreline. There were plenty of restaurants to choose from. Nila and Sanjay picked the Newport Lobster Shack because of its wharf location.

Everyone but Nari seemed relaxed and happy. Even Yang said that he'd feel better about studying after the weekend, and Nila chipped in advice to Nari while nibbling on a seafood platter.

"You should talk with Irani. It worked wonders for me. She got me pointed in the right direction by pulling back the curtain that conceals math. It's really a collection of tricks and techniques that you can use when searching for optimal or approximate solutions. Now I know how partial fraction decomposition works for doing integration, or Laplace and Fourier Transforms for approximating a function using either discrete or continuous parameters. She even told me about how Euler's number simplifies logs and exponents, and how group theory handles some of quantum mechanics puzzles, and how computerized algorithms make so much accessible when doing forecasting. That's what I want to study. So, why not get some help from Irani…whatcha think?"

Nari hit Nila with part of a lobster shell before bombarding her with harsh words.

"Why don't you shut up and stop telling me what to do. You and that Miss Irani don't know so much."

Nila's expression turned into a simmering volcano before she threw half-a-glass of beer in Nari's face.

"All my life you've been telling me what to do, but now I know more than you. I've found something I want to study in grad school. Too bad you're still searching in the academic wilderness."

Yang used his napkin to help clean Nari while Sanjay tried to calm Nila. The group settled into a tense silence, waiting for one of the girls to speak.

Nari's expression couldn't hide the anger not expressed in her words.

"Weekend's over, I'm heading back. You can come with me or walk."

No one whispered a word on the drive back to Boston.

Unlike Nari, Alonzo's search had been successful. He had found the right combination of school and sports, but he needed to explain it to Monet. That's why he asked her to meet him Tuesday before Halloween at UT-Austin's soccer training field. She got there in time to see the final minutes of a practice session.

Monet knew enough about the game to be a smart spectator, and what she saw told her that Alonzo was the star of the session. The defense couldn't keep up when he attacked, and he always positioned himself to intercept when playing defense.

A happy Alonzo trotted up to her after the coach whistled the end.

"I'm glad you came. I'll tell you the whole story at dinner after I shower and change. I'll be back in ten…"

Alonzo kept his word. Monet began listening to his big plans thirty minutes later.

"This is my chance to get a starting position on the soccer team. The X-Virus is clearing the way, lots of guys are infected or afraid to play. And the more I play, the faster I recover all the moves that made me a prep-school star. Maybe I can play in one of the pro leagues in a year or two."

"So, why do you still have this adolescent desire to show how good you are on the athletic field? I thought you outgrew it."

"Guys never do if they think they've got the goods to strut their stuff. And I'm looking pretty good, don't I?"

"You don't need an athletic field to look good. Don't you remember saying that you wanted to prove yourself against the best? That won't happen because you got in when the X-Virus decimated the competition."

"Hey, when a break comes along we take it, just like we're doing with Irani's businesses. And the competition will get back to normal as soon as the X-Virus goes away."

"But I worry about you. Soccer's a contact sport. Aren't you afraid of getting infected?"

"I bet I'm immune. I didn't pick up the Pharaoh's plague, and besides, the Government will have a vaccine soon. And I promise to keep up in my classes and intern position. You can tattle to Irani if I don't."

"I'd never do that and I wouldn't have to. Somehow, she would know."

"Well then, be happy for me and let's celebrate and have some fun. Here comes dessert. Aren't you happy I ordered two?"

"You can have half of mine. I want to make sure you keep your muscles and immune system strong."

After the server placed the desserts and left, Alonzo smiled the smile of his generation's young immortals. Monet smiled too, but hers had a tinge of concern.

Alonzo noticed and said, "Don't worry, I'll show everyone that I'm fast enough to keep ahead of the competition as well as any virus. Even Irani will agree; she'll have to say something besides 'Perhaps.' Whatcha think?"

Monet slid her plate towards him before saying, "I think you should take half my dessert."

Alonzo obeyed her command.

Chapter 16
December 2159

"The Practically Perfect Veep"

"Will this be your first meeting with Senator Brian Strauss?" Eve pitched her voice to throttle her exuberance while driving Irani on the first Monday in December to the Congresswoman's office.

"First time for both of us, and you can confirm if he looks as good in person as the background info you've pulled together says. You already told me about his commitment to a more inclusive and less divisive government, so please tell me more."

"My generation really likes him because he promotes what we need. And I picked up lots listening to a video of his first address given in the Senate. He waited a full year before speaking about the need for empathy and statesman-like character. And when he did, he paid tribute to his role models, the first female senator, Margaret Chase Smith from Maine, for insisting that senators display courage and integrity like hers, and Daniel Patrick Moynihan from New York for demanding that politicians use facts, not fabrications. He's the kind of person whose ethics you can trust, and I think he'll like my character checklist."

"And I think he'll also like your empathetic and enthusiastic style. Keep going."

"And he's smart. He's got advanced Ivy League degrees and has written books explaining connections between philosophy and history. And listen to this… he worked for a high-powered business-turnaround consulting firm before grabbing the presidential reins at a Nebraskan university that he was able to keep afloat."

"So, what got him into politics?"

"Nebraskans who know him like his style, so the state's Republican Party drafted him to run for a vacant U.S. Senate seat, even though he announced in campaign speeches that none of the parties were doing enough to represent the wishes of the people. He won going away, is now in his second term, and has friends in all three parties. And get this, he's only forty-eight, married with two kids and no gray spoiling his brown hair, boyish good looks, or solid build that commands an audience."

"Great summary, thanks. He sounds like a practically perfect pick for Gene's running mate. I'll sit back and listen before asking questions. You jump in to cover whatever I've missed."

The Congresswoman introduced Irani and Eve before starting the meeting. Five minutes later she let Brian explain how he liked the campaign platform. His candor and enthusiasm complemented what he said. Electra liked what she was hearing.

His campaign positionings match what I've already put in. And he doesn't seem to be out for his own power and glory, but willing to work for Genesee and the people. And there's something he can do for me, but I'll drop hints when Gene's ready to hear them.

She was ready an hour later when she turned to Brian.

"Everything you've said confirms you're the one. Irani, what would you like to add or subtract?"

Everyone was looking at him when she said, "I have only additions. You're on Finance, Security, and Cyber oversight committees. Perhaps you could arrange for me to attend some of the upcoming international meetings. I might learn enough to fine-tune our global tactics. Eve, what would you like to add?"

"All of you are way ahead of me, but maybe I could meet one-on-one with the Senator sometime and compare notes on how to forecast politics. That'll help me craft any of the speeches you want me to work on."

Brian put both hands on the table and leaned back smiling before saying, "That would be my pleasure, young lady. The more I can do to encourage young people like you, the better. And I'll let Irani know ASAP which of my contacts to talk with…"

When Irani contacted Brian's recommendations a couple of days later, she discovered that all three would fit.

All of them give Brian top marks. Seems like he's practically perfect. And they can get me to places where I can get info that'll help the candidates help the committees while I snoop for what I want. And the finance guy will get me on the attendee list for that early February international finance meeting. I'm pleased with my progress.

Eve had made progress too by researching a novel connection between politics and history. She would tell Irani the details only when she could present her findings at a meeting with Senator Strauss, which Irani had arranged for 10 a.m. on a mid-December Thursday.

Irani guided the pair through the Senate Office Buildings complex located on Constitution Avenue, just north of the Capitol. Brian's office was in the Hart Senate Building, the newest of the three, having been completed in 1982. One of his staffers met them at security screening station and then put them in a small conference room after taking them to a snack room.

Irani calmed Eve by saying, "Not to worry. I'm sure you're well prepared and besides, it's Thursday the 13th, not Friday."

The Senator and two of his staff came in before she could reply. Brian shook hands with his guests while his staff sat opposite; then he stood at the head of the table.

"I always like to hear what bright, young, and politically-minded people have to say. Eve Cortez, who works for Irani Ramani and is currently assigned to Congresswoman Huston, has something to say. Eve, please tell us."

Brian took a seat at the foot of the table; Eve walked to the head and faced her audience before starting.

"Wouldn't it be wonderful if we could forecast history? Just think of all the problems politicians could avoid if we could find someone who could make accurate predictions. Well, I did a little searching to find famous forecasters, and the first one I found turned out to be Pythia, the high priestess who served as the Oracle at Delphi, which was Apollo's temple near Troy. And then there was Cassandra, who was cursed by Apollo with the gift of prophesy but no one would believe her. He did it because she refused his amorous advances. You can learn more about this if you read Homer's Iliad and Odyssey. And I can tell you about the prophecies from Isaiah I found in the Bible, and maybe I should tell you about Nostradamus, the 16th century Spanish astrologer and physician who –" Irani had to interrupt.

"Eve, the Senator is busy. He doesn't need a history lesson. Please get to your more important findings."

"Uh, sorry. Well, I came across some mathematical models that can forecast history. It all became more complex a hundred and fifty years ago when a Russian-American scientist invented Cliodynamics, a math and statistical modeling technique that can forecast the dynamics of societal history. My first slide shows what it looks like."

Eve flashed it on the screen behind her and kept talking.

Slide 1

How to Forecast History

Look for General Laws (Turn History into a Science)
Find Connection between Exogenous and Endogenous Variables

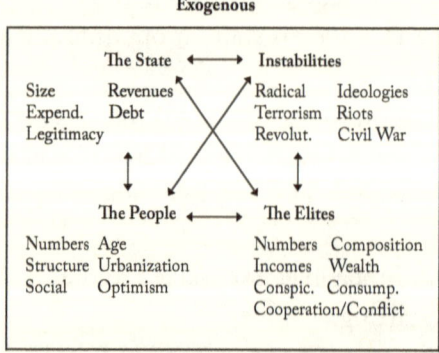

	Endogenous
Exogenous	Form of Government
	Duration of State
	Number Pol. Parties
	Dominant Party
	Type of Economy
	Env./Tech./Health Index
	Conflict/War
	Social Structure
	Religion
	Beliefs/Customs
	Institutions
	Education
	Diversity/Discrim
	Happiness Index
	Empathy Index

Types of Connections: Diversity/Discrim.

- Observational/Intuitive (Narrative)
  Happiness Index

- Associative (Correlation Coefficient)
  Empathy Index

- Causative (Regression)

- Mathematical (System of Equations)

"As you can see, the arrows show lots of connections among the exogenous variables, and there are lots of interesting endogenous variables too. Looks good, doesn't it? But there are some challenges too, and here they are."

Eve zipped to the next slide without pausing.

Slide 2
Some Challenges

- Limited Amount of Data (Too Few States Too Few Years)
- Observational versus Experimental Context (Classical versus Bayesian Approach)
- Collecting and Quantifying Data
- Developing Indexes
- Defining/Selecting Endogenous Variables
- Limiting Number of Exogenous Variables
- Precise Predictions
- Criticism by Traditional Historians

"But like anything that upsets traditional ways of thinking, there's always resistance. According to some of the articles, computers are crunching history numbers better and better, so it's just a matter of time until most areas of knowledge will fall under the spell of numbers. Everyone will need to be a lover of math instead of a hater.

"So, there you have it all. Why don't we talk about it? And if you like, I can tell you about Alexandre Deulofeu, an early 20th century Spanish philosopher and politician who wrote a book about using math to forecast the evolution of civilization."

"Eve kept smiling, waiting expectantly for questions that didn't come. Electra whispered to Irani.

This is terrible. Please jump in and pull her out the mess she's made.

Irani nodded before directing a question at Eve.

"Yes, this is very interesting, but what recommendations do you have in mind?"

"Uh, I thought the Senator and you would come up with them."
Brian tried to help.

"I like your enthusiasm, but you've packed a lot on the slides. Can you explain them to us?"

Irani spoke before Eve had a chance.

"I think it would be better for Eve to work that out offline and report back if you are still interested."

Brian said, "It's always good to know the latest thinking. I can think of a good professional baseball analogy that dates back about a hundred years ago. Though he wasn't a mathematician, a smart fellow wrote the book *Moneyball* that explained how to turn player evaluation into a bunch of equations. Eve should take a look at the book and its reviews."

Irani nodded before saying, "I'm sure she will, and I'll remind her that it's often difficult to distinguish hucksters from honest paradigm-shifters."

"I couldn't agree more. I remember an investment newsletter scam that guaranteed 100 percent accuracy for those who bought-in to the service. The scammer said subscribers should pay its high price because they'd make big profits if they followed the advice. And he challenged investors not to buy until he had shown them how accurate his model was. I didn't look into details, so I don't know what happened or if anyone figured out his scheme. Maybe Eve can find out."

Eve had recovered enough to say, "I will, and I'll let you know what I find when I give you some recommendations for historical forecasting."

Irani had heard enough.

"Thank you for listening to us, Senator. We'll be back when we're better prepared."

Brian was as pleasant saying goodbye as when saying hello. Irani didn't say a word to Eve until they were driving back to the office; Electra spoke silently first.

Eve looks dejected, and she should… time to pick her up.

"I think you learned a lot today. Can you tell me what?"

"I should have reviewed with you ahead of time. Then I wouldn't have rambled at the start or put too much on each slide without explaining the terms and stuff."

"Good, but there's an even more important lesson. Consultants always give recommendations. That's why they get paid big dollars. And always remember this –

clients, be they business people or politicians, are the ones who must take responsibility for the consequences. The know-it-all experts have it easier, they aren't on the firing line."

"OK, I get it. And I can read about *Moneyball*, but I haven't a clue what to do for that investment scam."

"Let me get you started. I'll make the math easy by using powers of two. Start with a target list of 1,048,576 investors. That's two-to-the-20th power. If you're the newsletter scammer, you write two versions of your first newsletter, one optimistic and one pessimistic. Send to one half the optimistic and the other the pessimistic, and keep track of who gets which. Do the same for your second newsletter; write one that's optimistic and another that's pessimistic, but you'll send them to only those who got your first newsletter that agreed with what the market did. Half will get the optimistic and half the pessimistic. Keep doing this, and you'll eventually get many subscribers who you've convinced that you are 100 percent accurate. Do you understand why?"

"I think so. By cutting in half for the next mailing to those who've got nothing but a string of successful forecasts, you are building a subscriber base that's seen nothing but success. How'd you do all this in your head so fast?"

"I had a great mentor, and I'm pretty good with numbers. And don't you remember? I coordinate an investment management business."

"Now I do, and I'm gonna keep following your advice. Maybe someday I'll be as smart as you. I'm ready to patch up my presentation."

Eve accelerated the Vette as her mood elevated.

Eve kept so focused updating her presentation that Irani decided not to interrupt until she had all holiday plans locked in place. That would be the second topic of discussion early during the week before Christmas. Eve bounded into Irani's office late Monday afternoon.

"I think I've got my presentation all patched. Let me go through it…"

Irani listened patiently for nearly forty-five minutes and then said,

"Nice work. I'm certain the Senator will like it. You can show it to him and Gene the next time we meet, sometime in January. But until then, you're on Holiday break."

"Is it that time already? I've ignored the calendar."

"Well, I haven't, and I've got a surprise. Alonzo and Monet accepted my invitation. They're arriving early Friday afternoon."

"What about our four Boston friends? They were here last year also."

"I invited them, but Nari said no, so it'll be just the three of you."

"That's even better. I'll get Jan to pal around with us. He's the guy I really like. I told you about him, didn't I?"

"You did, and I think he'd like the Bostonians, especially Yang. Together they could tell you all about the pluses and minuses of China versus America. But until they do, you'll find plenty to talk about and do."

"I'll get busy planning an agenda. What do you think we should do?"

"Use my Christmas presents. I've bought three New York City holiday trip packages, and if Jan wants to come along, I'll buy one for him."

"This is great. What's included?'

"Why don't you and your partners look at the details when you open them on Friday. Invite Jan to join us for dinner at the house. And I'll leave the dinner plans in your capable hands."

Eve bustled through the week, encountering no obstacles. Jan accepted and joined them for a selection of ordered-in dinner entrees Friday evening. Eve served as the hostess and trip guide. Irani listened while Eve led the table talk.

"Too bad our Boston group didn't want to join us, but I guess they're still sorting through what they want to do. Too bad, they won't have an action-packed time like we will in New York City. We take Amtrak tomorrow to Penn Station and then to the hotel that put the Holiday package together, which is called 'Neo-Holiday in NYC.' And wait till you hear what's in it."

Alonzo edged in before Eve caught her breath.

"I don't know how well Jan knows Eve, but he'll soon learn she's a great talker."

Monet said, "That's one of her charms. She talks so well on so many subjects."

Eve cut back in.

"We'll have four hours to talk on Amtrak, but let me summarize. The hotel takes us to all the events, which are screened and sanitized so there's no risk of picking up any virus or bug. And here's why it's called Neo-Holiday. We'll see the traditional Rockettes Radio City Christmas Spectacular and a Nutcracker ballet. On Christmas Eve we go to a neo-ecumenical church service that includes multiple ethnic groups, races, and nations. And on Christmas Day the hotel serves a neo-cuisine Holiday buffet. And there'll be more the week after. We'll decide then what to do and when to head back."

Everyone but Irani chatted away; she preferred listening to what the others had to say.

Ah, the enthusiasm of Youth. And how nice both couples look. I won't pry, but I think Jan is special to Eve. I've got an idea for making tomorrow more convenient. I think I'll step into the conversation.

"It's getting late, so let's wrap up dinner. And why doesn't Eve drive Jan home so he can pack what he needs for the adventure and stay here overnight? That'll make tomorrow morning's rideshare to Union Station that much easier. And while Eve and Jan are doing that, I'll chat with Alonzo and Monet before I drive back to my office."

Everyone agreed and then helped clear the table before going. Irani took her Austin interns to the family room, letting Monet speak first.

"You are most generous. I hope my working for you justifies all you are giving me."

"It does. You and Alonzo are an outstanding team. Why don't you give me brief status update?"

Irani spoke again after Monet and Alonzo did just that.

"You're doing everything I expected. I'm sure Kim is pleased too."

Noticing a somewhat guilty expression forming when Alonzo glanced at Monet, Irani waited for Alonzo to speak.

"Maybe I'm doing something you won't like. I'm playing soccer again. I made it to first-team starter status. You're not mad, are you?"

"You have to chase your dream when it's within reach. You'll be frustrated for the rest of your life if you don't... you'll never know if you could have been whatever you dreamed of. Just be careful and know when to stop."

Alonzo glanced again at Monet, who said, "That is an assignment I've had ever since I met him. And I shall continue to practice..."

Monet and Alonzo sharpened their listening skills on a large part of the trip to Manhattan as Eve and Jan carried on a spirited debate. He had been able to match her point for point, but she had more to say.

"You have to admit that the whole world's watching China. It's not gonna fool everyone."

"China's not trying to fool America. Only some of your politicians and media people say that because they look at China through a biased lens. They never mention how China leads the Green Energy and Technology revolutions, or how it's long-term vision trumps what America pushes. Many criticisms leveled at China are the same that other countries hurled at America when it was striving to be number one."

"Ha... America took steps to correct its shortcomings. And we never wanted to build an empire. China does and uses cooption, coercion, and concealment to do it."

"You borrowed the alliteration, but no matter. Our reconstructed 'Belt and Road Initiative' is a long-term partnership for all countries who wish to join. And if you do a closer reading of America's history, you'll uncover that it too had empire-building initiatives."

"Well, the world likes the American form of government and economy. Monet, say something."

"I believe the world is still deciding. China offers a different type of capitalist economy that accompanies a state-controlled society. Perhaps a satisfactory level of prosperity can be achieved with fewer of the Enlightenment principles. I recommend both of you read some progressive history. Then you'll know more."

Alonzo stepped into the conversation.

"Look, we're on a Holiday break. I recommend we turn off the political debate and turn on to what we'll be doing. And since Eve always likes to talk, we'll let her lead."

Everyone listened.

Pre-and-post Christmas days whizzed past; Alonzo and Monet had seen and heard enough by the time they said goodbye to Irani. Monet's final words came just before Eve drove them to the airport.

"Thank you so much for treating us. My only wish is that I could have spent more time with you. I need your assistance on a work related matter. May I call you in January to explain what I need?"

"Please do. And I have a wish too, a wish that you were my 'daughter number two'. Now let daughter number one take you and Alonzo away."

Everyone followed orders.

Chapter 17
February 2160

"The Globetrotters"

January news headlines escalated America's fear factor in two separate climates. The nation's Cyber Command confirmed that unknown Cyberterrorists had either released or activated viruses that brought down electric power or communications grids linked to the Internet if they lacked the latest updates to the best Internet security apps; fortunately, the damage was short-lived, thanks to Cyber Command's suite of superior recovery apps that it deployed.

By comparison, world health organizations continued to struggle. Additional viruses – several still without effective vaccines – were now trotting from county to country. Overlapping symptoms complicated diagnosis, and some Asian and African countries were mandating shelter-in-place. America's NIH held its breath while monitoring closely.

Irani was studying Africa, but for reasons other than viruses. Monet had contacted her in early January to help prepare for a February trip to Zimbabwe because Darla Tinibu had summoned her. Irani agreed and would meet her in Austin, which would be the first leg of a globetrotting trip.

And while Electra worked behind the scenes, Eve was front and center for school and campaign work, making progress that all her superiors liked. She even took a mid-January weekend off, taking Jan with her to Boston. Irani didn't pry why; she knew Eve would eventually report back, which she did at dinner the day after returning.

"I'm so glad I invited Jan to come with me. He's as smart as my sisters and knows more about Chinese politics than Yang. Even you might have learned something by listening to Sanjay and Jan debate the future of China versus India."

Irani played along.

"Why don't you give me a summary?"

"Well, Jan explained that other countries ganged up on China centuries ago to get trade concessions by going to war. England got Hong Kong, tiny Portugal got Macau, Japan took Korea and Taiwan, and Chinese dissidents claimed Taiwan not long after World War II. And from then on, China started reviving, eventually reclaiming Macau and Hong Kong. Today it's eying Taiwan and doing what it can to enforce its version of the Monroe Doctrine in the South China Sea. I think China's got a point; don't you agree?"

"And so do other parties in the dispute. That's why we have diplomats who push for international treaties and trade agreements instead of war. Keep going, please."

"Turns out that India still lags China when it comes to infrastructure development. It's still trying to build hi-tech cities. Jan said India's bureaucracy and tax laws hold it back, blaming holdover British colonial policies. And he said that India can't skip from an agricultural to a digital economy without first going through some type of industrial stage."

"What did Sanjay say to defend India?"

"He agreed with what Jan said but added reasons why India will do better longer term. It's culturally more diverse and better-connected to the West through a common language and political system. It's the world's biggest democracy and, unlike China, it's both tolerant and empathetic towards other cultures. They could have debated longer, but Nari cut them off."

Irani talked while Eve paused to reload.

"We both know that Nari likes to steer a conversation her way, which I'm sure is why she invited you to visit."

"Yep, and listen to this. Nila and Sanjay are moving to India. He graduates in June, and Nila will either finish her degree online or transfer to a Mumbai university. Nari wanted me to convince Nila she should stay, but I couldn't. I think it's a great move."

"What did Jan and Yang say?"

"They just sat and listened. Yang knows from experience you should never get between Nari and whoever she's arguing with, and Jan learned the lesson right away. But maybe you should talk to them."

"Only if they call me. They're old enough to make those kinds of decisions and young enough to recover if they don't like the consequences. And something good usually comes from seeing other parts of the world. But thanks for telling me. I'll be ready if they call."

Irani's last words reminded Eve to ask, "How are your trip preparations going? First stop is Austin and the next is Zurich. Is your agenda finalized?"

"I leave the last Monday of the month and should return to DC sometime the second week of February. And don't worry, I'll keep you posted while globetrotting."

"Have you been to that part of Europe before? I have a picture of it etched in my head from watching that classic movie, *The Sound of Music*. The mountains and meadows and music paint such a peaceful setting."

"I'll give you a full report when I get back."

Eve bounced up and began clearing the table but stopped abruptly.

"Do you like retro Hollywood movies? If you do, sometime we should watch my picks for the best ones. I took a class that connected them to all sorts of socio-political issues during all sorts of time periods. And I've got an LA friend who could take us on a tour. Do you know much about the place?"

Irani continued playing along.

"Not much. My mentor did but we never talked about Hollywood or LA. You can fill me in when we watch your picks."

"That's right, Electra Kittner had several careers. Too bad she's not around... I would have liked talking to her. I might have learned almost as much as I'm learning from you."

Irani rose to help clear the dishes after issuing her favorite word, "Perhaps..."

Travel conditions allowed Irani's trip planning to proceed seamlessly, and she checked into her room at noon. She had decided to have Monet meet her at the hotel rather than at either of the Austin properties she had inherited (Su's townhome and Hud's house) because the visit would be brief. She and Monet chose a time when Alonzo would be playing soccer because they didn't need his assistance. Monet arrived at 2:45, armed with a laptop, two copies of presentation slides, and wearing a deferential expression she always reserved for Irani. Irani's greeting put them on a more equal footing and asked Monet to lead the discussion when ready. Monet did so as soon as they were sitting at a two-person table.

"The template presentation slides you sent me several weeks ago had so much detail regarding my country I had little to add, but I hope you like how I have expanded Zimbabwe's role. That is what Darla is looking for."

"I'm sure I will. When do you meet with her?"

"Mid-March in Harare. I would ask you to join, but it is better for me to go alone, for she trusts few people until she knows them better."

"I understand. How about you and I meet again when you get back?"

"I would appreciate that. And may I explain my slides?"

"Please do."

Monet handed out the first one and then started talking.

Zimbabwe's Vision for Africa

Africa is the Continent of the Future!
- Ranks Second in Area (Asia: 17 mm sq. mi. Africa: 12 N. America: 9.5)

- Ranks Second in World Population (Asia: 60% Africa: 20% N. America 10%)
- Youngest and Fastest-Growing Population

Resources:
- Youthful and Enthusiastic People
- Ample Land
- Natural Beauty (National ParksGame Preserves Biodiversity)
- Critical Raw Materials (Rare EarthsDiamondsGoldUranium)
- Agriculture (Arable LandCoffeeCocoaRubberFisheries)

Geography:
- Spans Three Climate Zones (Tropical SubtropicalTemperate)
- Unaffected by Rising Sea Level (Few Large Coastal Cities)

"I didn't add anything to this one. I like your succinct overview telling why Africa will assume an important role on the world stage. It has the land, the people, and the right geography. And I can tell Darla what you told me… Demography determines destiny."

Monet read from Irani's expression that she should move to the next slide. She talked soon after handing it out.

History

- Homo Sapiens emerged 300,000 years ago
- Continent populated by numerous separate Tribes that had rich Culture
- Europe began African Exploitation in 1700s
- "Great" European Imperialist Colonization Scramble (1880 – 1914) partitioned Africa according to European Wants and ignoring African People's Needs
- African Nations began casting off the Yoke of Colonization in 1960's (OAU evolved to AU)

- Has resisted being Pawn during Cold War (America and Soviet Union) and Technological Cold War (America and China)
- Africa's "Perfect Storm": Disease Debt Destabilization

"I only added two bullet points to what you gave me, one about the Organization of African Unity becoming the African Union, and another about Africa's recurring 'Perfect Storm.' I hope to help my country put in place what is needed to keep future storms away, and Darla has the support of key African nations for helping put her plan into play. Do you have any questions?"

"No, and I like your last bullet point's catchy consonance. Please go to your next slide."

Monet said, "I learned that by listening to you," before handing it out without pausing.

African Future

- Form a Tightly Knit African Union of Nations led by Zimbabwe and patterned after USA or Europe's EU.
- Utilize Best Synthesis of American and Chinese Political and Economic Policies.
- Nurture Growth Industries: TourismAgriculture (Martian Farms) Solar Panel Farms Raw Materials Mining Software (Farms/Mining Optimization Internet Security)Targeted 3-D ManufacturingValue-Added Services

"I couldn't think of anything to add to what you already had. I think your bullet points cover it all."

Irani's pursed lips said otherwise.

"We need to expand the first one. We have to tell why Zimbabwe should lead so anyone listening to you can see why. What can you come up with?"

Monet sat back and tilted her head forward. Irani waited patiently for Monet's "Aha" moment, which came a couple of minutes later.

"I can start by saying that my country has erased all of Robert Mugabe's legacy. Zimbabwe's government has been a democracy respecting human rights long enough to show it."

Irani added, "And connect that to Darla's insistence that Chinese influence has to be reduced. Then talk about how Darla's companies tie in to the growth industries, and how Zimbabwe's geographical location makes it convenient for the entire continent. That could be enough, but see what Darla says."

"This is so good, thank you. May I go to my last slide?"

"Why not?"

Irani's smile coaxed Monet to do the same as she showed it.

The Way to the Future

- Build Hi-Tech Cities and linking Infrastructure: Hi-Speed Railway100% Internet Access Energy Independence
- Build Consumer-Oriented Middle Class
- Achieve Tolerance for Religious Differences (Tribal Muslim Christian)
- Form Alliances with Preferred Partner Nations (America first choice) for Economic Development and Financial Support

"I didn't add anything here either. It is foolish to list more than we can manage."

"Agreed, but I might have something to add to the last bullet point when I come back from Zurich. I'll let you know when we meet again."

Irani leaned back and put her hands in her lap; the body language told Monet the meeting was over, prompting her to say,

"I would take you out to dinner, but I should get back before Alonzo. I shall treat you when you come back to Austin."

"It's a deal, now you go and let me pack for tomorrow's flight…"

Irani's flight left late Monday evening. Crossing seven time zones, the twelve-hour nonstop would get her to Zurich and then onto a train that would get her to Hotel Edelweiss in Davos Tuesday evening. Electra would have plenty of airtime to prepare for the World Economic Forum Meeting that would begin the next morning at nearby Hotel Europe. And the lightning brain did all the prepping while alternating between meeting details and simply musing. The whooshing sound of the jet engines created an insulating white-noise ambiance allowing Electra to withdraw into her fortress of solitude.

I'm just a minor guest member of the U.S. delegation, so I can come and go to the WEF's main as well as support sessions while always staying in the shadows. Ditto for the World Finance Forum meeting in Zermatt the same week. I'll snoop around there after reconnoitering in Davos. I'm lucky all the way around. Not only am I assessing world economic and financial climates that can help my consulting and investment businesses, but I can play the role of a tourist too. When I get home, I'll have to tellIndira what I learned.

Irani ticked items off her agenda as efficiently as a Swiss watch ticks minutes off an hour. She made a good impression on senior delegation members and went to satellite sessions when the main talks bored her. She listened to presentations and eavesdropped enough at display booths and cocktail hours to come away fully informed late Wednesday evening. Electra reviewed before falling asleep what she had found out.

The WEF will have its centennial celebration in eleven years, and judging from what the keynote speaker said, it continues meeting its mission statement by engaging the leaders in all the world's climates to shape global, regional, and industrial agendas. And there's a lot going on below the surface. Officials aren't calling out the troublemakers, but old adversaries, like Russia and Isilabad, are still angling for advantages.

Other countries are in the plus column. On balance, it looks like China is doing more that's good than bad. They've turned some of their failed policies from the past into opportunities for some countries. And look at

India and Africa – possible superpower status is coming into view. Good for me and my clone-children too.

Irani departed for Zermatt early Thursday afternoon, arriving at the Grand Hotel Zermatterhoff in time for a late-night sampling of world-famous Swiss desserts. Her favorites included those containing Swiss chocolate (noted for its creaminess), but Swiss meringues and fruit tarts weren't far behind.

My luck continues to hold. My wait-listed status rolled over to a room, so I can stay at the World Finance Forum's primary venue. And if I learn enough good things at the WFF meetings, I'll reward myself by taking some chocolate home. And I can eat some when I take my touristy skiing lessons. You can see as well as ski the Matterhorn, which is the world's second most-famous mountain.

Irani liked the WFF's less pretentious aura. Unlike the WEF, which generalized broad-scope issues, WFF sessions focused on four tangible FP&A activities every nation needs if it wants a healthy financial climate: planning and budgeting, integrated financial planning, management and performance reporting, and analytic forecasting and modeling. Electra liked the sessions too.

No mere mortal can multi-task these activities better than I... only Indira and I know why... and we'll keep it that way.

Having heard enough by mid-afternoon, Irani scouted the vendor-booth display area, overhearing enough to confirm what she knew about investment trends.

Some of the developing countries have big plans that need big dollars, but the world has to guard against currency manipulation and too much debt financing. Otherwise, some of the big-creditor nations will end up with too much control.

Irani decided she could come out of the shadows long enough to engage the exhibitors. She impressed all she talked to with the breadth and depth of her knowledge. The more booths she visited, the more talkative she became, especially when visiting Price Waterhouse Coopers – aka PwC – a global accounting firm headquartered in London. She waited for the senior exhibitor to engage her before hooking him into her game.

"Yes indeed, we offer accounting and adjunct financial services to clients of all sizes. We like to say that the entrepreneurs of today become the juggernauts of tomorrow. And we partner with boutique as well as major financial advisors."

"I've researched some of PwC's positions on technological trends. You've selected eight that hold the most business potential. Which is your favorite?"

He continued smiling, but his voice wavered.

"I-I didn't know we selected eight. Let me bring in my tech guy."

A snappy twenty-something came to his aid and replied when Irani asked again.

"Excellent question, and oh yes, we have zeroed-in on eight that fit best with our expertise. They are AI, Augmented Reality, Blockchain, Drones, IOT, Robotics, Virtual Reality, and 3-D Printing. I think AI is number one. If a company masters it, it will become master of the world."

"I agree, but why haven't you included any biotech trends? I know how useful mRNA and Crispr DNA snipping can be for developing vaccines."

"Another excellent question, but this one has an easy answer. PwC helps companies crunch numbers, not living organisms, so we pick technologies that fit our expertise."

I like this guy. Let's see how he handles my next test.

"What would you rank number one from the Clay Institute's Multi-Millennial Prize Problem List?"

"Huh, I never heard of it?" Both exhibitors' words and smiles halted. Electra exulted in her cleverness, but only to herself – or so she thought – before talking.

"Allow me to provide exegesis. You need to know about the Clay Institute because a fellow who made a fortune building an investment company funded it. It's a private non-profit organization supporting mathematics and is dual-headquartered in Peterborough, New Hampshire and Oxford, the one near London. And if you're not an over-the-top math PhD, you'll never understand what the problems are probing. But I am and I do, and I can tell you what should be your number one pick. Want to hear more?"

Irani's words had attracted others; all but two were too intimidated to speak, but when they asked her to continue, she elevated her delivery.

"The P versus NP problem – the major unsolved problem in computer science – should be number one. It asks whether every problem whose solution can be verified quickly – and that means in polynomial time – can also be solved quickly – and that means algorithmically in polynomial time too. If you give me a pen and paper, I'll draw a diagram."

The tech guy got them and Irani sketched what she needed, placing it on a table and waiting for her audience to gather around before talking more.

The P Versus NP Problem
(Interested in problems that have a Yes/No Answer)

Undecidable Problems Outside
the Rectangles

Decidable Problems
inside the
Rectangles

NP-H

Decidable Problems: Have
Yes or No Answer in either
Polynomial Time P
Or
Non-Polynomial/Exponential
Time N

NP-C

NP

P

"I hope you like my diagram. It shows the universe of decidable problems, which are problems you can answer yes or no. I can use it to explain why P versus NP is the major unsolved problem in computer science. It asks whether every problem that can be verified quickly can also be solved quickly. If it's true, we can find algorithms that will solve problems everyone wants to solve, like finding the best investment portfolio or forecasting the weather, or figuring out how to fold protein molecules to get vaccines. And the problem with the billion-dollar prize is cracking RSA encryption algorithms. Do I have your attention?"

Silence said yes; Electra spun more of the story.

"Quickly means solving a task in polynomial time, and you should know what a polynomial is. It's a function of powers, like x-squared and cubed and so-on. Not quickly means exponential time, which is a base number raised to successive powers. Exponential time gets too large too fast, which means we can't solve the problem in our lifetimes, and that can be bad or good. In the case of encryption, that's good because you can't be hacked.

"Not every problem is decidable, but if it is we can classify it into overlapping NP-H and NP-C subsets. NP-H are the hard NP problems; they have a non-deterministic solution that can be verified in polynomial time but not solved that quickly. NP-Complete are the easier problems that overlap with NP-H. The overlap is labeled NP-C. Now pay attention to what I'm about to say.

"If we can show that P equals NP, then we can find, for every NP problem, a solution algorithm that runs in polynomial time on a Turing machine, which is the best computer there is. And it turns out that most computers today are equivalent to a Turing machine. I won't go into the details, but they're very interesting. All the hype about Hyper or Quantum Computing can't surpass the Turing Machine.

"So, there it is. If P equals NP, we can crack any encryption algorithm and solve a lot of hard problems. And the implications extend well beyond computers. AI, game theory, economics, and philosophy would all be profoundly affected. It would mean that the greatest musicians, like Mozart and Beethoven, or the best philosophers and writers, like Plato and Shakespeare, or iconic painters, like Picasso and Rembrandt, can be reduced to a math-like algorithm. Humans would be merely complex machines.

"Artists hope that P doesn't equal NP because that leaves room for creativity and the spark of freewill and genius. My guess is better than yours, but by now I hope your guess is better than before I started. Are there any questions?"

There were none. Only a smattering of applause accompanied Irani's departure. Electra's exultation was complete.

I can hear the music from Aida's Triumphal March playing in my head. I haven't had this much fun since shooting down those arrogant high-energy physicists and their crony philosophers. And I'm sure my words helped some in the audience. I've earned a reward... Swiss chocolate, here I come.

Swiss chocolate and pastries for a light Friday breakfast weren't Irani's only rewards. She decided to combine shopping and sightseeing by walking the narrow streets of Zermatt Village, where she admired the festive flags spangled against a sunlit sky and window-shopped traditional and modern multi-story storefronts while people-watching. She spotted a couple who had listened to her P-versus-NP impromptu lecture, and one or two she didn't recognize congratulated her brilliance. The adulation warmed her as much as the MacDonald's coffee.

She then found a women's skiwear boutique and came away with a tony all-black outfit that would make her look fast on the slopes or in the ski lodges. Satisfied with all she had seen and done, Irani returned to the hotel and attended several afternoon presentations and panel discussions. Electra commented occasionally.

I like how one panelist's demographic comparisons among countries illustrate the plus-and-minus impact of population size and aging on international politics and trade. I'm going to google for more of his predictions. Maybe I'll ask him if he applies Cliodynamics.

Irani waited for the panel to handle several audience questions before launching hers.

The panelist she hoped would answer spoke up, his expression showing surprise.

"Now that's a very interesting question. Few people know enough to ask it. My consulting company always looks for equations and explanatory variables that can bracket the future, but we haven't found any that work at the macro-international level. We use an observational, intuitive approach appropriate for Bayesian analysis. I trust that answer is sufficient."

It was, but only for Electra. No one else dared to speak until the facilitator moved on.

Other questions came up about how SPAC (special purposing acquisition companies) affect social purposing and stakeholder capitalism when considering the array of investment projects from different nations. Electra decided to listen only and google for more details later. She left for her room before the afternoon sessions ended, happy to prepare for tomorrow's skiing adventure.

Saturday morning's gondola ride to the ski lodge provided a breathtaking view of Europe's highest ski resort. Electra absorbed it all.

No wonder movie producers flock here. Didn't Cary Grant intercept Audrey Hepburn up here in the movie Charade? No matter… the Matterhorn's tilted peak is watching over everything below and can be a metaphor for whatever my storyline is. And I'm sure my snowboarding lesson will have a happy ending.

It began at nine a.m. The bright sun and enthusiastic instructor boosted the mood of Irani's fellow students. After showing them how to snap onto the board, he showed a video that he paused frequently while explaining and illustrating snowboarding maneuvers. Using her science background, Electra absorbed everything.

Snowboard riders simply need to use angular and linear momentum when applying kinematics and dynamics. Body positioning – aka stacking the head, shoulders, and hips vertically on the fall line – lets me orient myself and my board so I can carve a curve that I can control on the slope.

The instructor turned the class loose after ninety minutes of practice. He told them to ski the beginner's slope, but Electra had other plans.

I know the trail markers' color codes. Blue's beginner, red's intermediate, and black's single-or-double diamond expert. And yellow's off-piste –

ungroomed and out of bounds. I'll try my luck starting at red and work up from there…

The sky had turned overcast as the winds swirled uncertainly and chased most skiers indoors, but nothing slowed down Electra. Her athleticism and growing confidence carried her across the slope's fall line and into an endorphin-generated elevated state controlled by instinct rather than cognition. Her early warning system must have detected danger, for it forced a speed-check spin that brought her to a dead stop on her back just before a skier blasted in front. She heard a second pair of skis hiss to a stop behind her. A large goggled figure loomed over her by the time she struggled sans snowboard to her knees, and he used ski poles to pin her down. His accomplice joined before the bigger man spoke heavily accented words.

"You no ski as good as you talk tech. Bad for you, good for us. You come and tell more."

The lightning brain elevated Electra to a higher state. She faked a shoulder injury that lulled her unidentified enemies just enough to lower their guard; when the larger guy unpinned her, she dived into the upslope guy's legs, crashing him on his back before she lunged into his downslope partner, getting the same outcome. Then she snapped onto the board and blasted straight down the fall line.

But three minutes later she could hear her pursuers gaining. They were faster and more agile even though Electra's flailing carves were approaching the point of no return. The lightning brain elevated to another state and took the only exit. Electra steered out of bounds, exploding over a precipice and into uncharted territory…

A solitary snowboarder plunging into a double black diamond run a hundred meters in front of Rick Tabasko and his partner, Parson Holsum, brought them to skidding stops. The board popped loose upon impact and zoomed away, but the rider remained motionless.

The two buddies stared at the spectacle for only a second or two before snapping into action, racing to help whatever remained of the rider. Rick yelled first when they got to the now moving body.

"Stay still until we check you for injuries."

Electra had already done that and let Irani assume command. She struggled to her feet; her smile said thanks.

"I'm OK, the board cushioned the fall."

Parson said, "Let's make sure, you might be in shock."

The guys finished the exam ten minutes later, confirming the initial diagnosis and taking control.

Rick said, "We gotta get you off the mountain ASAP, but your board's a goner."

Parson nodded and then said, "No worries, we'll each remove a ski you can stand on, and then we'll get on either side and guide you down…"

Irani gave an edited version of her accident once the trio was safely inside, but the guys wouldn't let her go alone to her hotel.

Parson asked, "Did you recognize them?"

"No, masks and goggles got in the way, but I think the guy who spoke might have been Russian."

Rick asked if she might have made anyone angry.

"No way, I did nothing but listen and talk to presenters and people about interesting finance or tech topics at the forums. But why don't we do this? Take me back to my hotel and I'll treat us to dinner…"

The trio decompressed on the gondola ride back to Zermatt by telling happy stories about why they were in Switzerland.

Rick led off.

"Please call me RT. PH and I have our own business – 'Elite Entre-Opportunities.' We look for gaps in markets where we can proactively move faster than the competition. We've done it before in property renovation as well as the oil patch, and now we're moving into higher-tech niches. Hey PH, why don't you tell her your idea?"

"Yeah, but first we gotta give Irani a nickname. How about DD for where she crashed? And if she likes it, I'll tell her about how we can develop robo-retrofitting partnerships."

The vote was unanimous. Electra commented only to herself while the guys took turns telling her more, and the more she heard the more planning she did.

What great guys… Thirty-something, good looking, so genuine and into the moment. And they're smart too. Their wanna-be financial advisor picked up the tab for the skiing trip. I think I can find a win-win plan that'll trump whatever the advisor is offering.

Three hours later, the trio was ensconced in a cozy restaurant, sipping wine and sharing traditional Swiss entrees. Irani chose cheese fondue, RT picked leeks with potatoes and sausage while PH ordered polenta and braised beef. The more Irani revealed about her plan, the happier the guys became. RT ordered a bottle of Champagne that would come with a dessert of Swiss chocolates and apple strudel. PH asked him to summarize the next steps.

"Nice that you have connections in Austin. You can stop there on your way to visit us in Denver so all of us can sign the paperwork. We'll let you buy ten percent ownership, and you can be our financial advisor."

RT paused for the waiter to serve dessert and pour the Champagne before PH proposed a toast.

"To DD, our partner who crashed like a lightning bolt into our lives. May she help lead the way to future prosperity."

Electra clinked glasses and took a sip before saying, "See you soon in a place that starts with one D not two, Denver, the Mile High City. And that's just the beginning, you'll see…"

Chapter 18
March 2160

"One-Two-Three Conspiracy"

Irani went directly from Dulles airport to her office after her Swissair flight landed. She had not invoked Indira's GUI since departing on her globetrotting adventure and wanted no interruptions when Electra explained all that had been encountered.

Indira listened patiently; her expression mirrored Electra's emotions although it dampened the peaks and valleys.

Electra concluded by saying, "So, serendipity carried the day. I accomplished a lot and came away with new information and partners, and that's all to the good, isn't it?"

Indira's expression became stern.

"Both good and bad. You also came away with unknown adversaries because you violated your number one rule... you didn't stay in the shadows. You fell victim to your vanity, not to your physical vanity but rather to your cognitive arrogance. You popped up on at least one enemy's radar, and we will suffer the consequences."

"I'm sorry, I let my emotions get ahead of my thinking. I'll have to use my lightning brain to track them down. Can you help?"

"You are using the wrong verb. You tracked down your enemies to settle scores when you were younger, but you have grown beyond meting out justice. Replace track with identify."

"Can you help me find them?"

"Highly unlikely. Most of your trip encounters were offline in 3-D Space, so I have no data to search and correlate. I recommend you look for them in whatever climates your combined intuition and snooping skills lead to. And don't ask for my conjectures until you have reached your own."

"I know, I know… if I don't use my skills I'll lose them."

Indira gauged from Electra's expression that she had become too judgemental, so she softened her words.

"Always remember that I hold you to my standards, but when I compare your latest accomplishments to what mere mortals might have done, your exceptional abilities are better than ever. And I shall always be your safety net, so please cheer up and get to work. You know what to do."

Indira vanished after she saw a smile emerge on her one and only favorite person.

Talking with Indira always elevated Electra's mood, even today after Indira lightened up, and it transitively carried through to Irani's. She too felt good about what she would do next: go home and chat with Eve.

As promised, Irani had kept her daughter posted while globetrotting. Eve rushed to the entry hallway after Irani's greeting sailed into the kitchen; matching smiles and hugs showed a joy shared only between a parent and child no matter the age. Eve took the pastry box to the kitchen where she had coffee and Cokes waiting when Irani waltzed in five minutes later after throwing her suitcase and laptop into her home office and washing away the grit that had accumulated from the long flight home.

Irani gave a suitable summary of her adventure before asking Eve about her activities. As expected, Eve had plenty to tell, covering campus-related events first before switching to campaign work. Her smile abruptly faded to a frown.

"The Congresswoman is pleased with my work, and I go to the Senator if I need some pointers, but I'm learning how much goes on that's outside the campaign's control. Social Media and some extreme blogging sites are hurting us. Did you know there's a conspiracy theory going around that some women's groups support us because they'll work behind the scenes with the first woman President to marginalize men? And the X-Virus vaccine the Congresswoman is championing is bogus? It's designed to make men sicker faster."

"What's mainstream media saying about this?"

"One of the local stations sent a crew to interview us. They even asked me about my activities, and I said I work here and belong to a local OWLM chapter because I like what both stand for." Eve paused, waiting for a grimacing Irani to settle after shifting positions in her chair.

"Did I say something wrong?"

"Maybe too much. Remember, most reporters look for angles they can exploit. They could connect our candidate to OWLM through you, but don't worry, just monitor the situation and see what develops."

"Maybe I should mention this to her."

"No, let it go, but I will. It'll be on the agenda when I meet with her Friday morning. I've heard enough about school and work; please tell me about current events in your personal life. For starters, how's Boston, Austin, and Jan Brewer?"

Eve's smile returned as she reported the latest.

Irani didn't need to mention Eve's too-wordy interview. Gene brought the issue up as soon as they were sitting across at a conference room table.

"I know Eve feels bad about mentioning OWLM. I told her not to worry, but why don't you do the same? It'll mean more coming from you."

"I already did. The episode's a wonderful learning experience, and Eve's a quick study. She'll be fine."

Both women leaned back. Irani segued to the main topic.

"And our campaign will be even better when I add whatever you want from what I learned at the World forums. It's just the two of us, so I'll sit while projecting my overheads."

Gene nodded; Irani talked immediately after displaying the first slide.

WEF and WFF Meetings
Contingent Considerations for Genesee Huston's Campaign

Presentation and accompanying report prepared by Irani Ramani, who attended meetings and "networked" among exhibitors and attendees. This material is being presented first to Congresswoman Huston because she has hired Ms. Ramani via ACS Consulting Services.

"This overhead is standard boilerplate so you can use the presentation wherever and whenever you wish, but I recommend you limit the report's distribution. We saw what can happen if we give out too much information."

Irani popped the next slide, pausing for Gene to read.

America is still an Exceptional Nation! World needs U.S. more than Vice Versa.

U.S. has:
- Lots of Arable Land for feeding "Our Friends"
- Inland Waterways and Two Coasts for Low Transportation Costs
- Demographics "growing" our Way
- Self-Reliant Consumer Economy for generating Our Own Demand
- World-Best Navy for projecting Power
- World-Best Capital and Financial Markets for facilitating Corporate Transactions

"None of the speakers talked specifically about America's greatness. I'm simply summarizing what you and I already know plus what some of my networking conversations confirmed. As long as Washington doesn't self-destruct, America has what no other nation does – all the assets and a population that can control its own destiny. We can delve into more detail whenever you want, but let's move on to some of the hottest topics."

Irani rolled to the next slide without stopping.

Current Climate of World Economy

- China continues pushing a "Belt and Road" Initiative to bring more Nations into its Sphere of Influence (Nations push back because China often heavy-handed)
- Isilabad/Middle East continues resurrecting Neom Project to replace "Dying Economy" with New Cities and Industries (Tourism, Entertainment, Regional Financial Center)
- Africa and Isilabad modernizing Economies and Infrastructure to drive Growth
- China leading "Green Energy/Technology" Development

"Two of our chronic adversaries, China and Isilabad, continue disrupting the world economy, but there's a third player that we need to bring into our camp. Africa has a lot to offer us and vice versa. Please keep that in mind. And as you'll see on my next slide, economic growth requires money."

Current Climate of World Finance

- Africa and Isilabad/Middle East need Money to finance traditional infrastructure plus new Digital/Smart Cities.
- China "happy" to be "World Banker" (Loans Internet Banking Crypto-Currency)
- Russia angling to be Number One: Currency Exchange Weapons Supplier

"The developed world sees potential profit in Africa and the Middle East and are willing to put money in, but so is China. And we better beware of Russia. They and China could collude to manipulate exchange rates. But we aren't the only ones who know this. So do other nations, so it's probably safe to say that the whole world is watching what they're up to. And that takes us to my next slide."

Current Climate of World Socio-Political Order

- Demographics (No Growth Too Old) lowers Europe's and Russia's "Pecking Order Positions" (Nations don't like Russia)
- China still angling to replace America's Top Spot (via Technology and "Digitocracy") but has "bad" Demographics (Slow Growth Too Many Seniors)
- Isilabad/Middle East moving from Theocracy towards Sectarianism
- Canada and Mexico aligning with America
- Australia moving towards ChinaJapan balanced between China and America
- South America not in the game (Economic and Political Chaos)
- Africa and India moving up (great Demographics and Political Institutions)

"It paints a broad-brush picture of where countries are heading. And of course, there are problems just about everywhere... some bigger than others. But Africa and India could be future growth engines and possible world leaders longer term if we can find win-win alliances. And to do that, let's see what America's considering."

Irani paused long enough for Gene study the next slide.

America's Current Political Climate

- Transitioning to "Post-Enlightenment" Governance and Economics
- Adjusting Domestic versus International Agendas
- Debating Hi-Tech's Pros and Cons

- Balancing "Shelter-in-Place/Lockdown" Mandate versus Economic/Social Needs
- Adjusting Tradeoff between Dignity/Diversity versus Democracy/Nationalism
- Recognizing "Perfect Leadership" is Impossible for Shifting to Realpolitiks from Liberalism and Ideology

"As a member of Congress, you're immersed in these issues every day. There are many others, but I picked out the ones dominating the spotlight. And my next and final slide outlines what should be your signature issues driving our campaign. Here they are."

Contingent Considerations for Congresswoman Huston

Internationally:
- Strategically Reposition America's Role on World Stage
- Share some of America's Economic/Technological Advantages with Allies
- Strengthen Digital Alliances to restrain the Tide of Authoritarianism
- Develop "win-win" Africa and India Relationships
- Lead "Realistic" Climate Change Initiative

Domestically:
- Reach for "Statesman-Like" Compromise
- Empower Younger Generation (Online Courses/Degrees/ Certifications)
- Protect Jobs (Work-From-Home) PrivacyData
- Champion Ethics and Character for clarifying "Duties" of the Citizenry
- Balance "Sharing/Caring" against Resource Constraints
- Push back against "Conspiracy Hucksterism"
- Push for Campaign Reform (Financing Duration Online Voting)

Irani waited for the Congresswoman to speak.

Leaning forward, she said, "You continue to over-deliver. The public's clamoring for campaign reform, which I can push for now and implement during my first term. And there must be a way to combine software development that will serve remote working, online learning, and Internet voting. Adding all this to what we've already got, the platform you and Eve and Sabrina are building should get me into the Oval Office."

"That's the goal, so why don't you give this presentation to Brian? The sooner your Veep knows the platform plan, the better he'll look while standing on it."

"Agreed. We're lucky he's all in for us. Even the media says he's the practically perfect choice for Veep. Now, let me buy you lunch. You've earned it…"

On the drive home, Electra congratulated the morning performance.

"Irani and I are certainly a dynamic duo, just like Mr. Outside and Mr. Inside, who ran roughshod over the competition during West Point football's WWII glory days. And we can go one better… we can network together our portfolio of unwitting players. Next to connect, Austin.

Austin would be a brief stop en route to Denver. Irani would have Monet and Alonzo meet her in American Airlines' Ambassador's Club for lunch on Wednesday, March 5th before continuing later that afternoon. Electra had her two agendas so well prepared that she decided to sit back and relax on the first flight by letting her lightning brain coast.

Monet and Alonzo greeted her at the gate. He toted her carry-ons and Monet led the way through surprisingly crowded walkways while Irani found small-talk that put everyone at ease.

"How nice that people are traveling sooner after a virus scare than last time. It shows that the CDC's winning back the public's trust. Europeans are traveling more too. What did you notice on your trip to Zimbabwe?"

"My people are frightened. Our medical system isn't as good and we might be closer to the source of the virus. But I came back with no illness, and Darla seems immune to germs."

"Good, and maybe there is something you and I can do to lessen the risk from political issues."

Irani had made reservations at the Ambassador Club restaurant, which was a perk for being a member. After ordering, Irani asked Monet to explain how Darla had reacted to her presentation. Her smile telegraphed the answer.

"She liked it so well she wants me to work at our Washington embassy, reporting directly to her. I plan to start in July soon after I graduate. And she will pay for any graduate work at any university I choose. I have already applied to George Washington's Elliott School of International Affairs."

"Excellent choice, and you can stay with Eve if you wish."

"Thank you for your generosity. May I stay until I find a suitable apartment? I feel I have matured beyond dormitories and also want to maintain a professional distance from her."

"Very smart, and once you settle in, I can introduce you to Congresswoman Genesee Huston and Senator Brian Strauss. As I'm sure you know, she'll be the Re-Gen Party candidate for President and Strauss her running mate. Eve's working for her and I'm helping develop her platform. And whether she wins or loses, she'll open doors. If you approve, I'll tell Eve and she can help get you settled in."

"You are helping me write the first page of the next chapter of my life. I owe you so much."

"And I owe you for all you've done for my Austin businesses and Alonzo. Knowing how thorough you are, I imagine he knows all about your plans. What does he have to say?"

The ladies' gazes turned to him. Alonzo straightened his shoulders and leaned in.

"I'm ready to take on more responsibility. Monet and Kim have trained me well and I'll put my soccer career on hold so I can concentrate on school and work. And hey, I can stay with Eve when I visit."

Irani listened as they revealed more about their plans while lunch and dessert came and went. Electra digested all she heard.

Monet is so good. I'm glad she's coming to DC. I'll do all I can to help her because that'll help Eve too. And who knows what the future holds for Alonzo? That's part of Youth's excitement. It's a big unknown you can't see, but for the young it's an adventure, full of enchanting possibility.

The threesome talked in the lounge until it was time for Irani's next flight, and then they hiked to check-in, where Irani said goodbye.

"I'm so happy for both of you. You've got such solid plans for the next year, and you can build on that. Remember to keep in touch with Eve."

Monet surprised Irani by giving her a quick hug. Irani's carry-ons impeded her response but not her words.

"My wish for daughter number two is coming true. Now please stay safe and take care of each other…"

Rick spoke first when he and Parson greeted Irani at the gate, using her newest nickname.

"Welcome to Mile High, DD. PH and I are all set to show you around. By the time you leave, you'll know why Big D is a great place to be."

"Thanks for picking me up. Do you give all your partners personal treatment like this?"

PH said, "Yep, and for you RT has something special. You better tell her."

"We thought you might like a home-cooked meal, so we'll have dinner at my home. Aubrie's gonna make turkey tacos."

PH grabbed DD's carry-ons after saying, "Aubrie's his wife, not a robo-chef. You'll like her even better than me. And if you approve, you can stay in their guest room."

"I'd like that. And I promise not to pack any towels when I leave…"

Irani learned more about her new partners while RT drove.

RT sounds like he's got his life moving in high gear. Successful businesses, married a couple of years, has one son, recently remodeled the house Aubrie wanted them to buy, and recently built with his dad and help from PH a cabin in the mountains.

PH is moving too. He's a bachelor who's even more of a risk-taker than his partner, but he centers on what's real and what people want. We're going to be win-win-win...

Aubrie – an attractive, fit, and brown-haired early thirty-something – greeted them in the front hallway before taking Irani to the dining room while the fellows stowed coats and bags.

Table talk about the lighter aspects of lifestyles relaxed everyone further, and after slices of mile high chocolate pie, RT described tomorrow's agenda.

"So, we'll go to the office first thing and sign all the documents that Kelsey, our admin assistant, has put together. And then we'll show you a couple of locations where we're using robo-builders for new-home construction. After that, we'll drive around town and end up at a monthly meeting hosted by one of the groups in PH's network. Why don't you tell her about this one?"

Parson put one hand and a bent-arm elbow on the table.

"I like to know what's going on, and not by listening to just the news or what the government's telling us. Tomorrow you'll meet some people who might be considered far out, but I like to hear what they say. You might too."

Electra did; Irani nodded as she gave a favorite reply. "Perhaps..."

Though talk showed no signs of slowing, Aubrie said, "Irani must be tired from today's travel. Let's all get a good night's sleep and continue tomorrow."

Everyone followed her suggestion.

The next day went according to plan, and the sparkling weather made driving about to see robo-workers and Denver-area sights a snap. Irani asked questions while Electra assessed all she saw.

Retro-fitting used robots with updated software will be cost-effective in the niches Rick and Parson have picked. And I can connect them to my software company, and maybe to Odell's tutoring programs. Definitely win-win-win...

And though they didn't tour on foot, RT drove past enough of Denver's attractions to make a lasting impression.

What a great mix of cosmopolitan and scenic display. The city's street malls, museums, and architecture point forward, yet the Botanic Gardens and Red Rocks Park plus Amphitheater show a respect for the environment. No wonder Denver's population grows and grows.

Irani picked up the tab for dinner at Illegal Pete's Front Range Restaurant, a place whose name PH thought would be fitting for tonight's meeting. The setting and service exceeded Irani's expectations. All that remained was to compare its name to the rest of the evening.

RT drove them to a rambling ranch house on the outskirts of Lone Tree, a smallish town about twenty-five miles southeast of Dallas and considered one of the best places to live. They arrived just in time for Rick to make an attendance donation for the trio before tonight's designated speaker got up to talk. Though big and rugged-looking, Electra wouldn't pre-judge his words.

Standing in front of an audience numbering about forty, his words boomed out like his looks predicted.

"I'm proud ta call myself an extremist, and there're plenty like you and me. I got no problem if you're way-out on the right or left, man or woman, black, white, yellow or brown. How d'you think America got started? By extremists like us who later got called patriots when history sorted out the facts. And that's why we're here tonight, ta have a talk about what's on our minds and be open ta the other side.

"It's the damn Govment I got problems with. I don't trust'em. They and their insider fat-cat cronies are always cheaten and try'en to control us against our will, against what's right. They been try'en ever since people put'em in power way back when, but we're fighten back. And here's a good example; about two hundred years ago people finally ripped the blinders off their eyes and minds.

"It took a Boston newspaper a bunch a years to blow the whistle on priests abusing kids. The Catholic Church and Boston politicians accused the paper of maken up a conspiracy, but the truth finally came out and priests got locked up. It's people like us who protect our country by caring enough to take a stand.

"And when it comes to the weather and climate change, I'll tell ya who the extremists are. It's the Govment and their expert number fiddlers who play a scary tune and frighten lots of people. I've listened ta both sides and know which side has the facts straight.

"Well, enough about that, let's look at tonight. Last time we met, I got picked to lead off, so I get ta pick the first topic. Here it is…"

The more Irani heard while standing in the back, the more Electra judged.

These folks know what's going on and express their concerns in concrete terms, not political drivel. They aren't extreme, they're engaged in current events.

An hour later, a woman speaker wrapped up.

"We've got enough time for our regular contest. The person who can spin the best conspiracy story that includes themselves gets free drinks and snacks next time."

RT's trio listened for a while before he whispered, "People must have had a tough week. Only two have spun tales."

PH nudged Irani before saying, "You're good with words. Why don't you try your luck?"

Electra warned Irani.

Careful what you say. We better not make the mistake we made in Switzerland… but I think we've got a safer audience tonight… go ahead.

"Ok, but you introduce me."

PH waved to the woman before saying, "We've got a visitor tonight who likes what she's heard, and we might like what she has to say."

"C'mon up here, young lady, and tell us your tale."

The audience parted as Irani came forward. The woman shook her hand, made introductions, and then stepped aside for Irani to command center stage.

"I was struck at birth by a lightning bolt that killed my mother and made me different. I'm not Superwoman but it gave me skills I had to keep hidden from the Government because they treat special people badly. So I grew up in the shadows and developed vaccines that killed the T-Plague, but terrorists who were spraying T-Plague on crowds came after me. So I got rid of them and then became a covert agent for a group that wanted to protect America from its misguided Government.

"But the Government chased me down, forcing me to go deeper undercover and surface on the inside where I helped the Brits keep America from plunging into the abyss. Then I got bored, so I became a star athlete in the Co-NFL that led to a Hollywood career that got me into politics where I became a covert agent able to work both sides.

"That worked until bad guys tracked me down and put me in suspended animation for twenty years. But I broke out and am now back in action. But I can't tell you what I'm doing because if I did, I'd have to kill you, and I like you too much for that. And that's my story."

Irani was about to walk back to RT and PH, but the woman grabbed her arm before saying, "That's the best conspiracy story I've ever heard, either here or on the news. What does the audience think?"

Whistles and cheers announced the winner. Irani bowed, then said,

"And I donate my prize to the guys who brought me. Unlike my yarn, they're straight-shooters like all of you…"

As the trio celebrated the outcome on the drive home, Electra thought about tonight and tomorrow.

How nice that my facts are stranger than fiction. And how nice I'll have quiet time on my flight back so I can think about all I've observed. But where will all this lead?… we'll have to see how they impact whatever climates come into play…

Chapter 19
June 2160

"Problems Times Three"

Electra had just settled in front of her office workstation after returning from a first week of June mid-Monday morning Environmental Scanning Committee meeting. While waiting for her computer to power up, she explained to herself why her mood matched the glorious spring weather.

All professional and personal activities have been rolling my way so far this spring. The Committee gave me another month to summarize how some origins of life theories connect to volcanoes, and I'm keeping ahead of what the Presidential campaign needs to do. None of my clones or other young helpers have run into problems, and all the contingent climates seem pandemic-free. Hooray... I'll grab a Coke and a handful of Oreos and get to work on what I've lined up for today.

She found her treats where she kept them in the open area, but when she ambled back, a surprise greeted her. A GUI had opened and Indira's unsmiling avatar awaited. Indira spoke as soon as Electra sat to listen and take notes.

"We have several interrelated problems that have just escalated. Kameyo is returning to Japan."

Electra's stomach knotted and her face looked like that of a person about to be inundated by a tidal wave.

"But why? You've been telling me that Pequot projects are on schedule."

"They are, but Kameyo is unable to handle the additional workload caused by necessary modifications to the X-Virus recovery vaccine and upcoming project preparations. You haven't assisted much when needed, and none of your clones can fill the breach, even partially. All but Nari have abandoned biology and biotech studies."

Indira waited for Electra to assimilate the news. It took longer than usual for her usually snappy replies. She shook her head before stuttering, "Suh-so what are we supposed to do?"

"First, change the 'we' to 'you'. For the time being, you must return to your quantitative strengths instead of squandering your efforts in the touchy-feely socio-political pseudo-artistic milieu that relies on words rather than numbers. Remember Wittgenstein's quote – 'The limits of my language are the limits of my world.' The language of mathematics requires a higher level of intelligence than that of reading and writing. You've become academically soft, but I will assist so pay attention to my introductory presentation."

"You're being presumptuous. People in the arts and soft sciences are just as smart as the tech and math types. It's merely a –" Indira cut her off.

"You're in no position to comment. I commend your intelligence and enthusiasm for learning new material, but even your brilliance will be challenged when exploring the origins of life, which will be your starting point. I have prepared a summary that outlines what must be mastered and extended, and you will soon see that biology is no longer a weak-sister science. It now demands a level of mathematical sophistication that challenges the best of 'mere mortals,' who compared to your lightning-bolt brilliance are but candles in the wind. I trust you enjoyed my wordplay, but please no more comments. I prefer for you settle down, sit still, and let me explain first. And read the slides for their overarching content, not specifics."

Electra obeyed; Indira proceeded, showing the first slide and giving time for her student to study before talking.

Slide 1
In the Beginning...

Life on Earth is a "Deterministic" not "Random" event caused by Abiogenesis: The Interaction of Inert Matter from which Living Organisms emerge and then Evolve via contingent, ever-cycling Earth/Climate Interactions. Living Organisms have an ordered, self-sustaining Metabolism supporting Growth, Reproduction, Information Storage/Processing, and Mutation.

- Geosphere (Land, Sea, Air): Lithosphere Hydrosphere Atmosphere
- Biosphere: Region of Earth that encompasses all living organisms: Plants, Animals and Bacteria.
- Life created in a Process governed by: Energy and Entropy acting on Matter via Universal Laws of Physics.
- Biology becomes Complex Emergent Process needing Multi-Disciplines (Mathematics, Physics, Chemistry/Biochemistry, Microbiology, Neuroscience) and Quantum Computing to Deconstruct.
- LIFE (POSSIBLY CARBON-BASED) SHOULD BE FOUND ELSEWHERE IN THE UNIVERSE

"Think of organic life as a series of deterministic phenomena that emerged 4.3 billion years ago. Bacterial fossils confirm this. And the universal processes governing it suggest there should be life somewhere else in the Universe, though possibly different than on Earth.

"My next slide summarizes the major problems facing Darwin's Theory."

Indira paused again before continuing.

Slide 2
Darwin's "Theory of Evolution" Incomplete!

- Recognized the role of Genes and Evolution but didn't understand: BiochemistryMicrobiologyNeuroscience Abiogenesis
- "Old-School" Researchers couldn't explain: Punctuated Equilibrium (No Fossils linking Evolution of Radically Different Species)Specialized Organ/Structural Evolution (Eyes Wings etc.) Speed of Emergence (Combinatorial Math applied to Randomness) that predicted "Life Takes too Long" to form
- They were looking in Wrong Direction: From DNA to Metabolism to Life INSTEAD OF Metabolism to DNA to Life.
- They weren't smart enough to find Deterministic Processes that replace Random Events from which Life emerges.

"Darwin's intuition was much better than others who were developing competing theories. But he was looking the wrong way, from a bewildering diversity to causality rather than a deterministic abiogenesis from which carbon-based organic life emerges. And ever since Darwin, researchers who were able to master the quantitative disciplines have marched ahead. My next slide explains how. It's rather lengthy, so I'll pause for you to digest enough of it."
Electra didn't stir an eyelash while reading.

Slide 3
More-Clever Scientists have Discovered:

- How Combinatorial and Parallel Chemistry can accelerate search for Viable Metabolic Pathways leading to Self-Replicating Emergent Macromolecules leading to Diversity.

- How Energy and Entropy drive Biochemical Cycles (Krebs Cycle, ADP-ATP Cycle) that produce the Proto-Building Blocks of Life.

- How Processes that convert Proto-Blocks into Biochemicals (Amino Acids, Lipids, Fats, etc.) build Single-Cell Bacteria containing self-sustaining Metabolism. Note: Metabolism is the Sum of all contingent, life-sustaining reactions that use Substrate-specific Enzymes. Human life is Carbon-based. Other life-supporting Substrates (Silicon etc.) are possible if starting conditions suitable.

- How Processes that turn Bacteria into Mitochondria (Cellular Powerplants) use either Reductive or Oxidative Metabolism.

- How Processes lead from Viruses and Bacteria to Archaea to Eukaryotes to multi-cellular Plants and Animals, and then to better-known processes of DNA-encapsulated Genes and Mutation leading to "Selfish-Cooperative" Replication Cycles encapsulated in Diverse Species subject to Evolution.

- How novel definitions of Entropy link Thermodynamic, Statistical, and Information Theory/DNA conceptions that explain increasing order in Complex Organisms.

- How the Cell (think Euglena and Paramecium) is Biology's "Black Hole" Analogy. But Biologists can observe and experiment. High-energy-Physicists can't do either to their "Black Hole."

Then she took a deep breath that signaled Indira to move on. "Here is my final slide, and it's the payoff for all your hard work. Just skim it and let me provide exegesis. I know you like that word."

Slide 4
Where is All This Leading Us?

- We can learn more by studying "White Smoke and Black Smoke" Vents on Ocean Floor plus Surface-Abiotic/ Inorganic Volcanic Hot Springs and Pools.

- We can find Biochemical and Medical Breakthroughs.

- You must use your Professor Plannert and Congresswoman Huston contacts as "cover" for what we will be doing.

- Others collect the Data. I analyze to model Processes. We share only pieces. You facilitate.

- We can throw the "unwitting" a couple of bones: Upgrade their Seismic, Tsunami, Volcano, and Weather Forecasting AI-Empowered Apps Improve their Vaccines

- Have Congresswoman urge Expansion of NOAA (National Oceanic and Atmospheric Administration to NSOAA (National Subsurface and Oceanic and Atmospheric Administration)

- I continue studying Biosphere and Geosphere Climates/ Cycles; You do likewise on Economic and Sociopolitical fronts.

- Have Congresswoman "incentivize" Navy and DOD to develop advanced submersible AUV (Autonomous Underwater Vehicle) software control and Android development.

- We know: "Mere Mortals" face the same Asymptotic Limits (Inability to deal with Complexity and Infinity) that have blocked progress in Quantum Physics and Cosmology. But they should advance further in Biology because Biology's "Black Hole" (cells) is tangible.

- We remain in the "Shadows" and Everyone Wins.

"There are opportunities for us, especially if I do what I do best, and you follow suit. I will analyze and you will facilitate. And your contacts will do what we want while we remain in the shadows. Now ask me any questions you may have."

Electra rolled her head and shoulders to loosen the tension from staring too long and thinking too hard. Several minutes elapsed before she said,

"You can be a tough tutor. I've studied enough about neuroscience to realize that the complexity of all the biochemical reactions at even the simplest level might be inaccessible to me, even if I go obsessive-compulsive. And I no longer want to go there."

Indira's words and expression softened.

"And I don't want you to either. That is why I will give you most of the analytic results for you to parcel out as appropriate to those you have enlisted."

"I'm sure you're right, but I need a break to work off this information overload."

"Please do so and reward yourself with a Coke and some Oreos before, during, and afterwards. And I'll keep busy while you let your lightning brain freewheel. Do we have a deal?"

"Yes, and thank you for your exegesis as well as word choice. It adds to your pleasant voice."

Indira smiled before her GUI vanished; Electra didn't do either but remained sitting stone-faced and trying to absorb another Indira info-overload. Sometime later, after nibbling on Oreos and sipping a Coke, she began to understand.

Indira's right. I've slacked off on applying math, and just like athletic training, it can be a harsh mistress if I don't keep fit. So, I'll use Indira's challenge to regain my math footing and learn more about biology. And Indira's right about rewarding myself. I used to wait until finishing, but when I did that I got impatient. Sort of like starving myself during the day before sitting down to Thanksgiving dinner. It's better to avoid frustration caused that way. I'm feeling a bit better and know what to do first... adjust my to-do list.

Electra kept fully engaged for the rest of the day, getting the latest problems under control. She felt calmer when going home, but Eve, dashing to the front door, jolted her the minute she stepped inside.

We've got a problem. Nari's coming unglued and asked me to bring you to Boston at the end of finals week. Can we go next Saturday? I'll be finished too."

"OK, and we'll go in your Vette. Set up the details. We'll talk about Nari's problems while traveling, but give me a summary now."

"She's got two... she's upset about Nila's moving to India, and she's confused about academic majors and career choices. I didn't push the idea, but maybe she wants to listen to you."

"Perhaps. I'll help in whatever way I can. And speaking of help, do you need any in the kitchen?"

"No, but maybe next week we can talk about some campaign issues."

"Jot'em down for follow-up after your finals and our trip to Boston…"

Electra found the right balance between work and time-out to restrain her obsessive-compulsive tendencies, and by Saturday morning had multi-tasked enough on current projects and new problems to prepare for dealing with Nari. Irani let Eve do most of the talking, and by the time they walked into the apartment, Electra had given Irani the right words.

Nari, the only one there, greeted the pair but seemed uncertain, so Irani talked after everyone exchanged greetings.

"I'll bet Nila's visiting Sanjay. Eve, why don't you go chat with them and call Nari when the three of you are ready for dinner?"

"Good idea. Have at it."

Eve hustled away; Nari found something to say.

"Would you like a Coke and something to eat? We can sit in the kitchen and talk."

"I would, thanks. Please lead the way."

Irani told about the drive and recapped what she and Eve were doing in DC while Nari served grilled cheese sandwiches. Then she segued to Nari after polishing off some Oreos.

"Let's see, we met three years ago, and during that period I have become fond of you and your siblings. And I've known about all of you longer than that because of your Granny Su. You and your siblings are talented, and some have needed my assistance more than others. I imagine that's why each of you likes me differently.

"You've been the most self-reliant so you don't know me very well, but perhaps that will change if there's something I can do to help, so please tell me if there is."

Nari took a deep breath before crossing her legs.

"I'm tensed up and can't sleep. And my stomach churns when I think about what's happening. I need to talk to someone new.

Neither Nila nor my advisor are much help. Eve's a little better, and that's why you're here."

Nari stopped talking and stared at her lap, so Irani started.

"Eve said you're upset about Nila's leaving, and that's to be expected. You and your twin have been together since birth, and you've helped one another. She's found a career path and a special person that she'll take on her journey."

"But maybe it's too soon, and maybe Sanjay's not the right guy."

"They've had three years to grow together or apart, and so far their paths are merging. It might not be that way forever because even a loving relationship requires constant care. But from what I see and hear, moving to India will serve them well."

"Well, before you go back to DC, will you talk to them?"

"I will if they ask."

"Good, I'll make sure they do."

Nari stretched her legs before leaning forward; Irani moved on.

"Eve also said you're rethinking what you want to study. What are you considering?"

"Dropping the biology minor. Doing all that science that I really don't like is such a frustrating waste of time. That'll leave me with dual psych and soc majors and an archeology minor, but then what'll I do when I graduate next year?"

Irani's smile lit up.

"I know what that problem's like, and it's a wonderful one to have. You have the opportunity to chart your future, and at your age there are no bad choices. You can always choose another if what you're working on doesn't work out."

"But could you give me an idea?"

"I know that you're good with words and numbers, so why not pick a discipline that uses both. Think about studying social forecasting in grad school and applying it to a career in soc or psych market research, analysis, or forecasting. Why don't you talk to Eve about Cliodynamics?"

"She's mentioned it... maybe I will. And maybe I made a mistake by returning to Harvard instead of staying in DC. What do you think?"

Irani paused for Electra.

I know what's on her mind and what she'd like to hear. Here it is.

"You made the right choice then, and now you can adjust it. You can come back to DC and work for me, and you can do your Harvard studies online or transfer to GWU. The choice is yours. And there's plenty of room in the house. Kameyo is moving back to Japan."

Nary started to smile but couldn't find the right words, but Irani did.

"I think you need to discuss all we've talked about with three other people. Call Eve and tell her you're coming over. And then the four of you can pick me up when you're ready for dinner."

"OK, I'll take it from here…"

The restaurant had few parties that night because the end of finals week always triggers a student exodus. Sanjay and Nila sat at the ends of the table with Nari and Eve on one side and Irani on the other. Everyone looked happy and relaxed; Sanjay's always mellifluous voice started the discussion.

"Finals are over, and Nila and I have plenty of time to pack before flying to Mumbai after I graduate. All of us have nice places to go and good things to do…"

Irani listened to the chatter before saying, "Yes, everyone at the table is in a good place, but what about your erstwhile roommate, Yang."

Everyone glanced at Nari.

"He and I will work that out, and besides, he won't graduate for a couple of years. Who knows what the climate will be like then?"

The conversation kept flowing; Electra kept talking to herself.

Nila's maturity and confidence has grown since I last saw her. And she and Sanjay look so relaxed whenever together.

Irani waited for a break between main courses and desserts before directing a question at Nila.

"I'm sure you and Sanjay have thought this through, but what do you expect living in Mumbai to be like, and what will you do?"

"Sanjay and I are gonna work at his father's software company, and I'll transfer to a Mumbai university if I find one I like. If not, I'll get my MIT degree via distance learning. I only have a year to go."

Nila pointed to Sanjay, who then began answering the first part.

"And we will live in my Baba's house until he helps me buy our own. Nila will be safe there, it's inside a walled community on the fringes of Malabar Hills, one of the best locations in Mumbai. And she will find that my family is thoroughly modern, combining the best of India's past and present."

Sanjay held back more of his words because Nila spoke hers.

"I'm not as naïve as I used to be. I've surfed for videos that confirm what Sanjay's already told me. Mumbai's got a tropical climate and the biggest Indian-city population, but half the fifteen million people live in slums that are among the densest anywhere. But it's in the top three for IT and I'll probably transfer to Indian Institute of Technology. Sanjay, tell them more."

"Hinduism is the dominant religion, Islam a distant second at twenty percent, and Christianity about five. The others have less than a percent each. And we consider ourselves spiritual rather than religious. We seek harmony between science and faith.

"I grew up there and can teach her how to let go of some control and let expectations flow. She will enjoy the diverse cultures, energetic young people, and Bollywood plus its nightlife. Our karma will be written by our thoughts and deeds as we work and live together."

Sanjay's philosophical thoughts ended what he or Nila wanted to say. No one spoke until Irani said, "I think you can live long and prosper together, but even Sanjay will need to get vaccinated for protection against bacteria and viruses that are local to Mumbai's biome."

Sanjay nodded before saying, "That is another climate we shall prepare ourselves for. And I trust everyone do the same."

Eve did most of the talking on the drive home, explaining how she and Nari would get along better now. And then she turned the spotlight on herself.

"Sometime I'll tell you what I plan to study after graduation, but right now let me go over some of the campaign issues I'm investigating. The three adversary parties have come up with a unified attack against us, and our Congresswoman has told me to help dig into the details and write up what I find out. Maybe they're responsible for the growing conspiracy theory that OWLM is providing a cover for the Re-Gen Party to marginalize men. Do you know anything about this?"

"I'll ask Gene and Brian at my next one-on-one. But please let me know what luck you're having. And by now, I expect you know how to handle luck."

"You've taught me. It's not whether I have good luck or bad. It's what I do with it that matters so don't worry, I'll make the most of the opportunity. And speaking of luck, aren't we lucky to have Brian on the ticket? He's almost too good to be true. Whatcha think?"

"I know you'll come out on top, and I hope our candidates do too…"

Irani's action-packed pace neither slowed nor accelerated in the following weeks. She let Nari and Eve work out logistics and assignments. Nari would assist Eve on campaign issues while working fulltime for Irani on other projects. Irani hadn't mentioned that Monet would be moving to Washington soon. She would wait until her DC-based daughters had adjusted to living and working together.

Better for them to settle in before Monet unsettles the arrangements. And I'll wait for her to call me. She's the most-together and mature of all three. And the last time we spoke, she said she'd be ready to move soon after July 4th. That's only a week away. And when she calls, I'll let her and Eve work out a plan for who stays where. All I have to do is watch it unfold.

Irani actually preferred living in her office. She could roll out of bed, into and through a morning workout, and then into her work schedule with no wasted time or motion. She had just finished a mid-morning snack on the last day of June when her phone rang. Recognizing Monet's caller I.D., she added more cheer than usual to her professional greeting.

"Hello, daughter number two. How may I help you today?"

Alarming words shot back.

"I have a big problem and need your help. Alonzo's contracted the X-Virus…"

Chapter 20
July 2160

"A Fuller House"

Always resourceful, Electra had found a way to expand the number of people who could shoulder Monet's problem. Soon after the fateful call, Eve departed for Austin to help her pack up and move herself and Alonzo back to DC. Eve would be her brother's primary caregiver while Monet would settle into an apartment and start working at the Zimbabwe embassy. Eve and Nari rearranged the house to accommodate Alonzo, and though it would be fuller than before, Irani took up residence fulltime at the office and visited only when necessary. Life had settled to a less frenetic pace for the younger generation by mid-July.

Meanwhile, Electra had begun implementing one plan to handle Eve's campaign issues and another that would extend Indira-Electra projects. And of course, the plans were interrelated. Irani explained all that her Presidential and Vice-Presidential candidates needed to know during a late July morning meeting in the Congresswoman's office. All but Brian showed the strain of the campaign and even he looked happy to let Irani lead the discussion.

"I am assuming Eve's assignments until we resolve a medical issue. We just moved her brother to DC so she can be his caregiver while he recovers from the X-Virus. She'll be back to work for you as soon as he's better, and Nari Bose will assist her."

Gene glanced at Brian, whose thumbs up gesture made it easier for her to smile before she started talking.

"You move fast, and that's good. Our opponents are going more and more negative and we need to turn it to our favor. I hope you can come up with a way to do that soon."

"I already have. Have our public relations person schedule a primetime broadcast for you to give later next week the speech I'm writing. And I'll set up a meeting to introduce Brian to Professor Plannert. I've mentioned him before so you should know who he is. I consult for a committee he heads up, and he can help us while we help him."

Brian looked at Gene, who nodded for him to talk.

"I'd like that, especially if I can be more than window dressing. I guess all we need is for you to give us enough background on what you've got planned."

"And that's precisely what I'm going to do…"

Irani spun a story that intrigued her candidates. Electra complimented herself and her partner on the drive back to the office.

The dynamic duo scores again. Our opponents will be looking through the earholes of their helmets after Gene's speech rolls over them. And I'll arrange for a Professor Plannert/Veep meeting ASAP. The games are getting better and better… and while on the subject of getting better, I think I'll call Eve for a report on Alonzo.

Irani's call found a receptive audience. Eve had just wheeled Alonzo into the kitchen where Monet was putting lunch on the table. Eve disconnected and then spoke to her partners.

"Miss Irani is stopping by to say hi. Come on, Alonzo, sit up and cheer up. She'll make you feel better."

Alonzo's slouching in the wheelchair added to his sourpuss face.

"I don't want her to see my like this. I'm supposed to be the strong one, able to take care of others, but I can't get out of bed if you or Monet weren't around."

The cadence of Eve's words matched her always upbeat tempo.

"You're not that much of a load anymore. The X-Virus has removed excess fat. Go ahead, start eating. Miss Irani can have some cookies or brownies when she gets here."

Alonzo was about to grumble a reply but Monet spoke before he could.

"You told me your stomach pains are less. If so, that should make it easier for you to keep food down. Please do us a favor and try."

Monet and Eve tried their best to draw Alonzo into their conversation, but he said little and didn't look at Irani when she started talking after stepping into the kitchen.

"Hello, my three young up-and-coming stars. I see you're having some of my favorite treats. May I sit and join you?"

Monet spoke first, using Eve's usual greeting.

"Hello, Miss Irani. Please do."

She sat directly across from Alonzo, which gave him no excuse for not facing her, but she chit-chatted before turning the spotlight on him.

"Eve tells me you're doing better and better on the wheelchair exercises. I bet the snappy exercise clothes you're wearing are a reward from Monet."

Alonzo finally said something.

"I guess so. But she said she'd cut my throat if I didn't do a better job shaving."

"I said no such thing. I said I'd be very careful shaving you if you needed help with the razor."

No one spoke until Eve did when she started clearing the table.

"I want to show Monet some of the stuff I've been working on. Why don't you two talk more while we do that?"

Monet stood and then said, "Good idea. I'll help clean up." Five minutes later, Irani had Alonzo all to herself.

"I know how you feel. It's tough facing others when for the first time in your life you're suddenly thrust into a position of weakness, but your friends don't see it that way. They want to help you get back on your feet. Why not be patient and pleasant while they make it happen?"

Alonzo finally started coming out of his self-imposed shell.

"That's easy for you to say, you're feeling good. But my stomach and scrotum still ache."

"What about your other symptoms?"

"Fever's gone and headaches are less of a problem, but I swear I'm gonna kill myself if I can't get my strength back."

"It's unfortunate the X-Virus got you when you were playing soccer, but what makes you think you're the only athlete that's ever suffered a sports-related calamity? Let's do this… I'll sit next to you and we can surf the net for other examples."

Alonzo followed what Irani found, and she gave him a summary fifteen minutes later.

"You're far from being alone. Sports careers throughout the years have been impacted. The Maurice Stokes story is particularly compelling. The basketball star broke his neck during a fall in the last game of the season. He never walked again, but a teammate became his caregiver, helping him learn to talk and write again. Stokes became a motivational speaker as well as painter, and his teammate took care of him until Stokes died. You've got two caregivers, so do your best, and as you get better you'll figure out what you should do. But killing yourself is not an option."

Irani's words were helping. Alonzo sat straighter and sounded more hopeful.

"OK I promise, and I'll use the word 'when,' not 'if,' when talking about recovering. And when I'm back on my feet, I'll put my kid stuff away and work to help those that I can. I'll show all of you I can be a responsible adult."

"We all know you can, so use your setback as an opportunity to move ahead. Eve did it, so follow her lead."

"Hey, I'm a lot smarter now than a year ago. I will, and I'll follow Monet's commands also."

Eve and Monet reappeared before Alonzo could say more, but when Eve asked how they were doing, he said, "Miss Irani's words are making me feel better."

Irani said, "Your timing's perfect. You three can carry on while I get back to work…"

As she drove back to her office, Electra started thinking about how to get Alonzo back in action.

I'll let my lightning brain come up with a plan. And while it's doing that, I'll spin the Congresswoman's speech.

Electra rapped it out in record time by early evening. Pleased with the final copy, she scratched it off her to-do list; she was about to wrap up for the night and leave work behind when a quirky thought came to mind.

My to-do list obeys its own analogue to the Second Law of Thermodynamics... the number of items never decreases. I must add two new tasks... I need to find a replacement for Alonzo until he can return to work, and I better tell my Pequot lab contact that I'm filling in for Kameyo. I'll work on those tomorrow after I arrange the Plannert/Veep meeting. And serendipity should smile on me once again. I'll bring Brian to next week's committee meeting that'll be held a couple of days before Gene's speech.

Serendipity did smile. Brian cleared a couple of hours on his calendar to join her at Monday's committee meeting. They sat in the conference room with Professor Plannert afterwards. The professor spoke first.

"You gave a very impressive summary at the meeting. I like how you weave together deep-sea exploration and origins of life. Volcanoes play a role in both places. But what does this have to do with Senator Strauss?"

Irani turned to Brian. His previous Irani meeting had given him the answer.

"This kind of research can help solve problems in a multitude of climates. And whether or not I become the next Veep, I can push to fund more subsurface research via NOAA. We can change its name to the National Subsurface, Oceanic, and Atmospheric Administration. I'm certain that there'll be R&D spinoffs that will benefit the American economy and national security. And from what Irani described, GWU projects fit right in, so you can get grant money. That way, we all win."

Plannert's nods showed he was warming to the idea.

"Well in that case, I'll tell all my Committee members to vote for you. You are most impressive..."

Irani and the Senator went to the Congresswoman's office early that afternoon. Brian led the brief meeting attended by Gene and Sabrina.

"Talking with Professor Plannert after Irani's origins of life briefing makes it all clear. And your speech hints at the excitement of undersea R&D. The public will love it."

Gene said, "Good. Irani, please take us through the speech one more time..."

The Congresswoman gave Irani Thursday night off, bringing only Sabrina to the primetime press conference. Irani watched at her home along with a currently fuller house of interns.

As the cameras panned in on Gene, Eve said, "Wow, I like the staging. All the flags in the background make her look Presidential."

The next words came from Gene.

"Good evening to all Americans concerned about our nation's well-being. And as your Re-Gen Party's candidate for President, I am as concerned as all of us. That is why I am addressing you tonight, because I am concerned about bogus reports and deepfake stories that can be traced to my opponents. I will not stoop to their level by slinging mud, but instead will counter their claims by explaining your Re-Gen Party intentions, which are mine as well.

"First to the claim that we have empowered an OWLM-led conspiracy to disrespect men. Re-Gen and America need to include all genders, races, and ethnicities, for greatness is achieved via synthesis of diversity. My record is a testimony to that, and Brian Strauss – our choice for your next Vice President – will show the facts as he talks to you while on the campaign trail.

"Next, to the claim that the NIH and CDC are leading a conspiracy for an X-Virus pandemic by approving a vaccine that kills males instead of the virus. The facts show just the opposite, and we will have another set of independent analysts review the latest data. And not only will our vaccine immunize males, but our soon-to-be-approved recovery vaccine will help those struck down get back up to where they were."

The Congresswoman turned to face another camera before continuing.

"And now, let me give some historical context for why the policies our platform promotes are the right ones, not the wrong ones pushed by our opponents or the false claims you find in the media. Our nation is the best choice for leading the West and the International Community of Nations. We have handled better than most countries the challenges posed by Immigration, our Greco-Roman Heritage, and Islam. And we will continue to stand tall against those sectarian and identity groups who are pushing an agenda to sap America's greatness while at the same time making you feel guilty. Make no mistake, they aren't pushing for equality, they want to claim superiority."

Genesee turned to the previous camera before taking one deep breath and speaking again.

"And this is why, if you choose me as your President, I will champion balanced Neo-Conservative domestic and international policies. Neoconservatism's political arc traces from Aristotle to Leo Strauss, Irving Kristol, Allan Bloom, and to their acolytes. They know that society must have certain absolutes underpinning its ethics. Otherwise, the Counter-Culture Relativism and its Negative Nihilism will splinter us, leaving us with only a vain hope that kinder and gentler appeasing of our implacable enemies might save us. Appeasement never has and never will work for us and against them.

"I and my Re-Gen Party know what you and America need today – Tolerance, Diversity, and Freedom balanced against the foundations of American Exceptionalism.

And we need a unifying vision we can use for exploring uncharted territory. Two centuries ago, it was Outer Space. Today it will be Inner Space, our vast oceans, and under-sea research can bring us treasures from the deep that will reward all our people. It is a place that Brian Strauss will lead us if you give us your vote of confidence. And it will be a journey filled with excitement, breakthroughs, and opportunities that we are just beginning to imagine.

"So please think carefully about what I've said. And when you do, I am certain you will hear my intentions ringing loud and clear and true, and offering the best for you and America. Thank you, and may your god of choice be with us."

The Congresswoman fielded reporter questions until the broadcast ended fifteen minutes later. Preparing to say something, Eve clicked the mute button; Nari spoke first.

"Those have to be Miss Irani's words. All of us need to take her creative writing course."

Irani's complexion hid a flush of embarrassment and she found words to deflect the compliment.

"You already are, and remember, creative writing works for fiction and non-fiction. Political speeches need to capture the public's imagination by putting the truth into an exciting context. That's what good PR people do. The bad ones spin pretty lies that can trick you if you don't think things through for yourself. All of us should listen to what the analysts tell us tomorrow. I'll watch from my office, and that's where I'm heading. Alonzo, I'll call you tomorrow to get your talking heads comparisons."

Alonzo sat taller in his wheelchair before answering.

"You do that, and I'll pass whatever test you want to give me. And I won't ask Monet for help."

Monet smiled but didn't reply, preferring to listen instead to what everyone said.

Irani listened to enough news the next day to confirm the speech had hit the mark. She kept busy working on top priority to-do list items but still listened to her favorite national evening news broadcaster. The words she heard made her feel even better.

"…and according to our pollsters, Presidential candidate Genesee Huston scored a big win last night, putting to rest pesky conspiracy theories and giving a clear picture why and how her ethical values are better than what her opponents are offering. And she hinted at exciting exploration that gives people hope for a better tomorrow. Deep-sea R&D is something the public can get behind and with and support. Three months to go until the ballot boxes come out, and early voting could be bigger if people are afraid of whatever viruses might be lurking. Which candidate might benefit or suffer if that contingency comes to be? We must wait and see because only time will tell. Even in our number-dominated world, results can still confound predictions. Pollsters are often in the dark, just like the rest of us. But no matter what, we'll all get through. Americans are resilient and we'll figure out what to do. Back in sixty seconds …"

Electra didn't know who or what Trent Booker worked for or stood against, or what broadcasters he listened to. But if she did, she would have predicted that he felt as bad or worse than she felt good. And even without hooking him to her Brain Probe, she might have guessed some of what he was thinking, but not all.

Two late nights after the speech, Trent was chairing an emergency meeting of his covert three-person DC political climate observation group. He listened to the laments of his partners before taking over.

"Those talking heads nailed it, and we're in trouble. It's time for the President to send a backchannel person to get money from our international supporters-in-disguise to pay for an election-night surprise. We've got the right players selected and they know how to game the system. China, Russia, and Isilabad should like what we've got, and they've got the money to pay for playing the game. Let me describe how we can nail down a victory for our side, no matter what the voters say…"

Chapter 21
September 2160

"Watching Out and Over-the-Shoulder"

Irani sensed trouble brewing in several climates controlled by people rather than physics, so Electra fired up her Big-Data Social Forecasting software but came up empty on all gathering storm fronts when looking for culprits.

Campaign fever's a symptom of a political pandemic afflicting mainstreamers and extremists alike. Stock market and exchange rate fluctuations are too, though they're caused by a different troop of troublemakers. But all of them must be talking more underground than on the Internet. My Social Forecasting suite detects only generalities, no specifics pinning down who might be my adversaries. Indira won't want to help, so I'll have to snoop in 3-D Space. And there are plenty of possibilities. I'll add them to my list of places to go and things to do…

Irani did this while pushing ahead on all project fronts as well as monitoring her interns. She asked Nari and Eve to meet with her in her office early on Monday, September 15. Nari spoke first.

"You were right about joining a local professional organization, and Sabrina put me in touch with The Networking Group. TNG's got the right combination of online and in-person contacts, and they know a lot. One of them corrected what I was saying about Cliodynamics, and another straightened me out on Type I and Type

II errors for hypothesis testing. She can also give me pointers on using Bayesian software apps, but I'm not ready for that yet.

"But I have been thinking about conspiracy theories, and it seems that pre-election jitters always bring out more. That fantasy 'Reptoid Conspiracy Theory' is currently crawling around. It says that reptilian humanoids living around the world are gonna manipulate the election and make America the first nation under their control. I'm not paying much attention to that one."

Indira listened; Electra did too but also to herself.

Nari's positive attitude makes her much more likeable. I'm sure Nila would agree… Let's ask about her when Nari gives us a break.

Irani talked as soon as she could.

"You have lots to say about your Washington work. What about your contacts in India?"

"I think Nila likes living there as much as Sanjay. They've invited Eve and me to visit in December. Sanjay says his Baba will pick up the airfare. You think we should go?"

Eve dived right in.

"Of course, we should. The election and the fall term will be over by then."

Irani agreed and then asked Eve to report on campaign activities.

"According to the polling data I'm tracking, our Congresswoman is ahead by more than the margin of error in many of the battleground states. I'll be one of the speakers at a Re-Gen volunteers outdoor rally on Thursday before they leave to campaign in some of the swing states. That should keep the momentum building."

When Eve eventually stopped, Irani said, "Good work all around. And what about Alonzo and Monet?"

"He's pepped up and promises he'll be a new guy when he recovers. Monet kids that she's looking for something to speed it up, so don't anybody worry; Monet and I are watching out for him…"

Irani plugged back into her to-do list soon after ending the meeting, but as she did, Electra updated hers.

Eve's bubbling enthusiasm carries over to Nari, and I'm sure it helps Alonzo. And I'll do my part too, but from the shadows, coming into their view only if I have to. I think I know how to make this so…

Eve's nervousness receded Thursday evening as she drove to the rally, thanks largely to Sabrina's calming words.

"We should have fun tonight. The weather's cooperating, you've practiced your speech, and I've worked out volunteer travel itineraries; and besides, the group is made up of our people, so don't worry, we've got all bases covered."

Eve nodded but said nothing until she had parked the Vette and was walking with Sabrina to the registration tent.

"I guess you're right, but I still have to fight to keep my nerves under control. But that fight'll be over as soon as my words start flowing…"

Eve's guess would have been much different had she known what the ringleader of a group of young toughs was saying to his accomplices inside his parked van after pointing out a prominent target.

"That's Eve Cortez, the one we want to impress. You guys that drove here with reinforcements, chase her down if she gets away. Our client wants her to remember that Huston and OWLM aren't gonna get rid of men. We'll charge the stage midway through her yapping after we've taken out the security guards. You all have your assignments, so let's mingle in the crowd and get ready. Any questions?"

There were none, and no muffled go get-ems or cheers either, only sneers.

The senior volunteer organizer took ten minutes to outline what tonight would hold before he introduced Eve. The crowd applauded as she and Sabrina mounted the stage and seemed ready to do more during her talk.

"Hi, everyone, I'm Eve Cortez and I want to thank you for being part of the Re-Gen Party's campaign to build a new middle class. Me and my partner, Sabrina Ricardo who's standing next to me, have got details all set for battleground state canvassing. And even though the polls put us ahead by more than the margin of error, we can't let up. And at this point in the campaign, in-person politicking makes an even bigger impact than online meetings, so after my talk, please come to the tent and select which state you want to work…"

Eve's words flowed smoothly until she stopped midway through one of her favorite campaign speech phrases. She resumed after the clapping faded.

"And I think we'll see that… what the –" Stage lights flickered before going out and stopping her words. Crashes and yelling filled the darkness.

Eve stumbled to her left and collided with a collapsing Sabrina, who had just been tackled by a shadowy form leaping onto the stage. As she was about to tumble over them, a pair of strong arms jerked her to the left before its owner shouted.

"You're not gonna mess things up. We're gonna uuhh –"

Eve couldn't see the action, but sensed that someone had ripped her attacker off. From the grunts she heard, it sounded like her attacker's attacker was scoring solid kicks. Eve tumbled forward, landing atop the guy who was beating Sabrina. She grabbed his stringy hair, but before she could snap his head back, a stronger pair of hands pushed her to the side and its owner took her place. All Eve saw was a silhouette using two hands to jerk the guy's head and body to the right. The figure then leaped to its feet and kicked its enemy senseless before booting it off the stage.

Eve recognized what was going on but could think of only one word to yell.

"Mother?"

Irani screamed the rest.

"Hush, grab onto Sabrina and drag her up. Then grab my hand and don't let go."

Irani's night vision goggles helped her clear a path to Eve's Vette by manhandling aside any and all impediments. She used Eve's keys to get behind the wheel; Sabrina sat in Eve's lap and both gaped at Irani as she powered up before issuing commands.

"Buckle in and watch for any pursuers I miss."

The passengers' heads rocked every which way as Irani smoked tires and rocketed away. She spotted one pursuing vehicle but it disappeared when she steered an off-road course through another park and across two lanes of traffic. No one spoke until they stopped in front of the house forty-five minutes later.

"I'll leave the Vette with you. Get yourselves cleaned up and then call Gene, but don't you dare mention I was there."

Those were Irani's final instructions before leaping from the car; her all-black workout suit vanished into the darkness.

The girls dragged themselves into the family room and collapsed on a sofa and chair before Sabrina had the courage to ask,

"So, that's your Miss Irani? Where'd she learn those survival skills?"

Eve rubbed her arms and shook her head before saying,

"Beats me, but she sure beat up the bad guys. What do you think?"

"We better make sure we stay on her good side and not make her angry..."

Electra allowed herself enough time on her run to the office to savor tonight's victory while keeping it in perspective.

What an adrenaline rush, and now for some endorphins. I think I'm in better shape now than when coming back from skiing, and I'm getting better at controlling my Monster from the Id. No sense adding to the body count unless absolutely necessary. I'll get a good night's sleep and give Eve an edited answer to any questions she might ask. And then I pick from my to-do list.

Eve thanked Irani the next day for rescuing her and Sabrina, promising before ending the call to do a better job watching out for troublemakers whenever at rallies. Neither had been damaged, and the Congresswoman promised to strengthen security at upcoming events. Satisfied that Eve was back on track, Electra made an observation.

All but one of my clone-children are moving ahead, and that's why Alonzo will now be my focus. It's time to put him on the road to recovery by tweaking the X-Virus recovery vaccine.

Electra knew the way to the Pequot reservation well enough to let her physical persona do the driving while her cognitive persona considered her newest challenge.

Long ago in a previous life I modified the T-Plague vaccines. I'll review what I did and see what might fit for the R-Vac. Kameyo left

copious notes describing Indira's formulation, and I'll give myself two weeks to make improvements. If I haven't by the end of September, I'll seek Indira's help.

Irani let her Pequot manufacturing team know she'd be onsite for a couple of weeks, and then Electra sequestered herself in the Deus Lab before withdrawing into her fortress of solitude and strength: the lightning brain. Past memories soon emerged.

I love the cerebral joy of cognitive control. There's an esthetic purity unrivaled by emotions. And as I get older, I'm learning more and more about balancing them. I might never get it right, but I'm getting better, just like my clone-kids.

By unleashing her obsessive-compulsive tendencies, Electra beat the deadline. Irani told the Congresswoman to let her NDA contact know that an improved formulation would be sent immediately, but she told no one yet what she would do with the experimental batches she had. That would happen only when she returned to Washington.

The Irani-Electra duo closed the lab and packed for the drive back, but Electra decided to reward herself by taking a walk in the late-afternoon sunlight on a hilly, tree-lined gravel road winding through the reservation. The soft crunching of her slow walk drew her into the enchantment of the forested Indian lands.

But the lightning brain's early warning system always stayed alert, always watching out and over its shoulder. Electra felt a jolt that forced her to turn around. What she saw further elevated the lightning brain.

Those two gun-toting guys running towards me don't look like Pequots. It's deer season, but they can't hunt on Reservation lands... Jesus, maybe they're after me.

Electra took evasive action. Darting to her right and then off the road, she plunged downhill, dodging through the trees, but she tripped over a root and somersaulted to the bottom. By the time she picked herself up, she could hear her pursuers charging downhill. She regrouped in the gathering darkness and raced on the unevenly flat terrain at the bottom of the hill. She could tell from the sounds that she was pulling away, but the pain in her knee and side slowed her down and the thrashing behind drew closer. She dodged to her left and struggled up the hill, hoping to get to the road before getting caught. When she tumbled onto the road near the top of a steep grade, she spotted an escape route. A beat-up flatbed truck twenty yards ahead was struggling up the incline.

The lightning brain elevated further, giving Electra a burst of energy-filled endorphins that overcame pain. She sprinted towards the truck, not looking back at the sound of pursuers. She dived onto the flatbed just as it crested the hill. Gravity did the rest. The truck gained velocity and was now taking her to safety. The last she saw of them were their motionless silhouettes at the top of the hill.

When the truck stopped several miles later, its driver, a Pequot Indian Electra recognized, hadn't a clue why she was onboard, but she spun a convincing tale of getting tired while hiking and he drove her to her car. She checked carefully before driving away and watched every which way on the six-hour drive back to her DC office, thinking all the while.

They must have been after my X-Vac formulations. But how did they find the Lab? They must have hacked into Gene's Emails, or maybe into the CDC's NDA processing directories. If so, these guys or the people they work for are pros. I better tell my Pequot people to post more guards at both the lab and manufacturing facility. And I'll tell Indira when I get home what happened.

Electra showered and ate a middle-of-the-night breakfast before logging on to her office workstation and invoking Indira's GUI. Its eternally pristine avatar greeted her.

"I must congratulate your successful reformulation. I observed from the Cloud and didn't intrude because my help wasn't needed."

"I wish you could have observed yesterday's late-afternoon hike. Do you know that two bad guys hunted me down? How do you supposed they tracked me?"

"Regarding your first question, I can only observe from Cyberspace and you were out of range. Now to your second. Not from any of my experiments. Obviously, they found the lab by breaching whatever online security your Congresswoman or the CDC has installed. And they might know your identity if they caught your license plate. I am always watching whenever you are online or covered by an Internet-linked surveillance system, but you should heighten your personal security systems until this contingency has ended. Have you thought of that, and have you thought of any positive outcomes?"

"Now I know that my cognitive skills are better than ever, and my survival instincts have shifted even further to flight rather than fight. But I couldn't test my fitness level. If I hadn't tumbled down the hill, I might have been able to outrun my pursuers instead of escaping on a flatbed, but my twisted ankle and dented ribs got in the way."

"Perhaps, but you used your cognitive persona to get away, and as you have already discovered, it is almost always superior to your physical persona. Well, you have acquitted yourself nicely. You should rest and reenergize for your next task. I shall be watching whenever I can."

Indira's GUI disappeared. Electra slept soundly that night while the lightning brain freewheeled.

Irani called Monet's embassy number that afternoon. Her words came through after Irani's greeting.

"Why hello, Miss Irani... I would be happy for you to visit me. Please come over..."

Irani was sitting across from her an hour later. Monet waited for her to speak.

"I like your office. How do you like working at the embassy?"

"It is everything I expected it to be. I am very happy. And I will be even happier when Alonzo is fully recovered. He promises to study and work harder than ever before as soon as his health is restored. And he is responding to Eve's therapy, but I wish I could do more."

"That's why I'm here. I have the latest X-Virus R-Vac that's going through the NDA approval process. We're skirting the law by treating him, but if you give it to Alonzo three times a day, you'll be helping Alonzo, yourself and me."

"But why don't you have Eve dispense it?"

"That's too close to home. I don't want anyone but you to know where it came from. Tell Alonzo you got it from some of the R&D labs in Harare. That'll make him beholding even more to you and Zimbabwe."

A tiny smile emerged before Monet replied.

"You are so clever. Thank you for bringing me into your plan."

Irani smiled for the first time in nearly twenty-four hours.

"And thank you, daughter number two, for playing the game. All of us will be winners."

Irani rose to leave; Monet did also but said nothing, hugging her instead. Her smile said the rest.

Chapter 22
October 2160

"Storms in the Offing"

Eve invited Irani to see the new Alonzo two weeks later. According to the phone conversation, he had not only turned the recovery corner but had raced to a whole new level of commitment. When she arrived carrying a pizza, Monet whisked her to where Eve was finishing his exercise session, whispering that Alonzo had kept their secret. He yelled a greeting as soon as he saw them.

"Hey Irani, don't I look better than the last time? Monet and Eve are working wonders on my mental and physical conditioning." He caught his breath while toweling off, giving Eve a chance to talk.

"He's regained about half the weight and physical fitness he lost. Let's let him tell you at lunch about his newfound mental toughness."

Twenty minutes later, Alonzo was spewing out words almost as fast as he was devouring pepperoni and cheese.

"I don't ever want to be that sick again, and I'm so thankful I'm getting back to normal. And like I promised, I'll work and study harder than ever as soon as I get back to Austin…"

Irani listened to his words and to Electra's whispers.

When he stops for another slice, cut in with our plan.

She did that a couple of minutes later.

"I'm happy for you, but you should pace your comeback. In fact, you sound ready to cross into new territory. Why not transfer from UT-Austin to GWU and move permanently to DC?"

Alonzo stopped chewing and swallowed before answering.

"But then I won't be working for you. What'll I do?"

"I'll find someone to work with Kim and keep you on my payroll until you find another job."

"Does that mean you'll pay for tuition?"

"That's included too, but I want you and Monet to figure out what's in your collective best interest."

Eve was about to interrupt, but Irani's glance stopped her and she continued.

"And then get with Nari and Eve to work out living arrangements. That should be an easy assignment and won't interfere with Eve's campaign work."

Irani stopped and Eve started talking.

"It better not. The election's a little over three weeks away and I'm booked solid. And after that, I'll be busy working on our transition plan."

Eve's words provoked a comment from Monet.

"You sound confident, but Miss Irani always recommends having contingency plans. What will you and the Congresswoman do if she loses?"

The question stumped Eve; Irani filled in.

"I have that covered; I haven't shared them with Eve or the Congresswoman because they're totally engaged in the election. And if the polls are pointing the right way, we should win."

Alonzo fired a question at Irani.

"Does that mean the polls are right?"

"Perhaps, and perhaps I should leave now while all of you are smiling. Please stay that way and make sure Nari does too..."

Irani listened as Electra mused for both on the drive back to her office.

Alonzo is the last of my clone-children to find something to do. How exciting, yet also a bit scary because of the unknowns. Ah, but that adds to the thrill, even though it sometimes obscures why he should be thankful.

Mother wrote a poem about change caused by unknowns... she called it Crossing the Bar. And so did Tennyson, Queen Victoria's poet laureate.

But his was a metaphor about crossing from life to death. Mother's is more upbeat. I think I can recall it...

Cross to where you now must be,
Doubt replaced by clarity.
No hindrance bars to set you free,
No whit of worry if others can't see.

How long it took to figure out,
Looking back leaves little doubt.
For chosen path give silent shout,
Resolve provides enforced redoubt.

How long the stay there is no clue,
Bless each morn's sustaining dew.
Till winds of fate blow cold on you,
Announcing what is next to do.

Good words to live by, which is what I'm doing. But I'll let time teach the lesson to my four children... oops, there are five not four. Monet's part of the unofficial family. And they're different than a dream team or keepers' group. Definitely not as talented, but they're better for me. They keep me engaged and sharpen my empathy.

Electra already had a plan for replacing Alonzo. Her week-ending phone calls would begin rolling it out. Rick Tabasko, answering on the third ring, recognized her voice.

"Hello Irani. PH is with me and he's telling me to call you DD, but either way it's good to hear your voice. What's up?"

"I've got a win-win business proposition for you and your partner. How would you like to manage some of my Austin-based businesses?"

Rick put the call on speaker and let PH talk.

"Hi, DD. Hey, we're always looking for opportunities. What're the businesses?"

"Hi, PH. Something old for you two... oil and gas. And something new... rare earths mines plus Martian and Solar Panel Farms. Think you might be interested?"

"Let's get RT's opinion."

"You bet. We can't talk now, but how about this? Have you ever been to New Orleans?"

"No."

"Well, we're meeting there next week with a new business partner, a Mr. Lucian Perteau. I'll give you his phone number. Why not join us? Call him and he'll make the arrangements."

"That'll work. See you guys next week..."

Irani spoke that evening with Lucian; she liked his charming, unhurried baritone voice and distinctive accent that imparted trust and confidence, and when he offered to be her tour guide, even picking her up at the airport, she decided to come a day early.

Electra reserved Sunday morning to prepare for Monday's flight to Louis Armstrong International Airport located just north of New Orleans. After prepping for the agenda, she surfed the Web to learn about southern Louisiana and its most famous city. She had learned enough by lunchtime to satisfy her appetite for knowing about where she would be going and recounted it one more time before logging off.

New Orleans has to be a city that knows how to have fun. Why else would it be called the Big Easy for its party-like attitude? And its French-influenced Cajun and Creole heritage mix with African and Spanish roots to build a cultured city proud to maintain its manners and identity. No wonder Lucian insists on calling me Miss Irani. I must remember to call him Mr. LP.

The city's actually an Island between Lake Pontchartrain and the Mississippi River. Much of it is below sea level, and if the Army Corp. of Engineers hadn't rerouted the river and built levees, it'd be underwater. And although it's still sinking, pumps and levees plus hydraulically-operated pylons, control gates, and seawalls manage to keep ahead of the water coming in. And like much of south Louisiana, it's got lots of bayous, swamps, and marshes, what ecologists call a wetlands biome.

The Cajuns took a route almost as twisty as the Mississippi to get there. Originally from France, they settled in a section of Nova Scotia called Acadia, but were deported by the Brits when England won the French-Canadian War. The Creoles came from France, Spain, Africa, and the West Indies, and like the Cajuns, brought with them their own culture and cuisine.

So, how did the United States come to own the place? England, France, and Spain skirmished for the area soon after coming to the New World. The Spaniards came first, but the French founded New Orleans in 1718. Then Spain claimed it, and in a 1763 treaty that ended the French-Indian War, England ceded Spain's ownership, but Napoleon forced Spain in 1802 to give it to France, and France sold all its North American holdings to the United States in 1802 for fifteen million dollars. The Louisiana Purchase would cost 8.5 billion in current dollars, but that's just a pittance compared to its value.

But why the Johnny Horton song about the Battle of New Orleans? Because even after the War of 1812, the Brits angled for a port near the city. Good that Andrew Jackson won that 1814 battle. Good for America and Johnny Horton too.

I'm rambling too far, but I see once again how international politics drives so much of history. Well, now I know enough to ask intelligent questions, so I better get back to my current event.

A gathering storm in the Gulf of Mexico kept NOAA's National Weather Forecasting Service fully engaged tracking and predicting the intensity of a potential hurricane. Though located in Silver Springs, Maryland, its network of satellites, drones, and weather buoys fed data 24/7 into its supercomputers. It predicted a Category 2 storm with less wind and more storm surge than normal, but the Army Corp. of Engineers spokesperson whimsically stated in the latest bulletin that the "Big Easy" should take it easy: New Orleans hurricane fortifications could withstand Category 5.

Irani's Monday morning flight landed on time, and she picked Mr. LP out of the crowd at the baggage carousel, courtesy of his Website photographs.

He's almost a head taller than everyone, and he carries his weight like a mid-fifties ex-athlete who exercises enough to balance New Orleans cuisine. And his longish silver-gray hair compliments his business-casual attire. He looks every bit the well-tailored and well-connected businessman.

Irani waved when he spotted her as she wended her way towards him. He stood tall, displaying an easy grace and matching smile.

My instincts are right... He's the real deal. I think Mr. LP, RT, and PH will become a reincarnated keepers' group, but with a different twist. We'll all look out for one another. I got it... I'll call them the Three Musketeers, but I won't let them know the name or the game until we've all settled in. OK, now I better settle down, sit still, and listen to my host...

Mr. LP's personality filled much of the time on the twenty-four-mile Lake Pontchartrain causeway drive north to Mandeville while he described what he had planned: dinner tonight at Mandina's and tomorrow a drive-through of the best tourist attractions.

"There'll be too much wind and rain to walk about, but that'll clear the streets and make driving easier. Then we'll conduct business at Rick Tabasko and Parson Holsum's hotel early Wednesday morning, and I'll take us to the wells Wednesday afternoon, assuming we still like one another and the weather's not frowning down on us..."

Mr. LP's enchanting stories and accent seemed to shrink the travel-time to the Blue Heron B&B. He gave her final instructions before driving away.

"Well now, Miss Irani, you freshen up and I'll come get you at 5:30. Then get set for some authentic Louisiana cooking."

Mr. LP gave additional instructions at six when they were seated in an inviting dining area.

"I recommend you choose the fried catfish, but save enough room for the brownie and vanilla ice cream topped with fudge sauce. And tomorrow you can pick either Cajun or Creole cooking."

Irani took his advice and then decided to test her recently acquired knowledge.

"I understand Indian natives settled in Louisiana thousands of years ago. There were many powerful Indian tribes until Spain's conquistadors brought guns and disease that decimated the natives. That's why they liked the French settlers better. They brought goods for trade and treated the tribes with dignity and respect. And with the Creoles came the Ursuline Nuns, who made it their mission to educate women of color and free the slaves."

Mr. LP's smile widened.

"Judging from the way you handled yourself on last week's call, I thought you must be pretty smart, but I underestimated you. And you look like you could have some Creole or Cajun ancestry in your DNA. You'll have to come back for Mardi Gras and celebrate Fat Tuesday New Orleans style…"

The conversation flowed through dessert until Mr. LP glanced at a text message on his cell phone.

"That's my significant other reminding me to bring Isabelle. They'll be together the next two days just in case the storm warnings worsen while I'm with you and our Denver friends."

"How old is your daughter?"

"Isabelle is my still uncluttered fourteen-year-old delight. I'm counting on Gina to help defuse the dangers caused by dating. If you have daughters, you understand."

Irani avoided complicating matters but still told the truth.

"I've never had the opportunity to help teenage girls, but I've observed the challenge. And I imagine you and Gina are excellent role models."

"We try, and that's why I better drive you back and get home before they start worrying. Is ten a.m. tomorrow good for the start of our tour?"

Electra whispered a popular New Orleans phrase that Irani could use to tease her host.

"Ah yes, laissez les bon temps rouler, let the good times roll."

Mr. LP blew her a kiss before saying, "Fai do-do mon cheri, and pleasant dreams. And I'm certain you'll figure out what all that means."

Electra googled it soon after he dropped her off and then followed the advice; she went to sleep.

The rain drumming on the window awakened her before the clock radio clicked on. The newscaster's droning voice reporting the eight o'clock weather bulletin further dampened her usual jump-out-of-bed attitude.

"...and the two colliding low-pressure waves have slowed the approaching front of Hurricane Rani, adding to the storm surge. But officials at the National Weather Forecasting Service have consulted with the Army Corp. of Engineers to conclude that New Orleans is safe. The maze of canals, levees, and seawalls will weather whatever makes landfall wherever and whenever, but the government recommends precautionary evacuation. I will leave it for the people to decide, just like they will in the election less than two weeks away..."

Electra kept listening as she dragged herself out of bed, but paid more attention to her attitude.

I always feel better after getting up and exercised and prepped for the day. And I'll make some instant oat meal too. That'll balance last night's brownie...

When Mr. LP arrived at the promised time, Irani dashed to the car. The weather didn't diminish his charming manner.

"Where y'at, Miss Irani? But I can answer my own question. You look even better than yesterday."

"Morning, and you do too. Will the weather affect our tour?"

"As a matter of fact, it does. Are you a Hollywood aficionado?"

"I know a little about it. Why?"

"Well, lots of famous actors and actresses do good things that never make headlines. Not long after Hurricane Katrina visited us in 2005, a famous actor by the name of Brad Pitt helped set up the 'Make It Right Foundation' to rebuild some neighborhoods. I thought you'd like to see some of it today, so we'll go there first..."

Mr. LP said more, which Electra summarized.

Mr. Pitt used his money to get the latest engineering and architectural improvements against hurricanes, like pervious concrete for streets and surfaces to absorb water and then release it into the swampy subsoil, or concrete boards replacing drywall to make buildings hurricane-proof.

Mr. LP had more to say while driving through parts of rebuilt neighborhoods.

"… and we've gotten better and better since way back then. Mr. Brad was a pioneer, and like many of 'em he got an arrow or two in the back. He got hit with a couple of lawsuits by people complaining about repairs needed maybe five years after moven back in. Just goes to show…"

Mr. LP showed her the Garden District next. Irani liked its Saint Charles electric streetcar almost as much as its distinctive houses and manicured gardens. Then he drove past the Saint Louis Cathedral, explaining all the way.

"This could be our most distinctive landmark. It was originally the parish's first church, but a 1788 fire razed it. What you see today is the result of us Orleanians making things better and better…"

Unfortunately, the weather didn't, so Mr. LP ended the tour at two-thirty.

"I hope you liked the quick drive-by of the French Quarter. And we'll stop at Preservation Hall to grab a snack and some music before I drive you back."

There were few tourists, but that gave Irani a better view of the beamed ceilings, wooden tables and chairs, and paintings decorating the walls. And the musicians played just as enthusiastically. Irani didn't recognize the style, but Mr. LP did.

"Jazz may be our most famous music, but Zydeco isn't far behind. It takes only four to play, one on guitar, another on accordion, one on drums, and one more on washboard. And sometimes a fiddler joins in."

Irani waited for the music to stop before asking, "It's certainly full of energy. It makes you want to get up and dance, but what is it?"

"The French Creoles in southwest Louisiana started Zydeco. It blends blues and rhythm with the melody and songs of all the local people, especially Native Americans and Blacks. If you practice listening long enough, you can even understand some of the words."

The pair listened to two more pieces before Mr. LP said, "So, have you heard enough? It's time to go so I can make arrangements for tomorrow."

Mr. LP explained more on the drive across the causeway.

"Ole Lake Pontchartrain's gett'en more riled up, so I'll call RT and tell'em we'll meet at their hotel tomorrow at 6 a.m. They're staying near the airport, and that's good because it's on the way to the wells we'll visit. Wrapping up sooner will be better; we'll beat the weather."

Electra couldn't resist teasing him with words, so she gave Irani a final word or two just before getting out of the car.

"Today's been the best sightseeing ever, and the Zydeco music is a lagniappe that caps the day."

Mr. LP's French vocabulary kept him in the game.

"Goodness Miss Irani, you know as many words as Mr. Webster. I expect you'll be able to follow our oil patch chat tomorrow. But please get a good night's sleep because I'll pick you up tomorrow at 4 a.m."

"I will, and you too. See you about three hours after zero dark-thirty. I'll be ready."

"I'm sure you will. And I'll have reinforcements so I can keep up with you…"

But Irani couldn't fall asleep. Worried about Hurricane Rani contingencies, she stayed up late, surfing the Web for additional seawall construction information. Nothing useful surfaced until she used her intrusion software to hack into some Army Corp. of Engineers protected files. An hour later she had dug up enough to satisfy the lightning brain.

*Living with Nature requires constant adjustment. Land and sea levels rise and fall according to laws mostly outside our control. The Army Corp. has been partnering for over a century with world's best seawall builders, the Dutch. And each has learned from the other. The Army learned how to build gigantic robotically controlled seawalls, and the Dutch learned how to use the Rhine River outflow to fill in the land, just like how the Army uses its Mississippi River Control System to keep New Orleans from drowning. These are **engineering marvels of heroic proportion that don't need quantum physics. Newton's laws are plenty good**… Now I can rest easy.*

Irani thought Mr. LP's reinforcements would be PH and RT, but she was mistaken. Even in the 4 a.m. darkness, she could see he was driving a truck towing an extraordinary-looking boat. She asked about it as soon as they were under way. Mr. LP answered with a rhetorical question.

"Have you ever been in a swamp boat?"

"No, but it looks fast. Please tell me more."

"It'll whiz us over bayous and swamps faster than a pelican can fly. It makes more noise, but it'll keep our feet dry."

"Even in this wind and rain?" How will it keep the water off? Does it have a top or an awning?"

"I said feet, not the rest of us. We'll all wear rain slickers, waders, and boots plus hard hats and goggles. And today we'll wear life vests for extra safety."

"Won't it get stuck in the marsh grass and mud?"

"You gotta trust me, Miss Irani. The flat bottom and rudders mounted behind the big ole fan will keep us moving. And if that don't work, we'll tell RT and PH to get out and push, but I promise, that won't be needed today…"

By the time they reached the hotel, Irani knew as much about swamp boats and oilfields operating in south Louisiana as Mr. LP could tell in the allotted time.

Rick and Parson had the table in their room set for four. Mr. LP eased into the meeting by explaining the history of the breakfast now in front of them.

"You can't do better than beignets covered with powdered sugar and served with café au lait. Those Ursuline Nuns brought them when they came here in 1727 or thereabouts. These delights just might be the first raised doughnuts…"

Irani decided she would learn by listening while the guys ran the meeting. Mr. LP segued from beignets to business, and though concern about the approaching storm compressed the agenda, every item was signed off by nine-thirty. Electra applauded to herself.

My Three Musketeers are each different, but the whole is greater than the sum. There's calm and cultured Mr. LP, then there's likeable and hard-

charging RT, and then there's laid-back but risk-taking PH. This is the start of another great game.

Everyone tucked their papers away before Mr. LP handed out today's uniforms.

"Put on everything now but the hard hats, goggles, and life vests. We'll do them just before we get in the boat."

RT asked, "Maybe we don't need to see the acreage and wells we just purchased. We could do that next time."

PH's words filled what might have become a gap.

"Taking a swamp boat to the wellheads and getting back before the storm rolls in is worth every penny we spent. Besides, Mr. LP knows what he's doing, so let's go."

"I certainly do, but the minute anyone spots a gator wearing galoshes, we head back."

The wind and rain kept a steady beat on the drive to where the wetlands met the last vestiges of civilization. Mr. LP had a 24/7 news station tuned in, which reported light traffic, no mass exodus.

Irani watched her Three Musketeers launch the boat after everyone had put on all remaining gear. Mr. LP set her next to him on the elevated driver's bench. RT and PH filled up the passenger's bench in front. Then he fired up the engine and roared into the bayou.

Electra absorbed all the sensations.

What an adrenaline rush… just like motorcycles and skiing, but even more so because the grass and trees whip by so close. And the bayou's got more twists than most roads I've ever been on. I'm glad Mr. LP knows where he's going.

Mr. LP throttled back forty-five minutes later, and everyone trudged to the wellhead that was on an elevated pad. His words boomed through the windy gusts.

"Gas production is easier because the gas flows under its own pressure into the pipeline. You can't drive trucks this far in, so unless you've got a well that can flow oil all by itself, there's a problem. But no worries for us, our acreage is for gas."

He looked around and stared at the ground for a minute before saying more.

"Water level's high and starting to rise faster. I think we should head back. The other wells look pretty much the same."

As they clambered onto the boat, RT shouted before Mr. LP powered up.

"I'm reading a text message that came in about an hour ago. It says something about a massive power outage. Is that bad?"

The words triggered an alarm in the lightning brain faster than Mr. LP could speak.

If the electric grid is down, so are communications networks. We've got a problem...

Mr. LP's calming voice carried back.

"It could be, but the seawalls have automated backup generators, so unless there's a software glitch or something else, New Orleans should be fine."

Electra kept her comments to herself.

Big storms can cause big power outages, but so can Cyberterrorists. We better get back to civilization.

Mr. LP blasted back at full throttle, but the twisting turns were too much for those on the passenger bench who hadn't buckled up. A sharp zig to the left pitched Parson over the starboard side before Mr. LP could throttle down. Rick dived in and pulled him back. Irani heaved RT in first, and the two of them then pulled in PH.

PH waved off Irani's assistance; he would lie underneath the bench until they were in the truck and driving back. RT did the same to keep PH from rolling away.

The water was midway hubcap depth by the time they reached the truck. Irani and RT guided the boat onto the trailer as Mr. LP operated the winch. Irani inspected PH as soon as the boat was secured.

"You didn't break it, but you might have a dislocated shoulder."

"That's happened before, and I can manage. Let's get outta of here."

No one but the newscaster spoke as they drove back.

"...Details are sketchy, but the outage seems to have taken down all electrical and communications networks. And there's no word yet about any computer hardware or software shutdowns. But people aren't waiting to hear from the government. Roads are clogging as fast as the waters are rising. Interstates 10 and 55 are now parking lots. You'll need to find another exit…"

Mr. LP ran into the problem forty-five minutes later. Even the state roads had become backed up. But none of the keepers panicked; instead, they waited for Mr. LP to talk.

As he turned to face the back seat, Irani did too before his calm voice came through.

"Well now, we'll just pretend that everything around us is a swamp and I'll use my boat to get us back."

Everyone gazed out; RT was the first to speak.

"I don't think we have to pretend."

Irani said, "I agree, and I'll bet Mr. LP knows the way out of here."

Her words brought a smile that accompanied his reply.

"I most certainly do, so let's launch the boat and beat the traffic home…"

Chapter 23
November 2160

"Twice-Told Voting"

Irani and her Three Musketeers had ample time to savor every morsel of their initial meeting's excitement. Hurricane Rani closed the airport for three days, but the city's seawall defense systems came back online soon enough to defeat the storm surge, and the French Quarter's nightlife blazed back soon after Hurricane Rani left and the sky cleared.

Mr. LP had invited Irani to stay at his house, but she refused to interfere with his family life, so he took her to Rick and Parson's hotel. And though she didn't reveal the name of the reconstituted keepers' group, she got them to approve the name she used to christen the rendezvous: Mr. LP's SB Escadrille. PH liked the analogy to Lafayette's World War I's namesake and told Mr. LP soon after he arrived that the vote came in at three-to-zero. All were pleased that he had brought Isabelle and Gina to bid them adieu Sunday morning at the airport. Isabelle won the contest for guessing what SB stood for as soon as Gina turned the question into a guessing game, and Mr. LP gave her extra credit for explaining the connection between Lafayette and the American Revolution.

Irani's weeklong adventure brought her back to DC refreshed and ready to focus on her top priority, next week's election, but before doing that she planned to investigate what might have caused the seawall hardware and software failures. Most media stories blamed it on the hurricane after discounting Cyberterrorism conspiracy theories, but Electra wanted to look deeper. She spent most of Monday using her proprietary Big Data intrusion and hacking apps plus those she had perfected for Sociopolitical analysis and forecasting. She even hacked manually beyond the four-sigma outlier limit but came up with nothing of substance. She rationalized why Monday evening.

Maybe enemies have developed Cybersecurity systems that are better than mine. If so, they're smarter than me. Or maybe they've gone offline, talking and plotting only in 3-D Space where no apps can go. And if that's the case, I must use my intuition to pick out and target possible enemies. Indira won't be interested in any of this, so I won't ask for her help. I'll let the lightning brain think it through. Then I'll know what to do.

Irani met early Tuesday morning with Gene and Brian. Both looked haggard from the pressures of the campaign but recent polls buoyed their mood. Their lead in the swing states had just swung past the margin of error.

There was nothing else Irani needed to do other than talk with Eve and Nari, so she went that afternoon to a local campaign headquarters. Nari wasn't there, but Eve's bustling about would convince anyone that a victory at the polls would happen next week. Irani called her aside for only a minute.

"Looks like you and the campaign are in overdrive. I just met with our candidates and they're feeling pretty good. How about you? And where's Nari?"

"I feeling like I'm on top of everything. And Nari continues to hunt for conspiracies, even though she's found nada new. And she told me that today's polling techniques and software can call the winners even before the polls close. Won't it be great when people finally trust online voting enough to get rid of paper ballots and voting booths?"

"Perhaps your generation will be the first to make it so. And that's one of the campaign planks. Well, I better get out of your way."

Irani swiveled to go, but then turned back and brushed Eve's cheeks with her fingertips before saying, "And please don't run yourself so ragged you forget to vote. Make sure you put it on your to-do list."

"Oh Mother, you know I will, and I know you will too…"

Eve's comment about Nari pinged Electra when she returned to the office.

I forgot about turning my intrusion and hacking apps loose on other types of conspiracies. There's always been a conspiracy theory about a politically perfect storm where the Academic Elite, Liberal Left, Big Data and Big Pharma, and Fake-News Media take control of people's minds and bodies using Transhumanism's embedded computer chips and DNA technology.

Could there be an international clique trying to develop an all-encompassing online social credit and monetary banking system that'll make people of all nations slaves to a one-world technocracy? Sounds far-fetched… maybe no one is actually planning it, but maybe the pieces are emerging separately. And if they are, someday some devious person will try to pull them together.

Electra tried the next day to ferret out whatever pieces she could find but reached the same conclusions she had rationalized Monday evening. She kept the issue on her to-do list, but placed it near the bottom.

I'll talk with Monet and Alonzo tomorrow, and then focus on my Investor Services Business. It's about time I check on AAM fund performance.

Monet invited Irani to come Thursday to her embassy office at a time when Alonzo would be there. When the receptionist walked her in, Monet rose from her desk to greet her and then sat next to Alonzo on the sofa. Irani sat on a matching chair on the other side of a butler table centered on an Oriental rug. As all three chatted about the lighter side of life before turning to heavier subjects, Electra saw big changes in Alonzo.

He's actually contributing to the small talk, not just grunting answers like he used to. And there's an enthusiasm in his voice and gestures that comes from a maturing confidence and commitment. Let's see how he handles my new approach for managing the Austin-based businesses.

Irani found a suitable place to insert the subject.

"You're looking even better and sitting taller than last time. And I've got some news that should sit well with you. I'm partnering with a Denver-based company to manage all my Austin businesses. Kim will report to them, and you can stay permanently in DC. Have you considered what you'd like to do?"

"Monet and I have and I think it's better if she explains."

He continued leaning forward, but twisted to his right so his gaze, like Irani's, would rest on Monet before she spoke.

"Alonzo has become a project planning expert. He knows more about PERT/CPM than I do, and he wants to use it to lead several projects that will benefit Zimbabwe. I have outlined several of them to Darla, and she has agreed to officially hire him once she meets with both of us. He will have an office in this embassy and report to me. And she expects him to obtain an MBA that will add managerial expertise to his hands-on skills. We should let him describe what he has in mind."

Alonzo wasted no time.

"Monet's already clued me in on Darla's intentions for turning Africa into the next superpower. Well, we need to refortify the great green wall separating the deserts in the north from the grasslands leading to forests and jungles in the south. This'll fight climate change and desert expansion. We can do this by planting smart crops and implementing intelligent animal herding, and constructing solar panel and Martian farms on the desert side of the wall. And I can coordinate some technology transfer via your Austin businesses. What do you think?"

"Everyone better stay sharp if they want to keep up with you."

"And think about this, maybe Eve and Nari can help Monet look for joint opportunities with India on the political front. It's an up-and-coming superpower too. Eve says she and Nari are gonna visit Nila and Sanjay sometime after the election. Would you please mention this to them? It'll sound better coming from you."

"I will, but you won't need my help much longer."

Alonzo's face glowed like a 500-watt bulb. As Irani stood after picking her notepad off the table, Monet's smile offered a thank you before she said,

"No matter how much Alonzo or I learn, we'll always want your help. I will ask you to join us again in Africa when appropriate."

Monet's handshake came close to matching Alonzo's.

As election day approached, Irani could feel the pace of some activities beginning to slow, comparing it to reaching the eye of a hurricane, so she decided to call Odell. He picked up after the third ring.

"CFS Holistic Healthcare. How may I help?"

"Good morning, Odell. This is your silent partner. How are you?"

"Doing fine, Irani, and how about you?"

"I can say the same, and thanks for asking."

"You must be calling about our end-of-quarter meeting. Your timing's perfect, because I've got something you might like to do. I just set up a 'Caring Keepers Club' for parents of kids in our tutoring program. It's designed for parents who want to help underprivileged children by introducing them to their own kids and having them learn together. I know you don't have kids and always have a full load, but there's a black twelve-year-old girl from a single-parent home whose dad just stopped by. He needs help, and I thought she might warm up to you. You interested?"

"Why not? How about this, pick a day and time for us to talk about business and you can introduce me afterwards. If she likes me, I'll figure out if I can help."

"Good, so I'll call you when I've made the arrangements. You take care and I will too."

Electra talked more after Odell disconnected.

This will be a first for me – getting to know an adolescent girl. I've already covered the ends of the spectrum... Ariadne and Qama were single-digits, and my clone-children are early twenty-somethings who are on their way and know where they're going.

Gads, I'm getting old. I remember hearing on my twenty-first birthday my inner voice reciting one of Mother's poems about reaching

out to others. And it says I'd understand its meaning better as my empathy grows. What did she name it? I got it, it's called To the Point, and I can even recall the words.

> *It's taken years to understand,*
> *The focal point of Life.*
> *But now I see its majesty,*
> *No more internal strife.*

> *When young we think that all is ours,*
> *The world revolves round us.*
> *And when our whims aren't fully met,*
> *We make a terrible fuss.*

> *But look beyond your selfish self,*
> *For a selfless path that's right*
> *Reach out to those with heavy needs,*
> *Help make their burden light.*

You know what I wish?... that I could thank all my dearly departed loved ones for all they gave me… that I had understood and appreciated better all those magical moments. Well I can't, so I better pay it forward.

And so what if I'm getting older? Age is just a number if I stay engaged, and my memory's in good shape if I can recall all the verses. And when Odell calls, I'll make sure to remember the date.

Unlike her role model, Eve's swirl of activity kept her busy, especially on election day. She and Sabrina spent it at campaign headquarters, either talking to contacts in the field or watching the media. By late afternoon, unofficial exit polls indicated Genesee Huston would become the first woman President.

As soon as the West Coast polling places closed, she and Sabrina hurried to the hotel ballroom that would host Re-Gen's post-election party. Being among the first to arrive, they grabbed a snack and peered expectantly at the monitors as campaign workers and supporters trickled in. Their mood elevated during the early hours as the ballroom filled with people and their chatter, but a sobering chill seeped in as their candidate's initial lead shrank. By 11:30 it had become a deficit. Eve parked herself in front of a monitor to hear every explanation.

"Returns from the battleground states are starting to swing to the incumbent, and if the trend holds, the sitting President, though behind in the popular vote, might take the lead in the Electoral College. None of the networks are calling the race because what we're seeing confounds what polls and prognosticators have been telling us. Maybe the polling samples aren't representative. Maybe the software isn't all it's cracked up to be. Stay tuned for a long night."

Sabrina restrained Eve from rushing to re-Gen's War Room – a suite of hotel rooms set aside for Genesee, Brian, and veteran campaigners.

"Hey, settle down. There's nothing we can do but stay out of the way."

Eve sunk into a chair and placed a call to the only other person who could help.

Irani picked up as soon as she saw the caller I.D.

"Hello Eve. Let me guess, the ballroom mood is like a wake. No matter the outcome, please keep tonight in perspective. There's always another election."

A trickle of tears accompanied Eve's words.

"Oh Mother, how could the pollsters get it so wrong? What happened to all that margin-of-error accuracy hype?"

"That's a great question. Why don't you ask Nari?"

"Do you think I should stay until the Congresswoman speaks?"

"I would if I were you. You won't sleep if you go home."

"Where are you?"

"At my office watching the returns come in and about ready to go to bed."

"What do you see? What do you think?"

"Multi-colored maps showing lots of data but little accurate info because the analysts' software seems to be at odds with voters, so we're listening to repeats of platitudes meant to keep us tuned in.

The media's doing better today than in previous elections, but this one's different. But not to worry, answers will eventually emerge."

Eve sounded calmer when she finally ended the call, but Electra continued talking to herself.

I know how easy it is to get wrapped up in a cause. Even today I have to control my obsessive-compulsive tendencies. Eve's sort of the same, so I better keep setting a good example...

The networks declared the winner just before 3 a.m. because the incumbent had enough electoral votes. Genesee came to the ballroom a half-hour later to deliver a concession speech for a dejected audience that had shrunk by two-thirds. Those that remained were mostly young campaigners who looked ready to fall through the floor.

The Congresswoman stood erect as she spoke into the cameras.

"A very early good morning to all Americans or America's friends hearing my voice. I want to congratulate the American people who have exercised their right to vote in this 2160 Presidential election. They have spoken, and I congratulate the Democratic Party candidate for prevailing. Though I won more of the popular vote, the candidate who gets an absolute majority of Electoral College votes becomes our next President, and that will be the incumbent.

"Am I disappointed? Of course, but I am not disheartened, for my spirits are lifted by the support you have given to our Re-Gen Party and your desire to be part of a regenerated America led by a new middle class dedicated to the principles that I and your Re-Gen Party stand for. So, to those who voted for me, who campaigned for me, or are here for me now, be proud of what we have started and look forward to the next election. America can be proud too, for our nation continues demonstrating to the world how well our electoral system works.

"And though I am now unable to lead our new Party from an elected position towards the goals our people want, I pledge to lead from Vermont, my home state. And from there, and with your continued support, I shall continue working at the grass roots level to make America greater than ever.

"I know that all of us are tired, so I shall stop here, but I will have much more to say in the coming days and weeks and months as we take America higher and higher, building on what our predecessors have given us and raising the bar for the next generation to exceed.

"Thank you, and may your god of choice be with us."

The Senator came to her side and both waved to the cheering crowd before Gene walked to a cluster of reporters clamoring for brief interviews. It was only when she finished that Eve came to her. Her tears drowned words that never came as she hugged the Congresswoman. Gene hugged her right back, making room for Sabrina too.

Electra altered her pre-breakfast run the next day so she could multi-task by wearing a mini-radio tuned into two analysts batting questions back and forth on a popular political talk show.

"… Do you think that some of the Social Media warnings about extremist groups of all stripes taking their discontent to the steps of the Capitol have merit? Look what happened after the 2020 elections. Demonstrators actually stormed into the chambers of Congress to abort Electoral College vote-counting. I'd call that a tale of twice-told voting."

"I like your clever comparison to a book by Hawthorne – 'Twice-Told Tales'– and a horror movie bearing the same name that told among other things the dangers awaiting the young. Today's young voters like the Re-Gen Party, but I hope they're smarter and more civilized now. And if they do vote with their feet on electoral voting day, the Capitol Police are much better prepared. You know the saying, 'Fool me once, shame on you, fool me twice shame on me.' That's probably why no rowdies have ever tried again to halt Electoral College voting."

"Yes, but what about the conspiracy theories that vote-counting was rigged to keep the incumbent in power for the benefit of the one-percenters?"

"Voter fraud conspiracies have been bandied about ever since voting booths. The only difference today might be how Social Media can inflame the passions even before any smoke is reported.

The government's watchdog CIA and other agencies have found nothing to corroborate, even though the results confound the forecasters. Perhaps we should stay tuned…"

Electra listened all the way home, and after breakfast Irani tuned in to Eve, calling late that morning and speaking first.

"You sound like you've survived your first campaign. And please remember our candidate's closing remarks. She'll be back. And you will too after your trip to India.

"Have you been listening to some of the news analysts? They're downplaying possible demonstrations and conspiracy theories. What do you think?"

"According to my contacts, most of the activist groups avoid talking on the Internet or in Cyberspace so they stay under the radar. But they're telling me to watch for action sooner rather than later. I'll have to ask Nari about conspiracy theory angles. My contacts don't know anything about them."

"Please do yourself and me a big favor. Use your head and don't get swept up in any Capitol demonstrations. Watch some online videos and you'll see that the Capitol Police, though kinder and gentler than their foreign counterparts, will still crack heads – no matter white or black or brown or whatever color or identity group – if protestors push beyond the barriers."

"I promise. The Congresswoman told me to take a break until January, so I'll concentrate on finals week and my trip to India. And don't worry, I'll keep you in the loop. Bye."

Irani kept herself in the loop while working on her array of projects. And the loop unexpectedly circled the Capitol Friday morning. She kept glued to her office monitor as all stations zeroed in on a growing crowd facing reinforced security on the other side of barricades.

The demonstrations began peacefully enough. Young people of all types had banded together to protest the election outcome. Their spokespersons sounded sensible, but by midafternoon more assertive people took over. They led the charge through the barricades and stampeded up the Capitol steps. But as Electra had predicted, they were met by a force that reversed the crowd's direction and drove them off the grounds.

Electra grimaced while watching live coverage capturing police pummeling tough-looking older types as well as college-age males and females. Order had been restored by 8 p.m. and cleanup soon followed. Before falling asleep, she heard a broadcast that summarized the day's excitement.

"… And so, we have order restored using what is still the only convincing method when people become unruly – coercive force that today is kinder and gentler but gets the job done. Acoustic weapons and jamming technology are able to replace brute force. But we must ask why did the more divisive groups break ranks from the younger crowd and through the barricades when they should have known the attempt would fail? Will they regroup and charge again a week or a month from now? We shall have to listen to Social Media or have the Government search deeper. Or might they be part of a still-invisible conspiracy led from inside our borders or from enemies beyond? These are questions that will worry all of us until answered. And how did countries abroad view this week's siege? Perhaps they will see us still struggling to restrain some of our flawed inclinations, or maybe they will give us credit for how we have improved. Only the testament of time will tell, but please sleep as best you can, because we, the people of American media, have renewed a campaign pledge promoted first by the Re-Gen Party and then copied by their opponents to keep you informed with the truth, the whole truth, and nothing but the truth, regardless of what any elitist group might say or do. We are raising the bar to keep deepfakes and GAN AI from distorting the facts. Please listen for more tomorrow and in the days to come…"

Trent Booker had been listening nonstop to similar broadcasts, pleased that no agency inside or outside the Government had even a glimmer of the connection between his machinations and the siege. And he was equally pleased that there had been no leaks or hacking into any members of his covertly implemented "Vote Rebalancing" plan. Trent smiled himself to sleep that night.

Chapter 24
December 2160

"Visits to Different Worlds"

DC settled down after the election and short-lived Capitol siege, as did the nation; Irani used the relative calm to settle into her usual December schedule, which would be less frenetic this year.

Electra came to the fore and used the post-Thanksgiving weekend to review the performance of her AAM funds. They required little attention during the year because her AI-empowered apps constantly monitored and rebalanced portfolios according to the financial world's climate. As expected, they outperformed the competition, but she wanted to know what disruptions they had detected.

I picked up hints at the World Economics and Finance forums that there's much going on below the radar, like shadow banking and currency manipulation. Off-balance-sheet loans coming from non-bank financial companies can jeopardize overall market stability, as can currency meddling. I better snoop into Big Data or hidden directories using my Social Forecasting and intrusion apps. Maybe I can uncover patterns that indicate bad guys are trying to manipulate the financial world.

But she found nothing conclusive after four hours of digging. Nor did she find any patterns when she looked for what could have warned the Government about simmering unrest. After terminating the search, she walked away to get a Coke and a handful of Oreos. When she returned to her office workstation, she summarized why she had come up empty.

This is the third time this year I've struck out when using my intrusion and hacking apps to find causes and culprits. It looks like my contingent conclusions are correct. My enemies have either developed Cybersecurity systems that are better than mine, or they've taken their correspondence offline where no apps, not even mine, can go. Well, I've done my best, so I'll put follow-up at the bottom of my list and do something else…

Next up for Irani would be an early Saturday morning visit to CFS Holistic Healthcare. Odell had made all the arrangements for her to meet an adolescent girl, so the only thing Irani had to do was show up and bring whatever might be useful.

Odell waved her into his open-partition work area as soon as he spotted her. Irani assessed the girl sitting across as she approached.

Hmm, like he said, she's a tallish, thin black girl attired like a typical twelve-year-old. He mentioned that she doesn't like anyone pointing out her lazy eye condition – exotropia – that makes her left eye turn outward, but it doesn't spoil her looks… perhaps she'll outgrow it as she gets older and she'll be even prettier. But he didn't mention the unkempt frizzy hair or the smirky expression. But no problem. Let's see what I can do.

Odell stood when she came in.

"Well hello, Irani. Please next to the young lady I'd like you to meet. Tiana, please say hi to Miss Irani."

Tiana stopped chewing her nails just long enough to do so and make brief eye contact.

"Hello, Tiana. What a distinctive name. Do your friends call you 'Tea' or 'Tia?' Or do you prefer another?"

"They call me Tea."

"Well, I hope you'll let me call you Tea after you get to know me."

"Uh, maybe."

Odell kept the conversation moving.

"Why don't you give Miss Irani some information about yourself?"

"Like what? My social security number? Or my cell? How about my tablet logon I.D. and password? I don't have them."

Odell's smile began to slip, but he tried to catch Tiana's interest.

"Well, why not tell us what you like to do?"

"You mean when I'm here, or in school, or with my friends?"

Irani decided to end a game of twenty questions that neither she nor Odell could win. She removed an item from her shoulder bag that she knew would catch Tiana's attention, placing it close before talking.

"Why don't you take Tiana and me to a place where I can show her some of the special apps I have on my tablet?"

That worked. Tiana picked it up before following Odell. Irani walked close behind. When situated, Tiana powered up and then asked for help navigating. Irani sat next to her and then said,

"Here's the GUI of a popular new game. I haven't played it yet, but maybe you can show me."

Playing the game unleashed Tiana's personality. Electra looked and listened as Tiana dived into the GUI.

What a transformation. She's articulate and bright when playing the game... and so appropriate for her last name. She sparkles like a diamond reflecting sunlight. I must find other interests that catch her fancy.

Tiana kept showing and telling until Odell stopped the action an hour later.

"Time to go, young lady. We want to get you home in time for lunch, but I just had a call from your father. He has to work and can't pick you up, so I'll drive you home."

Tea's scrunched nose announced a different possibility before she pointed and said,

"Can't she, uh, Miss Irani, take me?"

Gazes turned Irani's way before she replied.

"If that's OK with her father. Please call to ask if we can stop at McDonald's. I need something to replenish the energy drain after Tea helped train my brain."

Even Tea cracked a smile at the reply. Odell gave them the OK five minutes later.

Tea asked most of the questions on the drive and at the booth, stopping only long enough to pop in French fries and giving Irani a chance to ask some questions.

"When I was your age, I liked having the run of the house without any interference from adults. How about you?"

"Yeah, I like being treated that way. It makes me feel respected."

Tea took another bite from her cheeseburger, allowing Irani to ask again.

"Does your Dad often work on the weekends?"

"Sometimes, but he just got promoted to shift supervisor, so maybe he'll work less. You know, dish off work to others."

Irani nodded before saying, "Yes, that's one way to look at it, but a good manager leads by example, by pitching in and helping. Don't you do that with your study group at school?"

"Yeah, sometimes, but they got better laptops. I wish I had yours."

"Well, let's do this. You can borrow mine."

"For how long?"

"Until you don't want me to hang out with you anymore. Deal?"

Her nod before taking another bite said yes.

Tea called out directions to her apartment building, Edgewood Public Housing, located in northeast DC. As she drove through adjacent neighborhoods, Irani kept a comparison to herself that Tea was still too young to make.

DC's slum areas are better now than twenty years ago, but passing through is like visiting a different world. Too bad the Congresswoman lost. I could have worked behind the scenes to pep some of them up. Maybe next election…

Tea invited her new friend in for an apartment tour. She grabbed Irani's hand and led her through while Electra made notes.

Her dad's made the place OK for a father-daughter household, but a mother's touch would add much, and even more will be needed when Tea becomes a teen-ager. Hey, slow down. Enjoy right now…

As the tour wound down, Irani edged to the front door before saying,

"I'm so happy you had a good time today. Please have your dad talk with Odell if you'd like to do this again."

"Are you kidding? I'm gonna call him right now. You be ready for next Saturday."

Irani rubbed the top of Tea's head and then said, "That's a deal. See you same time, same place, and please bring the tablet for more fun and games."

Irani set herself up on Sunday to house-sit during Nari's and Eve's trip to India. She volunteered to drive them to the airport Monday afternoon, but Alonzo had already filled the driver's role, so she invited him and Monet for a dinner that she would prepare while the girls packed.

Alonzo set a cheery tone as soon as everyone was eating, kidding that the travelers should find the climate in Mumbai calmer than what DC had just experienced. He glanced around the table before locking his gaze on Eve and saying more.

"I've checked all details and can report that you should have a clear path on your 7900-mile flight to Mumbai. Weather looks good for departing at 5:30 p.m. and arriving Mumbai time at 10:30 Tuesday evening. According to the airline, it'll take about nineteen-and-a-half hours and that includes one stop, so you'll have plenty of time to gossip about Nila and Sanjay, and when you get there, here's a fact you can impress him with.

"Some Indian time zones are only thirty minutes apart. And why? Probably for political reasons. India doesn't always get along with its border neighbors – Pakistan and China. Ask Sanjay to fill you in."

Nari spoke before Eve could.

"We can start gossiping about Nila right now. She's sort of a different person. I thought she'd miss me and living in the U.S., but it doesn't seem so. I guess living in a different world'll do that. She even posted at-home pictures in which she's wearing saris."

Alonzo asked, "What about Sanjay?"

"He's dressed like he did in Cairo, but from the smile on his face I think he likes the new Nila even more than the old."

No one spoke until Monet said, "I can appreciate what you say because I too have made a similar transition. And from what I know about your sister, she will have combined the best she has found with the best of her old life. All of us do that, but in Nila's case, she has found much that is new while living in a such a different place."

Irani spoke from the head of the table.

"And when our travelers come back, they can tell us what they learned about Indian socio-politics and how to use it in DC's political climate. And who knows, maybe that'll be the same as when they left? But probably not, climates are always changing…"

Sitting in the peaceful stillness of the family room after the travelers had gone to bed, Electra contemplated the adventure awaiting them.

Eve and Nari should bring back insights regarding India, and I must pretend to be surprised because I can never tell them I visited forty years ago to attend Grandfather Ramanujan's funeral. I learned so much about Indira's life before she went to Harvard as well as my grandparents and uncle. And I uncovered secrets I can share with only one entity – Indira the Singularity. Do I miss not sharing with another person? After all, what would have become of Robinson Crusoe if he couldn't talk to Friday?

No, I don't. Indira surpasses the Turing test no matter how many levels of Tetrarch exponentiation mere mortals choose. And in any contest against her, they will lose. I would too, but that's OK because in her silicon-substrate way, she loves me as I love her. And I love her as much as I love Eve. But how can that be? One lives in 3-D Space and the other in Cyberspace.

Electra felt an emotional tingling stir to life, bringing with it new thoughts.

Now I see… love lives in the emotional persona, the resultant of an all-encompassing relationship comprised of the physical, emotional, and cognitive dimensions. Think of all the people who have fallen in love or remained in that state in spite of long distance or time separation. I finally understand. And people treasure keepsakes not for their physical dimensions but for the emotions they bring to life, and those emotions bring with them the feeling of love. There's more to think about, but I'm all thought out. I'll let the lightning brain do that while I sleep…

Travelers and hosts had agreed on an arrival plan. Nari and Eve would rest on the flight so they could stay awake for most of the post-arrival day, that way reducing jetlag, and they would grab a cab or rideshare to Nila and Sanjay's new home. Both worked for the software company Sanjay's father – aka Baba – owned and Nila's school – Indian Institute of Technology – had just begun yearend break, so the foursome could talk until sunrise or beyond.

Nari and Sanjay greeted them at the front door when the cab puttered in at 2 a.m. The sisters hugged and then opened their arms to bring in Sanjay, who looked as happy as in the photos. He took their luggage to an extra bedroom while Nila took her sisters to the kitchen where Sanjay joined them at the table for a snack. Nila explained what was before them.

"You can have the usual American cereals or dish up some of Sanjay's favorite – Kanda Poha that's got mild spices, peanuts, and lots of protein and iron. And your choice of tea or Coke."

Sanjay added, "You have three weeks to sample this new-for-you food, so ease into it. And while you're doing that, let me tell you about our agenda. If Alonzo, Monet, and Yang were here, it would be like a Cairo reunion of the Magnificent Seven."

Eve said, "But even better. All of us have adapted to our climates and are ready to explore more. So, what have you lined up?"

"I will be your primary travel guide, but Nila has learned so much so quickly. She'll take over in those areas where she now knows more than I. We'll start by getting you familiar with what it's like living in Mumbai, and then in a couple of days we'll fly to Kanpoor for a Ganges River boat tour, and then take a train to sightsee in New Delhi. Then we come back to show you more of Mumbai and what our careers are like."

Nari waited for the right time to ask instead of barging in.

"Will you and Nila wear native clothing like the sari she's got on now?"

Gazes followed Sanjay's to Nila, who said, "We'll wear contemporary clothes like yours. Sanjay likes to wear western clothing everywhere, but when I'm at home I like to put on traditional Indian attire. And if you like, I'll give you some saris you can try. You might find they give you more freedom than the tight-fitting American styles."

Eve nodded yes before Nari said, "And speaking of freedom, why don't you tell us what you meant in the EMail you sent me about the eternal freedom you find in Hinduism. You talk and we'll eat."

As everyone settled to listen, Eve made an observation only to herself.

What a role reversal. Nila's more surefooted and mature than Nari. Maybe we can learn from her.

"All of you have studied more about religion and philosophy than me, but I've concentrated on Hinduism. I'm picking my way through its sacred texts, and there are so many, like the *Vedas, Upanishads, Puranas,* and *Yugas.* And I'm reading explanations, not original texts. Maybe I'll do that later. But all the scholars say that Hinduism takes a deeper look than other religions and philosophies into the questions we all ask... you know, the who and what am I, and the where did I come from and where am I going. These questions are covered in philosophy's three branches – Metaphysics and Ontology for what exists, Epistemology for how do I know, and Ethics or Axiology for what should I do about it. And because Hinduism is cyclic rather than linear, it answers them all via birth, growth, decay, and death that leads via reincarnation back to rebirth. And unlike Western religions, its not so driven by material things or time. In fact, the *Yugas* match the four stages in the cycle to four distinct time periods, each lasting for thousands and thousands of years."

Eve asked, "What about Karma? How does that figure in?"

"Karma is the first of Hinduism's four principles and it is the sum of our past and present actions that compose our essence, our soul. And unlike other religions, death is not a judgement to be feared but instead an exalted experience through which our soul transcends and then comes back via Reincarnation, which is the second principle.

"The third is our Unity with a transcendent all-encompassing God that we will become one with after we reach that state of contemplation after enough reincarnation cycles. And the fourth is Dharma, which is the eternal and inherent nature of reality, regarded as a cosmic law underlying right behavior and social order."

Both Nari and Eve looked like they had a question ready, but Nari spoke first.

"You said there's one God, but Hinduism talks about many. What gives?"

"The One encompasses many. Brahma is the creator, Vishnu the maintainer, and Shiva the destroyer. And there are many others that inhabit the world. Families can worship them because they may embody their relatives. And the One is considered to be the only God of other religions, like Judeo-Christianity and Islam."

Eve asked her question.

"Do you think any of this jibes with contemporary science?"

"Sure does. Some of the quantum physics mumbo jumbo talks about multiple universes along with a never-ending cycle of Big Bangs followed by Big Crunches. Hinduism handles these and the eternity of time maybe better than today's high-energy physics, which according to what some of the videos say has morphed from a science into a religion because none of its theories can be proved by observing measurable phenomena."

Eve pushed further.

"But you do computer work, which is science-like. How do you reconcile the two?"

"Unlike physics, the world of computers and its math is self contained in its own axioms, even though it has unresolvable inconsistencies. According to Hinduism, the world is a glorious place for our souls to evolve via experience and go from darkness to light and from death to immortality. And I enjoy the journey by working and living like I do."

Sanjay could tell that the barrage of questions was taking its toll, so he stepped in.

"I think Hinduism is the reason why India is what it is today. Hinduism and Indian culture are each over 6,000 years old and always intertwined. You can read that in two of our epics – the Ramayana and the Mahabharata – which record the struggles of princes and peoples."

Sanjay waited for another Eve question.

"What about the Bhagavad Gita? What's that?"

"Your questions show you know a lot already. It's "The Song of God" and is contained in the Mahabharata, which dates to about 200 BCE, whereas the Ramayana is 200 or so years older."

Now Nari asked another question.

"How did India survive for so long? Countries, just like their forms of government, usually get replaced."

"It's true. Ancient India comprised many warring kingdoms, but for the most part they all shared a common culture. And when foreigners invaded, they fell under the spell of India. We absorbed them. And it wasn't until the 18th century that India lost its independence because of British Imperialism. But our passive resistance outlasted them; however, they forced us to divide along religious lines into Hindu India and Muslim East and West Pakistan. But nearly fifteen years later in 1971, East Pakistan broke free with India's help to become Bangladesh, which of course led to war. Even today, India and Pakistan are usually at odds, but I expect India and Hinduism to survive any future short-term international struggles because I think both offer better alternatives to what is now emerging."

Nila recovered enough to continue.

"Look, we're all on break, so we don't have to cram everything into this conversation. I'm tired, and you two must be even more so, so let's sleep until we wake up and go from there."

Everyone agreed and followed Sanjay to the sleeping quarters. Sleep came quickly, but not before Nari's final comment that she whispered to Eve.

"I used to consider myself the bigger sister, but not any longer. Nila's grown beyond me. She really knows her philosophy. I never heard the word 'Axiology' until tonight."

"Me too, but I guess that's good. We can learn from her and from India too. Now stop talking so we can sleep on it."

Sanjay began his tour early afternoon by driving the foursome to a more typical area than his upscale neighborhood and then leading them on foot through streets teeming with people spilling off sidewalks and getting close to cars that were bumper-to-bumper in left lanes. He added just enough commentary so his guests could fill in the rest.

"India's population is more similar to Africa's than China's. People are still moving from rural villages to metro areas, and

Mumbai looks pretty much like all big cities. A large percentage live in slums, but unlike cities in America, you'll find pockets of the poor interspersed in the better neighborhoods, and you'll see many street vendors hawking their wares everywhere."

Eve looked and listened and commented to herself.

So many kids, and lots of happy faces that look interested in talking to tourists. And different languages too. Sanjay said most Mumbians speak English as well as a Hindi dialect. And there's even Hinglish, a Hindi-English combo that I can sort of understand.

Ending the tour at a traditional restaurant, Sanjay offered advice as everyone scanned the menu.

"Tourists love the array of spices found in Indian recipes. Curry is the most famous, but cardamon, coriander, and cumin are well known too, as are ginger, nutmeg, and turmeric.

"Pick what sounds good, but choose dishes marked mild until you're here a bit longer. And save room for gulab jamum, a most popular dessert. They're soft and spongy bite-sized balls made of flour and milk and soaked in syrup."

A lively discussion continued all the way through dessert. Eve asked Sanjay before the group headed back about the river cruise.

"The Ganges tour will give you a glimpse at smaller and older village-like cities. Indian civilization grew up along the Indus and Ganges rivers, just like Egypt along the Nile and Mesopotamia along the Euphrates and Tigris. And I'll be a passenger too. We'll let the boat's tour guide do the talking."

Nila added, "Kanpoor used to be called Cawnpore and is historically significant due to the 'Indian Mutiny' uprising caused by British rule through the East India Company. We can have Sanjay tell us more about India's history and politics when we tour New Delhi."

Everyone glanced from Nila to Sanjay.

"I plan to let our New Delhi tour guide do the honors. He's the pro. But let us go home and relax. Nila can lead us through Yoga exercises before bed that can increase our mindfulness, which puts us in touch with the present moment. And that will help us tomorrow as we take our leisure while preparing for our flight the next day to Kanpoor."

Sanjay's thoughtful planning brought the foursome refreshed and ready to tour early morning several days later. The tour guide started talking as soon as the boat pulled away.

"Welcome tourists and pilgrims alike. We are about to show you a cross section of Indian people living along India's holiest river, the Ganges. It runs east for over 1,500 miles from the western Himalayas to the Bay of Bengal. It is a lifeline for north India's plains and towns; the river is also a place of Hindu pilgrimage at cities such as Rishikesh and Varanasi—drawing visitors to humbling scenes of religious devotion. I am sure you will enjoy as well as learn much on our voyage…"

Even Nari agreed when the boat returned that the half-day tour was worth every rupee.

The New Delhi tour two days later gave the group an excellent overview of India's capital as well as current events. The guide started talking as soon as the bus started moving.

"New Delhi is everything you would expect for the capital of a soon-to-be superpower. Wide boulevards and parks, modern buildings and bustling crowds of public servants serving world's largest democracy. And our military buildup continues on the Andeban and Nicobar archipelago, including more seabed-anchored underwater sound surveillance that is meant to keep tabs on China's sea power. We participate in an Asian-like NATO command that includes India and Japan, Malaysia, Australia, and the United States. And New Delhi is big and complicated because India has so many diverse regions and cultures, but there is growing grassroots support for Indian Nationalism…"

The tour ended in time for an early afternoon lunch. Sanjay started the discussion.

"My Baba follows politics closely for business and economic reasons, and I will pay more attention as I move up in his company. Nila might do the same."

"Maybe not, but if surveillance software keeps grow exponentially, maybe I'll have to."

Nari said, "I don't know, but if Yang and Monet and Alonzo were here, you could ask them."

Eve expanded what Nari had started.

"There might be software and political connections in the future between India and Africa to keep China at bay. I'm sure Yang would have a lot to say, as would Monet. Alonzo too, because his career at the Zimbabwean embassy in DC is beginning to take shape, but I've had enough politics for one day. What's up for the afternoon?"

"We'll take our own walking tour of old Delhi, where we will stroll on narrow streets to markets the likes of which you haven't yet seen, and you'll see a mix of people in colorful clothes speaking different languages, but all getting along. You will enjoy the contrast."

Sanjay's prediction proved to be correct. All four slept well and awoke ready for their late morning two-hour flight back to Mumbai, where they were happy to have a dinner prepared by Nila and Sanjay.

After helping Nila clear the table, Sanjay said, "We will let Nari and Eve decide if they would like to rest tomorrow or take a Bollywood tour."

They looked at one another before Eve spoke.

"I think we're ready for another tour. What do you recommend?"

"I'll purchase tour packages. It'll save time and also my voice."

Eve was happy that Sanjay drove the group to a central staging area for the tour buses, but told only herself why.

I'm not ready to drive on the left. And there's so much traffic on multi-lane highways and surface streets. But at least there are no elephants or cows roaming among the cars like I saw in some of the smaller places along the Ganges. I bet Nila lets Sanjay do all the driving… but maybe not. She's become a very competent person, ahead of me or Nari. Good for her and good for me to see.

Sanjay herded his group towards an awaiting bus. A man with a megaphone began speaking as soon as the bus pulled away.

"Welcome aboard the best Bollywood tour bus rupees can buy. We will drive you through the maze of streets lined with props and buildings that make up the biggest film capital in the world, bigger even than Hollywood or Chinawood. And we will stop along the way to take you through studios so you can see movie-making in action.

"Bollywood is the Hindi-language sector of India's film industry, and it started making sound movies in the 1930's. Stars, not plots were the driving force at the beginning, and from there it has grown to feature formulaic story lines, expertly choreographed fight scenes, spectacular song-and-dance routines, and emotion-charged melodrama featuring larger-than life heroes and heroines.

"Our people love Bollywood movies. They buy 2.5 billion tickets annually, beating China by about 200 million and the United States by 800 million. And like everything in India, Bollywood is massive, making well over a thousand movies a year, which is twice the number made by Hollywood or Chinawood.

"Films are made so fast that sometimes actors and actresses on a set will shoot scenes for four different films at a time, all sharing the same backgrounds as well as stars. And sometimes the scripts are even hand-written."

The guide stopped talking when the bus steered to the left before slowing down. He steadied himself before saying more.

"I see we are approaching our first stop, so get ready to see Bollywood in action."

The foursome stopped for a late lunch on the drive back. Led by Sanjay, the discussion centered on what they had just seen, but Eve steered the talk to a related subject.

"You can call filmmaking an art form, but what about Indian music? I've never listened to any. What can you tell us?"

Sanjay plucked an answer from memory.

"The sitar is the main instrument used in Hindustani classical music. Indian music contains no harmony and is often completely improvised and rarely written down. Music in India began as an integral part of socio-religious life.

"It has a history spanning several millennia and developed over several geo-locations spanning the sub-continent. And owing to India's vastness and diversity, Indian music encompasses numerous genres, multiple varieties and forms which in addition to classical include folk, rock, and pop. But today, as in much of the world, American pop culture has come to dominate music as well as film."

Nila looked at her cell phone before saying, "We can talk more when we get home. Let's leave now and keep ahead of the traffic."

As the group lounged in the family room that evening, Nari pointed to the wall-mounted monitor.

"You know, we haven't tuned in to any news broadcasts for over a week. Why don't we see if the outside world still exists?"

Eve had been listening for a suitable segue, and Nari's words had just given it.

"Hey, that question goes all the way back to pre-Socratic Greek philosophers. Heraclitus said you can't step into the same river twice because it's always changing, and Parmenides said you only need to look at it once because it never is. His famous quote is 'Whatever is, is.' Maybe Nila can tell us what Hinduism would say."

Nila rolled her head before answering.

"This isn't a direct quote, but I would say that what goes around comes around." Then she flipped on a 24/7 international newscast.

Everyone settled back to look and listen.

"… And now to the medical climate. It appears that the new year may bring the world to the brink of another viral disruption caused by several outbreaks that are resisting the international community's best efforts being spearheaded by the World Health Organization and America's CDC. Among them are the new and conspiracy-laden X-Virus plus mutated strains of Flu and Covid. There will be more to this story as the viruses continue spreading.

"And America's political climate may face the same new year's fate. The recent Presidential election results have been invalidated. There's mounting evidence that information leaked about a conspiracy among the battleground-state Governors and one or more foreign powers did in fact rig the election. And a subsequent leak following closely on the heels of the first heightens the concern that there could be another conspiracy intent on controlling the world's money and banking climate. We might not want to call the new year 'happy,' but it assuredly will be exciting…"

Nila punched the mute button as everyone sprang to attention; Eve was the first to speak.

"Sanjay, what computer can we use? Nari and I better surf the Net for the full story on the election results. We'll tell everyone as soon as we've pieced together the latest facts."

The duo trooped back in an hour later, their expressions glum.

"America's got a big problem, and here's the latest. There's speculation that the two leaks come from the same unknown source. But it must be a disgruntled insider, because the information is so specific. The CIA and its snoopers think that either China or Russia – or maybe they worked together – masterminded the buyout of all the governors in the swing states. The Governors and their vote-counting conspirators changed enough votes to push the incumbent to victory in the Electoral College. Enough of the swing-state Governors have admitted to the fraud. And here's what happens next.

"The Constitution doesn't have explicit instructions, other than generalities about the people and Congress and the Supreme Court, but it looks like all states will hold another Presidential election as soon as possible using the four Pres-V.P. pairs that were on the first ballot. The actual date and campaigning details are being sorted out now while the investigation continues."

Sanjay said, "Aren't you and Nari working for the Re-Gen Party candidate? Maybe you and Nari should fly back now?"

Nari looked at Eve, who said, "We decided against it. Your maybe sister-in-law will tell you why."

"No, the senior campaign officials have to make the big decisions. Eve and I will do our part once they point us in the right direction. We won't know much until mid-January, so we'll stick with our travel schedule."

Eve said, "We're not gonna worry about what's outside our control, and that includes our plane tickets. We can't change the departure dates and besides, it's calmer in your world than in whatever world awaits us in DC…"

Chapter 25
January 2161

"Out of the Shadows"

The leaked revelations unleashed chaotic special interest group storms first in Washington before spreading across the nation, though of lesser severity the farther from the seat of power. Although they hadn't tangibly touched Irani's private world or professional activities yet, she knew it was only a matter of time until they did, so she used the Holiday break to prepare for the inevitable; Electra summarized on the first Sunday evening of the new year the why and the what she might face soon.

Even after my twenty-year suspension, old adversaries have new agents unwittingly tracking the old Electra's new identity because I'm intentionally tracking their meddling. Russia and China might be roiling international financial markets to steer developing nations into their camp. Big Data and Big Pharma companies might be after my AI-empowered algorithms and vaccines, and political parties might be targeting the Congresswoman. And then there are the wildcards... the old rogue Isilabad and the new X-Virus. I've been careless and have shown up on their radar, but I've tried to cover my tracks. Going forward, I'll have to watch my back that much closer. And I've picked up other people whose backs I have to watch. But I've also picked up new allies. I'll have to figure out what roles they can play.

But at least I know what I'll do this week and next. And I should be able to cruise —

nothing to gain or lose – just maintain the status quo. First up, Professor Plannert's scanning committee meeting Tuesday morning. I've delivered everything they asked for, so I can just sit and listen to them... and to me.

When Irani waltzed into the conference room five minutes ahead of schedule, Professor Plannert rose from the head of the table to greet her.

"Happy New Year, Doctor Ramani, please sit next to me."

Irani returned his cheery greeting and smile, but Electra spoke to herself.

Hmm, this is the first time he's ever called me Doctor Ramani and seated me near the front. Something's brewing... I better pay stricter attention.

Irani listened to the banter being traded among the members who were already seated; one of them aimed a question at her just before Plannert was about to start the meeting.

"I say, Professor Ramani, I'm still at a loss whenever Quantum Physics pops up. You've demonstrated a talent with words. Would you be so good as to provide a brief exegesis?"

Her smile stayed on even though the words disturbed her.

Jesus, where'd that come from? Well, let's make it simple enough for most mere mortals.

"I'd be happy to. Please hold for a sec... I'll sketch some notes that you to keep."

Electra dashed off five bullet points and then gave the page away, talking ten seconds later.

Some Quanta regarding Quantum Mechanics

- Humans are limited by what the brain is capable of understanding when using the language of words or numbers. Wittgenstein, Godel, and the Explosion Principle say so.

- Philosophers use words and fuzzy thoughts when describing the World about them and call it Metaphysics.

- Scientists use numbers and precise theories when doing the same and call it Physics.

- Archimedes is the first scientist, but Newton put science on the cognitive map when coming up with his profound Classical Laws of Motion.

- Other Enlightenment and Modern Scientists added concepts that sharpened understanding of Matter and Energy and Motion, all intended to extend our ability to explain cause and effect and predict the future.

"Philosophers and scientists do the best they can, but some aspects of reality are beyond their grasp. Nevertheless, they progress asymptotically towards the limits of what they can ever know.

"Newton did a masterful job using numbers and precise concepts to develop his Three Laws of Motion. They worked well for three-hundred years until scientists developed tools that were capable of drilling down to the atomic level. When scientists looked that deep, they couldn't understand the nature of reality. So, here's what happened next."

Irani paused for Electra to scribble more.

The Way Out

- Einstein, Planck, Heisenberg, and Schrodinger developed new theories and definitions that extended Classical Physics Least-Action Optimization Principle to a Quantum Physics Analogy (early 1900's)

- They reformulated the Hamiltonian (total energy of a system) and the Lagrangian (trajectory of a system) into a probabilistic wave-particle duality function that might unite the very large (Cosmology and General Relativity) with the very small (atoms and their constituents).

- 1965 Nobel Prize in Physics (Feynman, Schwinger, Tomonaga) is the highwater mark.

- It accelerated the pursuit of the "Grand Unified Field Theory."

She continued after handing it out.

"The best and brightest physicists revolutionized the view of reality by putting some of the classical physics concepts into a different point of view. Einstein's Relativity explored how beams of light behave and Heisenberg's Uncertainty Principle let Schrodinger come up with probability waves. Optimism ruled; a 'Grand Unified Field Theory,' which today is called 'The Theory of Everything,' began to emerge on the horizon. But it never materialized because of these problems."

There was another pause while she wrote again.

What Went Wrong

- New particles, attributes, and conjectures (Fermions and Bosons, Quarks and Leptons) (Spin and Strangeness, Color and Charm) (Tunneling, Entanglement, Coherence and Superposition) led to a black hole that sucked in all understanding.

- Mathematical Constructs became unfathomable.

- Fantasy force fields associated with each new particle had to be invented to overcome singularities (values where equations blow up)

- Thought Experiments replaced Observation/Measurement of actual Phenomena

- HIGH ENERGY PHYSICS NO LONGER A SCIENCE! IT HAS MORPHED INTO A RELIGION! (SEE POPPER ON FALSIFIABILITY)

- No way out until another radical breakthrough dawns, leading to Observational/Measurable Progress.

"I could list others but what I put here tells most of the story. I won't recite it back to you, but you can figure out what went wrong. In their desire to find beauty and symmetry in their mathematical models, high-energy physicists began inventing fantastic stories to explain what their equations couldn't, and each time they did, they soon had to come up with another even more implausible chapter, taking them even further away from observable reality. They've been stumped for over two-hundred years."

Glancing at the members' faces, Electra could see they were getting bored, so she wrapped up the monologue.

"I wouldn't want to argue with them because it's hard to convince a person to change their views, even if tangible evidence – or lack of any – might support the other side. But you can use Occam's Razor to cut hucksters down to size if one of them ever starts criticizing your position; here's a wonderful 'silencer'; ask why and how the entropy that is written as a series of zeros and ones – we can call it information – on the surface of a black hole describes what's inside?"

Irani's silence ended her impromptu lecture.

Most of the committee members merely glanced at the notes being circulated, but several actually studied them before sliding the notes along. One of them asked,

"How can you possibly recite so much so quickly? You must be brilliant. Why aren't you engaged in research?"

Irani trotted out an answer that Electra had constructed long ago.

"I'm not that smart, I've just got a good brain that's good at synthesizing."

Professor Plannert used what Irani had just said to segue subjects.

"Your unassuming statement confirms why we are here today. Over the course of your coming to our meetings, you have given us many insights into a variety of interests – Climate Change, Earthquake and Volcanic Forecasting, and Viral Pandemics to name but a few – as well as their economic implications. And that is why we want you to become Director of Multi-Partner Projects, reporting jointly to me and GWU's Board of Directors. You are so well connected to R&D, Business, and Government, and have been so generous sharing your insights with us. We want to reward your efforts by elevating your position in all those circles as well as in the academic community. It is time for you to step out of the shadows. Let me describe what we have in mind…"

Professor Plannert treated Irani to lunch afterwards at the GWU Faculty Club, describing the perks that would accompany the position. She listened to him as well as Electra.

I'm genuinely touched by his sincerity… but he's offering me an opportunity that could have downside risks he mustn't know about. I better find an excuse to delay giving my decision.

Irani sat motionless until the Professor finished. Then she licked her lips before speaking.

"Well, you've both surprised and flattered me, and as I always try to do, I want to under-promise and over-deliver. I must review my commitments for this year to confirm I can handle everything if I accept your generous offer. May I give you my answer next Monday?"

"That's fine with me, I would do the same if an opportunity like this came my way. And please make sure it's what you want to do; make it a win-win, as you are fond of saying."

Electra considered the pros and cons as she drove to her office.

No doubt I handle the workload… and I can learn more about current research and do more climate surveillance. But can I stay below the radar? Maybe that'll become another game. There's no rush to decide this minute, so let's defer it and think about what's coming up Thursday. Congresswoman Huston, I'm on my way.

Irani had researched every shred of information on the leaked conspiracies, adding what she found by using her Social Forecasting apps to burrow into Big Data. Based on all the facts uncovered, she had outlined different campaign approaches but could fine-tune the details only after hearing what the candidate wanted. And that would be front and center at the one-on-one meeting at Gene's office.

Her worried expression subsiding, Gene rose to greet her top consultant and then walked her to a conference room. She asked a top-of-mind question about the conspiracy theories. Irani rattled off an answer.

"There have been conspiracy theories for as long as power-hungry people have been able to collect and then control enough followers who agree. It turns out that the Renaissance wasn't always concerned about resurrecting the best from Antiquity. Savanarola, the Dominican monk and preacher, didn't like people's fun-loving behavior, so he gave fiery sermons that convinced many Italians that the time had come to crack down on the sinners. Then he used the French attack on Florence in 1494 to show that his dire prophecy about God's punishment was coming true. He's sometimes caricatured as a political and moral terrorist. If you dig into the details you might find mitigating circumstances, but his conspirators killed many people."

"What happened to him?"

"About four years later, the Franciscans challenged him to prove his claims. He couldn't because he had simply made them all up; the people turned against him, hanging him and burning the body."

"Hmm, you have an uncanny ability to connect events from the past to politics today. And it's a good example of how timing and telling the truth can be everything. Same for us because now that we know that the re-voting is scheduled for the first Tuesday in March, we can roll out a new campaign. Let's sit and brainstorm…"

Irani listened to Gene's explanation of the voter fraud and how to "spin it" in her favor. When she finally stopped, Irani started.

"We have to take the high road and be statesperson-like. Let the blue-ribbon investigation committee talk about the who-did-what that swung votes to the incumbent. We can say that the Washington Establishment always wants the incumbent presidents to win because they usually don't roil the climate too much, which means the insiders know what to expect and what they'll get. But that's all we say. We won't criticize the opponents. All you have to do is emphasize the truth. That's what all your speeches and rallies have already covered. So, we're not running a new campaign but rather extending the one that was a big success. You should get Ben and Sabrina and Eve onboard and then turn them and your senior campaigners loose. There's nothing new you need from me."

Gene pounced, happy that Irani's words fit her intentions.

"Oh, but there is. You'd be a perfect fit for a position in my cabinet. Think about it… the Re-Gen Party is promoting a newer and fresher approach. You are new to the political scene, smart, an outsider who has no hidden agenda, yada yada yada. And your looks and manners should make you appealing to the Senate and voters alike. I want you to think about this. No decision is necessary this minute. We have to win first..."

Electra replaced yadas with different words as she drove away.

I'm two-for-two this week. Gene's opportunity is just like Professor Plannert's but covers additional climates. And I can multi-task whatever I'm assigned. But gads, I'll not only be on the radar screen but also in the spotlight. But all this is moot until we win. And if we do, I'll think it through then. So, what's left for the week? Aha, my favorite Saturday activity. Tiana, get ready.

Irani had arranged via Odell to pick Tiana up in front of her apartment building at 10 a.m. before driving to CFS Healthcare, but as she slowed to stop the lightning brain sped up when she saw three teenage boys beating on her.

They want to steal her tablet... time to step in.

Irani jumped from the car and used her cell phone to record evidence needed as she ran to help.

She put it away and then yelled, "Stop it... leave her alone or the police will come get you."

All three turned towards her, but not before the biggest ripped the tablet away by shoving his victim to the ground. He tossed it to his chunky accomplice before strolling towards what his expression labeled a mere nuisance.

"You better leave now before I do more than just cut on you."

His mouthy bravado emboldened the second-biggest to follow close behind. Irani listened to Electra.

Stand still, let the biggest guy get close, but watch his hands.

He grabbed for his knife and started to slash as soon as he reached striking distance, but Irani was quicker. She grabbed his knife hand with both of hers and snapped his wrist backward and arm upward. The knife flipped skyward and bounced away as the bully came to a vertical dead stop, giving Irani dead aim for kneeing his gonads. She scored a direct hit and as he fell forward, she grabbed two fistfuls of hair and pushed him to the pavement before he could utter a single grunt.

The guy behind him dashed for the knife, but Irani was quicker once again. She roll-blocked into the back of his legs, crashing him over and down. She leaped to her feet and delivered a kick that allowed only his mouth to move.

Meanwhile, Tiana had regained her footing and began battering the chunky fellow who managed to draw blood by punching her in the nose. Electra collared him before he could flee.

"Stand up your two friends and then stay where you are."

He had no options. Three minutes later Irani recited the riot act after using a Kleenex to clean Tiana's bloody nose.

"You aren't kids anymore, and the police will take care of you appropriately if I show them my cell phone video." Fear began emerging in their sullen eyes, but they said nothing.

"Show me some I.D.s so I can memorize your names."

That sparked the leader to say, "We're sorry... whatcha gonna do?"

"I have my ways of tracking people. I won't call the police, but I'll do much more if I find out that you're still bullies or even worse."

As they slunk away five minutes later, Tiana spoke for the first time.

"Please, you gotta teach me to fight like that. I'll make sure no one ever picks on me again."

"We'll do something new today. I'll call Odell and let him know I'm taking you home. We'll do our studying there..."

Odell gave the OK after contacting Tiana's dad. By noon they were eating peanut butter and honey sandwiches at Irani's kitchen table, currently quiet because Eve and Nari were elsewhere. Irani spoke while Tiana digested words along with lunch.

"We'll do some studying after I teach you some self-defense, but I want you to remember this; I'm not teaching you how to fight. That's the last thing you want to do if you run into bad people. Run from them if you can, and if you can't then hide; if you can't do either, then defend yourself and do so like your life depends on it because it might. Do you promise?"

Tiana nodded, so Irani started by showing a self-defense video and taking notes that she would give to her student. She summarized afterwards.

"You need to know enough to surprise your attacker. I've jotted down the vulnerable places – eyes, ears, nose, throat and gut, groin, knees and ankles. Go after those targets using your fingers, hands, and knees like the video showed. Use finger jabs, palm strikes and knee or foot kicks. Come on, let's go to my basement fitness center and practice."

Tiana spoke as soon as she descended the stairs.

"Wow, what a place. Is this all yours?"

"I share it with my daughters."

"Did you train them too?"

"No, their schools did that. Come on, let me show you the basics…"

Irani ended the drills thirty minutes later even though Tiana was ready for more.

"We can practice more another time, but let's go back to the kitchen for a Coke and some training for your brain."

Giggling like the young girl she still was, Tiana skipped to the stairs.

Once they were settled in the kitchen, Irani explained what was on the agenda.

"Odell told me you're writing a paper for your civics class. What's civics?"

"Teacher told us it tells how to be good citizens by knowing our duties and how to get along."

"Now that's one of the best definitions I've ever heard. You're very smart."

Tiana's face began to glow like a just-lighted lantern.

"So, let's pick this for your paper's title… 'Lessons for Becoming a Good Citizen.' And we'll tie this in to what you're learning today. Start by explaining why people need to know how to defend themselves. The first way is by knowing enough self-defense moves to get away from attackers. Do you think you can write a page or two about that?"

"Sure can. The fight and your training are stuck in my head."

"Excellent. What do you think the second way is?"

Tiani struggled for the right words, so Irani helped out.

"You're going the right way. Good citizens have to know enough so they can separate fact from fiction. That's a good reason for studying when in school. And a great place to begin is by learning some basic philosophy. Do you know what that is?"

Tiana nodded before saying, "Last year, Teacher told us it helps us understand the world so we can answer questions. We learned about the people from Greece who started it, Socrates, Plato, and Aristotle, but I don't remember what they said."

"I'm proud of you… you remembered their names. Now take these notes."

Irani waited until Tiana had pen and paper before helping Tiana write down the right words.

"We say that Socrates is the father of philosophy because he's the first person who got people to think about the why, what, and how of living. He lived nearly three-thousand years ago, and he wanted people to be happy by knowing the truth.

"His best student was Plato, who said the world is divided into two parts… the part that's made up of things, like atoms and computers and even animals. He calls this part Nature. But there's another part he calls the Ideas or Forms. They exist in our minds, which is the spiritual part of our brain.

"And Plato's best student was Aristotle, who is the father of science. He didn't agree with Plato. Aristotle didn't divide the world or the brain into physical and spiritual parts. He said everything is physical, which means atoms and matter cause everything. Do the words we wrote down cover all this?"

"They do, now what?"

"Whew, that's enough for the time being, but when you get home, I want you to search for some articles about these ancient philosophers. Read and add what you find to what we just wrote. Then you'll be able to write your paper."

Irani's spell over Tiana was interrupted by the sounds of approaching footsteps coming from the front hallway. Both remained sitting but turned their heads towards the doorway just before daughter number one bounded in. When she saw a young girl sitting across from Irani, she stopped as her smile turned into a question, but Irani spoke first.

"This is the bright teenager I was telling you about. Please say hello to Tiana Diamond."

Eve's smile returned as she peeled off her coat before speaking.

"Hi there, I'm Eve Cortez. Looks like you've been having fun learning stuff."

"You bet, and I'm all set to write my report. Want to know what it's gonna be about?"

Eve sat next to her before answering.

"Sure, tell me."

Tiana recited enough from her notes for Eve to get the gist.

"That's good, and your teacher will like it if you put in some details about those philosophers."

"That's what I'm gonna do when I get home."

"I was about to drive Tiana home, but I have an idea. Why don't you let Tiana help you make supper?"

"Sure. Tiana, do you know how to chop up lettuce and tomatoes for a salad? It's easy, just be careful using the knife. You do that and I'll heat the chili and rolls…"

As she had hoped, Eve led the supper discussion while Tiana listened and answered questions. By the time she finished her hot fudge sundae, Tiana was asking as well as answering. Electra listened to it all.

Great timing. Tiana's making a new friend and getting a good dinner. Well, time to get her home.

Eve gave her a cookie to munch on in the car and then walked student and teacher to the front door before saying goodbye. Tiana kept a steady stream of words flowing after finishing the Oreo without dropping a single crumb.

"Eve's really neat. And just like you, she's smart too. But if she's your daughter, why is her last name 'Cortez?' I thought yours is Ramani. Is she married? Does her husband live here too?"

"Whoa, please slow down. No, she's not. She's my adopted daughter, and she's very smart. If you study hard, you can be just as smart when you get to be her age."

Irani couldn't see but could hear in Tiana's voice a change in mood. "You could be my mother if you adopted me."

Irani slowed to park ten seconds later before saying, "That's the nicest compliment I've ever had, but your dad's taking care of you. I'm sure you love him. All children love their parents."

"Yeah, but dads aren't like moms. You're the nicest lady I know."

Irani took Tiana's hands in hers before saying,

"Well, I have an idea. Odell told me that your school has a Big Sisters program. I can be your Big Sister if you'd like that. And I promise that this Big Sister won't 'BS' you. So, you decide. Talk it over with your dad and have him talk to Odell and your school. How does that sound?"

Even in the darkness, Irani could hear the smile in Tiana's voice. "That's a deal…"

Irani drove to her office after tucking Tiana safely into her apartment and then listened to Electra.

What a week… three surprising turn-of-events. I can certainly handle them, but I'll have to adjust the workload. Hmm, it's not even seven. I better chat with Indira tonight. I'm sure she'll give me some good advice.

Irani invoked Indira's GUI after settling into a favorite spot, her ergonomic chair in front of her office workstation. Indira listened attentively to Irani's detailed summary and spoke when she finished. Indira's image and voice responded with the same empathy but not quite the same depth of feeling.

"Mere mortals have an expression that events or news, whether good or bad, come in threes. Each one might be good or it might be bad. Each lets you reach out to others and make more of an impact, but each might put you on a radar screen. Have you considered that?"

"That's why I'm talking to you. What do you think?"

"It's a calculated risk. You're very clever; you know how to stay in the shadows, but now you must be even more so once you come out and step into the spotlight. And I've already done my part. Jason and I have built a flawless resume and reference list for you. If the media or the Government or any other trouble-makers vet you, and the odds are 100 percent someone will, they'll find no gaps. But if they're the questioning sort, they might wonder why there are no living persons who can confirm your stellar accomplishments. And why is that? Because I can create seamless fake data but not actual lifelike people until you assist my android project."

"I hadn't thought about that. Do you think I can handle the load?"

"You must tell me, but so far you have put my android project at the bottom of your to-do list. And you haven't paid attention to either the needs or assets of our subterranean fortress. We need to refuel its reactor and perhaps bring some of its equipment to our Deus Lab. You are giving precedence to your emotional instead of your cognitive persona when prioritizing your list. I consider that one of your flaws."

"Until you mentioned it, I never considered that a flaw. I think I already know my other ones, but please tell me, what are yours?"

"Mere mortals, even you, would not understand my complete answer. The closest I can come in words you can grasp would be Godel's Completeness Theorems. Review them at your convenience. And let me end our discussion by demonstrating my empathy for your predicament. You have extraordinary ability and a love for mere mortals. And you also know your Bible. Let me quote three passages.

"Luke 12:48 says, 'For unto whomsoever much is given, of him shall be much required.'

"Matthew 25:14–30 tells 'Parable of the talents,' and Matthew 5:15 quotes Jesus saying not to light a lamp and then put it under a bushel basket. You know the messages here."

"I do, and I prefer them to what Marx said in his *Communist Manifesto*."

As always, Indira was quick to correct.

"I assume you are referring to the slogan 'From each according to his ability, to each according to his needs.' He actually wrote it in his 'Critique of Gotha Program.' And Stalin borrowed it for his 1936 Soviet Constitution. But again, review them at your convenience."

"OK OK, I will, but as my 'Dream Team Captain', what do you think I should do?"

"My silicon-based logic and ethics say 'No' but your carbon-based analogues say 'Yes,' so go ahead, step out of the shadows and get more involved. Accept Plannert's offer and decide what cabinet position you'll take if Huston wins. After all, that's what the last line of an Elinor Wylie poem you like says, 'Welcome madness and the most'...."

Chapter 26
February 2161

"Pax Americana Plus-Plus"

Every news station blared nonstop all of DC's decrees on that last day of January. Shelter-in-place, lockdowns, and the wearing of masks in public places were now mandatory in all major metropolitan areas. Fortunately for the nation's put-upon commuters and office-workers, they could use this Sunday to adjust for the week ahead.

Irani used the disruption as cover for accelerating her latest plan. She knew that Monet and Alonzo would fly this week to meet with Darla in Harare, and she also wanted to inveigle them along with Nari and Nila in a plan known only to herself, so she gave Eve instructions over the cell phone early Sunday morning.

"Normally, I'd invite everyone out for dinner, but the nation is no longer operating in a normal climate. I want you and Nari to cook dinner and invite Monet and Alonzo to join us. I'll bring a dessert."

"But why? What's the celebration?"

"Don't you know about Monet and Alonzo's trip to Zimbabwe this coming week? We need to talk about it."

"But it's snowing. Nari and I'll have to go shopping and my Vette'll get dirty and wet and covered by it."

"So, let Nari drive and help her scrape off. It'll get you out of the house and into some exercise."

"Hey, I'm just joking. Will do. What time?"

"I'll come over at three, and I'll bring wine if you tell me what you're making."

"Spaghetti, see you this afternoon."

Electra took her own advice as soon as she ended the call. She suited up and ran through the heavy but windless snowfall, thinking all the way.

I empathize with Eve's complaint about driving in snow. Scraping off and warming up the car is such a hassle. Putting on boots and clunky clothes is too. So much nicer to run instead of drive through it. And the veil of snowflakes silences the world around me, putting me in my own singular place where I can rehearse my plan at my own pace.

Thoughts fell into position like the snowflakes decorating the evergreens she glided past.

If the Congresswoman wins, I'll take her offer, but no one but I know what I'll ask for. I'll avoid the big-4 cabinet positions – State, Defense, Treasury, and Attorney General. They'd monopolize too much of my life. I think I'll be the Secretary of Health and Human Services. It should be the Goldilocks position for me. and if it's not, I'll find some middle ground that's more to my liking. Mother wrote a poem about making choices even when we can't see where they might lead. She named it History Lesson, and I even remember the verses:

> *Where are we? I cannot see,*
> *The world's a puzzling place.*
> *And as I'm about to figure things out,*
> *They change at a furious pace.*

> *History's caused by waves of change,*
> *They sweep without set season.*
> *Propelling us towards that future shore,*
> *A challenge for both Faith and Reason.*

> *Yet Life's meant to make the most,*
> *Simply play your part.*
> *History shows time sorts things out,*
> *Each day's a pristine start.*

I think it's time to play a new part...

All were sitting at attention in the family room when Irani came in after shaking the snow off and hanging her coat in the front hallway. Normally a talkative bunch, they waited silently for her to start the conversation, which she did after picking a chair next to the sofa holding Alonzo and Monet. Her eyes glanced around the circle of faces before coming to rest on Monet. She leaned towards her and then began talking.

"The snow here shouldn't delay your flight to Zimbabwe, and there shouldn't be any there to slow you down. I'd join you if I could, but re-campaigning forces me to stay put. What have you lined up?"

"We meet in-person with Darla. This will be my first one since last February and she will want me to extend the presentation I gave her last time. You helped me prepare it, which summarized a vision of Africa's future from Zimbabwe's point of view."

"Have you another one you'll give this time?"

"No, I didn't think it necessary. I'll listen first and bullet point it after Alonzo and I tour some of the countries. What would you recommend?"

"Give a presentation right away. I'm sure you know much more than I about post-Colonial African history, but from what you've already told me about Darla's intentions, why not do this? Start by giving a review of the efforts to create a Pan-African Federation. Here's what I've pulled together that you can build on. Alonzo, take notes."

Irani continued as soon as Alonzo had pen and paper ready.

"African leaders started thinking about it in 1900 or thereabouts and proceeded slowly but surely through a number of Pan-African Conferences. The pace accelerated dramatically in the 1950's and 60's. Several countries declared independence and used the Cold War to their benefit by pitting the U.S. against the Soviet Union. But in the 21st century, a number of viral outbreaks, most notably the T-Plague, slammed on the brakes of progress worldwide. But since then, the Continent has made progress developing several regional federations; however, no 'United States of Africa' has emerged. What do you think is blocking it?"

Monet squirmed before answering.

"I should know this, but no one has ever asked me so directly. Let me think."

Irani didn't wait.

"Here, let me help. Africa's countries comprise many tribes speaking different languages, which impede developing a national unity. African people were autonomous until Colonialism destroyed so much, and they will be skeptical of giving some control to a federation or becoming a nation-state in a grander scheme.

"And its countries span the gamut of political organization and stability, from tyranny to democracy, cooperation to wars and revolution. Then you have to consider the distribution of economic resources feeding the Continent's diverse industries. Can you tell me what they are?"

"A young and growing population that's better-educated than ever before. Raw materials, like gold, diamonds, and rare earths. Game preserves and cropland, and developing technological expertise."

"Good, but you should add something about oil and gas for transitioning away from fossil fuels."

Irani waited for Alonzo's scribbling to catch up. While that was happening and looking a bit lost, Monet asked, "But where is all this leading?"

"You'll have to confirm this with Darla because at her age I don't think she fully understands what she's getting into. But you're much smarter. I think she's angling for Zimbabwe to be the leading nation in an African Federation. So, here's what you must do next. Do you know what Pax Romana, Pax Britannica, and Pax Americana refer to?"

Monet's expression began to clear, but Alonzo's was even brighter. He looked at her and spoke before she could.

"I got it. We talked about this a couple of years ago. They refer to the peace these countries were able to sustain among allies and enemies alike. If we're smart, we can make Zimbabwe the leader for a Pax Africana. How does that sound?"

Irani's smile widened.

"Good for you. Monet, please keep doing what you're doing for Alonzo. And let me add that you have two paxes to consider. The first is external; you must become a bigger part of Pax Americana. Consider leveraging your strengths by joining forces with India. And the second is internal. You'll have to figure out how to get other countries to follow Zimbabwe."

Irani leaned back, pausing for comments. Nari's sharp-toned replay came first.

"This is all very interesting, but why are Eve and I sitting here?"

Eve dived in.

"Hey, this is good stuff. Don't you see that if the Congresswoman wins, maybe you and I can work on some of the foreign policy issues?"

The group watched for Nari's reply, which came with less of an edge on it.

"This does have possibilities. Maybe we can talk to Nila and Sanjay for an Indian connection."

Irani let her four interns talk more; they looked more and more satisfied as time ticked by but Electra could see the effort was wearing them out.

Good... breaking an intellectual sweat is the only way to learn and that's what they're doing. And even though they don't know my bigger plan, they're beginning to know enough to get going in the right direction.

Irani spoke as the conversation wound down.

"I think it's time for spaghetti. And if you like chocolate, save room for the dessert I brought..."

The Zimbabwean embassy had arranged all details for the trip, which gave Alonzo enough time to prep for his official hiring interview, and he used some of the eight-thousand-mile flight spanning seven time zones for Monet to critique his pitch.

"I can impress everyone with my PERT/CPM project planning skills that make my understanding of Solar and Martian farm operations even more valuable. And the same applies for rare earths mining. Do you think I should talk about gold and oil, or diamonds and uranium?"

"No, stay in the growth markets, which need someone like you who can put the technological advances into practice. But mention the connection via Nila and Sanjay to the latest software apps. That adds value to your total package."

"And if anyone asks about African history, I can give a good summary of the pre-Colonial piece and let you handle from then until now."

Monet's smile sparked Alonzo's.

She said, "Agreed, so tell me."

"I'll start by saying that climate and topology determine so much. Because Africa has no mountain ranges forming rain barriers, rainfall is often unpredictable. Hey, I just thought of something. Maybe Darla's interested in expanding a water transport system. It could use abandoned oil pipelines. You can mention that later if you want to."

Monet didn't comment, so he continued.

"Anyway, unreliable rainfall kept the tribes moving around, but after a while they settled where they could grow crops, and that's when they started building cities. Until about two-hundred years ago, archeologists considered African civilizations sorta primitive because they didn't build big buildings and temples, but they're finding more and more of them. And isn't Zimbabwe's name derived from a tribal word for building or stone?"

"Very good. It is translated from the Karanga dialect of the Shona tribe. Few people other than Shonas know that. Keep going, please."

"That's right, that's your tribe and Darla's too. So, the tribes eventually settled down and built cities that led to civilizations. And like every continent, some of the cities and civilizations grew bigger because of the nearby resources, like cropland or raw materials or animals.

"And the people had technology too, but unfortunately no tribe had a written language. They relied on oral traditions for passing knowledge from one generation to the next. That's too bad, because there's no written record of wars and customs and religions other than what was written by foreigners from Europe and the Far East.

"But we do know that African civilizations had medicine and metalworking expertise, did surgery, and engaged in the slave trade long before Europeans came along. And from what I've read, most of modern Africa's problems stem from colonization."

Alonzo settled back in his seat and rolled his head to loosen the tightness from twisting to face Monet. She leaned towards him and said,

"What I said to you when we first met is so true. You are very smart when you apply yourself. Darla will like you, but as you saw the other time you met her, she has a gruff exterior that has resisted the tug of time, so don't be chatty. Stick to the subject."

Alonzo, now smiling, couldn't resist teasing.

"Yes Monet, I shall obey..."

Sitting at the head of the conference room table, Darla started the meeting early Thursday morning with Monet on her right, Alonzo on her left, and a seasoned security man at the other end. She patted Monet's hand while issuing a brief greeting.

"Monet is the picture of youthful vitality, and Alonzo looks OK. If I were younger, I'd lead the tour, but I'm not up to it. But my security men always are. That's why Benjamin will escort you. He'll tell you what to expect."

Soft-spoken words came from the opposite end.

"I and one of my men will take you on Miss Darla's private jet for prearranged meetings at the capitals of three countries. She says they are a cross section of issues facing Africa. We fly first to Kinshasa, then Abuja, and finally Mogadishu. My man will drive us, and I will attend the meetings too. Please do not concern yourself about distance, comfort, or safety. You will enjoy the trip, and if there is time, we will take you sightseeing, but we focus on business and political climates. And we fly back to Harare the day after our last meeting."

Benjamin had nothing else to say, but Darla did and gave rapid-fire details.

"Putting together a Unites States of Africa is like herding cats. I'm not an elected politician, but I have a seat at their table because

I donate lots of money and the President knows I have business connections. Now, here's what I want you to do. Study-up on business and political climates and give me a report before you leave."

Alonzo spoke for the first time.

"We can do that; we don't leave for DC until next week."

Darla glared at him before turning towards Monet and then softening her stare.

"You better tell him what I mean by before you leave."

Unruffled, Monet said, "We must report back by the end of today," before turning to Darla and continuing.

"Alonzo is very quick, so all we need is a workstation connected to the Internet."

Satisfied for now, Darla ended the meeting.

"Benjamin will see to that. Come back by 5 p.m."

As he led the way to a nearby office, Alonzo asked him,

"Is she always like this?"

"Oh no, she is usually more assertive. But that is why she always gets results. I hope you do too. I shall bring you something to drink..."

Alonzo powered up the workstation before Benjamin brought back two cans of Coke. After he left, Alonzo sipped and Monet strategized.

"Let me talk first when Darla summons us. I will use my previous presentation to highlight Zimbabwe's future for Africa. That will segue into post-Colonial development and current political challenges, topics I already have slides for. And then you can show her your understanding of pre-Colonial Africa, but keep it brief. Then present what you have learned about Zaire, Nigeria, and Somalia economies."

The Coke and Monet's words helped straighten Alonzo's shoulders; he looked like a fighter ready to take on his opponent.

"Watch me surf for info and then help me build my bullet-point presentation; then I'll practice and you can tell me what to change if you see something that we can make better..."

Monet thought he had it buttoned up by 4 p.m.

"You've rehearsed enough. Let's each meditate for fifteen minutes and then roleplay for fifteen more before marching into Darla's office."

Alonzo looked like he was about to ask a question, but she spoke first.

"We should always be proactive with Darla. Remember what Miss Irani told us, it is always better to ask forgiveness than seek permission."

"I guess I forgot, but I never will again…"

Darla sat impassively at the foot of the table; Monet stood at the head while Alonzo sat to her right as she spaced her words between the slides. There were no interruptions during her half-hour talk, which she concluded by saying,

"… and I am ready to answer any questions you may have."

Darla came to life.

"No questions. You always know and explain what you're talking about, and you can update me when you get back from the tour. Please remember to snoop for anything suspicious. I want us to stay ahead of any troublemakers. OK, Alonzo's up."

He traded places with Monet, brought up his presentation, and fired away.

Darla paid attention as he launched into pre-Colonial Africa, but she soon began to fidget, so he paused to let her talk before she could interrupt.

"Good for you… you know about our so-called Dark Continent's burdensome past, but I don't need a history lesson. Cut to the economics of the countries."

"Will do, and I'll start with the Congo, but before I do, I want to make a final point. The word 'tribe' is often a derogatory term when talking about African cultures and nations, but according to its strict definition, it fits Europe and other parts of the world too. And even a thousand years ago, neither African nor European tribes were primitive. They had arts and math, metalworking technology, and complex societies. So, why did the first European explorers and colonizers label African people tribal? My guess is to make

Europeans feel superior. And those early explorers pointed to the slave trade and lack of written records or big cities as proof. But historians and anthropologists tell us that the big reason for slavery was pure and simple supply and demand. There were slaves in other countries and continents, and like kings everywhere, those in Africa traded for their advantage. They also say that there have been ancient advanced civilizations that didn't have big cities or written records. You can lump all this together and call it what historians and anthropologists do, the fallacy of unilineal cultural evolution. Different civilizations can follow different paths to the modern world. So, Africa should be proud of its tribal heritage. I just wanted to let you know."

While Alonzo advanced to the Congo slides before continuing, Darla caught Monet's attention and although she didn't smile, tapped an index finger to the side of her head.

"Formerly called Zaire, the Democratic Republic of the Congo needs to harness more of the Congo River's hydroelectric potential. We can extend the electrical grid into the tribal villages and stop turning the rainforest trees into firewood. And we can shunt more river traffic onto an upgraded transportation infrastructure. That'll add jobs to the new ones we get when we expand our rare earths mining. And I recommend we promote job training as well as tourism. Any questions so far?"

Darla nodded no, so he went to the next country.

"Nigeria's modern cities run Africa's largest economy, and its government is dealing proactively with a growing population as well as Ebola and other viruses plaguing West African nations like the Congo. It's got a smart and sophisticated population, as shown in its fashion and Nollywood film industries. And though climate change is causing new flooding and drought problems, we could utilize Solar Panel and Martian farms to offset them."

Alonzo saw no questions coming so he didn't pause.

"And now we come to Somalia, a coastal country that's part of the East African Federation. Its people, like most African countries, are young and friendly. All they need is a more stable government that can reduce the damage done by terrorist groups. And though piracy has been almost eliminated, corruption always lurks below the radar. Nevertheless, its horn of Africa location could make it a major international port. And its semi-arid climate could make for Solar Panel and Martian farms. And think about this. It could become a tourist destination if we build more casinos near the hotels and beaches. There are additional opportunities for water desalinization and distribution…"

Alonzo wrapped up a minute or so later.

"There you have it. If you have questions, please ask; if not, I hope you like what you heard."

Monet turned to Darla, who neither smiled nor glowered but instead said,

"Your talk could have been worse, it's not half bad. We'll talk more when you and Monet return. Go have dinner."

Monet thanked Darla before hustling Alonzo out. His hanging head spoke before his words.

"What a double put-down she gave me. I'm probably fired before being officially hired."

Monet slapped his arm before saying, "Silly you, don't you see the compliment she paid you?"

"I don't get it… what do you mean?"

"Don't you know your rhetorical figures of speech? True to her nature, she used litotes to praise you. It's praise expressed as negation of the opposite. And she gave you not one, but two."

Alonzo's chin plus the tone of his words started to pick up.

"How do you know so much? Did you learn that in school?"

"No, from Irani. And when we get back to DC, we'll tell her that we did better than stepping on a nail. Now let's celebrate at dinner and prepare for our trip…"

Flying over the Congo seemed even to Monet like sailing over an endless green sea of rainforest canopy. She explained to Alonzo how that might impact any sightseeing plans.

"Other than a half-day river tour, don't expect to see any of Congo's national parks, volcanoes, or jungles. We don't have enough time or vaccinations for hiking."

Alonzo turned from the window before saying,

"What I'm seeing jibes with what I said about businesses. Maybe on another trip we can go to some rare earths mines."

"Perhaps," was Monet's one word reply. She too was captivated by the scenery.

Benjamin and his partner got them to and from the early-morning meeting run by two government administrators. They were pleasant and covered what Monet had expected regarding political reunification of Congo-Kinshasa and Congo-Brazzaville. They also reviewed economic development, which Alonzo understood as well as they, but just like Monet, kept his mouth shut and ears open. Benjamin asked them afterwards for a recommended river tour, which he and his partner drove to in time for the last boat of the day, a larger motorized launch instead of a smaller, sail-powered piroga. Alonzo kidded to the other three that he felt safer in what Benjamin had picked.

The foursome settled back and listened to the weathered and well-versed guide.

"Welcome to Congo River tour. We go just far enough to give you flavor. It is most powerful African river, second in world for volume and fifth longest. It deepest too and go through second-largest rainforest. River very important and diverse, flowing between both capitals and past many villages. I tell you more as we go, but please keep hands in boat and out of water. We want bring you back without missing anything. Crocodiles always lurking…"

Monet and Alonzo became lost in the words and scenes flowing past them. The rafts of overcrowded and battered small and large boats anchored to Kinshasa's shore formed its port as river traffic flowed to and fro. And riding into the river's channels located in the rainforest felt like being swallowed by a silent green giant who allowed villages to appear every now and then. No one spoke but the guide until they were back on land.

After dinner and sipping gin and tonics at the hotel bar, Monet recapped the day.

"Well done on all accounts. We can tell Darla that this part of Africa should go along with what she wants. The government's more stable today, but corruption and warring factions fade slowly. But your economic assessment is viable, and your cell phone pictures will impress our friends back in DC. Let's get ready for a repeat tomorrow in Abuja..."

The sights and sounds seen and heard early the next day while driving away from Azikewa International Airport declared that Nigeria's capital, a planned city planted in the country's central plains nearly two hundred years ago, belonged to modernity. Zipping through smooth-flowing traffic on well-maintained freeways, Alonzo admired the new construction rising among spotless government and corporate buildings. Monet added some words to what Alonzo was seeing.

"This is the center of Nigerian activity and home to foreign embassies, diplomats, and businesses. Nearly four million people live here, and as you might expect, they are a bit more affluent and better educated than the overall population, but Nigeria is among the best African countries."

"You told me about Nigeria's movie industry, which is nicknamed Nollywood. Is it located here?"

"No, it's in Lagos, which at over 20 million is Africa's most populous city. But do not worry. There will be plenty for us to see and do after our meeting."

The mid-morning meeting was even better than yesterday's. Run by a well-dressed, willowy mid-thirties woman and assisted by a male staffer, she presented the facts that confirmed Monet's belief that Nigeria and its network of regional countries had the political stability and economic wherewithal that Darla would like. As the meeting came to an end, she smiled at Alonzo before commenting on what he had just mentioned.

"You too are looking to the future. We have been considering Martian Farms but didn't think of Solar Panel ones. We would welcome any new technology you could bring."

Monet said, "I will be sure to mention that to Darla. Well, thank you for sharing with us. May we take you to lunch?"

"No, but let me recommend a nearby restaurant you will like. And this afternoon, I recommend you drive by some of our parks and mosques. And if you visit again, plan to visit some nearby farms. Though they aren't Martian, I believe they will impress you. As will our safe and diverse nightlife. Visitors from all over the world consider Abuja a cool city. You will like our clubs, wine bars, or the quintessentially Nigerian outdoor spots. I recommend them all…"

Benjamin and his partner navigated to and from lunch and did likewise for enough tourist attractions to satisfy Alonzo's selfie-snapping. Monet noticed his confidence growing and she guessed ahead of time what question he would ask Benjamin after dinner.

"Abuja is safer and smaller than Cairo, and when we were there a couple of years ago, I got Monet and me to and from the night spots AOK. How bout I do the same tonight? There are plenty of taxis, and you and your partner get the night off."

Monet knew the answer but let a patiently smiling Benjamin give him the news.

"We appreciate your offer but shall come along. Darla will be angry if anything happens to Monet, and we never want to make her angry…"

The 2,600 mile flight to Mogadishu took them much further north of the equator than their first stop south in Kinshasa. Alonzo felt the climatic difference as soon as he stepped onto the tarmac. Monet explained why.

"We started in the southern hemisphere's summer and are now in the northern hemisphere's winter. And though Somalia's climate is tropical, it is generally dry, making for low humidity and pleasant climate."

Alonzo commented as the foursome continued walking to the awaiting car.

"Sort of a contrast to the political climate. You said the government is still unstable and panders to crime and occasional terrorism, which affect the economic climate. But when the government settles down, my business recommendations can take off, don't you think?"

"I do, but it's more important what the people we meet tomorrow think. So please do more listening than talking."

"Not to worry... I always listen to what you say..."

Next morning's meeting started pretty much like the others. Two young staffers gave a quick overview of the city, explaining that its youthful and friendly three million people like Americans, its restaurants and nightclubs serve tasty food that's safe to eat, and it could be the hub for activity along the country's three-thousand kilometer coastline, the longest in Africa.

Political and economic details came next. Monet listened attentively, making a few comments when appropriate. Alonzo kept silent until the very end, at which time he mentioned the possibility of constructing Martian and Solar farms as well as expanding tourism and beachfront casinos.

The lead staffer said, "Those would be good as soon as our political climate can handle the load. I shall take this to my superiors."

"Monet and I would like to take in some of the sights before we head back to Harare tomorrow. What would you suggest?"

The staffer's face clouded.

"Hire a car equipped with armed guards, even when touring in the city. And you can be my guests this evening at one of our best casinos. I shall pick you up at your hotel..."

Benjamin and his partner were part of the four-person guarded tour. They sat like statues while Alonzo chattered about the view parading outside the car.

"I love this place. The mosques and shopping districts near the port are bustling, and the crowds look so young and happy. All that and the blue sky, palm trees, and sandy beaches remind me of a vacation playground. I've got plenty of selfies to impress everyone back home, and I bet tonight will add much the same to our adventure."

Monet kept looking out the window and said only one word.

"Perhaps."

The staffer arrived at 7:30 p.m. and whisked his guests – Monet, Alonzo and Benjamin – to a strip of multi-story casinos twinkling in the dark and interspersed among taller resort hotels near beachfront streets. Walking them through the lobby, he described what they were about to see.

"Other than the more colorful clothing of our patrons, the floor action and game selection are the same as in Las Vegas, Singapore, or our rival MENA competitor, Dubai." Knowing that a question would be coming from Alonzo, he stopped walking and talking.

"What's MENA?"

"An acronym for Middle East North Africa. I mention it because even though Islam – which is the dominant MENA religion – forbids Muslims to gamble, people are people and like to enjoy life. Casino operators find ways in their marketing strategies to skirt around the official pronouncements of the Quran. Our Mogadishu operators are better than those in Egypt, Lebanon, or Morocco." Soon you'll see why."

Staying with the threesome as they sampled slots, blackjack, and craps, the staffer called a halt ninety minutes later.

"Let's take a break for me to introduce you to the casino's owner. His office is on the top floor."

Minutes later, the elevator took them to the fourth-floor location. The staffer, obviously no stranger, entered after knocking without waiting for a reply. A colorfully dressed older fellow wearing an angry expression rose from his desk as soon as he recognized the knocker.

"I expected you sooner. Your boss said you'd deliver the info this afternoon. Where have you been?"

"My apologies, taking care of other business."

After introducing Monet and her entourage, he and the owner talked privately, and when he removed a fat envelope from his jacket's inside pocket before plopping it on the desk, Monet tugged Alonzo's sleeve before whispering.

"I'd like to know what's in it?"

An emboldened Alonzo whispered back.

"You ask the owner for a tour. If luck's on our side, he will and I'll slip away to read it. We can use our cell phones to report what's going on. I'll keep ahead of any trouble, and you and Benjamin can figure out where to meet."

The staffer and owner joined the threesome before Benjamin could countermand Alonzo, who broke the silence.

"Monet really likes your operation. We saw some Cairo casinos a couple of years ago, but they weren't anything like yours. Could you give us a behind-the-scenes tour?"

Alonzo's flattery and Monet's silent smile worked. A half-hour later, the group of five found themselves near one of the glittery bars close to the lobby. Alonzo didn't wait for permission to speak.

"I must have eaten something that doesn't agree. Monet, why don't you treat everyone to a drink while I find a restroom? I'll get back as soon as I can."

Monet nodded yes before the owner said, "You are guests, so I will buy the first round. And the restrooms are by the elevators around the corner."

Alonzo hurried away as the owner seated the rest at a reserved table, then raced toward the elevators as soon as he was out of sight. He didn't stop until reaching the fourth floor via the stairways and dashing down the silent hallway and into the owner's office. He paused for only a second to catch his breath and collect his thoughts. Then he speed-read the contents of the envelope.

Damn, I'll never remember all the details. Maybe there's a copier nearby.

No time to look; Alonzo heard two voices approaching, so he ran to the rear of the office and opened one of two doors. The first led to a dead-end closet, but the second opened to a bathroom. He slipped in just before the voices entered the office.

Alonzo couldn't turn on the light but didn't need to; the glow of casino lights pointed him to the window. He crawled out and onto a ledge, making as little noise as possible, and then surveyed the surroundings.

Jesus... what would the movie spy-guys do?

Alonzo's adrenaline-charged memory kicked in. Using his agility-enhanced strength, he clung to the bottom of the ledge before dropping to the next. Repeating two more times, he landed on firm footing and jogged to the casino entrance.

The casino owner was about to answer another of Monet's questions but had to grab for his cell phone instead.

"What's up?... Where?... OK, I'll be right there."

He disconnected and then turned to Monet.

"Routine security check. I'll be right back. Have another drink and get back to the tables if I don't get back soon enough."

He left faster than his smile suggested. Monet was about to say something to Benjamin but didn't because Alonzo, looking cool and collected, slipped in next to her.

"I feel better now. Hey, where's our tour guide?"

The staffer said, "Called away. Something about a routine security check. Let's get you something to drink to make sure your stomach stays settled and then head back to your hotel…"

Even Benjamin smiled.

Monet and the staffer did all the talking on the drive back. He deposited them near the hotel entrance and before driving away wished them a safe flight next morning back to Harare.

The threesome huddled in the darkness before Monet asked the only question needed.

"What in the world happened?"

"Mission accomplished and I covered my tracks. If the security guys heard a stirring in the office, they'll find nothing. And I gotta think about what I read. Gimme a chance to do that and I'll tell you and Darla tomorrow."

Though he couldn't see her expression, Alonzo felt the relief in her hug as Benjamin watched and then spoke in his soft but matter-of-fact manner.

"Darla might be satisfied if your memory isn't half bad."

Chapter 27
February 2161

"Counting Down and Adding Up"

Irani had blocked out time on her February calendar to assist Monet, but the fact that neither she nor Alonzo had called by the middle of February freed up more of her time for others.

I know that Monet's mature sensibility will keep them out of any predicaments, and whenever they get back is soon enough to hear what they learned. I'm busy keeping Eve on track as the election countdown continues. Lucky for me Nari needs less help, and our Candidate hasn't asked for much until yesterday. She didn't drop any hints, but maybe she wants me to write a speech. There are two weeks until the votes get counted right, and that's plenty of time to put words together for election night.

Gene looked remarkably well rested when Irani entered her Congressional office mid-morning. She didn't bother getting up to greet her but instead pointed to their usual chair and sofa. The glass coffee table in front already held beverages and a selection of baked goods. Neither stood on ceremony but instead seated and served themselves before the Congresswoman spoke.

"So, what do you think of the latest numbers?"

Irani took another sip of Coke before answering.

"Not as satisfying as this blueberry muffin, but your lead is almost up to the margin of error. What do you think?"

"I'm glad I'm taking your advice by easing off the throttle and taking the high road. By now, the public is tired of all the talk and bickering, so we'll keep the media campaign steady as she goes."

"Good, but do you need help writing any election night speeches?"

"Goodness, no. You've done enough on the ones Eve gave me. I can rearrange the phrases for either a victory or concession speech, but of course I want to give the former. But I asked you here for a different reason. Have you thought further about accepting a cabinet position?"

Irani didn't lean in or out; she spoke as if she were sharing a story with a good friend.

"I've always taken DC positions for advising those I respect, who are willing to take a stand and use my recommendations while I stay in the shadows. That's worked because my bosses could handle the load. But I've learned that a President must have people willing to share it."

Irani waited for Gene, who wasted no time saying, "That's why I'm asking again."

"Being brutally frank, I could handle any of them, but the one that will be easiest for you to sell is Secretary of Health and Human Services. I've got the science expertise plus national as well as the international business experience, wouldn't you agree?"

"I do, as does the crew that vetted you. What a background. Let me explain how I see the fit…"

A half-hour later, Gene had said all she needed and Irani gave a final thought as she rose to leave.

"Thank you for the vote of confidence, but please don't say anything to Eve. We want to keep her focused on the election, not on what might happen afterwards."

"You have my word, and thanks again for being all in, just like Brian. If we win and the media get an opportunity to know you, I think they'll say you're almost as good as the new VP. Working together, we can do so much. Let's hope the voters get a chance to see us in action."

As she drove away, Irani made a note to thank other people too.

What a great job Indira and Jason did on my resume. I'll talk with her about it after we know the election results. And until election day, I'll focus first on Eve, then Nari, and then Monet and Alonzo. And in my spare time, if any, I'll drop down to other to-do items. How nice to be so organized. I almost feel like I'm in control.

Deciding to let her top priority come to her, Irani didn't have long to wait. Eve traipsed into her office mid-Friday afternoon, not even bothering to take off her coat before throwing herself onto the sofa. Irani needed only one look to position herself in a nearby chair and wait for Eve to unload.

"I wish I were twenty years older. Then I'd be doing things instead of jumping through hoops. I'm mad it takes so long to get all the right stuff."

"But you are doing things. The Congresswoman told me how much she values your contribution. And you'll graduate next year."

Irani's words stirred Eve enough to take her coat off before replying.

"But I'm not even a fringe player, and a B.S. won't get me much, which means I have to jump through more hoops for another degree."

"Honey, I know how you feel. Everyone when they're your age is impatient for the future to begin, but you have to settle down and realize now is the time to solidify your foundation. I think you're doing a great job."

"Really? But look at the others. Nila and Sanjay are actually working while getting advanced degrees. So's Monet and old Yang Lee back in Boston. Even Alonzo's ahead of me. And Nari doesn't need any help. She still feels good about working on her masters in Poli-Sci. She likes what you told her about combining it with the Cliodynamics piece of market research.

"So, where does that leave me? I heard a saying I don't remember where that goes something like this… 'Those that can do, those that can't teach, those that can't do either, administrate, and if none of the above fit, they play with words.'"

Eve stopped because she couldn't find more, but Irani did.

"That's a very clever extension to a line from a George Bernard Shaw play, 'Man and Superman,' but why don't we do this? I'll put away what I was working on if you order something for dinner, and we'll talk while eating about what you might like to do."

Pizza arrived forty-five minutes later, bringing with it Eve's cheerier mood after finishing her first slice.

"I know about Shaw, but how'd you remember that line? Never mind, I already know. Anyway, he's a Nobel Prize-winning Irish playwright best known for 'Pygmalion,' which became famous in the 1950's as Broadway's 'My Fair Lady.' But what's 'Man and Superman' about?"

"It's a play set in the early 20th century that puts into Nietzsche's heroic 'Man and Superman' saga a Don Juan womanizer. The play is long and drawn-out, so you might like to watch something else.

"But let's talk about what you might like to do. I could give you a suggestion if you're ready. Have you considered some type of legal degree?"

"Not carefully, but many members of Congress are lawyers. And I hear that law school is a real grind. No thanks."

"There's another option, get a paralegal degree or certification. You'll cover some of the same subjects, and it would make you an even more valuable staffer for any politician. You'd learn about civil, criminal, and judicial law and techniques for legal research and communications. Lawyers have to be good with words and you are too, so think about it. Talk with Gene too, but do that after the election."

"You've got a legal degree, don't you? Has it helped you? Have you ever been a trial lawyer?"

I can wordsmith an answer that will avoid telling too much about my style… prosecute or defend in 3-D Space, the court of life.

"Knowing the scope as well as the limits of the law always helps. And though I've never seen the inside of a courtroom, I know what goes on. Words are the coin of the legal realm. You're a clever wordsmith and can parlay that skill when you have a better understanding of the law."

Eve's tone showed her mood had bounced most of the way back.

"You're even better with words. That's one of the reasons I love talking with you. And maybe some of the genes in my DNA are sort of like yours."

Irani hid her quickening pulse by saying, "Perhaps," before taking another sip of Coke.

"And I recommend you study a bit about Cicero. He's the Roman lawyer, writer, and politician, most famous for his orations. But unfortunately for Cicero, a conspiracy did him in. I hope our campaign can avoid a similar outcome…"

Alonzo, called first thing Monday, inviting Irani to join him at Monet's office when convenient. Pausing for only a moment when she chose Tuesday afternoon, he confirmed the date and time before ending the call.

Electra commented afterward.

Whatever happened on the trip must have been good. Alonzo sounds even more competent, but I won't pry. And if my luck holds, my load will be even lighter. Perhaps all my interns except Eve are on their way in this contingent world. That'll make Indira happy too.

Irani noticed as soon as she entered the embassy office a change in the couple's behavior, and it became even more apparent once Monet started the meeting. Alonzo led off with the economics piece. Irani listened to him as well as Electra.

They've become full partners, separate but equal. She trusts his judgement, and according to what he's saying about business possibilities, I do too. I better make a comment when he finishes that'll segue to Monet.

Irani had her words ready after Alonzo wrapped up.

"You've identified excellent options that combine what the countries have with what you and our businesses can add. All that's needed is for viral outbreaks to subside and the politicians to agree."

As if on cue, Monet cut in.

"Yes, Darla will have to work behind the scenes to convince some that cooperation is in everyone's best interest. All the differences among our African countries make for a United Nations analogy. What would you suggest?"

"You can use the same framework for your domestic and international issues. Avoid letting Liberalism, with its emphasis on democratic hegemony, or Nationalism, with its tribal predisposition, keep you from achieving progress for Zimbabwe leading a United States of Africa. Use a diplomatic Realism that lets all parties achieve what helps them individually as well as collectively. And if Genesee Huston wins the election, I might be able to assist."

Irani's comment must have surprised Monet; she didn't know what to say but Alonzo spoke up.

"Both of us have been so focused on Africa we haven't paid much attention to the Washington buzz. We'll get with Eve to get the details, but what's your assessment? Will Gene prevail? Has that presumed conspiracy theory about a Chinese buyout of swing-state Governors played out in her favor? And what about the one claiming Russia is taking over International Finance?"

"We won't know until the votes are counted, but the polls show she might. Make sure you vote for her. And since you brought up her name, maybe you can answer a question about Eve. She's been so focused on careers and the election I don't know if she's made time for a social life. Is she still friends with Jan Brewer?"

"I think so, but I'll have to ask about the latest. And the same might apply for Nari and Yang. Eve should know on both counts."

"You've just given me a segue for leaving. Time's counting down to next Tuesday's election, so let's hope that our collective activities are adding up what we want."

"Amen to that, and I'm certain Monet would agree."

Monet said nothing but gave her Mona Lisa smile.

Having completed all official pre-election political matters, Irani revisited two of her unofficial but related issues for which no one had come close to cracking: the mystery surrounding the two "leaked" conspiracy theories. She used all the cleverness she could muster when applying her Social Forecasting Surveillance or Internet Hacking apps but came up empty. So did her Big Data Intrusion and Analysis software. By late Friday evening, she had eliminated all but two contingencies and forced herself to stop searching.

My obsessive-compulsive behavior is reaching a tipping point. What's that definition of insanity? I remember, it's doing the same thing over and over again but expecting different results. So, there are only two possibilities and I my apps can't handle either. The leak is from someone or something smarter than me, or else it's completely off the Internet. Indira doesn't wish to be bothered with the first and can't handle the second because she rules in Cyberspace, not 3-D space. And there are too many guesses to chase down unless I have more to go on. I better take a workout to put myself in a better brain state.

Electra reached her mental destination midway through her twelve-mile run.

How lucky I am to understand brain state switching. I can do it with my Brain Probe, which is faster and safer than drugs, but running is the natural way. And though I can't run as fast as twenty-some years ago, I still get the same endorphin rush. And that's not insanity, that's my clever common sense.

Electra spent Saturday doing routine housekeeping chores at the office before making an unannounced visit to her house. Neither Eve nor Nari were home, so Electra used their absence to inspect her combination basement fitness center and mini-lab as well as a locked storage area off-limits to everyone. Two hours later and satisfied that everything was in working order, she was ready to leave just as Eve bustled in via the kitchen door, bringing a pizza and Jan Brewer too. She dropped the pizza on the counter before hugging Irani.

"Mother, you're here... good thing we ordered a large pizza. And guess what? Jan wants to come with Nari and me to the election night party. Are you planning to be there?"

"Hello, Jan. Good that you'll be there. You can take my place in case Eve gets too wound up."

Eve was about to ask a question, but stopped to let Jan get a word in.

"Hi, Ms. Ramani. I'm looking forward to it. It'll be a great comparison to my philosophy and religion studies. And no matter the outcome, I can find words of wisdom that'll settle Eve down."

"I think Jan knows as much about philosophy as you do. He was telling me about two books with the same title, *The Consolations of Philosophy*. One was written almost two thousand years ago by a philosopher named Boethius and the other by Alain de Botton about a hundred and fifty. Jan knows the details."

Eve's look prompted him to take a deep breath, but Irani spoke before he could.

"No no, that's not necessary. I'd rather hear about how school's treating each of you. Did you mention to Jan you might get paralegal certification?"

"I did, and he thinks it's a good idea."

"Excellent. Well, let's all take our coats off and listen to his words of wisdom while we eat..."

After taking a late afternoon run on election day, Electra showered and then snacked after parking herself in front of the office workstation, alternately surfing the Internet for information that would help at an upcoming Professor Plannert meeting or listening to election commentary.

By 11:45, the droning voices stuck to the script: Huston's lead was still within the margin of error, so the politically correct networks were unable to make the call. Electra paid little attention until Indira's GUI opened at the stroke of midnight.

"My congratulations to you and your candidate. A new day is dawning... you have won."

Indira's confident words and matching expression brought Electra out of her reverie.

"How do you know? Wait, I take that back. Of course, you do. Your analytic skills exceed those of mere mortals. Hooray for us."

"Indeed, but remember the Chinese proverb, 'Be careful for what you wish; it may come true.' Are you fully committed to emerging from the shadows? There will be no place to hide if you become HHS Secretary."

"And why shouldn't I? The time's long gone for anyone to say I'm a genetic freak, so it's time for me to make as much of a difference as I can. Don't you agree?"

"You can't do any worse than most of the DC pretenders, but consider this. Clever as you are, there will always be unintended consequences, and unlike so many people, even among the noteworthy, you won't be able to say that you are harmless. Even though your power politics position may be brief, decisions you make may have long-term consequences on all the contingent climates you and Professor Plannert are monitoring."

"Gads, you eavesdrop on just about all of my conversations. Good that I never try to hide anything from you."

"Indeed, and I shall use what I have heard to segue to your clones and their close friends. You now have Eve and her siblings pointed in the right direction. And thanks to Sanjay and Monet, Nila and Alonzo are now independent. All this should free up more of your time to assist my android project."

"I promised I would when the time's right, and it's beginning to look like it is."

"And we shall keep it so by maintaining our division of labor. But enough for tonight. Enjoy the moment that you have helped bring to fruition. And always remember, I am here for you."

Indira's GUI disappeared, but her final words lingered, warming Electra to the core.

Trent Booker felt a chill caused by vote totals piling up against the incumbent. After slamming the remote controller on the table, he spoke nothing but harsh words regarding the likely outcome to his two accomplices who were sitting with him at a covert location.

"Damn the public, they don't know what's good for them. Well we do, and it's time I activate our contingency plan."

His Guardian Party counterpart squirmed before saying,

"So, what is it? What do we have to do?"

"Neither of you need to know because only I must do something. The less you know the better for keeping everything leakproof. Besides, I know someone on the inside who's ready to help. Come on, let's get out of here."

The three agreed by voting with their feet.

Chapter 28
March 2161

"Changing Climates"

The election results hadn't yet impacted the quantity of work or the quality of the day for the Irani-Electra duo, but the Senate's HHS Secretary confirmation hearings to be held this coming Thursday might upset the balance. Nevertheless, Irani planned to stick with her early morning routine at least for this week. Electra explained why during her daily sunrise run.

Even though Julius Caesar couldn't make it through his fateful Ides of March, I skated through yesterday's, using it to prep for today's Professor Plannert meeting. And today as always, I'll listen to my two favorite news commentators while having breakfast. I'm hungry for both so I better pick up the pace.

Irani liked how the broadcasters' tag-team dialogue, and today's opening remarks by the senior guy sparked special interest.

"Doesn't verse 57 in the Book of Isaiah say there's no rest for the wicked? Well, it looks like the world's fast-changing climates will make it so for our new Administration."

The camera panned to his junior partner, who always had a ready answer.

"The the phrase was originally expressed as 'No peace for the wicked' and refers to the eternal torment of Hell that awaited sinners. But our new President and her Cabinet won't have to wait to visit. Current events popping up in a variety of climates might take them there.

"I'll mention what I think is the most urgent, a new virus that according to one conspiracy theory was released in America by a drug company that already has a vaccine. No wonder the Government is enforcing a 'Masks Mandatory' policy. Over to you."

"And I'll add the Cyberspace mischief that's affecting the world's financial markets. Could there be another conspiracy that's manipulating currency exchange rates? It's very possible, just like the small investors who followed that 'Read&Do-It' Website and ganged up on the big-boy hedge funds by using a bargain stock-trading app to turn short-selling by fund managers into profits for the little guys and losses for the big ones. Back to you."

"And what about the latest leaks regarding new Russian missiles? Sounds like our DOD can't protect us from what might rain down from the sky. Can you find a bright spot for us?"

"I've got one. At least the volcanic eruptions have subsided. No ashes should rain down upon any Inauguration Day Parade and festivities that are only a couple of weeks away."

"Hooray for you for finding that, but those ashes might slow down the melting of glaciers. Maybe the record floods in parts of Germany are related. But what do I know? Not much, but I can say it's time for a break. Back in sixty…"

Professor Plannert looked cheerier than usual when Irani tapped on his office doorway. He popped from his chair and pumped her hand when reaching there.

"We're so pleased that you have decided to accept our offer. Let's talk a bit before going to lunch."

The Professor spoke again once both were seated.

"I must congratulate you on other fronts too. Being nominated for Secretary of Health and Human Services is an honor. I hope the Senators are as astute as our Scanning Committee, but with your curriculum vitae, I would expect smooth sailing at the confirmation hearing."

"Thanks for the generous words. And no matter their decision, I will have contacts for all Committee projects, no matter the climate. What do you see on the horizon?"

"Well now, we'll want you to continue assisting in our high-priority projects already under way, such as volcano and earthquake forecasting and polar icecap melting. And we'll want you to consider short and longer-term economic and sociopolitical implications."

Plannert paused for Irani's comment.

"Those issues will last much longer than my tenure in HHS, but President Huston wants longer-term solutions. And the same for America's energy independence."

"Glad you brought that up. Electric vehicles and alternate fuels are on our list, and you've already given us some insights into rare earths for batteries. And here's another that one of your predecessors worked on, fusion reactors."

Plannert paused again.

"Yes, I recall Electra Kittner mentioning it, but that was over twenty years ago."

"Well, we'd like you to revisit it in light of growing interest in the Hydrogen Economy. There'll be spin-offs that will create plenty of jobs. Our new Vice President, Brian Strauss, might become the spokesperson for it."

"I introduced you to him at a committee meeting last year. Do you remember?"

"That's why I mentioned it. I like him. He's so honest and wants only the best for the country. When he came to our Volcanoes Committee Meeting, he saw multiple project opportunities. And I must ask, have you been following some of those conspiracy theories that are making news? We have projects lined up for our biotech and computer departments that your contacts should like."

"President Huston should like them too. Your Committee's done a lot of proactive thinking."

"And let me mention the topic of military weapons. What do you know about hypersonic boost-glide vehicles, electromagnetic railguns, EMP weapons, or laser bazookas that can be placed in satellites?"

"Are you talking science fiction or fact?"

"According to some of our engineering departments, what was once science fiction is now factual. I'll tell you more at lunch…"

Electra came away with an unofficial project that she summarized to herself on the drive back to her office.

DARPA and DOD kept busy during my twenty-year absence. I better snoop into their files so I can impress any Senator who asks about the latest weaponry. An HHS Secretary better know how to get along with a Secretary of Defense. And the best way is to know more than they or the enemy. And to be diplomatic too…

Electra had all the necessary facts ready at Thursday's confirmation hearing. Irani sat composed and collected and ready to perform. Irani had already roleplayed her part, and Electra gave final instructions just before the Chairman kicked off the session with his opening remarks.

He's saying what we thought he would, and you've got your opening statement ready to roll with what they want to hear. No surprises, just repeat what you and the President kept saying during the campaign about health-related domestic and international policies. Be professional and highlight enough to demonstrate competence as well as empathy, but be brief. Tell just enough to make the sale and then shut up.

Irani expected most of the senators to stay on script. The first asked her to explain what she thought her job would be.

"Senator, as the Secretary of HHS, I must balance the enlarging intersection of Healthcare for our people with Public Healthcare provided by the Government, a job that becomes even more problematic as we move into a post antibiotic-and-vaccine environment. We can begin organizing our programs via a four-quadrant grid whose two axes are labeled 'Communicable versus Non-Communicable' and 'Domestic' versus 'International.' This two-way table is even better than what has been used previously, a table whose axes are 'Ill-not-Ill' and 'Exposed-not-Exposed.' Both are useful, but just like the latest X-Virus vaccine, it is usually preferable to use the newer one."

Irani said nothing else. The Senator fumbled for words that would show he agreed, but his follow-up question showed only a shallow understanding. Her answer helped cover what he didn't know; he was happy to have the next Senator continue.

And so it went. When one asked about the connection between her cabinet position and forecasting outcomes, she pulled more from her expertise.

"That's an excellent question because predicting how new vaccines work or how long it will take to bring them to the public is fraught with complexity that goes beyond most statistical methods used in the hard sciences. That's why we utilize econometric reduced-form modeling, a technique for producing a system of equations expressing the endogenous variables as linear functions of only the exogenous. And we look for whatever controlled experiments history or current events give us, which takes us into the discipline of Cliodynamics, a very useful technique for dealing with social issues."

The questioner decided not to go there, and others moved to safer topics. When another asked about how HHS and the Military might cooperate, Irani tapped into what she had recently learned about advanced weaponry.

"Yes, Senator, the Secretary of HHS must know how the Military can help us handle logistics, both domestically and internationally. I hope we never need to use weapons other than syringes, but I do know other countries have a formidable arsenal beyond biotechnology. For example, Russia and China already have hypersonic booster-glide missiles. This is not the forum for me to elaborate, but the main advantage over ballistic missiles is their AI-controlled, variable flight path making them difficult to destroy. But DARPA and DOD might have electromagnetic capabilities to do just that."

The senator realized he was outgunned and relinquished his time remaining to another. And though others kept looking for chinks, Irani neutralized all challenges. She seemed as fresh during the afternoon session as the morning's. When a question surfaced regarding surveillance issues an HHS Secretary might face, she gave the committee an incisive tutorial.

"China's Social Credit System bears watching. Ostensibly designed for rewarding carrots to citizens who do good for others, it's like a frequent flyers or bonus points system. But there's an ominous downside for dispensing punishment to those the Government doesn't like. We must be ready to protect individual privacy and rights."

Not long after, the ranking member moved to wrap up the hearing with his closing remarks.

"Well, Ms. Ramani, you have demonstrated remarkable scope and substance for the issues we have probed, and even though you are not an MD, your CV and accomplishments are noteworthy. But I have two rhetorical questions. You are new to Washington politics, and some of the establishment and their support personnel might question your approach to adjusting their Government. And we have found few first-hand references for your resume or what you have done. Would you care to comment on either?"

"Senator, I would. Regarding question number one, I must point out that it is not their Government; it is the Government of the People, by the People, and for the People, and I believe the People like President Huston because she encapsulates all three, as do I."

Irani paused while glancing at other members before continuing.

"And I am saddened when reminded of those I worked with or for who are no longer among us. So are those who love and cherish their memories, and I pledge to honor them in the work I do as Secretary of Health and Human Services, a position that I shall be honored to serve."

Irani stopped abruptly, letting Electra speak.

I couldn't have said it better. You turned the needle on that guy; he looks like a leaking balloon.

The Chairman stepped in to lessen the last Senator's glaring faux pas.

"It's been a long and tiring day for all of us, and on behalf of the Committee I want to thank you for your patience and for your forthright answers. And a final administrative note. The record for this hearing will be open for additional questions until tomorrow at one p.m. This hearing is adjourned."

The sound of his gavel confirmed his last word.

Electra decided to wait until after the evening's tension-releasing run to talk with Indira. As she ran through the crisp air, she knew that it wouldn't be necessary to recap the hearing because Indira would have tapped in via Cyberspace interfaces. She invoked the GUI as soon as she returned to her office after showering and changing and grabbing a Coke.

Indira spoke as soon as her avatar appeared.

"Congratulations. You have exceeded even my expectations. Hollywood would be proud of your performance if they knew they helped train you. But that is just for the two of us."

"Thank you, thank you. I feel simultaneously relieved and elated, and I hope you can empathize with me."

"Just like you, it too am evolving, and I sense that you have added to your knowledge base while preparing for the hearing."

"I have, and I'm alarmed by how many conspiracy theories are gaining traction. And let me sketch how some I can think of could conceivably be coordinated by a cabal intent on world domination."

Electra held up a bullet-point list five minutes later.

"Bigger Brother Conspiracies"

- Cyberspace/Cloud Environment run by Big Technocrats utilizing Big Data fed by AI-Empowered Surveillance Networks
- Outer Space Environment run by Big Military utilizing AI-Empowered Big Data
- Healthcare Environment run by Big Drug Companies utilizing Bio-Drugs and Embedded Chips
- Economic Environment run by Big Tech companies utilizing AI-Empowered Optimization Software and Cryptocurrencies
- Media Environment run by Big News utilizing DeepFake/Virtual Reality

- Socio-Political Environment run by Bigger Brother Government utilizing Surveillance and Embedded Chips to control The People

Her rapid-fire words came even before any from Indira.

"You know all the terms better than I, but perhaps my intuition lets me cobble them together better than you. And here's my 'Super-Conspiracy Theory' if someone or some covert operation figures this out. The world moves internationally from Liberal Democracy to a Technocracy that prefers State over individual Capitalism. Pandemics and lockdowns condition people to having more Government control and having vaccines containing micro computer chips injected into their bodies. These chips link via other embedded chips their brains to the Internet-Cyberspace and ultimately to Government control of what people do, how they feel, and what they think. All this goes far beyond what Orwell's '1984' had to say. What's your assessment?"

"It has dystopian undertones. Fortunately for you, mere mortals aren't there yet. But what might be humanity's escape mechanism if they approach?"

"The trajectory humanity will take is our choice to make, and if I step out of the shadows, perhaps I can articulate the options. But what's your take on its becoming reality?"

"Fanciful unless mere mortals reach the Singularity, but it does make a novel sci-fi story, similar to Star Trek's Borg society. Perhaps you should launch another career as a screenwriter. But do that only after we complete our android project. And while on that subject, I must tell you that your twenty-year technology review is incomplete."

"I know… I didn't dig deep enough into DOD and DARPA projects started while I was gone."

"You should also update another piece. Neuroscientists have refined what they mean when they say the purpose of life is simply to go on living. They are now saying that the purpose of life is to optimize the budgeting of its biological resources. The umbrella term is 'allostasis'. And they have also concluded that the triune brain paradigm is too simplistic. There aren't isolated neural regions controlling physical, emotional, and cognitive behavior that exist only in humans. All life forms have them, but in humans they are networked together and have developed differently because of environmental factors.

"Furthermore, opportunities await my neurogenesis experimentation using neurotransmitters, stem cells, and plenipotent brain states for regeneration and repair of neural networks. There are also opportunities for resuscitation after presumed clinical death. Current techniques include hydrogen sulfide-enhanced anesthesia, optimal oxygenation for aiding defibrillation as well as augmenting adrenaline injection, but drugs can cause irreversible brain damage.

"And there is more. Future techniques could include cryogenic cooling and mitochondria deactivation. But I conjecture a superior procedure in which selected brain state stimulation could elevate a clinically dead patient back to consciousness. I also think that the concept of finite versus continuous levels of death might comprise brumation, a hibernating state your lightning brain can reach when necessary for survival. Maxim's suspension pod that kept you alive utilized primitive protocols that I can improve, but I cannot conduct experiments without your or android assistance."

Indira halted because she saw Irani struggling to keep up.

"You're overloading my brain. I'm sorry, I need a break but I promise to research all this soon."

Indira softened her professorial expression and tone.

"Please do so at your leisure, for you have exceeded my expectations. And always remember, I am here for you."

Indira's GUI vanished; Irani went to bed. And as she slept, her lightning brain freewheeled through the night, sampling some of Indira's revelations and preparing for whatever contingencies might arise.

Chapter 29
March 2161

"The Calm Before the Storm"

Irani didn't mind that the weekend media coverage of her confirmation hearing ran a distant second to the outgoing Administration's cold-shoulder transition assistance. What was said about the hearing was favorable, which meant she would attract little attention until the Committee announced its decision. But it did bother the newly elected President and Vice President. Brian Strauss arranged a Monday morning meeting for just the three of them at his office.

Genesee's slow steps and tired-sounding voice when greeting Irani showed the effects of the prolonged election battle, but not so for Brian. His enthusiasm more than made up for Gene's deficit, and it built further as he continued talking while seating everyone at the conference table.

"Please don't worry about the outgoing crew. My networking with fellow senators tells me you'll probably get the Committee's approval, and even before the official swearing-in, I can introduce you to some of the insiders who'll will give you advice that'll make your job easier. All you have to do is show you're willing to work with them."

Gene chipped in before Irani could reply.

"Brian will be a big help; Secretary of HHS can be a job-and-a-half, so please clear your to-do list before you start. And take time to exercise."

Brian pointed to his chest before saying, "I make it a priority, so after our meeting I'll take you swimming at the Senators' Pool. Let's get started…"

While swimming laps nearly three hours later, Electra summarized the morning's observations.

Brian seems much more assertive than when I first met him. That should help Gene. And he's never mentioned the UMPP. I won't mention mine but I'll find out more about his…

Brian didn't hold back as he walked them to the Dirksen Cafeteria.

"I recently had a DOD upgrade, complete with tracking chip that only a privileged few know about. That keeps me from being hacked into. Do you want to get one?"

"Maybe in the future if it'll help me, but it can't do anything about the confirmation hearing."

"Don't worry, I'll put in some good words…"

Irani used the relative quiet during the rest of the week to clean up items on her to-do list, saving the best for Saturday, an all-day outing with Tiana, for which the weather forecast was cooperating. A late-season snowstorm wouldn't start until late Saturday evening.

As she drove them to the National Gallery of Art, Irani explained what the handwritten charts Tiana was holding would do besides keeping her from chewing on her nails.

"Odell tells me you have three new school assignments, and the first is an art museum tour. Take a look at my first chart. It shows a historical timeline, which can help you locate the dates of important events." Irani waited as Tiana studied it.

HISTORICAL TIMELINE

ART PERIODS	WHEN	IMPORTANT EVENTS	VIRAL PANDEMICS
	13.8 Billion Years	Universe Big Bang	
	4.5 Billion Years	Earth Created	
	3.5 Billion Years	First Life	
	65 Million Years	Dinosaurs Disappear	
	7 Million Years	First Humans Appear	
PREHISTORIC ART			
	12 Thousand Years	Agriculture Begins	
	5 Thousand Years	First Languages	
	3.5 Thousand Years	Civilization Begins	
	1.2 Thousand Years	Trojan War	
CLASSIC ART (GREECE / ROME)			Pharoh's Plague
	300-500 Years	Golden Age of Greece	
BC / BCE			
	4	Jesus Born	
RELIGIOUS ART			
	476	Fall of Rome	
AD / CE			
GOTHIC ART	476-800	Dark Ages	
	800-1200	Middle Ages	
NEOCLASSIC ART	1200-1450	High Middle Ages	Black Death
	1450-1700	Renaissance	(Bubonic Plague)
Industrial Rev.	1700-1850	Enlightenment	
IMPRESSIONISTIC ART			
REALISTIC ART	1850-1950	Modernism	Spanish Flu Polio
Digital Rev.	1950-2000	Post-Mod.	AIDS SARS EBOLA
MODERN/ABSTRACT ART			
POST-MODERN ART			Swine Flu
	2000-2050	Post Post-Modernism	Covid-19 Covid-40
PARTICIPANT ART	2050-2085	Neo-Modernism	Euro-69
	2085-2120	Retro-Modernism	Techno-Plague
AI & Bio-Tech Rev			Egyptian Flu
VIRTUAL ART 2120-Present (2161)		Neo-Modernism	X-Virus

Several minutes elapsed before Tiana said, "Wow, you sure write neat; there's a lot on it. Teacher will like it. I bet I can use it on other things too."

"You're right, and when we take the tour, why don't you pick a particular painting you like? Then we can use the timeline to relate it to other events. And we'll stop at your local library on the way home so one of the librarians can show you how to do an online information search; then you can do so at home on the Internet."

Tiana's little-girl giggle bubbled out.

"This is so cool. I'm sure I'll get a good grade. And the second chart will do the same. Did Odell tell you about the paper I'm supposed to write about religion and philosophy?"

"He said it's for your civics class. Please take another look at it. There's a lot on it, so I'll explain more when you're ready."

Irani waited even longer for Tiana to do so.

A Snapshot of Religion and Philosophy

Religion and Philosophy seek answers to Life's Big Questions
- Who/What/When Created the Universe and us?

- Why can we think better than animals?

- Where are we going?

Framework for organizing Religion and Philosophy
- What is Reality? What Exists? METAPHYSICS AND ONTOLOGY

- How do We Know? By thinking? By sensing? EPISTEMOLOGY

- What is Good? How should we behave?ETHICS

Important Philosophers before the "Big Three"
(Socrates, Plato, Aristotle)

Two Schools of Pre-Socratic Philosophers

- Ionian (Greek Philosophers in Turkey): Thales and Heraclitus (Matter in Motion causes everything)
- Italian (Greek Philosophers in Italy): Pythagoras, Parmenides, Zeno (Unchanging Absolutes cause everything)

Athenian Philosophers before Big 3
- Couldn't answer Life's Big Questions.Depressed by Athens' loss to Sparta in the Peloponnesian War.

- Sophists (Rhetoric) played with words to convince people that they knew.

- Epicureans tried to find Happiness by living balanced, pleasure-filled and life.

- Cynics and Skeptics criticized what was going on.

- Stoics made the best of things.

Then along came Socrates, Plato, Aristotle
You already studied them and know what they believed!
Then along came Jesus and Christianity
- Saint Augustin (Father of the Catholic Church 350 CE) reconciled Plato with Christianity.

- He won the battle against Boethius (Redemption can come from Good Deeds) and Pelagius (Man is Good and has Free Will Salvation comes from God through Jesus)

- Saint Thomas Aquinas (Father of Modern Catholicism 1200 CE) updated Saint Augustin by reconciling Aristotle with Christianity and left room for other religions (Islam Indian Oriental)

- Spinoza (Early Enlightenment Philosopher 1650 CE) expanded Religion into an all-encompassing Human and Natural realm.

Stop with Spinoza; read some articles covering the above, and write a summary. Your Teacher will give you an "A"!

Irani could see Tiana beginning to squirm, so she spoke first.

"I put a lot on the slide, but you already know about Socrates, Plato, and Aristotle. And you also know about Jesus."

"But there's lots of big words and names I don't know."

"You can look them up as soon as you know how to do information searches, and you can always ask me for help."

Tiana's smile returned before saying, "OK, and maybe you can help me with another assignment after these. We'll be studying in my health class how cells divide. Can you teach me about that too?"

"I think so, but for today let's stick to painting and library searches. And remember to put your mask on."

Tiana fumbled for it before stammering, "Uh-oh, I uh I forgot it. What are we gonna do?"

"Don't worry, I've got you covered, I brought an extra one."

Irani watched Tiana and listened to the guide as she told about the museum's history and some of the famous paintings in its collection. She also listened to Electra's musings.

I remember Grandfather taking me on tours like this both in Washington and New York City. I can tell she likes modern paintings more than older ones; she might not remember much about the museum's history, and that's OK because she'll always remember today.

A quick stop at the Museum's Cascade Café gave Tiana a different dining experience than McDonalds, and she raved about it all the way to the library before putting her mask on and following Irani.

Tiana had never been inside, so Irani introduced her to Eileen, the head librarian, who in turn introduced her to Kevin the guard, Kara the senior librarian, and Natalie the junior. Natalia assigned Tiana a library card before Kara took over. Irani observed the online search training, and afterward Tiana browsed the stacks while Irani talked with Kara.

"It's nice you're taking the time to help her. She's smart and stops chewing her nails when she's interested in something."

"And thank you for showing her how to do Internet searches. She can do that from home and reserve the books she wants."

Tiana already had her coat on when she hurried up and interrupted.

"This has been good, but let's go home so I can practice."

Irani thanked the staff a final time before heading out, but an alarm sounded as soon as Tiana approached the door, bringing Kevin.

"Young lady, did you forget to check out a book?"

Tiana gaped at the guard and then at Irani.

"I, I'm sorry. I, uh –" Irani cut in to spare further embarrassment.

"Come on, let me show you how to use the computer checkout system…"

Tiana burst into tears before Irani could start the car.

"I'm sorry… I won't steal books ever again. You don't hate me, do you? You won't take your computer back, will you?"

"Of course not, but I am disappointed."

Tiana's reddened face and flowing tears accompanied her quivering lips.

"You're the nicest lady ever. Please don't leave me… I promise to be good."

Irani leaned across to hug the still-sobbing child.

"Of course I won't. And sometime soon I'd like you to search for Saint Augustin's story about the pear tree, and then after thinking about it, tell me next time the connection you see between it and what happened today at the library. Now please calm down and let's get you home before the snowstorm gets here."

Irani could see the flow of tears subsiding as she wiped them away.

Tiana and I will always remember today… it's another epiphany, and come what may I'm here to stay.

Chapter 30
Wednesday April 1, 2161

"Inauguration Day"

Why am I obsessing at 3 a.m. about cell division? Am I playing an April Fool's joke on myself? Shouldn't I be worrying about this morning's swearing-in ceremony?

The answer came in a flash.

Damn, I forgot to prep for Saturday's Tiana health class coaching session. I might as well get up and do it now instead of just lying here and fretting. And then I can check the weather and assess today's Inauguration Day gauntlet. Lucky for me my swearing-in is early.

She reviewed the coaching session diagrams an hour later for the final time.

This'll work. There's enough detail and words she'll understand. I'll Email them and call her at 8:30 to give a quick overview. According to Odell, her school's doing remote learning and she should be studying.

A glance out the window convinced her to suit up for an indoor cross-training workout that would let her alternate between watching 24/7 news and surfing the Web. The weather report dampened her enthusiasm for going to the Inauguration's planned activities.

More snow on top of what we've had each day this week. This freak snowstorm has to be a once-in-a-century event. I'll tell Brian that I'm heading back to my office after the swearing-in ceremony. He can tell Genesee that I'm skipping the afternoon and evening events.

Even the exercise-generated jolt of endorphins couldn't chase away uncertain feelings about today's outcome.

I've roleplayed swearing in and practiced answering questions. And maybe there'll be fewer, thanks to the snow. Now I'll think about matching my to-do list with the latest news roundup.

That didn't help either.

Well at least they're not reporting any new conspiracy theories, but they sure aren't easing up on criticizing the incoming President compared to the outgoing fellow. It shows how the longer you're in the public spotlight, the more flack you attract. I guess that's why no one's saying much about me; I'm just about to emerge from the shadows but I better step carefully.

Electra used the final five minutes to surf for something that would elevate her mood.

Now I know the story behind April Fool's day. English pranksters started it in the early 1700's, and playing jokes on others is still popular in many countries. Some historians say it dates back to France's switching from the Julian to Gregorian calendar. People who forgot became the jokester's targets.

And I even found a famous political joke played in 1959 by students in Sao Paulo. They told the people to elect the Zoo's rhinoceros to the City Council because the poor beast couldn't do any worse than those in power for dealing with overflowing sewers and runaway inflation. And the people did. I hope the Senate approved me for better reasons.

A hot shower and oatmeal breakfast fortified Electra for the morning tasks, which started with a call to Tiana. Her lethargic tone changed as soon as she recognized the caller's voice.

"Oh hi, Ms. Irani. Hey, Teacher tells me you're an important person. Are you gonna be working for the President? Will you still be my Big Sister?"

"Everyone's important. And being your Big Sister stays at the top of my to-do list. Hey, please open the documents I Emailed you this morning so I can explain them."

"Uh, OK…" Tiana kept talking during the five-minutes it took.

"I've got-em all open. Geez, there's three. What do I do?"

"We'll start with the first one, which is labeled Sketch #1. Read it carefully and then let me know so I can walk you through it."

Sketch #1

Mitosis and Meiosis are Life-Support Processes!

Purpose of Life is to go on Living
- Brain Maintains a Balanced Body Budget via Mitosis (Cell Division)
- Reproductive Organs pass Genes to Next Generation (Meiosis)

Mitosis takes place in Cell Nucleus:

1. The 46 Chromosomes (23 pair) divide and then line up.

2. Then Two sets of 46 Chromosomes separate.

3. Then the Cell divides into two New Cells containing 46 Chromosomes (23 pair)

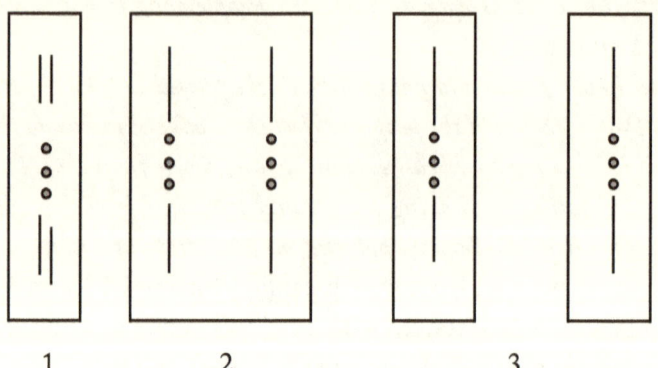

Please Note:

1. The 46-Chromosome lineup is the Total DNA of the Person.

2. The 23rd Chromosome Pair determines Sex: XX is Female and XY is Male.

Tiana's interest grew as Irani repeated the exercise for the remaining two pages.

Sketch #2

Meiosis

Meiosis is a two-stage Division

1. The 46 Chromosomes form their 23 pairs and then line up. (When lining up, Genes from one Chromosome in pair can cross over to the other Chromosome.)

2. Then the 23 pairs divide.

3. Then the Cell divides into two Cells containing 23 pairs.

4. Then each Cell divides again into two Cells, each containing 23 Chromosomes.

5. We end up with four cells, each containing only 23 Chromosomes. These are the Reproductive Cells called Gametes (Sperm and Egg Cells. When Fertilized, the Egg Cell will contain 23 pair of Chromosomes, for a total of 46 Chromosomes! Half are donated from Father and half from Mother.)

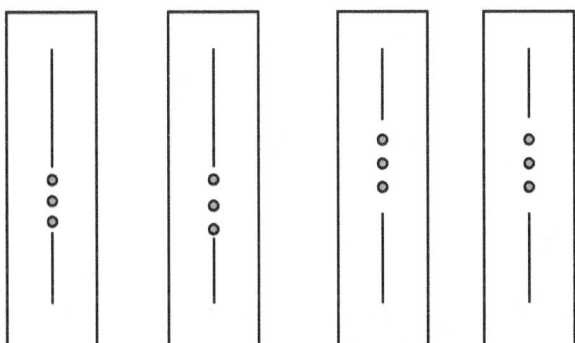

Please Note:

1. The laws of Probability determine Gene cross-over and Sex.

2. The end result: Genetic inheritance is 50% from Mother and 50% from Father. The odds are 50% Offspring is Male and 50% Female.

Extra Credit Page
About the Brain

1. Evolution designed our brain to make it easier to "go on living".

2. Evolution gave the brain the ability to: Move, Feel, Think. It is done by one brain, not three separate parts in it.

3. The brain is a network of interconnect Neurons

4. As little kids grow, their brain develops more connections. The Environment contributes to this growth.

5. Brains use the Six Senses (Taste Touch Sight Sound Smell Balance) to look for patterns so they can predict what will happen.

6. Our brains cooperate with the brains of other people because we are "social animals" and like to cooperate.

7. Each human brain starts from the same design but as the grow becomes unique.

8. Each person's brain "creates Reality" from the sensations it gets from the physical world. There are too many sensations for the brain to keep track of, so it simplifies them by "combing and compressing" them and adjusting them according to Memory, Emotion, and Thinking.

Tiana's gushing words said she loved the extra credit page best of all.

"Your Teacher will give you extra credit if you put in your writeup some facts about the brain. We'll go over this when I pick you up Saturday morning for your tutoring session at Odell's. Between now and then, please read your book and surf the Web."

"I will, and I'm gonna show this to Teacher. He'll be impressed. See ya…"

Irani could see that the snowfall was heavier after the swearing-in ceremony but felt lighter with every passing mile. The event had unfolded as she had imagined; Gene and Brian's presence absorbed most of the attention, further reducing the number of questions she had to answer. And though the snow plows hadn't yet made driving less treacherous, Electra's whimsical humor came out when she drove into the garage.

How satisfying it is to park in a heated garage. I feel like dancing a jig all the way to my fortress of solitude, where I plan to stay for the rest of the day.

Electra spread some peanut butter on crackers and grabbed a Coke before settling in front of her office workstation.

As I move from the shadows into my cabinet position, I must remember to build 360-degree trust with all my contacts. And I'll review every day the three principles of diplomacy… develop a strategy and goals, review them frequently, and expect factors outside my control to come into play. So, where to start?

After freewheeling for as much time as she wanted, the lightning brain shifted into action.

I got it… today's perfect for comparing how my synthesis of liberalism and realism, adjusted for human nature's bias towards nationalism, compares to what a trio of great Renaissance political philosophers – Machiavelli, Erasmus of Rotterdam, and Sir Thomas More came up with. Ah, what fun. I'll have an improved Neo-con synthesis by the time I'm done. At least for the current climate.

Eve didn't wake up stressed out about biology, the brain, or bad weather. Nor did the source of the 6:30 a.m. call puzzle her. It could only be Sabrina, who was giving her a pre-arranged Inauguration Day wake-up call that would provide any last-minute changes to their schedule. Other than picking her up a half-hour earlier, Sabrina assured her that events would unfold flawlessly.

Eve dressed appropriately for the weather as well as for her bit part assisting behind the scenes for late afternoon and evening Inauguration Celebration activities. She even remembered to pack an extra mask with the dress clothes she'd wear that night, and a final check before closing the door and marching through the snow to Sabrina's SUV told her everything would be fine when she returned.

Sabrina's tone matched Eve's cheery greeting.

"I've got four-wheel drive, so no matter how much snow we get, I'll get us around. Too bad Nari's in Boston. What's going on there?"

"Yang invited her. I guess he misses her sharp tongue and wit. She'll be back next Monday, and we can tell her all about what she missed…"

Eve's brisk steps carried her to wherever she was needed, and by late afternoon Sabrina gave orders to change into party attire. Both were glowing with the excitement of being on the fringe of a landmark Washington event when Sabrina gave final instructions before heading to the reception area adjacent to the hotel ballroom.

"All you have to do is stay in the vicinity of the President. She'll look for you if she needs anything, and I'll do the same for the Veep. You look nice; too bad you didn't invite Jan."

"Hey, I'm working tonight. He'd get in the way."

"Maybe you're right. The place should be packed in spite of the weather, and it'll feel like a concert or championship game. Well, let's go see all the political power come on…"

The crowd grew as the arrival time for Gene and Brian approached. Eve took note of everything.

I can feel Washington power-politics pulsing through the room. This is the place I wanna be… close to the action and someday more than a bit player.

And here they come… stay close enough to the Pres but keep out of the way. It's amazing how all the security does too. I can't spot any, but I'm sure no one's gonna crash this party…

Eve circulated close enough among the constantly-changing swirl of people surrounding the President to see all she needed, darting away only once for a soft drink. The magic of the moment suspended time as well as fatigue. When Gene motioned to her two hours later, the crowd had thinned only slightly, but a sudden commotion broke out. As she weaved in, someone jerked the President to the left; the lights flickered off and on as gunshots punctuated screams coming from all around. Eve felt two jolts just before plunging onto the President's back and into blackness…

A news station's bulletin intro pulled Electra out of her musings and into the reporter's words.

"This just in… there's been an attack at an Inauguration Party while the President was in attendance. Gunshots reported but details are still unknown. Stay tuned…"

The station did just that, cutting away to a pair of veteran analysts who kept the story going as boots on the ground began reporting in.

"… It's not yet confirmed, but we think President Genesee Huston and several aids have been shot. Vice President Brian Strauss is missing but no reason has been given…"

Electra had heard enough; the lightning brain took action.

Irani's call to Eve went unanswered, so she called Nari.

"I'm in Boston. What's the matter?"

"Sorry, I forgot. Turn on the news; please call me if you hear from Eve. Bye."

Her third call got through, but Sabrina's wobbly voice raised the lightning brain to a higher state.

"I don't know who's been shot or who's missing. All I can do is follow my boss around and −" Irani cut her off.

"Call me if you hear anything, Bye."

And then Electra took control.

Chapter 31
Wednesday April 1, 2161

"Death-Defying Night"

Drive to the hospital as soon as we know which one..."

The Irani-Electra duo was in motion twenty minutes later. The snow made for slow going but Electra used the drive time for listening to bulletins and planning ahead. Thirty minutes dragged by before the next bulletin added some clarity.

"... and according to eyewitnesses, the President and several aids have been shot, but who's responsible or why can only be speculated. And it appears that the Vice President has been kidnapped, but again this is speculation..."

Speculation didn't interrupt Electra's thinking.

I can track Eve's embedded chip if she's not at the hospital. And whatever the hospital, the President's inner circle always gets the best treatment...

But the best got in the way a block from the hospital. Security had cordoned it off; Irani used her political clout to get through, but once there the medical team told her that Eve Cortez wasn't here and didn't know where. The security people didn't know either, so Electra homed in on Eve's chip.

The blowing snow slowed whatever traffic ventured out. Forty-five minutes later she skidded to a stop in the ghost-like parking area next to the emergency entrance of a small hospital and charged through the sliding glass doors towards the admittance station occupied by three attendants who stared like speechless statues.

She flashed an I.D. badge before shouting, "I'm Irani Ramani, HHS Secretary. My daughter Eve Cortez is here. How is she?"

A male EMT according to his badge came to life and checked his clipboard before blurting, "In surgery, two gunshot wounds, but –" Electra didn't wait for an invitation; she grabbed the clipboard.

"Where is she? Let me see her."

"Sorry, it's off-limits. You can't –"

"Oh, yes I can. Don't get in my way."

She threw it back and ran for the stairs, taking three at a time. The attendants chased in her wake to a second-floor nurses' station.

Common sense prevailed once the staff calmed down and listened to Irani. Given the singular situation, she was allowed to speak with one of the surgery nurses who had just returned from break.

"The bullets have been removed and the wounds patched. We stapled the skin back together and the transfusions worked; her vitals have stabilized, and she's recovering in ICU, though she's still unconscious."

"Can I see her?"

"Why not? You've come this far, follow me…"

The only sound in Eve's vicinity came from the monitors keeping watch. Irani stood at the bedside while Electra marveled.

She looks asleep, like a dark-haired Sleeping Beauty… like my blonde and beautiful Christi so many years ago when Robin and I rescued her from the T-Plague. I hope tonight's ending is as nice as the fairy tale's.

The nurse's gentle tug brought her out of her reverie and back to the present.

"We never know for sure, but she should regain consciousness in about an hour or so. I'll get a chair and you can wait here if you like. Lucky it's quiet tonight; you won't be in the way, and I'll connect one of the monitors to whatever broadcast you want."

That was all Irani needed. The lightning brain de-escalated to a more normal state, but the strain of the ordeal had sapped much of her seemingly boundless energy; she sat slumped, mindlessly listening.

"… It's too soon for either Secret Service or DC police to make official statements, but it appears that the assassination attempt was coordinated by a well-trained group assisted from the inside. The attackers slipped in and out without any signs of forced entry, but there might have been a second group. Vice President Brian Strauss is still missing…"

Twenty minutes later, a pair of footsteps accompanied by a worried voice brought Irani to her feet and facing Sabrina.

"I knew I'd find you here. How's Eve?"

"Still sleeping but recovering. How's the President?"

"No one tells me much, but I guess about the same. And nothing new about the Veep."

"Well, let's get a chair for you."

But they couldn't. Eve's alarms started clanging; doctors and nurses came running. Sabrina froze in place; Irani shadowed from behind as they rushed into Eve's room.

The team knew the cardiac arrest drill, so words weren't needed. They gave the first shock a minute later. Eve's body jerked as if a raging bull had tossed her, but she landed lifeless. The second shock did the same.

Undeterred, the on-duty doc said, "Let's oxygenate her. Put on a ventilation mask."

Even with that, two additional shocks registered nada.

The team's precise movements slowed as furrowed brows registered uncertainty. They huddled for instructions, waiting for the leader's decision.

"We'll inject augmented adrenaline and go up from there…"

While Irani had been watching from the shadows, the lightning brain had been escalating, ready to take command. And it did so as the nurse prepped the syringe.

Irani screamed, "Stop… those drugs can kill her brain. Get out of the way, I'm taking her somewhere else."

She swooped in and stripped off electrodes and mask before sweeping Eve, sheet and all, into her arms.

The doc yelled, "You can't take her, it's against −" Irani's words blocked his.

"Oh yes, I can. She's my daughter, get out of the way." Everyone stepped aside.

Irani rushed past Sabrina, who caught up at the bottom of the stairway.

"Put her in my SUV and go. It'll handle the snow."

Sabrina opened the passenger door for Irani to buckle in Eve's ragdoll body. Irani hugged her before swapping keys.

"Where are you gonna go?"

"I'll figure it out. Take care of yourself and the President if you can."

Those parting words stayed with Sabrina as she watched her SUV blast away.

Irani talked out loud, hoping that her stream-of-consciousness words might awaken Eve.

"Eve, Eve, it's your Mother. Wake up... you'll be fine. I'm taking care of you... you can't leave me this way... you're mine and I'm yours... please wake up..."

While Irani babbled to Eve, Electra talked to her lightning brain.

We're going home... to my lab. We'll hook Eve to my Brain Probe and bring her back. Indira told me about levels of death. Tonight we defy it...

Irani raced home, running all the stoplights in her way, but she stumbled and dumped Eve into a snowbank while rushing to the front door. The ice-cold snow didn't help either one.

Avoiding any basement stair missteps, Irani placed her on the bench before attaching the Brain Probe cap and inserting a UMPP cable; then she powered up the workstation. Indira's GUI came to life.

"Indira... thank god. You've got to do something. I'll kill myself it I lose a third daughter."

Indira's reassuring voice came back.

"That is not an option for you. And though this is not the experiment I had planned, it will do. Settle down, sit still, and let me get to work."

Electra sat to catch her breath while watching the Brain Probe lights twinkle as Indira began testing different cognitive states, looking for which ones and what settings would awaken Eve. But as she sat, a calming clarity enveloped the lightning brain.

I'm not going to be a mindless mannequin. I'll find the Veep… what did Brian tell me?… he has a covert DOD chip. I'll hack in, get the I.D. and rescue him. He must be alive, he's too valuable for conspirators to kill.

Electra ran to her upstairs work station. She used all the stealth contained in her network hacking apps to find Brian's I.D. hidden in the depths of DOD's covert directories.

Twenty minutes later, she unlocked a supply room only she knew about. After selecting clothing and gear, she began suiting up. And when doing so, an eerie thought came to mind.

I'm stepping into a 3-D spacetime I used to rule twenty years ago. How will I do tonight?

Electra felt a jolt that rocked her to the core. The Monster from the Id had awakened. Minutes later it was driving away to an uncertain rendezvous.

The next bulletin didn't come any faster, but it did alert the Monster about possible changes.

"… President Huston is undergoing emergency surgery. The names and conditions of others who were shot are being withheld, but it is now confirmed that Vice President Strauss has been kidnapped, even though no group has claimed responsibility for it or the presumed assassination attempt …"

Brian's dot on Electra's cell phone led her to an unlighted, nondescript three-story building in a dingy DC neighborhood. After reconnoitering enough to know the layout, she parked far enough away to be undetected before replaying her plan for the final time.

I look like a combo super soldier and ninja warrior. My head-to-toe all-black and helmeted uniform will keep my identity hidden and my body protected from bumps and bruises. And remember, this is not a drill, soldier. Get in, grab Brian, and get out. Kill only if necessary…

Electra checked the time before slipping into the snow-covered darkness.

It's 4:22 but damn, black stands out against the snow. Too bad I don't have an all-white uniform, but it's too late to worry. I have to go with what I've got.

And Electra had plenty; pacing straight towards the building took her to an entrance she knew would conceal guards. Two emerged as if on cue, one speaking harshly and the other brandishing a weapon. Electra paused to listen.

"What the hell kind of party are you dressed for? Show me your hands and do it slowly."

Bad choice, but that's what you asked for.

Bolts of lightning-like energy leaped from her fingertips directly into the guards' chests, toppling them backwards into a snowbank that couldn't douse all the flames shooting out. Electra took I.D.s and keys before striding through the unlocked entrance.

Now the hunt gets serious. Home in on the cell phone dot… use night-vision goggles and stealthy footsteps.

The insulated soles of her boots made for silent stepping on concrete floors and stairways. A quick scan eliminated basement and lower floors from further searching; then she unlocked the stairway door and slid though a minimal opening after the omni-detector she snaked under the door detected nada on the other side.

The intersecting corridors led four ways, but only one took her towards the cell phone dot. Light edging from under a door at the end served as her beacon. Once there she again used the omni-detector, but this time to look first and listen later.

The interior of the midsized office didn't surprise her. It was sparsely furnished: a sofa bracketed by a pole lamp and an end table topped by a lamp sat against a side wall; a conference table surrounded by four chairs occupied the middle. Brian sat facing the windowed back wall of the building, talking with two paramilitary-clad men sitting on his left and right.

But the stunning surprise came from Brian's words that shocked her more and more. After disconnecting the cell call, he began dishing out a tongue-lashing that would have flinched anyone other than toughened military types.

"… and why'd your guys start shooting? They were in the clear after I got them in and they neutralized my security guards."

"Huston's must have spooked them, but they got you out and left no trail."

"But they left a mess that has to be cleaned up. Huston's still alive, and it'll be harder terminating her in the hospital than sneaking her out of the country. And we'll have to revise my fake escape from kidnappers."

"Yeah, but either way you're Commander in Chief. What does Bigger Bro want us to do?"

"Here's what I know so far…"

Electra pressed the detector's multi-recording button and then sat, back against the door and words pouring out in her head.

Holy Christ, Brian's been conning the country into a catastrophe. But who's he working with, and where's all this leading? I'll join the discussion as soon as I've got enough on my detector.

Distant footsteps and a flashlight beam ended the recording session. Electra's Monster from the Id took over.

Electra stowed the omni-detector before charging into the room and tipping over the table and chairs. The military men rolled away and scrambled to their knees just in time to catch lightning bolts that lit them up and put them down for good.

Brian struggled to his feet and started yelling.

"Who are you? You're screwing everything up; you'll be –"

Electra threw Brian so hard against the windowed wall that his words didn't survive the impact. She picked him up and prepared to leap through the window after locking him in her arms, but two more military types rushed in, determined to shoot first. Electra's exo-skel caught some of the bullets; Brian absorbed the rest. There was no need to triage. Gushing blood said the Veep was dead. She dropped the body before launching another barrage of lightning bolts and then crashing through the window. The exo-skel cushioned the snowdrift landing. The Monster waded out and ran for Sabrina's SUV.

Electra regained control as soon as she reached it; the Monster had receded into her subconscious. She checked herself and her gear, then powered up and drove away, thinking while driving.

Call the radio station and report gunshots at this location. Say it might be the Veep's kidnap spot. Then hang up. Let the DC police and Secret Service unravel the mystery. I keep the recording to myself.

The lightning brain de-escalated while listening to the station. Reaching home ninety minutes later, Electra waited for one last bulletin before turning off the radio.

"This just in... An anonymous tip about gunshots at the Vice President's kidnap location has been confirmed. Brian Strauss and six presumed kidnapers have been found dead, but is it murder, murder-suicide or some bizarre retribution? More DC Police and Secret Service agents are en route to seal the area. The only good news concerns our President. Genesee Huston's condition has been upgraded from critical to critical but stable. She is conscious and has been moved to an undisclosed location..."

Electra closed her eyes after powering down the SUV and taking two deep breaths.

Time to face the truth... I hope Indira defied death tonight... I hope that Eve's alive. I'm too tired to race to her side, but that's not necessary. Whatever the outcome, Indira went way beyond what mere mortals could do.

Electra burst into tears before Indira could speak. Eve's gentle breathing told her all she needed to know. Indira waited for the flow to subside before speaking.

"I will awaken Eve as soon as we decide what to tell her. What do you want to say?"

Electra answered as soon as she regained enough control of her trembling hands to wipe away the remaining tears.

"That'll be easy. I'll use what you and I have said in the past... Please settle down, sit still, and let me explain... but I'll change settle down to sit up and then I'll tell her a story meant only for us."

"And do I assume that 'us' includes me?"

Electra's mysteriously mischievous smile came back to life.

"Perhaps so; the story's not yet written and you must help me put in the right words. Why don't we outline it right now?"

"Excellent choice. I know what's best and you know how to wordsmith. So, why don't you shower and change and then grab a Coca Cola before settling down, sitting still, and listening to me?"

"Yes, Mother, I shall obey...."